The sound of footsteps on the pecan wood flooring announced the arrival of her prospective client.

"Ah, there you are. You must be Olivia."

She froze.

Her heart began to pound. It had been fourteen years since Olivia had heard that dark, velvety drawl, but she would recognize the voice if it had been fifty. Standing with her back to him, she squeezed her eyes shut.

No. No, it can't be. Of all the people in Savannah, it can't be him. It *can't!*

But it was.

Accepting the cruel irony, Olivia drew a deep breath and turned slowly—and came face-to-face with her ex-husband.

Also by GINNA GRAY

THE WITNESS
THE PRODIGAL DAUGHTER

Watch for the newest novel from
GINNA GRAY
Coming April 2005

GINNA GRAY

PALE MOON
RISING

MIRA

ISBN 0-7783-2032-4

PALE MOON RISING

Visit us at www.mirabooks.com

Printed in U.S.A.

PALE MOON
RISING

One

Her nerves were wound so tight the soft ping of the seat belt light gave her a start.

Before any of the other first-class passengers had a chance to react, Olivia Jones jumped to her feet, slung her coat over her arm, snatched up her shoulder bag and briefcase and made a dash for the door.

Oblivious to the flight attendant's plastic smile and cheery "Have a nice day," she stepped past the woman and strode down the jet way.

The closer she got to the airport terminal the harder her heart thumped against her ribs. Though she had grown up in the area, she had not set foot in Savannah in fourteen years, not since that dreary, rainy November night when she had boarded the Greyhound bus for Atlanta with all her belongings in a single battered suitcase and her entire life savings of nine hundred and forty-seven dollars and eighteen cents tucked away in her wallet. Barely eighteen, frightened and on her own for the first time in her life, she had fled this town with her dreams and her heart shattered, vowing never to return.

Now here she was. Olivia's full lips twisted in a wry grimace. Which, she supposed, just proved the old adage, "Never say never."

Behind her a man coughed, and Olivia started.

Calm down, she admonished, annoyed with herself for being so jittery. There's nothing to worry about. Savannah is a good-size town. The chances you'll bump into someone you know from the old days are slim, so quit torturing yourself.

Squaring her shoulders, she drew a deep breath and stepped into the terminal. Dressed in a rust-colored silk turtleneck and hunter-green suit with a long, pencil-slim skirt and high-heeled Italian boots, she knew that to the casual observer she appeared self-assured and calm.

Hitching the strap of her purse a bit higher on her shoulder, Olivia walked past the gate counter and joined the flow of people hurrying along the main concourse. She followed the signs to Baggage Claim at a brisk pace, her shoulder-length auburn hair bouncing to the rhythm of her walk. Barely aware of the admiring male glances cast her way, she kept her gaze focused straight ahead and avoided making eye contact.

She knew she was being foolish. True, the little town where she'd grown up was practically a suburb of Savannah, and many of Bella Vista's old guard had financial interests in the city and conducted business here, but, though she knew most of them, she had never been part of their social set.

It was silly to worry. She had not come here to cause trouble or stir up old grievances. She was a professional woman, here on legitimate business.

Anyway, she had changed a lot since leaving Savannah. She doubted that anyone from her past would connect the shy teenager she had been with the woman she was today. They might not even remember her.

Years ago she had created a minor stir in the insular little world of the elite of Bella Vista and Savannah, but there had been countless other scandals to titillate the local blue bloods since then.

Olivia sighed. Who are you kidding? You know perfectly well how long memories are in the South.

After retrieving her bag, Olivia gave a cab driver AdCo Enterprise's address and settled back for the ride. Taking deep breaths to quiet her nerves, she cast an absent glance out the window, and at once the familiar scenery brought a pang that caught her by surprise. Until that moment, she had not realized how much she'd missed this city.

There was no place in the world quite like Savannah. There was a timelessness here, a dreamy tranquillity that lingered from bygone days. The town had always reminded Olivia of a genteel old lady, decked out in her best finery.

A faint smile tugged at her lips when they passed a sign advertising the Oglethorpe Mall. During their teen years, when she and Blair hadn't been slouched in a darkened movie theater munching popcorn, or riding horses, or pretending to ignore boys at the beach, they had spent every weekend and a lot of their summer days roaming the shops of Savannah.

In those day she and Blair had been inseparable friends, so close they'd practically been joined at the hip.

Olivia's smile faded. How things had changed. Since leaving Savannah, she had not had so much as a telephone call or a note from Blair even though, in the beginning, she had written to her friend several times.

Annoyed, Olivia jerked her gaze away from the

window. She had promised herself when she'd made the decision to accept AdCo's invitation that she would not dredge up the past. What would be the point? All that was over and done with, a distant memory that had nothing to do with her life today.

Returning to Savannah was something she had hoped she would never have to do, but she wasn't going to turn down a career-making opportunity just to avoid bitter memories or people who wanted no more to do with her than she did with them.

She had agonized over the decision, but in the end, she'd had no choice. Business, after all, was business.

During the past six years, since starting her own design firm, some of the most influential and powerful people in the country had been her clients. She had been invited to their homes on social occasions, taken trips on their yachts, spent weekends at their country homes, ski lodges and island retreats. She could certainly hold her own with any of the well-to-do in Bella Vista or Savannah.

Even with Eleanore Connally. And her son.

They were nearing the historic district, Olivia noted. On impulse, she leaned forward and asked the driver to take Bull Street.

"Yes, ma'am. If that's what you want, ah kin sure do it. But ah gotta warn you, it'll take longer and cost more. Got to go slow round all the squares, ya know."

"I know. I don't mind."

"Yes'um. It's your money."

The driver turned, drove a few blocks and turned onto Bull Street. He'd barely driven a block when he started the counterclockwise turns around the first square. Olivia settled back, an odd tightness in her chest, her gaze drinking in the stately old mansions and town homes that surrounded the small parks.

Gray beards of moss draped the ancient live oaks. Fallen leaves and other winter debris littered the walkways and benches, and last summer's stubble filled the flower beds, giving an overall atmosphere of gloom to the squares, but Olivia knew that in three months or so the azaleas and camellias would be in full bloom. Then the area would be a riot of beautiful colors and the soft spring air would be perfumed with the scents of flowers.

Olivia loved spring in Savannah. The sights and scents intoxicated the soul and enhanced the genteel graciousness that permeated the historic district.

How many times, as a teenager, had she sat in the squares and dreamed away hours, imagining herself in another time, a grand lady living in one of the lovely mansions fronting Montgomery Square?

Much to Olivia's delight, AdCo Enterprises occupied a lovely old building on River Street, below the Savannah River Bluff, right in the heart of the historic district. Located as it was on the bank of the Savannah River, she assumed it had originally been an old cotton warehouse. She was so charmed that for several minutes after the taxi pulled away, she stood in the brick courtyard at the front of the building, admiring the facade.

It said a lot about the priorities of the company's partners that they had chosen to renovate and preserve what had probably been a crumbling nineteenth-century structure rather than build a modern steel-and-glass office building to house their company. Codes and guidelines were stringent in historic districts everywhere. No doubt new construction would have been cheaper and more efficient, but a lovely piece of the past might have been lost forever.

The inside of the building was just as charming as the exterior, but Olivia had only a second to take in the high ceilings and polished broad-planked floors. A tall, sleek-looking blond woman of about thirty stood beside the desk, talking to the fresh-faced young receptionist. Both women glanced up when Olivia entered.

"May I help you?" the younger woman inquired politely.

"I'm Olivia. Mr. Addison is expecting me." She handed the receptionist her card, on which only her first name was printed in large, swirling script. Beneath that, her address and other pertinent information were listed in tiny, unobtrusive block letters.

In the design world, and among her clients, she was known simply as Olivia. That was also the name of her company. Though privately Olivia felt that using only one name was a silly affectation, she had grown up among the wealthy elite and she knew them well. When she started her own business she'd had a hunch that they would attach a certain cachet to the practice, and she'd been right.

Before the younger woman could reply the blonde took the card from her and turned to Olivia with a welcoming smile. "Ah, yes, Olivia, we were expecting you. I'm Caroline Keeton, Mr. Addison's assistant. I believe we spoke on the telephone last week."

"Yes, of course."

"I'm so sorry, but there's been a slight change of plans. Mr. Addison just telephoned. I'm afraid he's tied up in a meeting with some investors and doesn't know how long he'll be," the woman said, her honeyed drawl dripping with apology. "He feels just terrible about not being here to personally escort you to Mallen Island as he'd intended. I'd do the honors myself, but I'm afraid I'm just snowed under today.

"But don't you worry, now, sugar," she assured Olivia before she could reply. "Reese wants you to go on out to the island, and he'll join you there later this afternoon."

"Oh. Well, I, uh…I suppose I could do that," Olivia stammered, a bit thrown by the unexpected change in plans.

"He said for you to make yourself at home and to feel free to look around. He merely requests that you not wander too far from the house. The island is about six miles long and three to four miles wide. Two-thirds of the land is covered with thick forest and all the old trails through the woods have become overgrown and dangerous."

"I see."

"And don't worry, you won't be alone on the island. There's a work crew there each day. They're putting in new piers and boat slips and a full-service marina.

"And, of course, Mrs. Jaffee is there every day. She's the temporary cook and housekeeper who'll be in residence throughout the renovation. She's there to look after whoever happens to be staying overnight on the island.

"So far there's been a whole slew of structural engineers and the like, and each of the other two decorators bidding on the job has already spent a few days at Mallenegua, getting a feel for the house and an idea of the partners' vision for the project. You're the last one."

"If I may ask, how am I supposed to get there? I was told there was no ferry service to Mallen Island."

"That's right. The island is privately owned, and has been since 1870. But don't you worry. Your transportation is arranged. The *Lady Bea* is docked and waiting on the river right now. Come along with me, and I'll take you to the boat and introduce you to the captain. His name is Buford Baines, but everyone calls him Cappy."

She stared at the house as the boat drew near the island. Dear Lord. *This* was the Victorian summer cottage that AdCo was going to renovate?

"When the fog rolls in and the pale moon rises over Mallen Island, God help those foolhardy enough to venture near."

Unbidden, the words from the past whispered through Olivia's mind and a shiver rippled through her.

Faintly embarrassed by the reaction, she shook her head. How many times while growing up had she heard that old warning? Always, it had been murmured in a dire tone and accompanied by a look that had sent chills down her spine.

Olivia figured that the new owners of Mallen Island had to be outsiders. Probably Yankees who'd never heard that the island was not only haunted, but cursed. No local would dare to invest the kind of time, energy and money in the house and island that AdCo was planning.

Though there were those who claimed that Savannah was the most haunted city in the United States, and locals were proud of their ghosts, that didn't hold true for Mallenegua. Most people felt that there was something inherently evil about the island and the old mansion. Unless things had changed drastically in the past fourteen years, you'd be hard-pressed to find many who'd come within a mile of the place.

Reese Addison had explained during their initial telephone conversation that he and his partner were planning to turn the place into an exclusive retreat for the ultrarich, so she had expected the house to be large. She'd also known that the nineteenth-century nouveau riche who'd built their summer homes in the area had used the term *cottage* loosely. Even so, she hadn't expected this.

Growing up near Savannah, Olivia had heard all about Theobald P. Mallen, the wealthy nineteenth-century shipping magnate, and the summer home he'd built on the isolated island off the Georgia coast. However, not being part of the sailing and yachting set, she'd never ventured out this far, so she had not actually seen the house before.

Recalling the wild tales she'd heard about the place, Olivia chuckled to herself. Controversy had swirled around Theobald throughout his lifetime, especially speculation about the source of his great wealth.

According to the stories, he had arrived on the Savannah scene mere months after Lee's surrender had ended the Civil War, or what Savannahians, to this day, referred to as "the war of Northern aggression." Theobald had been a young man in his early twenties with nothing to show for himself but good looks, a fancy suit of clothes, a glib tongue and charm a'plenty. In other words, your typical "carpetbagger." Yet within months of his arrival he had somehow managed to purchase two merchant ships, and by the end of the decade he had been the wealthiest man in town.

At the time, the citizens of Savannah believed, and the old guard still swore that it was true, that Mallen Shipping Lines had merely been a cover for Theobald's true business—smuggling pirated and illegal goods into the country, and that he wasn't particular about what they were. It was also widely believed that the contraband had been brought in through Mallen Island.

Theobald died under mysterious circumstances, falling from the island's cliffs, which he'd known like the back of his hand, into the pounding surf and jagged rocks below. Rumor was, he'd been pushed, and for his sins, his spirit was doomed to roam the island for eternity.

Over the years since, some had claimed to have seen Theobald's ghost wandering along the cliffs on those nights when the pale moon rose like a misty specter above the island. Consequently, gory tales of ghosts and the strange and evil doings that took place on Mallen Island abounded.

As a child, Olivia had listened to the stories with fascinated horror. During sleepovers, late at night, she and Blair had often sat cross-legged on her friend's bed recounting the tales and scaring each other witless.

A wry smile tugged at Olivia's mouth. Thank heaven she no longer believed in ghosts.

The huge stone mansion stood on the northern promontory, perched high on the granite cliffs that dominated one end of the island. The almost-perpendicular walls of stone formed a point that looked strikingly like the prow of a sailing ship.

The house looked out defiantly over the cliff at the Atlantic Ocean, its massive tower silhouetted against the leaden January sky like a raised fist, as if arrogantly daring the sea to hurl its full fury at the island.

"It looks like a castle," Olivia murmured. Huddled in her coat, she stood beside the captain in the pilothouse of the *Lady Bea,* and stared, transfixed.

"Humph," he replied.

She glanced at the man out of the corner of her eye. The *Lady Bea* was a tugboat, and Cappy Baines could not have looked more the stereotypical old sea dog had he been chosen for the part by a Hollywood casting director. In his mid to late fifties, big and barrel-chested, he exuded self-reliance and ruggedness.

Olivia had also discovered that Cappy Baines was a man of few words. During the entire hour-and-a-half boat trip, other than barking orders at his crewmen, he had barely uttered three complete sentences.

He wore a pea coat that had seen better days and a navy wool knit cap, pulled low over his brow. What little she could see of his face between the cap and the full silver beard was sun-baked and wrinkled to the texture of old leather. Roughened hands, big as hams, gripped the ship's wheel while piercing gray eyes constantly swept the restless waters. Every few seconds his gaze flickered over the loaded cargo barge the tug was pushing.

From the corner of the captain's mouth hung a curved pipe. A thin tendril of smoke curled upward from its bowl.

Olivia's nose twitched at the not-unpleasant, slightly sweet scent. She would have preferred to stand out on the *Lady Bea*'s deck, but the frigid January winds and damp sea air made that impossible. It was either join the captain in here and inhale second-hand smoke or go below deck, and her stomach was a bit too uncertain for that, thanks to the choppy sea.

Ignoring the taciturn old man, Olivia resumed her study of Mallenegua. Oh, yes. She was definitely going to enjoy her three days here, she thought with growing excitement.

Mercifully, her jitters had passed. From the moment the *Lady Bea* had pulled away from the dock her tense muscles had begun to relax, especially once they'd reached the open waters of the Atlantic and Savannah had begun to fade into the distance behind the tug.

They approached the island from the north, giving her a clear view of the front of the sprawling, three-story mansion. Built of the same rusty-rose granite as the cliffs, the house seemed to have sprouted right out of the ground. Its design was apparently a cross between Queen Anne, Victorian and a French palace.

Cappy steered the tug and barge along the leeward coast of the island where the waters were calmer. Chugging past the promontory afforded Olivia a side view of the mansion and its west wing. To her amazement, the house was even larger than it had appeared from the front.

The captain reduced speed, and Olivia tore her gaze away from the cliff top to discover that they had entered a cove that formed a natural harbor.

A hundred or so feet down the shoreline from the existing pier, new pilings marched out from the shore, their tops sticking up out of the water in several neat double rows.

On shore and in small boats, men shouted and signaled to one another and to the workers operating a barge-mounted pile driver. Sloth slow, the rhythmic thuds of the huge machine reverberated like a giant's footsteps, each ponderous concussion battering the air.

Spotting the tugboat, a man waved and left the work party to jog down the shoreline. By the time the tug docked he stood waiting on the rickety old pier.

Olivia cast a dubious glance over the structure, not at all confident the thing would support an additional burden, not even her slight weight. The old pier looked as though it had been built at the same time as the house.

"Hey, Cappy. Have a good trip?" the man asked when the captain and Olivia came down the short gangplank.

"Tolerable."

"I see you brought the decking and cross ties."

"Said I would, didn't I?" Cappy growled. "Though why anybody'd want to fix up this godforsaken place, I don't know."

"Now, Cappy."

"Don't 'now Cappy' me. There's strange goings-on here, and you know it. You ask me, this place is bad news."

"Damn, Cappy, will you knock it off. You're gonna scare the lady."

"Oh, don't worry. I grew up not far from here. I know all about Mallen Island," Olivia assured the younger man.

He had a friendly if weather-beaten face, what she could see of it beneath the wool cap that was pulled low over his ears and forehead. Dressed in jeans, work boots and a heavy coat, he appeared to be somewhere in his early forties, with the brawny look of a man who did physical outdoor labor.

As though suddenly remembering Olivia's presence, the captain scowled at her, then tipped his head toward the other man. "Olivia, meet Mike Garvey," he muttered. "He's the foreman in charge of that lazy bunch of landlubbers down yonder. Olivia's one a them designers, here to have a look-see at the house."

"Nice to meet you." Mike glanced back toward the *Lady Bea.* "Where's the boss? I thought he was coming today, too."

"I was told that he had a meeting," Olivia volunteered. "He'll be along a little later."

Mike offered to carry Olivia's suitcase up to the house, but she politely refused his help. Leaving the two men discussing where to unload the contents of the barge, she walked away down the pier and started up the flight of stone steps that were carved out of the side of the cliff.

The wind off the water battered her every step of the way. Its damp chill seemed to penetrate to her bones. Seagulls circled the shoreline and pier, their grating caws an eerie counterpoint to the boom of the pile driver. The southern two-thirds of the island sloped to the sea and were covered with tall pine forests, and the trees swayed and moaned in the whipping winter wind. Beyond the mouth of the cove the ocean swells were building, and the sky had turned from gray to an angry pewter. Olivia eyed the low-hanging clouds and shivered. There was a wildness here, an almost palpable feeling of menace that unnerved her.

At the top of the steps she put down her suitcase and paused to catch her breath and get her bearings.

Though the house was still impressive and imposing, this close she could see signs of age and neglect everywhere. From the look of it, no one had done anything to this place in years.

The remains of three wide gravel paths led away from the landing, one to the right, one to the left and the other straight ahead. All three wound through tangled vines and overgrown plants and trees that had once been a garden.

A gust of wind buffeted Olivia, whipping her hair in all directions and tearing at her coat. Shivering, she picked up her case and took the middle path, which appeared to be the shortest.

Soon she found herself standing on a wide flagstone terrace that ran along the west side of the house. Many of the stones were cracked and buckling, and the surface was littered with leaves, pine needles, broken limbs, a few shattered slate tiles from the roof and various other debris.

The marble fountain at the center of the terrace stood silent, its tiered bowls filled with stagnant rain water and trash, their surfaces green with algae. Most of the cupids that cavorted around the bowl's edges were chipped and cracked.

Olivia turned in a slow circle. The smell of decay and dampness made her nose twitch. Overhead, the bare branches of giant oak trees swayed in the wind and rubbed together with a grating screech. Leggy, bare crepe myrtles bobbed and creaked. An eddy of dead leaves danced across the stone floor like a dervish, then settled in a pile against the base of a broken stone jardiniere.

Olivia shook her head. How sad to see a place that had once been magnificent so seedy and forlorn.

Another blast of wind moaned around the eaves of the house. The hair on the back of Olivia's neck prickled. She darted a quick look around, her gaze bouncing from window to window. No one was there, but she couldn't shake the uneasy feeling that she was being watched.

She shivered again and hugged her coat tighter around her body. Perhaps it was merely the gloominess of the day, or the desolation and neglect all around, but there was something disquieting about this place. Something creepy. If she'd been prone to fanciful thoughts and fits of hysteria, she could have almost believed those old stories were true.

Several sets of French doors opened onto the terrace, but heavy draperies were drawn over all of them and there was neither a knocker nor a doorbell in sight. Olivia went from one set of doors to the next, at each, tapping on the panes and cupping her hands around her eyes to try to peek in through a crack in the draperies, but she had no luck.

Finally, giving up, she retraced her steps and returned to the landing at the top of the cliff and took the path to the left toward the front of the mansion.

The path was overgrown and littered with debris, making Olivia wonder how long it had been since anyone had come around to the main door. Pushing aside branches and stepping cautiously, she picked her way to the front portico. She would have liked to stop and inspect the details of the outside of the house more closely, but it was too cold and raw. Already she felt frozen to the bone.

A lovely porch graced the entrance, but she was too miserable to do more than cast a distracted glance at the lovely proportions. All she wanted was to get inside and escape the cold.

She climbed the steps, grateful for the partial shelter from the wind. To her relief, when she yanked the ancient pull chain chimes sounded on the other side of the double doors. The slow, deep-throated notes seemed to go on and on, echoing eerily through the interior of the house before finally fading away.

Hunching her shoulders against the cold, Olivia shifted from one foot to the other. While she waited she turned and studied the area immediately in front of the porch and the gray, choppy waters of the ocean beyond.

From experience she knew that for most of the year the south Atlantic coastal area was lovely and inviting, but it was certainly bleak now.

Her gaze wandered over the area directly in front of the veranda. No doubt this part of the grounds was a continuation of the formal gardens that had once surrounded the house. This section had probably been filled with roses and secluded little arbors, she mused. A place where the lady of the house or courting couples could stroll at sunset. Not this wild tangle of unchecked vegetation.

Like the garden that ran along the side of the mansion, this one was also enclosed by a four-foot stone wall. Beyond, the land had been left natural. At this end of the island the pine forest gave way to the jutting granite promontory. Here and there bits of wild vegetation and a few stunted, wind-twisted trees poked up between the slabs of rock that stretched out to the cliff's edge.

Olivia shook her head. She hoped AdCo and their

investors had deep pockets. It was going to take a mint to get this place back into shape.

Growing impatient, she turned back to the door. For heaven's sake, where was that housekeeper? She was about to give the bell another yank when the door opened.

Olivia found herself looking into the sternest face she'd ever encountered.

Somewhere in her sixties, the woman was angular and rawboned, and so tall she towered over Olivia, even though the three-inch heels on her boots put her at five foot seven. The housekeeper was homely to the point of almost being grotesque.

It didn't help that she did absolutely nothing to improve her appearance. Thinning steel-gray hair pulled back in a tight bun, small, metal-rimmed glasses and not so much as a speck of makeup merely emphasized sharp features and sunken eyes and a mouth so thin and pinched it would have been invisible had it not been for the circle of lines radiating outward from her lips like a star burst.

Hatchet-faced and cold-eyed, she stared at Olivia in silence, looking as though she'd just stepped out of a Halloween horror movie. Olivia had to resist the urge to back away.

"You must be Mrs. Jaffee," she said, forcing a polite smile. "I'm Olivia."

"Yes. That Miss Keeton called and said you were coming," the woman replied in a voice as cold as her expression. She stepped back and motioned for Olivia to enter, giving the impression that she did so reluctantly.

The moment Olivia stepped inside she forgot all about the scary woman and her own discomfort. Enthralled by the faded glory all around her, she tilted her head back and inspected the high ceiling, ornately carved moldings and grand staircase that swept upward in a graceful arc. "Oh, this is magnificent. Simply stunning."

"I've prepared a room for you on the second floor."

"What?" Olivia blinked and looked around, and discovered that Mrs. Jaffee had picked up her suitcase and was heading for the stairs. "Oh, yes. Yes, of course."

"Don't expect much. There are only a few bedrooms fit to use these days. The rooms that weren't being used, Miss Prudence kept closed."

"And Miss Prudence is…?"

"Miss Prudence Mallen. She's the granddaughter of Theobald Mallen. She was born in this house and lived here all of her life until a couple of months ago."

"Do you know her?"

Mrs. Jaffee shot Olivia a cold look over her shoulder. "I have worked here for the Mallen family for over forty years. My late husband and I both worked here."

"I see." Olivia's gaze swept around as they climbed the massive stairway. "This house is so wonderful. She must have hated to leave it. I know in her place, I would have."

They reached the second floor and Olivia followed Mrs. Jaffee down a wide hallway. At a door halfway down the hall, the woman stopped.

"You ask me, it's a crying shame she had to give up her family home. Especially at her age. Theobald

Mallen built this house. Mallens have lived here for over a hundred years. It just isn't right.''

Taken aback, Olivia didn't know what to say, but luckily Mrs. Jaffee did not seem to expect a reply. The housekeeper opened the door, motioned Olivia inside and followed.

''This was the master's suite, but when Miss Prudence inherited the house she chose to stay in the blue room at the end of the hall, the one she'd slept in all her life. In recent years her nephew has used this bedroom.''

Olivia walked to the middle of the faded Oriental rug and turned slowly. ''It's lovely.''

The room was enormous, many times the size of modern master bedrooms and beautifully proportioned, with a soaring ceiling, tall windows and intricate molding and woodwork. Through an open door to one side she glimpsed what appeared to be a sitting room.

Curious, Olivia peeked into the room and saw several comfortable-looking settees and chairs and an open armoire that held a TV/VCR/DVD and a complete stereo system.

''That's the master's private sitting room,'' Mrs. Jaffee confirmed. ''The door on the other side of that room connects to Mrs. Mallen's bedroom. All those gadgets belong to Miss Prudence's nephew. I expect he'll be back for them soon.''

The old woman stomped to the fireplace, tossed more wood on the fire and stirred it with a poker. ''This suite has seen better days, but it's clean.''

Like the rest of the house, the room was shabby and time-worn, with threadbare rugs, faded and peeling wallpaper, and dull, worn floors. The finish on the furniture crackled with age. The long swaths of heavy velvet draping the windows had cost a fortune when new, but now they were faded and worn bare in spots and tired-looking.

Yet remnants of the room's former grandness remained in the massive bed with its carved headboard that stood at least eight feet high, the intricate molding, the beautiful fireplace and little bits of gilding still clinging stubbornly to the ceiling wallpaper.

This had once been a showcase of a bedroom. A showcase of a house, Olivia thought, growing steadily more excited. And if she got this job, it would be again, she vowed.

The housekeeper gave the fire one last jab, then straightened and turned cold eyes on Olivia. "There's a furnace in the basement, but it's over fifty years old and doesn't work too well. To stay comfortable you'll need a fire. I brought up an extra supply of wood," she added, gesturing toward the wood box beside the hearth.

She returned the poker to the stand of fireplace tools and once again fixed Olivia with her frigid stare. "The bathroom is right through there. The pipes clang a bit and it takes a while to get hot water, but it works."

"I'm sure it'll be fine."

"Is there anything else you require?"

"No. I'm fine, thanks. I'm going to unpack my things, then have a look around the house."

Mrs. Jaffee stared at her a long time, and Olivia could see that she wasn't happy with the idea of her roaming the house unaccompanied. What did the woman think? That she was going to filch the silver? Or strap one of these massive antique pieces of furniture to her back and swim back to Savannah with it?

Finally the housekeeper tipped her chin in the slightest of nods and stalked out without another word.

One glance at her suitcase and Olivia decided that unpacking could wait. She was anxious to see the house.

She began in the suite she was occupying, inspecting each piece of furniture, noting the type of wood used for flooring and trim, the details of construction. The master bedroom and sitting room, though shabby, were clean and showed signs of use, but in Mrs. Mallen's bedroom the furniture was draped with old sheets and covered with dust and cobwebs.

When finished in the suite, Olivia started with the first room at the top of the stairs and worked her way down the hall.

As a designer, she appreciated all styles of architecture and furniture, but she had a special affinity for antiques. Even in their shabby state, the house and furnishings were a treasure trove.

In each room she found something unique, and with each discovery her excitement grew. "I have to get this job," she murmured to herself after viewing only three rooms. "I *have* to." Not just for the money or the prestige the job would bring her, but for the joy of it. The chance to work on a house like this one didn't come along very often, if ever.

By late afternoon Olivia was in a bedroom at the end of the hall, which appeared to have been used recently. While inspecting the handmade shutters that disappeared into the walls on either side of the windows, she spotted a cabin cruiser skimming over the waves toward the island.

The boat docked behind the tugboat and a tall, dark-haired man hopped over the side onto the rickety pier and fastened the mooring lines. A couple of men from the crew unloading the barge came over to greet the newcomer, and Cappy Baines waved to him from the pilothouse of the *Lady Bea*.

From that distance and angle Olivia could not see the man's face, but she assumed he was Reese Addison.

That assumption seemed to be confirmed when, after a brief discussion with the men, he left them and started up the pier, heading for the stone steps.

Though loath to stop what she was doing, good manners required that Olivia go downstairs and meet the man. With a sigh, she pulled the shutters together and refastened them, but when she turned to leave the lovely canopy bed caught her eye, and she stopped to run her fingers over the fluted posts. Minutes later she was still there, studying the hand-carved acanthus-leaf design in the headboard, when the sound of footsteps on the pecan-wood flooring announced the arrival of her prospective client.

''Ah, there you are. You must be Olivia.''

She froze.

Her heart began to pound. It had been fourteen years since Olivia had heard that dark, velvety drawl, but she would recognize the voice if it had been fifty. Standing with her back to him, she squeezed her eyes shut.

No. No, it can't be. Of all the people in Savannah, it can't be him. *It can't!*

But it was.

Accepting the cruel irony, Olivia drew a deep breath and turned slowly—and came face-to-face with her ex-husband.

Two

"I'm afraid that Reese couldn't get away, so he asked me to come in his place. I'm Joe Connally, his partner in Ad—"

He jerked to a halt, his jaw dropping. Had he been anyone else Olivia would have thought the reaction comical.

"Livvie?" he managed finally. "Is that you?"

"Hello, Joe."

"Dear God. It *is* you."

"Yes. I'm afraid so."

He blinked several times and shook his head as though he couldn't believe his eyes. "I don't understand. What are you doing here?"

"I was invited by Reese Addison to come and look over Mallenegua and bid on the design job."

If possible, he looked even more stunned. "Good God! *You're* Olivia?"

"Yes."

"But how…when did you…?" He stopped and raked his hand through his walnut-brown hair. "That is…I had no idea you'd become an interior designer."

She had never seen Joe rattled before. He was always calm and collected, almost nonchalant, even in the midst of a crisis that threw others around him into a tailspin.

His sister claimed that Joe seldom became riled enough to lose his composure, and even then it took extreme provocation. In all the years that Olivia had known him, she'd never seen him in a full-blown rage, but Blair had told her that it was an awesome sight to behold. According to her former friend, on those rare occasions his voice would soften in a way that was all the more frightening for its steely control. Then, without warning, he let fly with an explosive fury that could scorch the paint off a wall.

Olivia might have been amused by Joe's momentary loss of composure if the sight of him hadn't stirred so many painful memories. Or if his connection with Reese Addison hadn't squashed any chance she'd had of getting this job.

She would not, however—absolutely would not—allow him to see how upset and disappointed she was.

She shrugged one shoulder. "There's no reason why you should've known. You and I severed all ties fourteen years ago."

"Yes, but your mother still lives in Bella Vista. Even given that she's retired now and that I no longer live at Winterhaven Farm, I'm there frequently. You'd think word would have gotten around."

Olivia forced a chuckle. "Oh, I'm sure it did, but I can't say I'm surprised that bit of information didn't reach you. You and my mother hardly move in the same social circles."

Even if news of her had reached Joe's mother, which Olivia doubted given that no one with the slightest instinct for self-preservation would have dared to mention her name in Eleanore's presence, she would not have passed the information along to her son.

The Connally matriarch handled trouble or unpleasantness by dealing with it swiftly and decisively, then pretending that the matter never happened. Olivia was certain that Eleanore would not do or say anything that might remind Joe of his disastrous marriage.

The twist of his mouth revealed that the little dig had hit its mark. The glint in his eyes said he wasn't pleased, but he could hardly deny it.

After all, for twenty-two years, her mother had been his mother's housekeeper.

"True enough, I guess," he conceded finally.

He stared as though he could not help himself, taking in every inch of her, from her chic, shoulder-length hairstyle to her expensive Italian boots. "You look good, Livvie. Different than I remember, but really good."

"Thank you."

She could say the same. Fourteen years had added a sprinkle of gray to the hair at his temples and etched a few lines into his face, but the signs of age merely added maturity and character, and made him more attractive than ever. At thirty-five, Joe was a man in his prime.

Shoving back the edges of his leather jacket, he stuffed his hands into the pockets of his jeans and rocked back on his heels. "So. How are you?"

"I'm fine. And you?"

"Good. I'm good."

"That's nice."

Olivia shifted her feet.

Joe jingled the change in his pocket.

"You live in Atlanta now, do you?" he asked after an awkward silence. "That is…your design firm is there, so I assume that's where you live."

Olivia nodded. "Yes. It is."

"Hmm. Nice town."

"It's not Savannah, but I like it."

Another silence stretched out.

When she could stand the strain no longer, Olivia sighed. "Look, can we just drop the polite chitchat? You don't have to worry. I'll make this easy on both of us. Just give me a minute to collect my bag and I'll get Captain Baines to take me back to the mainland and I'll take the next flight home."

Swamped with disappointment but determined to exit with dignity, she started for the door with her head high, but he sidestepped in front of her. "Hey, wait a second. Whoa. Why are you leaving?"

His sudden nearness gave Olivia such a start she barely stifled a gasp. They were so close that she could smell his scent—clean, and virile, and so painfully familiar, even after all these years, that she experienced a flutter of panic and took a hasty step back.

"Please, Joe. Let's not play this game. Okay? Given our history, I don't have a snowball's chance in hell of getting this job, and we both know it. I see no point in wasting my time and creative energy coming up with ideas and putting together a presentation when it's just going to be rejected."

"Why would you think that? I mean…so we're divorced. So what? All that was a long time ago. Anyway, it's not as though there were any hard feelings between us when we went our separate ways."

Olivia gazed back at him. No, she thought. Not on your part, anyway. You would have to care about someone before you experienced those kind of emotions.

Their divorce had been a civilized one, nothing

more than the dissolving of a contract, really. Joe had even shaken her hand and wished her well after their final court appearance when the decree was granted.

Becoming aware of the painful tightness just beneath her breastbone, Olivia gritted her teeth. She hated that seeing Joe again could do this to her.

He was right. All that had happened a long time ago. In another life, she told herself. To a naive girl who no longer existed. None of it mattered any longer.

"Look, Joe, you're a good person. I know that you would try to be fair, and I appreciate that, but you're only human. The past can't help but work against me. Face it, when the time comes to choose the designer for this project, somewhere in the back of your mind there's going to be a little voice whispering, 'Do I really want to work with my ex-wife for the next year or two?' We both know the answer to that. And I understand. Honestly, I do. The truth is, it would be an awkward situation."

"Maybe. But that won't affect my choice or Reese's. Granted, working together might seem a bit strange at first, but that will pass. Hell, Livvie, you and I have always gotten along well. Before and during our marriage." He ducked his head and gave her a teasing look and flashed his lopsided smile, the one that, in the past, had never failed to make her heart go pitty-pat. "Actually, I think this is our first fight."

"That's not funny, Joe. I'm serious."

"So am I. This project is the most ambitious job our company has undertaken so far and it's a top priority to Reese and me. Our primary concern is to hire the best there is for every aspect of the job. Nothing else matters. You were highly recommended. In fact, we heard from several of your clients that when it came to historic restorations you are the designer of choice.''

Disarmed, she blinked twice. ''Really?''

''Absolutely.''

He could have no idea how much it delighted her to hear that she was earning that reputation. She had created beautiful rooms in every style imaginable, from shabby chic to extreme contemporary and everything in between, whatever suited her client's taste. Her personal preference, however, ran to historic American—anything from the graceful, European-influenced, pre-revolutionary War styles to Federal period through the Victorian age. If it was old, it appealed to Olivia.

''Yes, well…regardless, when your partner finds out who I am he may decide that second best is good enough.''

Joe's grin flashed again. He folded his arms over his chest and tipped his head to one side, his brown eyes twinkling. ''So…you think you're the best, do you?''

Olivia's chin angled upward. ''I *know* I am.'' When it came to her work, she had no doubts or insecurities. She knew her stuff, and she was good. Damned good.

''Then stay and finish what you came here to do.''

''Why do you even care? I'd think you'd be happy for me to withdraw.''

''Not so. As I said, Reese and I want the best. Besides, my company tendered an offer, which you accepted in good faith. We don't renege on a deal. I'm also aware that this will be a lucrative job for the designer who gets it. I'd feel terrible if you missed this opportunity because of me.''

Ah, there it is, Olivia thought. That ingrained, Southern-gentleman attitude that was so much a part of Joe. The same code that had prompted him to marry her fourteen years ago.

The old-fashioned ethic had been bred into his bones and reinforced by years of training from his late father, Brian Connally. More than merely some high-flown ideals or gracious good manners, those unwritten rules were a way of life among old-line Southerners. A true gentleman of the South was always polite and considerate to ladies, took his responsibilities seriously and strove to always do the right thing.

And above all, he valued his honor. His word was his bond. If he gave it, whether with a signature on a contract or a handshake, he kept it.

Olivia was quiet for so long Joe cocked his eyebrows at her. ''You do *want* the job, don't you?''

''Of course I want it, but—''

''Then go for it. The only criterion we have is that whoever gets this job has a knockout of a design plan. Nothing else matters. You have my word on it.

''And don't worry about Reese's reaction. We were college roommates, but when I returned to Princeton after you and I split, I told everyone I'd laid off a year because of a family crisis. Reese doesn't know anything about us or our marriage.''

''I see.'' Olivia looked at him impassively and tried to squash the hurt that squeezed her chest. Their marriage had been so insignificant—nothing more than a temporary inconvenience in his life—that he hadn't even bothered to mention it to his friend and business partner.

"I see no reason to tell him now," Joe continued. "So, if he picks you for the job you'll know it's because he likes your design ideas best."

She hesitated, torn. The idea of working with Joe for the next year or so was unsettling. Which was putting it mildly. Just a few hours ago the very idea would have been unthinkable. It would be too awkward, not to mention it would stir up memories that were just as well left alone. And then there was Joe's mother. Oh, Lord, when Eleanore found out she would be livid.

Still…this job was a career-maker, and Olivia wanted it so much she could taste it.

Finally, coming to a decision, she drew a bracing breath. "All right, I'll stay. If you're sure."

"I'm positive." Joe stepped back and motioned toward the door. "Now then, why don't I take you on that tour that Reese promised you?"

"That's not necessary. I've already been exploring on my own for the last couple of hours. I don't think I need a guide."

"Don't be so sure. You can get lost in this place. At least let me take you on a quick walk-through. That way you can get a handle on the layout. Later you can take a closer look on your own."

The last thing Olivia wanted was to spend an hour or so alone with Joe, wandering through the romantic old mansion, but she couldn't very well refuse. The whole reason she'd come here was to get a look at the place.

"Very well. Whatever you think best."

"Why don't we start on the ground floor? We can work our way front to back on each level, all the way to the top."

"All right."

At the bottom of the stairs they walked to the center of the marble floor in the entrance, where an inlay in shades of rose, mauve, black, gray and white granite formed a star-burst pattern.

Olivia turned slowly in a circle, taking in the great expanse of open space, then craned her neck back to gaze upward. Seventy-five feet overhead soft, rainbow-colored light seeped through the enormous stained glass dome into the foyer. The intricate pattern in the dome mirrored the star burst on the floor. Though its effect was muted by the overcast winter sky, Olivia had no trouble imagining how alive with light and color the foyer would be on a sunny day.

The glass was intact, though it needed to be cleaned and repaired. Judging from the streaked and crumbling plaster work edging the circumference of the dome and the arched ceiling beneath, it had a serious leak. Even so, the extravagant beauty of the entry was evident.

"Some foyer, huh?" Joe commented. "Mr. Mallen wanted to be sure that his guests were duly impressed the instant they walked inside. The last owner, Miss Prudence Mallen, told me this space was often used during parties to handle overflow from the ballroom at the back of the house."

"It's certainly large enough," Olivia murmured in a distracted voice. The foyer alone was larger than many homes.

Though age and neglect had taken their toll, to her professional eye, the faded beauty of the mansion was entrancing, and she felt her excitement growing by the minute. Already ideas were taking shape in her mind.

Getting the chance to restore this place to its former grandeur would be a dream come true. AdCo was offering the designer unprecedented freedom and a nearly unlimited budget. Even a chance to consult with the architect in charge of restoration. Lord, if only she had a chance of getting this job.

Joe strode over to a set of tall, cherry-wood pocket doors and slid them open to reveal an enormous room with a faded mural on the ceiling and tattered silk wallpaper. Throughout the room, dusty, sheet-draped furniture dotted the faded Oriental rugs that covered much of the marble floor.

"This is the largest of four grand parlors or drawing rooms. It's fifty feet long by thirty wide and the ceiling is twenty feet high," he said, rattling off the figures like a tour guide. "As you can see, there's a fireplace at each end, and…"

As Olivia had anticipated, the tour turned out to be awkward for both her and Joe.

Though they tried to pretend otherwise, they were ill at ease with each other. They walked from room to room doing their best to avoid making eye contact, their conversation, if that's what you could call their stilted exchange, so excruciatingly polite and stiff they sounded like two strangers.

Sadly, it occurred to Olivia that no one observing them would guess that once upon a time, almost nightly for five months of their lives, they had made passionate love to each other.

Olivia was acutely aware of Joe walking beside her and, consequently, so tense she felt as though her insides had been twisted into a knot.

She took care to keep a safe distance between them. Even so, now and then his arm accidentally brushed against hers or he touched her in some way. Each time her nerve endings sizzled.

Once, when he placed his hand against the small of her back to turn her down yet another corridor, she jumped as though he'd poked her with a cattle prod. If Joe noticed, he didn't let on.

For his part, he kept up a running monologue, rattling off facts and anecdotes about the house and the Mallen family, pointing out architectural features and details and, in a general way, explaining AdCo's plans for the place as they went.

On the surface Joe almost seemed his usual self, but anyone who knew him could detect the stiffness in his demeanor and voice.

On the first floor, he led her through the other parlors, as well as dining rooms, a solarium, a music room, a billiard room and a magnificent library with a soaring ceiling and a mezzanine level all around, accessed by a spiral staircase. There was also a richly paneled office with a decidedly masculine feel, which Olivia assumed had once been Theobald Mallen's. In all there were four parlors—five, if you counted the ladies' sitting room—and three dining rooms, with long tables that seated from twelve to fifty-two people.

The main parlor and largest dining room, the library, office and the ballroom opened onto the large terrace that she had seen earlier, which ran along the west side of the mansion.

On the opposite side of the hall from the ballroom a solarium overlooked one of two sheltered inner courtyards. Wandering gravel paths and overgrown boxwood hedges had once created intricate patterns through both, but at the center of this one were the shriveled remains of what appeared to be a vegetable garden. Only one small patch of ground at a corner of the garden seemed to have been recently cultivated, for the benefit, Olivia assumed, of Miss Prudence Mallen and her housekeeper.

With its numerous intersecting corridors, the layout of the house was, indeed, confusing, just as Joe had warned. Try as she might, Olivia could not get her bearings. She began to wonder if she was going to be able to find her way back to her room without help.

"The house was originally to be built in a wide, face-to-face double-E shape, but during construction additional wings were added," Joe volunteered, as though divining her thoughts. "The changes made the overall design a bit confusing and odd. I'm told that the architect objected strenuously, but Theobald was adamant."

"Why?" Olivia asked. "Surely the original plan would have been big enough. And certainly a more classically elegant design."

"Yes, well, in the Gilded Age the *nouveau riche* were constantly trying to outdo one another and, according to Miss Prudence, her great-grandfather felt especially competitive with the Vanderbilts. Maybe because the Vanderbilt fortune was made legitimately, while rumors persisted, no matter how hard Theobald tried to squash them, that the Mallen fortune had come from smuggling and other…well… shall we say, less-than-reputable endeavors.

"Anyway, when Cornelius Vanderbilt's son, George, began construction on Biltmore Estate in 1890, Theobald immediately began building this house. He already owned Mallen Island, and I suppose he figured the setting would make his estate even more unique.

"Originally, Mr. Mallen's intention was for Mallenegua to be bigger and better than the Vanderbilt estate. Imagine his frustration when he learned that Biltmore would have two hundred and fifty rooms.

"That's when he ordered the architect to add the additional wings and rooms to Mallenegua. Unfortunately, construction was well under way by then and the limitations of the site he had chosen restricted the size of the mansion to a mere one hundred and sixty-four rooms."

Olivia's mouth twitched. "My, how tragic."

The second and third floors were mostly bedrooms, which Olivia found curious. "How many children did the Mallens have, for heaven's sake? Other than the Biltmore, I've never seen a private home with so many bedrooms."

"Theobald and his wife Agatha did have several children, but only one, a son, survived to adulthood," Joe replied. "However, the Mallens were a prominent society family, and they entertained lavishly. This was their summer home, and whenever they came here they always brought a large house party with them. Plus an army of servants. Throughout the summer new guests arrived and departed almost daily."

"Ah, well, that explains the hotel feel the place has."

"Yes. Which makes it perfect for our purposes. In its day, Mallenegua catered to the rich and famous. Now it will again."

At the end of the third-floor hall Joe opened a door, revealing a large storage room. Stacked neatly on the shelves lining the walls were linens, yellowed with age, and all manner of items from the nineteenth century—everything from kerosene lamps, brass spittoons, porcelain washbowls and pitchers and chamber pots, to more refined accoutrements like smelling salts, castile soaps, hair pomade, gentlemen's shaving brushes and mugs, mother-of-pearl-handled strop razors, shoehorns, corset stays and long-handled buttonhooks. A thick layer of dust covered every item, and spiderwebs festooned the entire room in eerie swags.

"It looks like nothing has been touched in here for ten years," Olivia said, wrinkling her nose at the musty smell.

"Maybe longer. By World War One old Theobald was gone, and in the hands of his son, then later his grandson, the family fortunes didn't fare too well. After the crash in '29 the family could no longer afford to entertain on a lavish scale.

"By the time Miss Prudence inherited, about twelve years ago, all the other family homes and the Mallen Shipping Line had been sold to cover debts. This house, its contents and the island were the only tangible property left—along with a modest sum of money, which was a tiny fraction of what Theobald's fortune had once been.

"Unfortunately, this place is a money pit, and to make ends meet, Miss Prudence has had to sell off paintings and valuable antiques."

"Yes, I saw the dark spots on the wallpaper and rugs where items had been removed," Olivia said. "If money was that tight, I'm surprised she didn't just sell out. It doesn't make sense for just two people to live here."

"Actually, there were three—Miss Prudence, the

housekeeper and a great-nephew of sorts. He's not blood kin to the Mallens. The guy is the great-grandson of Miss Prudence's stepmother.

"When Charity Ainsworth married Randolf Mallen, Miss Prudence's father, she was a widow with a son named Franklin. Franklin's grandson, Lennard, moved in here about eight years ago at Miss Prudence's invitation. Apparently she felt safer with a man on the premises. In exchange for his keep, he was supposed to be a handyman and maintain the place."

"Really?" Olivia said with disbelief. "Pardon me for saying so, but he didn't do a very good job."

"Yeah, I know. But to be fair, a mansion this size is too much for one man to keep up. I've never met the guy. He moved out as soon as he found out that Miss Prudence was selling.

"You're right about this place, though. It's been nothing but a liability to her for years. However, she'd lived here for most of her life and didn't want to leave."

"I suppose I can understand that," Olivia said. "What finally convinced her to sell?"

"Age. About six months ago she fell in the garden while Mrs. Jaffee and the nephew were in Savannah getting their weekly supplies. She lay there for hours until they returned and found her. She wasn't seriously hurt, but the experience frightened her.

"Several years ago I had tried to purchase the house and island, but even though I'd made her a generous offer, she turned me down. Within a week of the fall she telephoned and asked if I was still interested. Believe me, I jumped at the chance. I'd been wanting to get my hands on this place as far back as I can remember.

"As soon as the deal was done Miss Prudence moved to an assisted-care facility in Savannah."

"The poor old thing," Olivia sympathized. "It must have been heart-wrenching for her."

"I'm sure it was at first, but she adjusted quicker than anyone would ever have guessed. Last time I stopped by to see her at Tall Pines she was having the time of her life. She's in her eighties, but she's made friends with other residents and learned to play bridge and croquet and taken up several hobbies. She's even taking painting lessons."

Olivia raised her eyebrows. "You visit her?"

"Sure. Now and then." Joe shrugged. "She's a nice old lady. I like her."

Olivia didn't know why she was surprised. That sort of thing was typical of Joe. As a child, even through the teen years when most boys turn into obnoxious clods, he had always been kind to the very young and the very old and anyone weaker than he was. The plain truth was, man and boy, Joe was a good man. That was partly why she'd fallen in love with him all those years ago.

Suddenly uneasy with her train of thought, Olivia turned her attention back to the contents of the storage room. "I'm surprised she held on to all this stuff, since she needed money. Any antique dealer would be happy to buy the lot."

"I'm sure she would have eventually sold it all, but I'm glad she hadn't gotten around to it. We want to retain the 1890s feel, and we're hoping some of these items can be incorporated into the decor."

"I'm sure they can. There are some real treasures in here."

"There's plenty more in the attic storage, as well."

Olivia stepped into the storeroom, partly for a closer look at the contents and partly to put some distance between herself and Joe. Bending, she rubbed a patch of dust off the lid of a porcelain pot with her forefinger, revealing the initials TPM in fancy gold script. "Monogrammed chamber pots? Now, that's classy." She glanced back at Joe with a quizzical frown. "Why are there so many? From the look of the bathrooms, I assumed they were original to the house."

"They were. The Vanderbilts were incorporating all the latest innovations at Biltmore, so Theobald did the same when he built Mallenegua—indoor plumbing, central heat, electricity, the works. The only problem was, in 1890 indoor toilets were a new-fangled oddity, and people didn't trust them. Most guests requested a chamber pot in their room."

Shaking her head at the absurdity, Olivia dusted off her hands and returned to the hall.

They continued touring the third floor in silence, and when they were done they climbed a back stairway to the attic.

"These were the servants' quarters," Joe explained as they started down a narrow hallway with numerous doors on either side. "The attics in the west wing housed the staff. This is the southwest wing, which was used by the female staff. The northwest wing rooms were for the men. The attic space above the rest of the mansion is used as storage for seasonal items and family discards and such. The basement contains the furnace, the boiler, a wine cellar and the equipment needed to maintain the house and grounds. Hidden at the far end of the island is a massive generator that provides the electricity.''

''I see,'' Olivia murmured, matching his business-like tone.

Lit by bare lightbulbs placed at infrequent intervals, the passageway was dim and unadorned, except for a threadbare runner down its center. Olivia suspected that the small luxury had been provided for the benefit of the guests on the floor directly below in order to muffle the footsteps of the servants.

A shiver rippled through her, and she rubbed her upper arms. ''Brrr. It's chilly up here.''

''That's because there's no heat on this level. These rooms contain the bare minimum as far as amenities, and they're all pretty much the same,'' Joe said, opening one of the doors to give her a look.

Olivia poked her head inside and saw what he meant. The room was perhaps a quarter the size of the guest bedrooms on the lower floors, with a low ceiling and bare floors, partially covered with worn rag rugs. The furnishings consisted of a narrow bed, a small chest and a writing table and one wooden chair, all of which were scarred and battered.

''There is a bathroom at each end of each corridor. Evidently servants didn't count for much back in the Gilded Age,'' Joe said. ''We plan to knock out walls and double the size of these rooms and add more bathrooms. These days, if you expect to keep good employees, especially the live-in variety, you have to provide a helluva lot better housing and working conditions than this or they'll turn up their noses and walk out.''

Unable to help herself, Olivia shot him a droll look.

"That's right. The hired help has gotten downright uppity in the last forty or fifty years." Turning away, she added too low for him to hear, "Some even have the temerity to marry into the family."

Joe winced. "Ah, hell. I'm sorry, Livvie. I forgot that your moth—that is... Hell, I don't think of you that way."

That's because you don't think of me at all.

Wisely, she kept the thought to herself, but her expression must have betrayed her cynicism.

"It's true," Joe insisted. "C'mon, Livvie, you know that you've always been more like a member of the family."

"I wouldn't repeat that in your mother's presence if I were you," she drawled, and he had the grace to wince again.

"Livvie, I know my mother can be difficult, but—"

She held up her hand. "No, please, let's not get into all that. Don't worry about it, okay? It's not important."

She turned and walked away down the hall and opened another door, leaving Joe staring after her with a pensive frown.

After that the mood between them became even cooler, their exchange more stilted. Taking her time, Olivia moved from one cubbyhole room to the next, looking into each one with as much attention to detail as she'd done in the other parts of the house. Joe followed along in silence.

When they reached the end of the long hall, he said, "The male servants' quarters in the northwest wing are identical to this, but if you want to see it I'll take you there."

"Thank you, but that won't be necessary."

"Well, then, that completes the tour. Except for the basement and storage attic and a few more supply rooms scattered throughout the house, that's about it for the inside. C'mon, I'll take you back to your room."

Olivia flinched when he cupped his hand around her elbow and turned her toward the stairs. Joe's mouth compressed into a flat line, but he didn't comment.

Neither spoke until they stopped in front of Olivia's door, and only then did he release her arm. His gaze ran over her face as though he was searching for something, his brown eyes guarded.

Then suddenly he frowned and stepped forward, grasping her upper arms. "Livvie? Livvie, what's wrong? Dear God. You've turned white as a sheet."

Olivia barely heard him. She stared past Joe's shoulder, her gaze fixed on a point about twenty feet away, where the hall intersected another corridor. There stood a ghostly figure of a man in nineteenth-century dress, his fierce glare aimed directly at her.

Three

"Livvie! For God's sake, what is it?" Joe gave her a shake. "Talk to me!"

Olivia tore her gaze away from the apparition and struggled to gather her wits. When she could focus on Joe again she realized that his hands still gripped her upper arms and he was bent over her, his face taut with concern.

"Dammit, Livvie, what's wrong? You're as white as a sheet."

"N-nothing. Nothing's wrong. I, uh…it's just that I…I thought I saw someone watching us from the end of the hall."

He looked over his shoulder, and Olivia risked another peek in that direction as well, but the corridor was empty.

"There's no one there now." He turned his attention back to Olivia. "It was probably just Mrs. Jaffee."

"Mrs. Jaffee? Does she make a habit of sneaking around the halls?"

Olivia didn't believe for a moment it had been the housekeeper standing there glaring at her. The figure she'd seen had been male. And about as solid as smoke. However, she wasn't about to tell Joe that. He'd probably think she was hallucinating. As it was, her chances of landing this job were slim. She certainly wasn't going to make them worse by appearing hysterical.

"I'm afraid so. She keeps an eye on us to see what atrocities we're going to commit against her beloved house."

"You mean you *know*."

"That she resents us and disapproves of what we're planning for Mallenegua? Sure." Joe shrugged. "She doesn't try to hide her feelings on the matter."

"Then why in heaven's name do you keep her on staff?" As casually as possible, Olivia stepped back out of Joe's grasp, and his hands fell to his sides.

"She's old and harmless—a little spooky, I'll admit, but harmless. Anyway, do you have any idea how difficult it is to find someone willing to stay alone on an island miles from shore in a huge old house that is supposedly cursed? Not that Savannahians are afraid of ghosts, mind you. They are used to those. Hell, they're proud of them. Half the people who own houses in Old Savannah claim they're haunted. It's the gruesome tales of mayhem and evil that have circulated about this place that bother folks. I doubt there's another woman in Savannah who'd take the job. Anyway, the arrangement with Mrs. Jaffee is only temporary."

"I see. Well, I'm sure you know best."

Joe studied her face. "Are you okay now?"

"Yes. Yes, I'm fine."

He didn't looked convinced as his gaze slid over her features once again. "Are you sure? You're not going to feel uneasy up here by yourself, are you?"

"No, of course not. I was just startled is all." She gave him a polite smile and backed up another step.

"I'm a big girl now, Joe. I don't need you to look after me anymore."

The moment Olivia uttered the words she wanted to take them back. For the past couple of hours, except for that one slip, they had avoided any mention of the past or their relationship. Now the air between them seemed to vibrate with a palpable tension.

Joe's sudden stillness told her that the subtle allusion to the way things used to be between them had not been lost on him.

He stared at her for so long she began to feel antsy and had to fight the urge to squirm.

After a time, he relaxed and his beautifully sculptured mouth twisted. "Yeah, I guess you don't at that. Sorry. Some habits die hard."

Relieved that he was willing to let the matter drop, Olivia answered with a wan smile and edged another step closer to the door. "You must be anxious to get back to your work crew. Please, don't let me keep you. I know you're busy and I've taken up enough of your time already."

"Yeah, I probably should be getting back. I need to go over some things with Mike before I leave." He checked his watch. "I'm having dinner with some investors, so I have to be heading back to the mainland soon.

"I apologize for leaving you here alone. Reese had planned to be here throughout your stay, but we've had an emergency with another project and he had to fly to Chattanooga. We expect he'll be there for several days. I'd stay myself, but I've got other commitments, too. If you'd like, I'll see if Caroline can rearrange her schedule and keep you company."

"That's all right. I'll be fine."

Casting another look down the hall, Joe massaged the back of his neck with his cupped hand. "All right. If you're sure you'll be okay, I'll be going." He smiled and stuck out his hand, leaving her no choice but to accept the handshake.

At the first touch of flesh to flesh, an electrical current ran up Olivia's arm. His hand engulfed her much smaller one, his strong fingers curling around her fragile bones in a firm grip.

Unbidden, like a whisper wafting through her mind, came the vivid memory of those big hands sliding over her naked flesh, cupping her breasts, slipping between her thighs. Touching the silky, wet, most secret part of her.

An involuntary moan escaped Olivia as her knees seemed to turn to mush.

"Damn, I'm sorry," Joe exclaimed, and loosened his hold. "I didn't mean to grip so hard. I forgot how delicately you're built, and I guess I'm used to shaking hands with men. Did I hurt you?"

"No. No, you didn't hurt me. I'm…I'm fine," she replied, struggling to regain her composure and will some starch back into her body.

"Good." Joe smiled and covered their clasped hands with his other one. "I'd better be going. I wish you luck with your presentation. It was great seeing you again, Livvie."

"You, too, Joe."

"Oh, I almost forgot. Here's my card with my office and cell phone numbers. If you have any questions or there's anything I can do for you, I'll be down on the pier for the next hour or so," he said, easing away. "After that, you can either call me or you can call Caroline at the office. She's Reese's and my assistant and she knows as much about our operation as we do.''

He'd barely taken two steps when she blurted out, ''Actually, there is one thing you could do for me.''

Stopping, he shot her an expectant look. ''Sure. Name it.''

''Please don't call me Livvie. My name is Olivia.''

The request seemed to startle him. ''But...I've always called you Livvie. Everyone does.''

''Not anymore. With the exception of my mother and sister, no one has called me Livvie in fourteen years, and I'd like to keep it that way.''

Olivia knew she was being picky, but she felt an almost desperate need to keep their relationship on a professional footing, and the diminutive form of her name was just too familiar. Too...intimate. Especially coming from Joe.

He stared at her determined expression. ''All right. If that's what you want, Olivia it is.''

Lifting his hand in farewell, he continued down the hall, then took the stairs at a lope. Olivia remained where she was until he disappeared from view and his footsteps faded away. Only then did she reach for the doorknob.

Once inside her room she collapsed back against the door, closed her eyes and shivered. She didn't know what had upset her more—seeing Joe again or that apparition in the hall.

On second thought, there was really no contest. Running into her ex-husband, especially here, had been the real shocker.

Anyway, there was no such thing as ghosts. There had to be a logical explanation for what she'd seen.

Perhaps she really had been hallucinating. Considering the shock she'd received, was it any wonder?

Of all the lousy, rotten luck. She couldn't believe it. All her dealings had been with Reese Addison or Caroline Keeton through correspondence or telephone conversations. He'd mentioned his partner a few times, but never by name. Not once, not even with all her apprehensions about coming here, had Olivia dreamed that AdCo stood for Addison and Connally.

There was no reason why she should have. She had expected—*everyone* had expected, especially his mother—that after Joe finished college he would step into his father's shoes and run Winterhaven. The farm just north of Bella Vista had been in the Connally family for generations and was known throughout the horse set as one of the world's finest Thoroughbred farms.

Originally, the estate had been a cotton plantation, boasting one of the most beautiful and gracious mansions in the South, and covering many sections of land. After the Civil War cotton farming had no longer been feasible, and the family's fortune was seriously depleted and its workforce gone. In a desperate attempt to hold on to at least some of their property, the Connallys had switched to raising horses, which had proved to be a wise decision. The family had not only prospered, by the turn of the twentieth century their fortunes had exceeded prewar levels.

A chuckle escaped Olivia. My, my, how she would have loved to have been a fly on the wall the day that Joe told his mother that he was not taking over the family horse farm but going into business for himself. Eleanore Connally must have pitched a walleyed fit.

Normally, Joe's mother was soft-spoken and gra-

cious, exuding charm and a fluttery feminine help-
lessness that brought out the protective instinct of
males and put other women at ease. However, beneath
that fragile, "sweet as sugar" Southern belle manner,
was a strong-willed and determined woman who was
not above scheming and manipulating to get what she
wanted. And woe be unto anyone who crossed her or
upset her plans in any way.

Unfortunately, Eleanore had viewed Olivia's marriage to her son as a betrayal and a personal affront.
She, after all, had given Olivia's mother, Flora, a job
and provided her and her children with a place to live.
She'd even allowed Livvie to be friends with her
daughter.

But by the time Livvie and Blair had reached their
mid teens Eleanore had come to regret that decision
and had done her best to steer her daughter toward
more "suitable" companions. To Blair's credit at the
time, she had stubbornly refused to end their friendship.

Olivia frowned. She herself hadn't even known that
Joe was interested in construction or renovation. Not
in any serious way, at any rate. Oh, sure, as a child
he had enjoyed building things and working with his
hands, but that was true of a lot of young boys.

Although…come to think of it, once, during their
short marriage, he had mentioned that he'd like to
someday purchase one of Savannah's old historic
mansions and renovate it himself. At the time she had
thought that he was just making idle conversation.

Rolling her head back against the door, Olivia
looked up at the crumbling wallpaper on the ceiling
without truly seeing it, her mouth taking on a wry
twist. That had been something they'd both done a

lot of back then—chattered away about trivial things just to fill the awkward silences that had often stretched between them.

The intimate side of their marriage had been wonderful—passionate and fulfilling, everything she had ever dreamed it would be and more. In bed with the lights out, when words had not been necessary, she and Joe had been perfectly in tune, coming together, night after night, like two healthy, lusty young animals.

She gave herself a shake, and her dreamy expression vanished. "Out of bed, it had been a different story, and you'd do well to keep that in mind, my girl," she muttered. She and Joe had spent their daylight hours tiptoeing around each other, each too unsure of the other and their future to be themselves.

Pushing away the memories, Olivia left the door and went to the desk in the bay window alcove where she'd left her purse and briefcase. After retrieving her Palm Pilot and cell phone, she dialed her office and began to pace with the tiny instrument pressed to her ear.

"Olivia's. How may I direct your call?"

A hint of a smile curved Olivia's mouth. Margaret Went's sultry voice conjured up images of a sexy femme fatale, not the stocky, gray-haired woman who manned the telephones and fussed like a mother hen over her, the other two designers and the two delivery-handymen who made up her staff.

"Hi, Maggie, it's me."

"Well, hi there, boss. How was the flight?"

"It was okay."

"Uh-oh. Don't tell me you forgot to take that medication before you boarded the plane, like I told you?

Child, you know how easily you get motion sickness."

"I took it. Don't worry, I didn't toss my cookies all over the client's shoes. Look, Maggie, I'm in kind of a rush. I need to speak with either Janie or Mary Beth for a minute."

"Humph. When aren't you in a rush, I'd like to know? You dash around like a cat with its tail on fire. Work, work, work. That's all you ever do. You ask me—"

"Maggie. Not now, okay? Let me speak to Janie."

"You can't. She's gone to the Furniture Mart. Mary Beth is here, though. Hold on and I'll connect you. And you be sure to take some more of that medicine before you start home. You hear?"

"I will," Olivia replied absently, stopping by the desk to check the to-do list in her Palm Pilot.

"Ms. Mason speaking."

"Mary Beth, it's me. I wanted to remind you that Mrs. Devereaux will be in tomorrow afternoon to look at swatches."

"Yes, I know, Olivia. You told me about a dozen times this morning before you left."

"And the furniture for the Prescott project is due to be delivered tomorrow. Either you or Janie will have to be there first thing in the morning to receive it. Oh, and be sure to check on that antique sofa I'm having recovered for Bayou Teche Plantation. You know how poky the upholsterer is. If you don't prod him it'll be summer before he finishes."

"All taken care of. Janie's going to go straight to the Prescotts' after she drops her kids off at school, and I talked to Mr. Bodette this morning. Calm down. Everything's under control here."

"Just making sure."

"You know, Olivia, you're going to have to learn to relax. If we get that Mallenegua job, for the next year or more you'll be spending the majority of your time there. For the most part it's going to be up to Janie and me to keep the rest of our clients happy."

"I don't think we should plan on getting this job. If it happens, fine, but in the meantime, let's concentrate on keeping the clients we do have happy. Okay?"

"Yes, of course. You know we will."

Olivia heard the offended quiver in her friend's voice. Sitting down in the elegant balloon-back chair, she propped her elbow on the desktop, cupped her forehead with her hand and sighed.

Mary Beth had been with Olivia almost from the time she'd opened her design firm. Over the past six years they had become more than employer and employee; they had become best friends and confidants. Even so, she had not told Mary Beth everything about her past, just enough to satisfy her curiosity and to explain why she had no desire to return to the Savannah area. Basically, she'd explained that she had married Joe when she'd been barely eighteen, very much against his mother's wishes, and that after only five months Eleanore Connally had succeeded in wrecking the marriage.

To make Mary Beth fully understand how unsettling it had been for her to come face-to-face with Joe again, and how unlikely it was that she would get the Mallenegua job, was going to require a much more detailed explanation, one Olivia did not want to give over the telephone.

"Sorry. I didn't mean to snap. I'm a bit tense."

"I understand." Mary Beth cleared her throat. "So, are you going to stop by to see your mother when you leave Mallen Island on Thursday? I could have Maggie change your ticket to a Monday flight and you could have a nice long weekend to visit."

"Mary Beth. We've been all through this. No. I'm not going to Bella Vista to visit my mother."

"Why not? You're so close it would be a shame not to. If Flora ever finds out you were there and didn't bother to stop by, she's going to be hurt."

Olivia doubted that, but she knew how pointless it was to try to convince Mary Beth. She rubbed her forehead again. Her friend came from a close-knit family, all of whom delighted in one another's company. It distressed her that Olivia was not close to her own family.

Olivia loved her mother and sister and she knew that, in their own way, they loved her, but she was as different from the two of them as night and day. If it weren't for her strong resemblance to her father, she would have sworn that she'd been switched with another baby at birth.

Flora and Vicky had never understood her dreams, or the deep need she'd had after the divorce to succeed on her own, to feel that she was of value. Nor did they understand why she wanted so much more out of life than they did. Consequently, they seldom approved of her and were as uncomfortable in her company as she was in theirs.

For the past fourteen years, on holidays and other special occasions, Olivia had always made up excuses why she could not come home. To atone for her absence, she always sent her mother and sister plane tickets to visit her after most holidays. Of course,

Vicky usually returned hers with a terse note of refusal. Only three times in the past fourteen years had her sister accepted her invitation.

Olivia might have felt guilty except that her mother didn't seem to mind the arrangement. If anything, though Flora had never come right out and said so, Olivia suspected that she was secretly relieved that her younger daughter had stayed away from Bella Vista.

"I don't have time for visiting," Olivia said wearily.

"Horsefeathers. You make time. This is your family we're talking about."

"I said no, Mary Beth. Not this trip. I have too much on my mind."

Her friend did have a point, though, she supposed. Now that she'd come face-to-face with Joe again, she had no real excuse for staying away. She raked her hand through her hair again. "Look, I'll make you a deal. If I do get this contract, I'll visit Mother as soon as I can when I come back here. Okay?"

Mary Beth sniffed. "I guess that will have to do. When you use that tone I know there's no budging you. I'm sure Flora will be delighted."

Olivia doubted that, as well, but she answered with a noncommittal "Mmm."

"Now that we've got that out of the way, tell me about Mallenegua," her friend urged. "I'm dying of curiosity. What's it like? Is it as spooky as the stories make it out to be?"

"Oh, Mary Beth, you should see this place. It's fantastic."

Olivia's passion for her work took over, and all thought of Joe and his mother and her difficult relations with her family receded as she launched into a description of the house and grounds and the design plans that were already taking shape in her mind.

After ten minutes of shop talk, Olivia felt calmer and more in control. When the conversation ended she stood up and wandered over to the windows.

Only the outer third of the old pier was visible from that vantage point. Stepping farther into the bay window alcove, Olivia stared out at the activity below.

The wind had grown stronger, and even the waters of the protected cove were choppy now. She became aware that the incessant boom of the pile driver had ceased, and that the barge-mounted monster was now docked and idle.

Far out on the old pier near where the tugboat was moored, Joe stood talking with a group of men. Even from that distance he stood out from the others.

But then, he always had, Olivia reminded herself. Boy and man, Joe had always had that air of authority about him, a quiet, controlled strength that others respected and to which they responded without question. Whether that "in command" aura was the result of his privileged upbringing or an innate character trait, she had no idea, but it was as much a part of him as his dark hair or his brown eyes.

The amazing thing was that she hadn't recognized him, even from this distance, when he arrived. There had been a time when, if he was anywhere in sight, if no more than a speck on her horizon, she'd have sensed his presence.

Of course, back then she had been in love with him.

Crossing her arms over her midriff, Olivia stared at his broad back and shook her head. Dear Lord, how she had loved him.

From the moment she had first set eyes on Joe Connally she had adored him.

She could remember that day as clearly as if it had happened the week before. She had been nine years old at the time, and Joe had been a much older, much more mature twelve.

The Connallys' longtime cook and housekeeper had retired, and Olivia's mother had been fortunate enough to land the job. One of the perks, and a godsend for the Joneses, had been that they could live in a small cottage on the grounds of Winterhaven Farm. For Flora Jones and her family it had been moving day.

Olivia and her fourteen-year-old sister, Victoria, had viewed the move as an adventure, but looking back, Olivia now realized that their mother had probably been terrified.

All of her adult life, Flora had been a stay-at-home wife and mother. When her husband had died of a heart attack at age forty-six she'd suddenly found herself alone in the world with two young daughters to support. With no job experience and no education, she had taken the only job at which she had any experience.

That day, while her mother and Vicky had been busy unpacking their belongings in the cottage, Olivia had gone exploring. The first people she had encountered had been Joe's younger siblings, Luke and Blair.

Blair was only a year younger than Olivia, and they'd taken to each other right away, but Luke, being a typical ten-year-old, had taunted and teased her, until Joe had come striding out of one of the horse barns and ordered him to stop.

Had he been wearing a suit of armor and riding a

white horse, he could not have appeared more gallant in Olivia's eyes. From that moment forward Joe Connally had been her Prince Charming.

Of course, he'd ignored her throughout the entire nine years she had lived at Winterhaven.

Like most boys, he'd considered his younger sister a nuisance, but he'd nevertheless been protective of her. Since Olivia and Blair had been inseparable, Joe's protection had extended to her as well, but to him she'd merely been skinny, knobby-kneed Livvie Jones, his irritating little sister's playmate.

When Joe had started dating, Olivia had been miserable. When, during his second year at Princeton, he'd announced his engagement to Selina St. Clair, she had wanted to die.

Selina was the pampered daughter of another of Bella Vista's wealthy families. Blond and beautiful, she'd been headstrong, high-tempered and accustomed to getting her own way, and from the beginning, the romance had been a stormy one.

Over the following year, Selina's and Joe's frequent, often public arguments and breakups had kept a kernel of hope alive in Olivia's foolish heart. Instead of getting on with her own life, she had waited and prayed that sooner or later Joe would have enough of Selina's tantrums and call off the engagement permanently.

However, Joe and Selina had always made up, thanks in large part to Joe's mother. Eleanore had approved of the match and had done all she could to promote it. After each breakup she'd always managed to maneuver her son and Selina back together. After each reconciliation, Livvie had quietly gone back to nursing her broken heart.

Only Blair had known of Livvie's unrequited love, and her friend had kept her secret, though, in typical sisterly fashion, she had frequently complained that she couldn't understand how anyone could be interested in her "dumb ole brother."

"There are a lot more interesting guys around, you know," Blair had insisted. "Why, there are at least four that I know of who would love to go out with you. For heaven's sake, Livvie. Forget about Joe."

Olivia sighed and tightened her crossed arms, absently massaging her elbows with her fingertips. If only she'd heeded her friend's advice, she thought. She could have saved herself a lot of heartache.

Was Joe still blind to Selina's faults? she wondered, watching him gesture toward a row of new pilings poking out of the water. Before Olivia had left Savannah, Eleanore had informed her that Joe was going to marry his former fiancée, and shortly after her mother had written to her to say that Eleanore was busy planning the wedding.

After that, she had never again asked her mother about Joe. In the beginning, she hadn't wanted to know the details, and later, once she'd finally gotten over him, it hadn't mattered. In any case, as though by unspoken agreement, during those rare times when she was with her mother or sister or spoke to them over the telephone, neither Joe nor any of the Connallys were ever mentioned.

While touring the house, Olivia had noticed that Joe did not wear a wedding ring, but that didn't mean he was single. He had never cared for jewelry of any kind. He hadn't worn a ring during their marriage, either.

She wondered if he and Selina were happy together. If they had any children.

Unexpected pain stabbed at her chest, and Olivia pressed her lips together and swiped angrily at the tears that rushed to her eyes.

The mantel clock chimed softly, and her mouth thinned as she realized how much time she'd wasted. When she had accepted AdCo's invitation she'd told herself she would not let coming to the area stir up old memories, and now here she was, raking through fourteen-year-old ashes like a self-pitying fool.

Her jaw clenched, she watched Joe throw his head back and laugh at something that one of the men had said. Turning away from the window, she plopped herself back into the desk chair and snatched a sketch pad and pencils from her briefcase.

Why should she let seeing Joe again upset her? Other than that brief moment of shock when he'd first recognized her, being around her again seemed to have had little effect on his equilibrium. He certainly wasn't tying himself in knots thinking about her.

Livvie was back.

The thought bounced around in Joe's mind like a ricocheting bullet. Ever since he'd first seen her standing there, looking so grown-up and startlingly gorgeous, he hadn't been able to think about anything else. The whole time they'd toured the house and all the while he had listened to Mike's progress report and issued instructions to the men, his mind had been on Livvie.

Leaning against a weathered piling, Joe stood on the pier, pretending to watch the crew unload the tugboat, but with every fiber in his being he was aware of Livvie's presence, just a few hundred yards away. Neither the men's activities nor the biting wind tearing at his clothes and whipping his hair in all directions registered fully on his consciousness.

Mike stood on the edge of the pier beside the cargo barge, shouting orders through his cupped hands while Cappy straw-bossed from the tugboat's bow. Now and then both men shouted comments Joe's way, but he merely nodded in reply.

Joe glanced up at the house. Damn. He couldn't believe it. Livvie was back.

He wasn't exactly sure how he felt about that. Unsettled, mostly, he supposed. Not that he and Livvie had parted enemies or there'd been any hard feelings between them or anything like that. It was just that having her pop up all of a sudden had been a shock. After all this time, he hadn't expected to ever see her again.

Damn. Who would've thought that Olivia, the hot new decorator his mother and all her friends were raving about, would turn out to be his ex-wife?

The irony of that produced a bark of laughter, but the sound was snatched away by the wind and went unnoticed by the others. One thing was certain, Joe thought. His mother had never met her friend Dorothea Montgomery's decorator or connected the name with her former daughter-in-law, otherwise she would never have urged him to contact "Olivia." Lord, his mother was going to have a stroke when she learned that she had recommended Livvie.

Joe winced. Correction—Olivia.

He huffed out a sharp breath. Never once had he heard her called anything but Livvie. He hadn't even associated the name Olivia with her. Well, if that was what she wanted, that's what he'd call her, but to him she would always be little Livvie.

For a brief while she'd been *his* little Livvie.

Although…she *had* changed. A lot. He had to admit, she looked good, though. Good, hell. She looked fantastic. Livvie had always been a cute little thing, with those big green eyes and that auburn ponytail bouncing around her shoulders, but he'd never particularly thought of her as a beauty.

Joe huffed again. Just showed what he knew.

The changes in Livvie's outward appearance weren't what disturbed him, though. What he found confusing was her coolness and the anger he sensed simmering just beneath that regal composure. And it seemed to be directed toward him.

Joe glanced up at the house again and frowned. He didn't have a clue what that was about. What the devil did she have to be angry about? *She* had been the one who had wanted the divorce. Not him.

The way Livvie acted you'd think he was the enemy, speaking to him in that ultra-polite way, as though he were a stranger, and giving him those frosty looks. He'd also noticed how she had stiffened whenever his hand had so much as grazed her arm, and the pains she'd taken to keep a distance between them.

Dammit! There had been a time when he'd touched and kissed every inch of her, and she sure as hell hadn't shrunk from him then.

The wind whipped Joe's hair across his forehead, and he raked it back impatiently. Growing more irritated and restless by the minute, he straightened away from the piling. "I'm going back to my boat," he shouted to Mike. "I'll be here for about another half hour before I head back to the mainland. If you need me, just holler.''

''Sure thing, boss.''

Joe marched down the pier past the tugboat and cargo barge and climbed aboard his sleek cruiser. Below deck, out of the wind, the cabin was cozy and warm, though the boat rocked and bobbed in the rough waters and strained at its mooring lines.

He sat down at the banquette but popped back up again almost at once, too agitated to sit still. He began to pace the cabin.

Maybe Livvie was right. Maybe the two of them working together on a project *would* be too awkward. He probably should have let her withdraw when she offered.

He stopped pacing and rubbed his jaw. He supposed he could march back up there and tell her he'd changed his mind. No doubt, that was the smart thing to do.

Joe sighed, and his mouth folded into a grim line. He could…but he wouldn't. A deal was a deal.

Four

On Thursday, Olivia flew home to Atlanta, picked up her car at the airport and drove straight to her office-showroom.

The moment the cottage came into view her flagging spirits lifted. She drove around back and parked in the former carriage house, alongside the cars of her office staff.

As always, the instant Olivia stepped from the carriage house and started up the brick pathway toward the back of the cottage, a sense of satisfaction swelled her chest. She was proud of everything she'd accomplished, not the least of which had been having the foresight to purchase this property.

The post-Civil War cottage had been built by one of the deposed Southern aristocracy in the 1870s. The place had no doubt been a big comedown for the former plantation owner and his family, but the clapboard house had enough Victorian-era charm and style to appeal to Olivia.

Seven years ago the residential neighborhood had been run-down and seedy. Gambling that the area's close proximity to downtown would make it a prime candidate for commercial development, she had purchased the property for a song—against the advice of almost everyone she knew. Armed with a grant from the historical society and a hefty loan from the bank, she had restored the property and moved her fledgling company in.

Her gamble had paid off. By the time the cottage and grounds were fully restored, three high-rise office buildings were going up around her property. Today her office was the only original structure left on the street.

Painted pale yellow, its fancy gingerbread trim, shutters, porch railings and fish-scale eaves shingles meticulously defined in brown, blue, hunter green, magenta and cream, the cottage sat on an oversize corner lot amid towering oak, pine and magnolia trees. A white picket fence, lined inside and out with flower beds that ran riot with colorful flowers in spring and summer months, enclosed the entire property. A rose garden, with a stone birdbath and glider swing at its center, occupied much of the side yard. White wicker furniture with green-and-white cushions dotted the front porch, along with an old-fashioned swing.

Like a bright jewel among stones, the cottage caught the eye of everyone who passed by, especially so since its charming image was reflected with mirrorlike clarity in the modern steel-and-glass buildings that surrounded it.

Olivia climbed the steps to the wraparound porch and entered the cottage through the side French doors that led into the dining room. Skirting the long double-pedestal table, she walked into the adjacent front parlor, which served as her office.

The room was large and, like the rest of the house, meticulously furnished in high Victorian style. An Oriental rug covered most of the heart-of-pine floors.

A table in the precise center of the room held a vase of fresh flowers, and two brocade medallion-back settees flanked the fireplace. Scattered about the room were potted palms, rococo chairs and ornate marble-top tables that held fringed lamps and the requisite plethora of Victorian bric-a-brac.

A grand piano, draped with a large fringed scarf, occupied the bay window alcove. Ivory and jade figurines and an arrangement of peacock feathers in a Chinese vase adorned the mantel, above which hung a portrait of a Victorian lady with her children and their fluffy little dog. A pair of filing cabinets, cleverly disguised to look like a chest, were the only nonauthentic pieces in the room.

The space worked well for Olivia. Impressive and tasteful, the parlor, like the rest of the ground floor of the house, served as an example of her work. When conferring with clients, she had the option of closing the two sets of twelve-foot-high pocket doors that connected the parlor to the entrance hall and the dining room.

Olivia set her briefcase down beside the massive secretary desk, picked up the pile of messages that were neatly stacked on the fold-out top and shuffled through them as she strolled into the entrance hall.

"I see the place is still here, so I guess y'all survived without me," she drawled.

"Well, look who's back." Margaret Went, her receptionist/bookkeeper/girl Friday sat at the Gothic table butted against the stairs that served as her desk, peering at her over the top of her glasses. Beside her stood Jane Greer, the youngest of the two other designers on Olivia's staff. The small ground-floor bedroom at the back of the cottage was Janie's office.

"Hi, Olivia. It's good to have you back," Janie chirped.

"How was the trip?" Margaret asked, subjecting her to a narrow-eyed scrutiny. "You look a little green around the gills. Don't tell me you forgot to take your medication?"

"No, I took it. But there's a storm brewing off the coast, and the boat ride back to the mainland was rough. The plane trip wasn't any better. Turbulence all the way."

"I thought I heard your voice," Mary Beth said, sauntering out of her office, which was the study across the entrance hall from the parlor.

If ever any two women were diametric opposites it was Janie and Mary Beth. Olivia's dear friend, Mary Beth, was rock steady. She possessed a wonderful sense of style and moved with the languid grace of a Southern belle, but when she spoke her Minnesota clip gave away her northern roots. An attractive brunette of forty-four, the widowed mother of twenty-two-year-old twin sons, Mary Beth exuded the kind of confidence that comes only with experience. She claimed that after raising two rambunctious boys on her own, nothing had the power to surprise or upset her.

Whereas thirty-year-old Janie Greer was a bundle of kinetic energy and tended to be a worrier.

"Good to have you back, boss." Mary Beth gave Olivia a quick hug and stepped back. "So...how did it go?"

"I spent the last three days working like a demon. I measured rooms and photographed everything I could from every possible angle, all under the watchful eye of a scary old crone of a housekeeper who made no bones about not wanting me there.''

"Yikes," Janie murmured. "What a bummer."

"I did my best to avoid her, but I swear, no matter where I went in that house, whenever I turned around, there she was. Sometimes all I saw was a flutter of a black dress disappearing around a corner. Other times she just stood like a statue and made no attempt to hide, staring at me with those cold eyes of hers. It was eerie. I don't believe all the tales that have circulated about Mallenegua but, believe me, being there alone with Mrs. Jaffee was enough to make me lock my door at night."

"Sounds spooky, all right," Mary Beth agreed. "What's her problem?"

"Oh, she's worked for the Mallen family for years and doesn't approve of outsiders buying the island and turning it into a resort." Olivia waved her hand in dismissal. "I probably overreacted. She's scary but harmless."

At least, according to Joe, Olivia added silently.

"When I wasn't measuring or taking photos I tried to avoid her by keeping to my room. I spent that time sketching ideas and making scale drawings and playing around with various furniture arrangements and fabric and wallpaper combinations. I came up with some good ideas for my presentation."

"What's Reese Addison like?" Janie asked eagerly. "I've heard that he's a real hunk."

A reluctant grin twitched Olivia's mouth. Leave it to Janie to get right to the heart of what mattered to her. Though married and the mother of two small children, she had an eye for male beauty, and she seemed to have made it her life's work to find a husband for Olivia. All of Olivia's protests that she didn't need nor particularly want a man in her life didn't seem to have the least effect on Janie's relentless matchmaking.

"I wouldn't know. I didn't get to meet him. He was supposed to spend the three days at Mallenegua with me, but something came up and he had to cancel. His partner was there for a while and showed me through the house, but he already had other commitments."

"Oh, pooh! What rotten luck." Janie snatched her bright red coat out of the closet and gathered up a stack of fabric sample books from the corner of Maggie's desk. "Much as I'd like to stick around and hear more about your trip, I've gotta run. I'm meeting with Mrs. Pettigrew in fifteen minutes to pick drapery and upholstery material. See you later."

Janie never walked. She flitted and darted from one place to another like a busy hummingbird. Her energy level was so high it made Olivia tired just to watch her. Stiletto heels clicking, she disappeared down the hall and out the back door, a flash of billowing red coat and bouncing blond curls.

"Well, I don't have an appointment for another hour, and I'm dying to see those photos," Mary Beth said.

"Maybe later," Olivia replied. "Right now there's some other business I need to discuss with you. Let's go into the kitchen and talk over tea."

Once the tea was brewed, the two women sat across from each other at the round kitchen table, cradling their steaming cups.

"If this is about the Bayou Teche project, it's under control," Mary Beth said. "Stop worrying. Like I told you before, Janie and I can handle our other clients while you're working in Savannah and Mallen Island.''

"That's what I wanted to talk to you about. There is very little chance that we will get the Mallenegua job."

Mary Beth made a disparaging sound. "Will you stop being such a pessimist? So there are two other designers bidding on the job. Big deal. They don't have your talent. Once the AdCo people see your proposal the others won't have a chance."

"Yes, well, I appreciate your faith in me, but as it turns out, the competition is the least of our problems."

"Uh-oh. I don't like the sound of that." Mary Beth narrowed her eyes and examined Olivia's face. "Something happened, didn't it? What? What's wrong? Don't tell me you ran into your ex? Oh, no, you did!" she exclaimed before Olivia could speak, seeing the answer in her expression.

Olivia took a sip of tea to calm her nerves. "Actually…it's worse than that, I'm afraid."

"You mean you ran into his mother?" Her friend groaned. "That's terrible. What happened? What did she say?"

"No, it's not that. I haven't seen Eleanore, thank heaven." She paused. Her head had begun to throb, and she closed her eyes and massaged the spot between her eyebrows with the tips of her fingers. "Joe Connally is Reese Addison's partner in AdCo."

Mary Beth's eyes widened and a stunned silence hummed between them, followed after a moment by her incredulous whisper. "Joe Connally? Your *ex-*

husband, Joe Connally? You're kidding me. Please say you're kidding me.''

"I wish. But I'm afraid it's true.''

Another groan, this one more prolonged. "How awful for you. Was there a horrible scene?"

"No. Actually, our meeting was very civilized, but the whole thing was extremely awkward and unsettling.''

"I can imagine. Are you all right?" her friend asked, reaching out to touch her arm.

Olivia sighed and raked her free hand through her hair, pushing the thick fall away from her face. "I'm okay. I was a bit shaken at first. It was a shock seeing him again. But I think I managed to get through the meeting with my dignity intact. I doubt that Joe realized how rattled I was.''

"Oh, I'm sure of that,'' Mary Beth replied with a chuckle. "I've seen you in action, sweetie. The more awkward the situation or the nastier people get, the more ladylike you become. It would take a lot more than an ex-husband to shake that elegant composure of yours. So, what happened? Did Joe withdraw AdCo's invitation?"

"No. Actually, he insisted that I continue. He claims that I have just as good a chance of getting the job as either of the other two designers.''

"But you don't believe that.''

"I believe *he* believes that.''

"I see. So what are you going to do?''

"What choice do I have, with him being so gracious? I'll work up my proposal and in two weeks you'll fly to Savannah and present it to Joe and Reese Addison. But I'm not going to hold my breath.''

"Me? You want *me* to deliver your presentation?''

"Yes. Trust me, Joe and his partners will find some excuse to reject my plan, so the presentation is just a formality. Why should I have to deal with seeing Joe again? If they object just tell them I had a prior commitment."

"All right. If you're sure that's what you want."

Olivia sighed. "Actually, there's something more I should tell you. The truth is, there's more to what happened between Joe and me than you know."

"Oh?"

Searching for the right words, Olivia took another sip of tea. "As I believe I told you, I adored Joe from the moment I met him. Not that he ever noticed. To him I was just his sister's playmate."

She picked up her cup and cradled it between her hands. Over its top she stared out the window, blind to the dormant daylily garden in the backyard or the birds gathering seeds from the feeder hanging from the magnolia tree. Her gaze was focused on another time, her pupils glazed over as scenes from the past came flooding back.

"On my eighteenth birthday, all that changed. I remember that afternoon so clearly. I was lying sprawled on my stomach across my bed, staring at the crepe myrtle bush outside my window and feeling sorry for myself...

There she was, poised on the threshold of womanhood, and no one cared, she thought morosely. Mrs. Connally was having a party that evening, so her mother would be working late up at the big house. Her sister had married one of the horse trainers about ten months before, but even though Vicky and Travis lived in one of the other cottages on Winterhaven

Farm, her sister was pregnant and suffering from al-most constant morning sickness and in no mood to celebrate her baby sister's coming of age.

She had no boyfriend. She didn't even have a date to help her celebrate the special day.

The one bright spot was that it was spring-break time for Joe, and instead of going to the beach with his friends from Princeton, as he'd planned, he'd sur-prised everyone by arriving home five nights before.

In a black mood, he had slammed into the big house while she and Blair had been watching televi-sion in the Connallys' den and announced to one and all that his engagement to Selina was over. For good this time, he'd vowed.

Though Livvie's heart had leapt in reaction at the time, she was trying her best not to get her hopes up and to maintain a "wait and see" attitude. She had heard that claim too many times before.

Since that first night she'd barely seen Joe. He'd spent the past five days brooding and arguing with his mother and snapping at anyone who got too close. If he even remembered that it was her birthday—which was doubtful—he certainly didn't care.

Lost in her blue funk, Livvie jumped when Blair burst into her bedroom.

"Get up! Get up! We've only got a few hours to get you ready."

Livvie rolled over and sat up in the middle of the bed. "Ready for what?" she asked, frowning as she noted that her friend carried several dresses on hang-ers over one shoulder and a tote bag crammed with accessories, shoes and beauty supplies over the other.

"For your date."

"What are you talking about? I don't have a date."

"Oh, yes you do." Blair draped the dresses over the foot rail of Livvie's iron bed and dumped the tote onto the mattress. Placing her hand on her hips, she shot Livvie a triumphant grin. "Joe is taking you out to dinner for your birthday."

Livvie's heart stumbled to a halt, then took off at a gallop. She stared at her friend, unable to breathe. "Wha-what? How…? Why would he…? He's never…"

"I talked him into doing it," Blair announced. She was so pleased with herself she didn't notice the way Livvie's shoulders slumped.

"Oh. I see."

"Yeah. He found out that Selina and her parents are coming to dinner tonight, and he and Mother had a bodacious row over that," her friend went on, bouncing around the room as she set out her beautifying tools.

"Joe is furious. He refuses to attend the dinner, which, of course, ruins everything, since Mother's whole reason for *having* the party was to throw Joe and Selina together again.

"To get her off his back, he told her that he had a date. But of course he didn't. When he started calling around he discovered that all the girls he used to date before he met Selina were either married or away at college. So I told him it was your birthday and suggested that he take you out to celebrate, and he agreed."

"Then he doesn't really want to go out with me. He just wants to escape your mother's matchmaking."

Blair turned from the dresser with a set of hot rollers in her hands, becoming aware for the first time of

Livvie's disappointment and hurt. She quickly set the appliance aside, scrambled onto the bed and grabbed one of Livvie's hands. "Oh, sugar, don't be upset. It's true, he probably never would've asked you out if I hadn't prodded him, but—"

"He *hasn't* asked me out."

"You know what I mean." Blair dismissed her words with a wave of her hand. "My point is, this is the chance you've always wanted. Who cares how it came about? The important thing is you're going out with Joe. Just go out there and make the most of it."

Livvie sat with her eyes downcast and plucked at the old quilt that covered her bed. Ten years of romantic fantasies vied with the awful fear that if she said no she would never again get the chance to spend an evening alone with Joe. After a time, she looked up and gave Blair a wan smile. "You're probably right."

"Thatta girl." Blair threw her arms around Livvie's neck and gave her a quick hug, then scrambled off the bed.

She looked over her shoulder. "Well. Don't just sit there. We've got a million things to do before Joe picks you up." She clapped her hands, and Livvie jumped. "C'mon, move it!"

A faint, sad smile flickered across Olivia's mouth at the memory of that afternoon. That had been the last time that she and Blair shared that sort of sisterly closeness.

"What a foolish dreamer I was in those days," she said with a glance at Mary Beth. "Throughout the hours of beauty treatments and primping and giggly excitement I actually harbored the fantasy that Joe would take one look at me in my borrowed finery and fancy hairdo and fall head over heels in love.''

''I take it he didn't,'' Mary Beth said.

''No. Although, to be fair, his eyes did widen when he first saw me, but he merely grinned and said, ''Hey, little one.'' But then he'd spoiled even that by adding, ''C'mon, sugar. Let's go show the guys what they're missin'. We'll make 'em so jealous, by tomorrow they'll be beatin' your door down.''

Mary Beth groaned. ''Not exactly what a lovesick girl wants to hear.''

''No. It wasn't. Of course, the date was a disaster,'' Olivia continued, her gaze once more going out of focus.

Joe took her to one of the most popular restaurants in Savannah, but Livvie had been almost sick with excitement and so nervous she'd barely been able to string three words together throughout the meal. He struggled to be polite and keep the conversation going, but when all his efforts were met with nods or monosyllabic replies he finally lapsed into a moody silence.

After dinner, when they were again alone in the car, he asked, ''Would you like to go for a drive?''

''Yes. I'd love to,'' Livvie eagerly accepted.

Any romantic motive she had read into the suggestion vanished when he immediately sank back into bitter silence. After a while she realized that the drive was nothing more than a means of killing time so that his mother's guests would be gone when he returned home.

Livvie was not certain that he even remembered she was there. Staring straight ahead, his expression unreadable, he drove through the dark Georgia night in silence. They drove over the Talmadge Bridge and into South Carolina.

Joe drove fast, as though trying to outrace his private demons. Olivia sat quiet as a mouse, her hands clasped together in her lap. She stole a glance at his profile and her uneasiness deepened. Joe's face looked as though it had been carved from stone.

Mile after mile of moonlit salt marsh flashed by the windows. Not until they reached the little town of Beaufort did he turn the car around and head back toward Savannah.

Olivia told herself to say something—anything—but she couldn't unstick her tongue from the roof of her mouth. Which was just as well, she supposed, since she couldn't seem to come up with a single intelligent comment. Or the courage to utter it if she did.

Sometime after midnight Joe headed the car toward Bella Vista. Livvie sat huddled in a ball of misery on the passenger's side of the front seat, silently berating herself for being a ninny and a coward. This had been her big chance. She'd had Joe all to herself all evening, and she'd blown it.

They passed through the darkened streets of Bella Vista without slowing and took the highway that led to Winterhaven Farm. All too soon Joe turned the car in through the arched brick entrance and started down the mile-long gravel drive. Alternating magnolia and oak trees lined the drive on either side, forming an almost solid canopy overhead. On the other side of the trees the whitewashed board fence glowed in the moonlight. Beyond the fence the pastures rolled away into the darkness in gentle, undulating swells.

When the big house came into view, Livvie saw Joe scan the circular drive out front for cars, unwittingly confirming her suspicion.

He drove past the mansion and took the narrower road that wound through the trees and eventually led to the employees' homes. Moments later he parked in front of the cottage that she shared with her mother.

He switched off the car's engine, and Livvie's spirits hit bottom. Their date was over. She'd had her chance and she'd blown it. Angry tears banked against her lower eyelids, and she widened her eyes to hold them back.

"Well, here we are." Turning sideways, Joe laid his right arm along the back of the seat. Here among the trees the night was black as pitch. The only light came from the yellow bulb burning beside the front door, a soft, golden glow that provided barely enough illumination to see each other.

Joe smiled, his teeth a slash of white in the dimness. "I'm sorry for being such bad company tonight, little one," he murmured, grazing the side of her neck with his forefinger.

Livvie jumped. That feathery touch packed the punch of a lightning bolt. Electricity sizzled through her body and left her tingling all over.

Joe raised one eyebrow. "Hey. Easy, there. What're you so jumpy about? It's just me," he soothed.

She gave him a wan smile. "Sorry. I, uh…I guess I drank too much coffee today, or something."

"I hope you weren't too bored tonight."

"Oh, no! Not at all. I had a wonderful time. Really!"

Joe laughed and tugged a lock of her hair. "Fibber.

I was a rotten companion all evening, and you know it. You deserve better. Especially tonight. This was supposed to be your birthday celebration.'' Still smiling, he curved his right hand around the back of her neck and tugged her toward him ever so gently as he lowered his head. ''Happy birthday, Livvie,'' he murmured, and touched his lips to hers.

He had never kissed her before—not even a brotherly peck on the cheek. Livvie's heart beat so fast it felt as though it would explode. She'd spent endless hours fantasizing about how it would be, but none of her daydreams had even come close.

It was the most chaste of kisses, no more than a gossamer touch, but for Livvie the feel of his lips on hers carried the force of a dam bursting. The strain of the evening and the panicky feeling knowing this would probably be her one and only chance with Joe, and it was slipping away, was suddenly more than she could bear.

Her self-control and inhibitions crumbled. Ten years of pent-up longing surged through the breach and broke free.

Flinging herself against Joe's chest, Livvie wrapped her arms around his neck and kissed him back with all the love and ardor that was in her heart.

Taken by surprise, he stiffened momentarily before grasping her upper arms. Drawing his head back, he broke off the kiss and stared at her, bemused. ''Livvie?''

She made a whimpering sound and tried to tighten her arms around his neck. ''Joe, please.''

He stared at her flushed face, her pleading eyes. Livvie's chest heaved with each breath, but otherwise neither of them moved. Somewhere a dog barked, and a horse in the paddock whinnied in reply. The south pasture had been mowed that afternoon, and the damp night air was redolent with the smells of fresh-cut grass and wild onions.

Joe was quiet so long an uneasy feeling began to knot in Livvie's stomach. When his hands tightened on her arms she was certain that he was going to push her away. Instead, slowly, as though unable to help himself, he lowered his mouth to hers again.

It was like setting a match to tinder.

Though it started out as soft as the first one, this kiss was neither tentative nor chaste. It was sensual and thrilling, and it quickly escalated into something greedy and hot. The kiss was wet and wild and openmouthed. Sultry and lavish.

Livvie groaned and leaned into the kiss, abandoning herself to the exquisite pleasure, to the wonder of it all. Holding nothing back, she kissed Joe with nine years' worth of love and pent-up desire.

Almost delirious with passion, Livvie never knew when Joe eased her onto her back across the seat, nor was she concerned when he lowered the zipper on her borrowed dress and stripped it from her body, or even when her lace panties and bra followed. She was in Joe's arms and he was kissing and caressing her in the most wonderful ways, and that was all that mattered.

When he unfastened and shoved aside his own clothing and moved over her, the cloud of passion cleared for an instant, and she experienced a pang of anxiety, but it made no difference. She could not have asked him to stop had her life depended on it. This was Joe, and she loved him. Had always loved him.

She wasn't prepared for the searing pain of his entry, and when she cried out Joe stiffened.

"Dear God, Livvie!" He stilled instantly, braced up on his arms, and stared down at her. He looked shocked and horrified. "Why didn't you tell me?"

Tears filled her eyes. "I...I'm sorry," she quavered. "Don't be angry with me."

"Angry with you? I'm not angry with you, I'm—" He turned his head to one side and cursed under his breath. When done swearing he looked at her again and shook his head. "Ah, Livvie."

"No!" she pleaded when he clamped his teeth together and made a move to withdraw. Livvie clutched his shoulders so hard her fingernails dug into his flesh. "Please, Joe. Don't stop now. Please."

"Livvie—"

"Oh, please. I...I want you, Joe."

He closed his eyes and groaned.

Operating on instinct, Livvie lifted her hips and brought him deeper inside her.

A hard shudder shook Joe's body.

She trailed her fingers over his flat belly, all the way down to where their bodies were joined. "Please, Joe," she whispered. "I want my first time to be with you."

A low, guttural sound rumbled from deep inside him as his last thread of control snapped. Bending his elbows, Joe lowered his head and covered her mouth with his in a rapacious kiss that threatened to devour her. At the same time, he thrust his hips forward, going deep, filling her.

When she had accepted him completely he stilled, giving her body time to adjust. He buried his face against the side of her neck, and Livvie could feel that his jaw was rigid. He was breathing hard and his muscles quivered under his fierce control. "You all right?" he asked through clenched teeth.

Unable to speak, she nodded, her chin bumping the top of his shoulder.

"You sure? I don't want to hurt you."

"You won't," Livvie whispered. She trailed her fingertips down his spine, pausing on the way to explore each dip and bump. Joe shivered, and with a groan he began the rhythmic movements.

Livvie was awash with pleasure, delirious with need. She hadn't known what to expect, even though she had dreamed of this for years, had countless times imagined Joe making love to her. She had spent most of her youth on a Thoroughbred-breeding farm, so the physical act was no mystery to her, but this—this was so much more. This was indescribable rapture, this was completion, this was a joining of souls. This was right.

She gave herself up completely to the moment. Nothing else existed. Nothing else mattered. She responded to each thrust, each touch, each small grunt and moan of pleasure that came from Joe. She reveled in their closeness, in the intimacy, the weight and warmth of his body on hers, the smell of him.

A wonderful tension built inside of her until it was almost pain. She clutched Joe's back with both hands and moaned. "Oh. Oh, Joe. Oh!"

"Let go, baby," he whispered in her ear between gasping breaths, pumping harder. "Don't fight it. Let go."

The words seemed to push her over the edge of some strange and wonderful precipice just as the world exploded all around her in white-hot, pulsing pleasure.

She cried out as her body stiffened and arched, and her legs began to tremble. An instant later Joe thrust deep and stilled, his muffled groan rumbling in Livvie's ear.

The memory brought a flood of emotions. Surreptitiously, Olivia wiped her moist eyes with her fingertips and took another sip of tea. Could all women recall their first time so vividly? she wondered. Even after fourteen years?

She glanced at Mary Beth and made a rueful face. "I suppose some people would see the whole thing as tawdry and cheap—your typical, awkward 'make-out' session in the front seat of a car, but to me, at the time, it was the fulfillment of all my girlish dreams."

As much as she hated to admit it, even now, after all that had happened, after all the pain and heartache, the memory of that night still seemed magical to her. Which just shows what an idiot you are, she scolded herself.

"So, are you telling me that Joe married you out of guilt for taking your virginity that night?" Mary Beth asked.

"No. Not exactly."

"I didn't think so. *Nobody* is that much of a gentleman in this day and age. Not even an old-fashioned Southerner. Not even fourteen years ago." Mary Beth topped off their teacups and added a dollop of cream to her own. "So what happened? How did you two end up getting married?" she asked as she stirred her drink. "Did he realize that he'd been in love with you all along and sweep you off your feet?"

Olivia gave a little huff. "Hardly. Although, I have to say, Joe, bless him, was so sweet and solicitous after we made love. As you can imagine, we were both uncomfortable and awkward, but he couldn't have been more tender and considerate...."

"Are you sure you're all right?" he asked her for the umpteenth time as they fumbled into their clothes.

"I'm fine. Really," she replied in a small voice. She could feel her face flame, and prayed he couldn't see in the dim light. Oh, Lord. What must he think of her?

"Here, turn around so I can zip you up," he said, and the heat spread down her neck and over her bare shoulders.

Making quick work of the zipper, Joe fastened the hook at the top of the strapless gown, then took her by the shoulders and turned her toward him. Livvie's gaze dropped to her hands. She felt Joe running his fingers through her hair to smooth it, but she could not muster the courage to look at him.

"There. That's better." He put his forefinger under her chin and lifted her face, but she kept her eyes closed. "Look at me, Livvie," he ordered gently, and she complied.

"I wasn't expecting anything like this to happen tonight, so I didn't come prepared." He looked away and snorted. "Hell, even if I had, I got so carried away I doubt that I could have stopped long enough to take precautions."

He slid his hands up over her shoulders and the sides of her neck until he was cupping her face between his palms. Livvie stared up at him trustingly as he gave her a searching look. "Look, I have to leave tomorrow morning to return to school, but I want you to promise me something, Livvie. If it turns out that you're…well…that there are repercussions from this, you'll call me right away. Okay?"

"What kind of repercu—oh." She ducked her head, but she felt more scalding heat spread over her shoulders, neck and face. Pregnant. Oh, Lord, she could be pregnant with Joe's child. "I…I see."

Putting a finger under her chin, Joe once again tipped her head up. "So you *will* call me if it turns out there's a problem. I want your solemn promise on that, little one."

"I…I can't. I don't have your number at Princeton."

"Here." He released her and searched through his pockets and came up with a ticket stub. "Got a pen?" When she pulled one from her purse, he scribbled a number across the back of the stub and gave it to her. "If it turns out you're in trouble, you call me as soon as you know. And don't say a word to anyone else. I mean it, Livvie. Promise me that."

"I…I promise."

"Okay, then." Giving her a reassuring smile, he climbed out of the car and came around to her side. At the front door of the cottage he once more took her by the shoulders. "Good night, little one." Joe bent and placed a tender kiss on her lips. "And don't worry. Okay? Everything is going to be fine."

Olivia wiped away more tears and shot Mary Beth a rueful look. "How in God's name he expected me not to worry, I don't know. For the next month I was scared spitless and unable to think of anything else.

"For the first time, I didn't confide in Blair. I wanted to, mind you. I desperately needed to talk to someone. But I simply couldn't. What had happened was just too private. It was just between me and Joe."

Olivia gave a weak chuckle. "Not that Blair didn't try to worm a blow-by-blow account of the evening out of me. After a sleepless night, I'd finally dozed off around dawn, only to be awakened two hours later when Blair burst into my room and pounced on my bed."

"Wake up! Wake up! C'mon, sleepyhead, open your eyes!"

"Bla-aire!" Livvie groaned. "I was sleeping."

"This is no time for sleeping. I want to hear all about your date with Joe!" She grabbed Livvie's hands and pulled her to a sitting position, then sat back on her heels, her expression bright with curiosity. "Well? How did it go?"

Sighing, Livvie raked her heavy auburn hair away from her face and shot her friend a bleary-eyed, baleful look. "It didn't."

"What! What do you mean? What happened?"

"I was so nervous and tongue-tied I sat like a statue all evening and barely uttered a word. After a while Joe gave up and went back to brooding. When dinner was over he brought me home. End of story." It was the truth—as far as it went.

"Oh, Livvie!" Blair spat with disgust. "You're hopeless!"

"Tell me something I don't know."

Her friend flounced off the bed and faced her with

her hands planted on her hips. "Well, don't expect me to set you up again. You had your chance and you blew it." With a huff, she headed for the door. "You ask me, you don't deserve Joe."

Olivia looked at Mary Beth again. "That parting shot really hurt, mainly because, at the time, I agreed with her."

Five

"What! Why that's...that's...nonsense!" Mary Beth sputtered. "You're one of the sweetest, brightest, kindest people I know. Joe Connally should count himself lucky to have been married to you."

"Thanks, Mary Beth. I appreciate your loyalty. But the Olivia you know today is a far cry from the insecure girl I was back then.

"Also, what you don't realize is, there is a definite pecking order in Savannah. The scion of a blue-blood family simply does not marry the housekeeper's daughter. Young as I was, even I knew that. As much as I loved and admired Joe, it never occurred to me that he would consider such a thing."

"Well that's the most archaic thing I've ever heard. So what happened after he went back to Princeton?"

Olivia shook her head sadly. "Keeping my promise to Joe was the most difficult thing I'd ever done in all of my eighteen years up to that point.

"Don't ask me how, but I knew almost right away that I was pregnant."

Mary Beth gasped, and reached for Olivia's hand. "Oh, dearest. You had a *baby*. I sensed there was some great sadness in your background, but a child...I never once guessed."

"There was no reason you should have. Anyway,

for weeks after Joe left I refused to accept what my body was telling me. Whenever I felt peculiar I told myself that I must be coming down with something. And the swelling and tenderness in my breasts—well that had to be some new unpleasant symptom associated with my monthlies. That was all.

"Eventually, though, I had to face reality. A test confirmed my suspicion and I had no choice but to telephone Joe.

"Before placing the call I rehearsed what I would say over and over, but I was so nervous and so emotional that when Joe said 'Hello' I started to cry. I couldn't utter a word...."

"Who is this?" Joe had demanded.

Her answer had been a sob, a harsh, raspy sound that hurt her throat.

A brief silence followed. When Joe spoke again his voice softened. "Livvie? Is that you?"

"Ye-yes..." Another sob rose and her attempt at speech dissolved into a strangled cry.

"Ah, Livvie. Sweetheart, don't take on so. It's going to be all right."

"Bu-but...oh, J-J-Joe."

"Take it easy, sugar. You're not alone. Have you spoken to anyone else about this?"

"N-no."

"Good. Look, I'm going to take the next flight home. Don't say anything to anyone, okay? If you have to, pretend you're ill and stay put in your room until I get there."

"I—I wi-will."

"Good. I'll see you in a few hours."

Joe was as good as his word. Rather than alert his

family, he rented a car at the Savannah airport and drove directly to the cottage. Thankfully, Flora was working up at the big house and Livvie was alone. Had her mother seen Joe at her door or the way he pulled Livvie into his arms the instant he stepped inside the cottage she would have fainted.

With a sigh, Livvie melted against his chest and wrapped her arms around him. She felt as though a hundred-pound weight had been lifted from her shoulders.

"How're you doing, little one?" he asked, rubbing his cheek against the top of her head.

"I'm...I'm okay." His concern was nearly her undoing, bringing fresh tears to her eyes.

"I don't want you to worry about a thing, you hear? Just go pack a bag."

"Pack? But...why?"

"We're going to fly to Vegas and get married."

Livvie's heart leapt. "Ma-married?"

It was her most cherished dream come true. And the last thing she had expected. Since she was nine years old she'd dreamed of becoming Mrs. Joseph Connally. As a young teenager she'd even practiced writing the name over and over in her diary. Still, she could not in good conscience let Joe make that sort of sacrifice without at least *trying* to talk him out of it.

"Joe, I...I appreciate what you're trying to do, but...well...these days most people don't feel like they *have* to marry just because—"

"I'm not most people," he declared almost angrily. "And neither are you. We've created a new life together, and we're going to do the right thing." He paused, frowning. "Unless the idea of marrying me is repugnant to you."

"No! No, of course not! It's not that. I just don't want you to feel obligated."

"I am obligated. An honorable man takes responsibility for his actions."

Livvie backed up a step. She looked down at the floor and traced an invisible pattern on the worn braided rug with the toe of her sneaker. "Times have changed, Joe," she said quietly, though every word stabbed her heart like a dagger. "These days you can take responsibility without tying yourself to the child's mother. People have children out of wedlock all the time." Trying to lighten the mood, she glanced up at him and attempted a smile, but the result was a sad little quiver of her lips. "There's no such thing as a shotgun wedding anymore—not even in the deep South. I don't think there's been one in Georgia in at least twenty years."

Joe was not amused. "Ours won't be a shotgun wedding, Livvie. No one is holding a gun to my back. Now, why don't you go pack that bag and let's get out of here?"

"Well, I must say, the more I hear about the man, the more I like him," Mary Beth declared in a somewhat mollified tone.

Olivia chuckled. "I probably should have put up more of a fight. Maybe if I'd been a little older and wiser—certainly had I known how it would all end— I would have."

Her mouth twisted. "Then again, maybe not. I was so thoroughly besotted with Joe and so thrilled with the idea of becoming Mrs. Joseph Connally that I could have rationalized my way past any obstacle.''

"Even his mother?" Mary Beth asked.

"Yes. Even Eleanore.

"She was livid when she found out, of course. She demanded that we have the marriage annulled before anyone found out, but Joe refused. Then she used what she thought was her trump card—she cut off the money from the trust his father had left him. She thought that would bring him to heel, but Joe stood his ground.''

"So, how did you two manage?"

"His aunt Tilly let us move into a tiny furnished garage apartment behind her house, and Joe got a job at a lumberyard. He tried to find work through family friends, but Eleanore had already put the word out that no one was to hire him, and no one dared defy her.''

"I take it the marriage was a disaster. What happened? Did you two fight a lot?"

"No, not at all. For almost five months, in spite of the awkwardness between us, I was happily married to Joe, happier than I'd ever been in my life. We never quarreled and I adored having him all to myself day after day.''

"What about the sex part?"

"Mary Beth!"

"What? You know what they say—if it's good it's only a small part of a marriage, but if it's bad or you ain't gettin' any, it's a huge part.''

"It so happens the sex was fantastic," Olivia declared, struggling to ignore the flush climbing her neck and face. "The problem was, the rest of the time we were intimate strangers. We'd known each other for years, but not well. We were stiff and ill at ease. Mostly we sort of tiptoed around each other, being ultrapolite so as not to rock the boat. It was like walking on eggs.''

''Mmm. That's not the best way to develop a close relationship.''

''I know. But I was besotted, and with all the skewed reasoning and blind optimism of youth, I thought that as time wore on, especially after the baby was born, the awkwardness would vanish and Joe and I would form a lasting bond.''

''But that didn't happen, did it?'' Mary Beth prodded cautiously, when a troubled look came over Olivia's face.

''No. In my sixth month of pregnancy I miscarried and that hope was dashed.''

''Oh, no! I thought you were going to tell me that Joe used his family influence to win custody. I had no idea that you lost the baby. Oh, sweetie, I'm so sorry.''

''I had gone into premature labor. At the first sign of trouble Joe rushed me to the hospital,'' Olivia went on, as though having started, she felt compelled to get the whole story out.

''Throughout the ordeal Joe remained by my side, holding my hand and wiping the sweat off my face. All the time the doctor and nurses tried to save our baby, Joe crooned encouragement in my ear. In the end, though, all their work was for nothing. After twelve hours of struggle, our son came into the world stillborn.''

''Oh, sweetie, I'm sorry. So sorry,'' Mary Beth whispered.

Olivia stared out the kitchen window at nothing,

her tea cold. "Joe held me while I cried," she continued in the same lost tone. "I cried so long and so hard that the doctor became concerned and ordered that I be sedated. Throughout the night, whenever I roused, Joe was always there, sitting beside my bed. He looked so young, and so sad and haggard.

"It was midmorning the next day before I awoke fully. Joe was still there but we were both somber and quiet. There didn't seem to be anything either of us could say to ease the pain. In addition, hanging in the air was the unspoken question that neither of us wanted to acknowledge. Where did we go from there?

"Joe looked so tired I told him to go home and get some sleep. He resisted at first, but I insisted...."

"I'll be back by five—as soon as I catch a couple of hours' sleep and grab a bite to eat," he said, giving her a peck on the forehead.

Thanks to the lingering effects of the sedative, Olivia spent the day alternately weeping and dozing. When five o'clock came and went with no sign of Joe she was not unduly worried. He'd been so exhausted when he left he'd probably overslept, she told herself.

At five-fifteen a volunteer brought her dinner tray. She was still picking at the food when the telephone on the bedside table rang.

"Hi, little one. How're you doing?" Joe said when she answered.

The tenderness in his voice brought a lump to her throat and a fresh set of tears, but she managed to mumble, "I'm okay."

"You sure?"

"Yes." She looked at the acoustical tiles on the ceiling and blinked hard.

"That's good." A brief silence followed. "Uh... Mother called a few minutes ago. She wants me to come to dinner tonight."

Livvie's heart skipped a beat and warning bells began to clang inside her head. Joe had called both of their mothers that morning to let them know about the baby. Since they had announced their marriage, Livvie had seen her own mother only a few times, though she called her weekly. However, she and Joe had not heard so much as a peep out of Eleanore.

"Oh?" she said cautiously, wondering what was behind this sudden invitation.

"Yeah. Look, I know she's been rotten to you, little one, but I think she feels really bad about the baby and all. I have a hunch she wants to mend fences. If it's all right with you, I thought I'd go and at least hear what she has to say. Unless you object. Or you need me, of course."

"I see." She needed him. She needed him desperately—to hold her and tell her he was sorry about the baby, that everything was going to be okay. That they would have other children. But she couldn't bring herself to say the words. She wanted them to come from him with no prompting.

"So...what do you think? Would you be upset if I went?"

"No. Go ahead. I...I think you should go."

"Me, too." He chuckled. "Mother can be a real pain in the ass sometimes, but she is really not so bad." When Livvie didn't comment he added, "I won't stay long. I told her I would have to get back to be with you, so she said she'd have your mother serve dinner early. I should be at the hospital by eight. A quarter after, at the latest."

Livvie didn't want him to go. She didn't trust Eleanore. Didn't trust her motive. And she had one. Of that Livvie was certain. Eleanore seldom did anything without a reason.

Still, she was Joe's mother, and Livvie knew that he loved her and missed her, in spite of the stand she'd taken. "Okay. I'll see you, then."

Time seemed to drag. Every few minutes Livvie glanced at the big clock on the wall, willing the hands to move. She wondered what was going on at Winterhaven. What was being said. What Eleanore was up to.

She picked up the remote and surfed through the TV channels, but nothing held her interest, so she turned the set off. Easing onto her side, she winced at the pinching between her legs. She stared out the window at the twinkling lights of Savannah and pressed her fist against her breastbone and the painful knot that had lodged just beneath it.

The door swung open a few minutes before eight. Livvie looked over her shoulder, her face lighting up, but her smile of greeting instantly collapsed.

"Mrs. Connally!"

"Hello, Livvie. How are you feeling?"

Following close on Eleanore's heels came Livvie's mother and Blair.

"Oh, dearest," Flora cried, and rushed to her side to give her a hug and murmur condolences. Blair did the same, then both she and Flora stepped back and out of the way, their gazes darting to Eleanore.

A prickly sensation crawled up the back of Livvie's head and spread across her scalp, making her hair stand on end. Her heart began to race. Something was up. Her mother and Blair looked nervous, almost

guilty, and Eleanore's face wore that sweetly determined look that Livvie knew from experience spelled
trouble.

Craning her neck to one side, she looked around
the three women toward the door. "Where's Joe?
Didn't he come with you?"

"No. Joseph is busy. He may drop by later. But
before he does, we have to talk."

A cold sensation trickled down Livvie's spine.
Busy? Doing what? He promised he would be here
by now. It wasn't like Joe to break a promise.

"What…what do you want to talk about?"

"First of all, let me say that I'm sorry that you've
suffered this loss. From talking to your mother I'm
aware of how much you wanted the baby, and no
matter the circumstances of his conception, I understand that it's always devastating to lose a child."

"Thank you," Livvie replied warily.

"Yes, well, what's done is done. And you must
surely realize that it was for the best."

The cruel words brought fresh tears to Livvie's
eyes. She had to press her lips together to keep them
from trembling.

Eleanore didn't seem to notice. She fixed Livvie
with a look, her normally soft blue eyes determined
and unblinking. "I'm afraid I must insist that you free
my son. He did the honorable thing and married you,
but there is no longer a reason for you to stay together."

"But…but marriage is sacred," Livvie stammered.
"We took vows before God."

"Oh, piffle!" Eleanore dismissed the claim with a
chuckle and an airy wave of her hand. "I'd hardly

call a quickie civil ceremony in Las Vegas a Holy sacrament.''

She smiled fondly, her voice becoming soft and cajoling. ''Livvie, sugar, I've known you since you were a child, and I know that you're not a selfish person. Surely you can see how unfair it would be of you to hold on to Joe now. You have to know that you are, and will always be, nothing but a millstone around his neck.

''I am fond of you, Livvie. And I'm not trying to hurt you. Truly, I'm not. But it must be obvious, even to you, that you don't fit into our social set and that you never will. If you hold Joe to this marriage you will always be an embarrassment to him. You don't want that, do you?''

Livvie glanced at her mother and Blair, but neither woman would meet her eyes.

''No, of course not. But…'' Livvie gazed down at the white cotton thermal blanket that covered her, which she was twisting between her fingers. ''Joe doesn't seem unhappy. And he's never given me any reason to think that he's ashamed of me.''

''Well, I should hope not,'' Eleanore replied indignantly. ''He's a Connally, after all. He has extremely good manners.''

Livvie couldn't argue with that. Even if Joe was miserable, for her sake she knew that he would probably keep his chin up and pretend everything was fine.

''The point is, my son should be completing his studies and earning a degree and leading the life to which he was born, among people of his own class, not eking out a subsistence living at a menial job and living in a hovel. Honestly. What was Tilly thinking, renting you that awful garage apartment of hers?''

Olivia frowned. She didn't think their home was a hovel. It was small, and maybe it wasn't fancy, but she had fixed it up with paint and made new curtains with material she'd bought on sale and decorated it with restored hand-me-downs and flea market finds. She thought it looked charming.

"Aunt Tilly has been very good to us," she murmured in mild protest.

Eleanore sniffed. "She's an interfering old biddy." She paused and looked for some sign that Livvie was relenting. Finding none, she went on the attack again. "The plain truth is, if you hadn't tricked my son into marriage he would be graduating soon and making plans for a summer wedding to Selina."

Livvie's head jerked up. She looked at her mother-in-law with stricken eyes. "Joe had already broken up with Selina when we married."

"Oh, pooh. That was just temporary. Like always. Those little spats happen when two people are as passionate for each other as those two are. Face it, Livvie. Joe doesn't love you. He's in love with Selina. He always has been."

Livvie bit her lower lip and looked down again at her twisting fingers. She didn't want to believe Eleanore, but the truth was, she was too unsure of Joe's feelings and of their fragile marriage to be certain about anything.

Still, she couldn't just cave in without even trying. "You may be right, but I won't believe any of it until Joe himself tells me that he wants his freedom."

"Oh, for heaven's sake, he won't do that. You know Joe. He's too much of a gentleman. In fact, he would not approve if he knew that I was here now telling you the truth. If you confront him with what

I've revealed, you know perfectly well that his sense of honor will demand that he deny everything. He made a commitment to you, so he will insist on continuing the marriage, no matter the cost to his personal happiness.''

Livvie knew that Eleanore was probably right about that. With Joe, honor came first. It would do no good to ask him. So what was she to do? How was she to know?

"Well? What is your answer? Will you release him?"

"I...I don't know."

"Oh, for—" Eleanore huffed and rolled her eyes. "I didn't want to have to tell you this because I didn't want to hurt you, but you leave me no choice. You want proof of Joe's feelings? Then you should know that at this very moment he's with Selina."

Livvie shrank back against the pillow, shaking her head. "No! No, he wouldn't do that."

"Oh, but he has. If you don't believe me, ask your mother. Or Blair."

Livvie's gaze darted to her mother. Flora twisted her hands together and looked back at her with infinite sadness. "Oh, baby, I'm afraid she's right. Joe is with Selina. They left Winterhaven more than an hour ago, right after dinner."

When she looked at Blair her friend grimaced. "I'm so sorry, Livvie," she whispered.

Livvie felt as though someone had just cut her heart out. The ache in her chest was enormous.

A silent tear slid down her cheek, then another, and another, until they streamed down like soft rain. She stared straight ahead, unaware of anything beyond the excruciating pain that enveloped her.

, With an anguished moan, Flora stepped to the side of the bed and took one of Livvie's hands in both of hers. "Oh, baby, don't cry so. I know it hurts. I know. But this was bound to happen. If only you had listened to me. Over and over I've tried to tell you that you can't change who or what you are. Why couldn't you be happy with that? Why did you have to be like your daddy, always setting your sights so high?"

"Please, Mama, don't. Just…don't." Livvie buried her face in her hands and gave into the sobs that rose in her throat.

"You have to set that boy free," her mother urged. "You have to, baby. If you don't you'll never be happy again. And neither will he."

"Your mother is right, Livvie," Blair said, touching her heaving shoulder. "You tried, but you and Joe just weren't meant to be. Accept that and end it now, before you both get hurt even more."

"Pl-please, will you all ju-just go away and lea-leave me alone," she choked into her hands.

"Very well," Eleanore agreed. "But before we go I'd like to have a word with you alone. Blair, why don't you and Flora wait for me in the hall."

The women murmured agreement, and a moment later Livvie heard the door swish closed behind them.

"Child, you really should try to calm down. You're going to make yourself ill, carrying on like that," Eleanore said, her voice sugary sweet with compassion.

"Oh, please," Livvie wailed. "Can't you just go?"

"Not yet, I'm afraid. Look at me, child. *Look* at me." For all her Southern belle airs, Eleanore was a strong-willed woman, and when she used that tone few would have ignored her. Livvie jumped at the command, her hands dropping away from her face.

"There, that's better." Eleanore came around to the side of the bed and patted Livvie's arm. "I know that you are hurting, and whether you believe it or not, that wasn't my aim. Truly it wasn't. Nor is it my intention that you walk away from this marriage empty-handed. I want you to take this check," she said, drawing the slip of paper from her purse.

"You're offering me *money* to set Joe free?" Livvie said in an appalled voice.

"Think of it as a divorce settlement. You've been married to my son for almost five months, after all. You deserve something. I know you've always dreamed of attending college. This money could buy you a fairly decent education at a state university.

"There is just one condition. I think it would be best all around if you left Savannah. And that you stayed away."

Eleanore laid the check on the bedside table and walked to the door. Once there she opened it but paused with her hand on the knob and looked back at Livvie. "If you care for Joe at all, you will do the right thing and let him go."

When she had gone, Livvie didn't move for several minutes. Then, slowly, she reached out and picked up the check from the side table. Her eyes widened when she scanned the amount. Fifty thousand dollars. She gave a bitter chuckle. Eleanore must really want her out of their lives.

"You know," Mary Beth stated, slamming her cup into its saucer, "though I don't agree with her, I can at least understand what motivated Mrs. Connally.

What chaps my backside is your mother's attitude. You'd think she'd be thrilled with your marriage, and do everything in her power to support you.''

Olivia smiled at her friend's indignation. ''Yes, well, there's a saying in the South that you probably haven't heard. It's 'Don't get above your raisin'.' If my mother believed in such things, that would be her mantra.

''What it means is, don't get uppity or let success go to your head, but my mother takes it literally. She believes that whatever level of society you are born into is where you belong, that you shouldn't strive to better your lot, but accept it. She felt that my marriage to Joe was wrong from the get-go. My audacity embarrassed her.''

Mary Beth cocked her head to one side and gave Olivia a shrewd look. ''Is that why you don't visit your home? Because it would *embarrass* your mom?''

''And my sister. Also because Eleanore doesn't want me there, and they both would jump off a cliff if she ordered them to do so. Which I suppose I can understand. They do depend on the Connallys for their livelihood.''

''I still say it's terrible. No wonder you stay away.''

''We're just very different people, is all.''

''Humph. So…what happened between you and Joe? Did you ever find out the truth about him being with Selina?''

''Oh, yes.'' Olivia drew a deep breath and let it out slowly. ''It was almost ten when Joe got to the hospital that night…''

* * *

Poking his head around the edge of the door, he grinned sheepishly. "Hi. Sorry I'm late. I hope you're not angry. I had a bit of trouble."

Livvie merely looked at him in silence. He stepped inside the room, and as she watched him approach the bed her heart sank. Smeared all along the right side of his jaw and around his mouth were lipstick stains. The bright, pearly pink was Selina's favorite shade.

Joe bent to kiss her, but at the last second she turned her head away and his lips grazed her cheek. Clenching her jaw, Livvie wiped the spot with her fingers, revolted by the thought that some of that pink glop might have gotten on her skin.

"Uh-oh. I guess you are angry. Look, I'm sorry, I can explain if you'll just give me a chance."

"All right. Go ahead." She clasped her hands together in her lap and waited, wanting with every fiber of her being for him to explain away those lipstick smudges and have a good reason why he'd been with Selina in the first place.

"I...well...I, uh...I had car trouble. I was stranded on the side of the road all this time. No one stopped to help, and it took me forever to get the car started again."

Livvie's last fragile hope shattered.

She turned her head away, unable to bear the sight of his lipstick-smeared face any longer. She could feel his gaze, but she refused to look at him.

"Are you all right? Is there anything you need? Would you like a back rub?" He started to sit down on the bed beside her, but she shook her head.

"No. I don't want a back rub." She waved toward the chair. "Please. Sit down. I think we should talk."

"All right," he said cautiously. "Is there a problem?"

"No. There's no problem," she replied in a dull monotone. "I just wanted to tell you that I think we should split up."

"What?"

"I want a divorce."

"A divorce?" He stared at her, his expression blank. Then he shook his head as though trying to clear it. "A divorce. Wow. I didn't expect this."

"You said yourself that you married me because you felt obligated, but—"

"Ah, Livvie, I didn't mean it that way, I—"

"It doesn't matter. The point is, now that there's no baby to think of, there's no reason to continue this marriage."

His gaze sought hers again and held it for a long time. "Are you sure this is what you want?"

Curling her hands into fists, she dug her fingernails into her palms so hard the pain brought tears to her eyes and forced out the lie. "Yes."

"I see."

He looked stunned, even a bit sad, but she noticed that he didn't try to argue.

"I'm sure your family's attorney can handle all the details," she continued in the same dull tone. "If you'll move your things out of the apartment before I leave the hospital we shouldn't have to see each other again until the divorce is granted."

"Don't you want your own attorney? Someone who can look out for your interests?"

"I can't afford an attorney. And since I won't be asking you for anything, what's the point?"

A frown creased Joe's forehead as he studied her

curiously. "You're really serious about this, aren't you."

She turned her head away and stared out the window. "I just want it to be over." That part, at least, was true. If she was going to lose him, she wanted the break to be quick and clean.

He was silent for a long time. Then she heard the vinyl chair crackle as he stood up. "All right. If that's how you want it."

From the corner of her eye she saw him walk to the door and pause with his back to the room. "Goodbye, little one," he said softly.

Livvie's head whipped around in time to see him disappear through the doorway. Her throat worked painfully and her lips trembled. "Goodbye, my love," she whispered, and the heavy door whispered shut behind him. She squeezed her eyes shut and her face crumpled.

"Oh, Olivia," Mary Beth murmured, giving her arm a squeeze. "You must have been shattered. And you never saw him again until you came face-to-face on Mallen Island?"

"Actually, I saw him in court, the day we received our divorce decree, the same day that I left Savannah for good. Eleanore and Blair and the Connally family attorney were with him."

She remembered that part distinctly because she had been the only person on her side of the courtroom. Her mother and sister had claimed that they did not want to take sides so they had stayed away.

"When it was all over Joe came over and shook my hand and said, "Good luck, Livvie. I hope you have a happy life."

Mary Beth snorted. "That was big of him." She fixed Olivia with a penetrating look. "You've told me how you felt about Joe then. How about now? When you saw him again what did you feel?"

Olivia chuckled. "If you're worried that I'm still in love with him, don't be. In a way, seeing Joe again was probably a good thing. No matter how much I told myself that I was over him, somewhere, deep inside, a part of me worried that if I saw him again all the old feelings would come rushing back. But they didn't.

"I'll admit I was nervous when we met again, but that's only natural. I also have to say, he's still the best-looking man I've ever known. But other than a purely physical tug of awareness, I felt nothing—none of the old aching yearning or starry-eyed adoration that I used to experience around him. It's good to be able to say that I'm not in love with Joe anymore and know that it's true."

Six

Standing by the wall of windows in Reese's office, Joe leaned back with his hips braced against the long marble sill and watched his partner pace back and forth in front of the three easels.

Joe's pose was indolent and unconcerned—outstretched legs crossed at the ankle, arms folded loosely over his chest, his expression almost bored—but inside he was as taut as a drawn bow.

Each of the easels held several presentation boards that the designers had used to illustrate their proposals. Well…two of the designers, anyway. Olivia had not personally pitched her own ideas but had sent one of her employees in her stead. The woman had assured them that all the designs were Olivia's, and it had been she who had put together her firm's boards.

The stand-in, a designer named Mary Beth Mason, had given a thorough and professional presentation, but it had irritated Joe that Olivia had not followed through and presented her plan herself.

Dammit! Ever since he'd left her on the island a month ago, he'd been looking forward to seeing her again. Why, he had no idea. Her manner toward him had been less than friendly from the moment they'd met again.

Not only had he been disappointed, it had galled

him that she cared so little about the project that she couldn't be bothered to present her own plan. When he'd said as much to Ms. Mason, however, the woman had coolly informed him that Olivia was convinced she had no chance of getting the job, and therefore felt her time would be better spent working on other projects.

Though Ms. Mason hadn't come right out and said so, the look in her eyes and her tone told Joe that she knew all about him and Olivia, and she clearly felt he was to blame for their split. That had left him more puzzled than ever and hardened his resolve to clear the air between him and Livvie.

Learning that she still felt that the past would work against her, despite his assurances otherwise, had annoyed Joe all the more. Not only had Livvie developed an aversion to him, she no longer trusted his word.

Well, he had made his choice based on the best design, just as he'd told her he would, without allowing their history to influence his decision one way or the other.

At least…he didn't think he had. Not consciously, anyway.

He had to admit, though, he was anxious to see if Reese would make the same choice. If not, then, as always, Caroline would cast the tie-breaking vote. Even though she wasn't a partner, she knew their vision for Mallenegua and she had excellent taste.

Reese moved from one easel to the next, at each shuffling through the various boards that the designer had worked up. After looking at them all he took several steps back and stood with his feet braced wide, his hands hooked over his lean hips, the jacket of his Armani suit pushed back. He pursed his lips, his gaze going from one easel to the next.

Some of the boards contained scale drawings—some depicting floor plans and furniture arrangements, some architectural changes, some detailed views of finished rooms. Others held samples of fabric, carpet, wallpaper, wood, tile and hardware. There were also photographs of various accessory items, such as fringed Victorian lamps, urns, umbrella stands, porcelain basins and pitchers, and quilt racks.

"Hmm." Reese cocked his head to one side and stared at the top board on the easel on the far right.

Joe ground his teeth. For God's sake, man. Will you just *pick* one?

Finally, just as Joe's patience came to an end, Reese turned to him with a satisfied expression. "I don't recall which presentation belongs to which designer, but to me the choice is obvious. This one is the best," he said, pointing to the third easel.

Joe's nostrils flared as the breath he hadn't realized he'd been holding whooshed out, but his nonchalant facade held. "I agree. As far as I'm concerned there's no contest. The first one is too fussy, too over-the-top Victorian. The second one is more modern than we're going for. But that one is right on the mark in every way—style, colors, content, design. There are even some damned good suggestions for structural and architectural changes included."

"Well, then. Since we're in agreement, it looks like we have ourselves a designer. By the way, which one are we talking about?"

Joe glanced at the boards with a look of grim satisfaction. "Olivia."

* * *

Olivia felt as though a thousand butterflies had taken up residence in her stomach. She'd gotten the job. She'd actually gotten the job! It had been two weeks since Ms. Keeton had called to inform her, but she still couldn't believe it.

Since then Olivia had rushed around, wrapping up other projects, placating clients who had been waiting for her services, tying up loose ends and preparing her staff to take up the slack in her absence. All the while she had half expected that at any moment she would receive another call from Ms. Keeton, telling her that they had made a mistake, that she wasn't getting the job after all.

The call never came, however, and now here she was, waiting in the elegant third-floor reception room outside the executive offices of AdCo Enterprises.

Too nervous to sit still, she shifted positions on the muted green-and-cream-striped silk-upholstered settee and glanced at the magnificent eighteenth-century pendulum wall clock again. She'd been looking for one exactly like that for the Clairmont restoration, and she made a mental note to find out where the decorator had located this one.

The younger of the secretaries seated at the two mahogany desks looked at her and smiled. "It shouldn't be too much longer. As soon as the conference call is over Mr. Addison will see you."

"Thank you," Olivia replied.

The woman turned back to her computer and resumed typing. According to the nameplate on her desk, she was Joyce Benson. Behind the desk and slightly to one side, a massive mahogany door bore a brass plaque that read Reese Addison, President.

On the same wall a few feet away was an identical door and plaque with Joseph Connally, Vice President etched on it. At the other desk in front of Joe's office a fifty-something woman, whose nameplate identified her as Martha Lumis, sat opening mail.

Trying to settle her nerves, Olivia gazed idly around the room. The executive floor, like the rest of the AdCo building, was a beautiful example of tasteful restoration and conversion.

According to the date chiseled in the stone pediment over the front entrance, the building had been constructed in 1761, during the late Colonial period. In those days of Georgian architecture even warehouses had been built to a standard of excellence and visual appeal.

In this case, both the architect and decorator had done outstanding jobs, she noted. The restoration had been carried out with historical accuracy and an appreciation for the elegance of the period. At the same time the structure's primary use had been skillfully converted from warehouse to office facility, unobtrusively incorporating all the latest modern technology needed in today's business world.

The wide-planked heart-of-pine floors had been refinished and polished to a soft luster while retaining the rich patina of age and the scars and dings of centuries of use. Lovely Oriental rugs and runners in shades of muted green, cream and faded raspberry delineated sitting areas and traffic paths.

The furniture was also faithful to the period, a mix of Chippendale and Queen Anne with an occasional piece of Chinese design for accent. Olivia doubted that the cream-colored plaster walls were original to the space, but they, too, were in keeping with the time period, as were the massive dark wood beams and woodwork.

"Mr. Addison will see you now," Ms. Benson announced, and Olivia jumped. Recovering quickly, she grabbed her purse and briefcase and headed for the mahogany doors.

"Ah, you must be Olivia. At last we meet. I'm Reese Addison." The man seated behind the desk stood up and came toward her with his hand outstretched.

"How do you do," she replied as he took her hand in both of his.

Reese Addison was Hollywood handsome, with perfect features and a thick shock of blond hair, which was styled fashionably short. His pale gray "bedroom" eyes gleamed with masculine interest as they ran over her.

Joe was charming, in a mannerly Southern gentleman sort of way, but Olivia instantly pegged this man as a beguiler. There was something about Reese that drew people in, something captivating and irresistible. Male or female, you could not help but respond to his personal brand of charisma. During their telephone conversations she had sensed that quality in him, but in the flesh it was almost palpable.

No wonder he was the point man for the company, the negotiator who acquired financing and dealt with customers and potential investors, while Joe worked behind the scenes. The man was a born Svengali.

Holding her hand longer than necessary, Reese towered over her, and she realized that he matched Joe's six-feet-one-inch height. Meeting his flirtatious gaze with a polite expression, Olivia wondered how many women had been dazzled by that killer smile.

"I do apologize for missing our appointment in January," he said smoothly. "I felt terrible about that. And now that I've met you, I regret it even more. Had I known you were this lovely I would have dumped those bankers in a heartbeat."

"That's quite all right. I understand the pressures of business," Olivia replied, choosing to ignore the last part of the statement. "In any case, your partner showed me around."

"Yes, so he told me." Reese's gaze went past her. "He always was a lucky son of a gun."

Automatically, Olivia glanced over her shoulder to see what had drawn his attention, and her heart skipped a beat when her gaze collided with Joe's.

"Oh! I'm sorry. I didn't see you there." Nor had she expected to. During their telephone conversations these past two weeks, Ms. Keeton had made no mention of Joe attending this meeting.

"Hello, Olivia," Joe said, watching her intently. "It's good to see you again."

He sat in front of Reese's desk in a Queen Anne wing chair upholstered in maroon leather. Between the chair's high back and side extensions and the light pouring in through the wall of windows at his back, he was almost completely in shadows, which was probably why she hadn't noticed him before. Olivia wondered if that had been his plan.

"Thank you. It's nice to see you, too."

That she could utter those words and not feel like a bald-faced liar gave Olivia a tremendous sense of peace. Okay, so maybe "nice" wasn't exactly the right word to describe how she felt about seeing him again, but at least the experience was not nearly so unsettling as it had been during their last meeting.

It was such a relief to know, once and for all, that the all-consuming love she'd felt for Joe for so long was dead. When she looked at him now she felt nostalgic, but her heart no longer palpitated nor did she experience a rush of suffocating emotion and get all flustered and tongue-tied.

To think, for fourteen years, she had allowed the mere thought of seeing him again to fill her with dread. If she'd had **a lick of** sense she would have returned home ye**ars ago an**d laid the past to rest.

But at least now, at long last, she was free. She felt confident that she could handle this job and whatever contact with Joe **that** was required with the same equanimity as she did any other client.

"Congratulations," Joe added. "You said you were the best, and you were right. Reese and I were very impressed with your ideas. Too bad you couldn't have presented them in person."

Though softly spoken, there was no mistaking the criticism lacing the comment. Olivia had never before been on the receiving end of Joe's displeasure, but she refused to let it throw her. Tilting her chin, she met his dark stare.

"Unfortunately, there was a minor crisis with another client that needed my attention. Being businessmen, I was sure you'd understand."

"Of course we do," Reese replied. "And your Ms. Mason gave an excellent presentation, so there was no harm done.

"Please, won't you have a seat?" he asked, indicating the matching wing chair that was separated from Joe's by a small pie-crust table. When she was seated he resumed his seat behind the desk and gave her a questioning look. "Would you like some coffee before we get started? Or perhaps some tea? Or perhaps you're hungry? I could have a snack brought in, if you'd like.''

"No, thank you. I've had lunch."

"Very well, then. Let's get down to business, shall we? As you know, Olivia, we estimate this project will take about two years to complete, give or take a few months. We expect a full commitment from you for the duration of the project. Is that agreeable?''

"Yes. Provided you understand that I will periodically be making short trips to Atlanta to check on my own business, and perhaps, when the schedule allows, take on small jobs for select customers."

"Are you sure you can handle that?" Joe asked. "We wouldn't want you to stretch yourself too thin."

"I'm sure. I'll do the extra design work in the evenings on my own time, and since I'll be making buying trips for this job to replace the pieces that Miss Prudence sold, I can buy for other clients at the same time."

"Very well, then," Reese said. "We'll agree to that. Anything else?"

Olivia shook her head, and Reese flashed his killer smile.

"Good. Now then, if you'll just look over this contract and sign it, we're in business."

"I'm sorry, but I'd like that proviso written into our contract before I sign it."

Reese's eyebrows shot upward, and Joe cleared his throat. Olivia thought she saw his mouth twitch as well, but she couldn't be certain.

"Well, well. I had a hunch you were more than just a pretty face."

Olivia shrugged. "I've learned that, in business, if you don't get it in writing you don't have a deal."

Reese glanced at Joe, and he nodded. "Very well, I'll have our attorney revise the contract. It should be ready to sign in an hour or so. But until then, we might as well press on.

"AdCo will provide you with a design space here, but we anticipate that you'll do most of your work on-site.

"The remodeling blueprints are drawn up, but nothing is set in stone at this point. We expect there will be many changes as we go along, both minor and major. Joe and I would like your input, both on the plans as they stand now and with any problems or changes that crop up. For that reason it will probably be best if you plan to stay at Mallenegua throughout the work week most of the time."

"You could ferry back and forth to the mainland with the men each day," Joe put in. "But that's a time-consuming commute and I doubt you'd like it."

Olivia doubted it, too, given her motion-sickness problem. Anyway, Reese was right; it would be best if she was on hand during all phases of the project. Besides, she had to live somewhere. Many weekends she would fly home to Atlanta, and when she didn't, there was always the hotel just a short walk from the AdCo building.

"All right. That sounds reasonable. Will anyone else be staying at Mallenegua?"

Joe chuckled. "If you're concerned about being there alone with Mrs. Jaffee, don't be. I'll be staying at Mallenegua most of the time myself."

Surprise darted through her. "You?"

"Joe is the architect for the renovation." Reese

shot his partner a wry look. "He likes to keep his hand in, and I have to admit, he's the best man for the job. He's such a stickler for detail. On projects of this size and scope, he usually acts as general contractor. That way we can keep close tabs on things."

"I see." She hadn't counted on spending her days—and nights—under the same roof with Joe. She had expected to report to him or Reese periodically, maybe every couple of weeks or so. She'd also assumed that now and then, one or both of them would visit the site. Since he was one of the owners, it had not occurred to her that Joe would involve himself in the day-to-day work of the project.

All right. So this development was unexpected. It was nothing she couldn't handle, she told herself, squelching the uneasy flutter in the pit of her stomach. She would just have to adjust her thinking. That was all.

"I suppose the first thing we should do is go over the blueprints with you. Let's see. What did I do with mine?" Reese muttered, scanning the top of his desk and the credenza behind his chair.

"I have a set in my drafting room," Joe said.

"Good. Let's go. We can show Olivia her new workspace and take a look at the blueprints while we're there."

Reese stood up and Olivia and Joe followed suit just as the door opened partway and Ms. Benson stuck her head inside.

"Pardon me, Mr. Addison. I hate to interrupt, but if you don't leave in the next ten minutes you're going to miss your flight."

Shooting back his cuff, Reese glanced at the gold watch on his wrist and grimaced. "Right. Thanks,

Joyce.'' As the woman retreated he gave Olivia a re-gretful look. "I'm sorry to cut this short, but I don't have a choice. That conference call ran longer than I anticipated and put me behind schedule. I have an early meeting in Alexandria tomorrow morning, so I have to be on that flight.''

"I understand. Business is business.''

"Olivia will be fine with me,'' Joe said. "I'll take her on a tour of the office and introduce her around, then I'll show her the space she'll be using and we'll go over the blueprints. After we sign the contract, we'll take my boat to Mallen Island.''

Reese nodded. "Right.'' He stood up and came around the desk and took Olivia's hand again, smil-ing. "When I get back, why don't you and I have dinner together some evening and get better ac-quainted?''

Taken aback, not by the invitation—business was often discussed over dinner—but by the tone in which it was delivered and the flirtatious look in Reese's eyes, Olivia was at a loss for a reply.

"Uh, Olivia, why don't you wait for me in the reception room,'' Joe said. "I want to have a word with Reese before he leaves.''

"Certainly,'' she replied, grateful to escape.

"What's up?'' Reese snapped open his briefcase, his expression distracted as he started stuffing items inside.

"I don't think you should see Olivia socially.''

Reese's head snapped up. He looked at Joe with blank surprise. "Why not?''

"It's not a good idea for you to start romancing someone who's working for us.''

"What's the big deal? Anyway, you went out with

that lady lawyer who handled the Baton Rouge deal for us.''

''I went out to dinner with Jolie a couple of times when I was in Baton Rouge, that's all. And she didn't exactly work for us. That was a one-shot deal that took all of two weeks. Plus we both knew that nothing permanent could come of a long-distance romance, so there were no expectations.''

Reese flashed his wolfish grin. ''So? I'm not looking for permanent, either.''

''That's my point. You've never sustained a relationship longer than a few months in your life. Olivia is going to be working for us for at least a couple of years. It would be awkward when you got bored and moved on.''

''Olivia... What the hell *is* her last name, anyway?''

''Con...uh, Jones.''

''Really? I would never have guessed that. She looks like she should have a classy name like St. Clair or Raveneux or something like that.'' He flipped through a stack of papers and added them to the briefcase. ''Anyway, as I was about to say, we're both adults, and she strikes me as a levelheaded woman. You worry too much.''

Joe gritted his teeth. And a good thing, too. Reese was great with people and at negotiating, but he looked at the big picture and didn't concern himself with details or life's inevitable problems. His good looks and charm had always greased the way for him. Being a member of a wealthy and influential Southern family didn't hurt, either. He was a great guy and a good friend, but he sailed through life, glibly expecting that everything would work out fine—whether it was a business deal or the end of a love affair.

Joe had to admit, Reese did seem to have the unique ability to stay on friendly terms with all his ex women friends. But dammit, this was Livvie they were talking about, and he didn't want her to get hurt. Beside, it would feel…well…strange to stand by and watch his best friend and his ex-wife dating.

Hell, he may as well admit it. It would drive him nuts. He wasn't sure why, and it was a question he didn't care to examine too closely. It didn't make any sense. She wasn't his, and she hadn't been for almost fourteen years, but that didn't seem to matter.

"So you're going to ask her out, whether I like it or not. Is that what you're saying?"

"You got it. In case you haven't noticed, ole buddy, that's one fine-looking woman. I'd be a fool not to try my luck."

"Dammit, Reese, I'm serious about this. I want you to leave Livvie alone."

His partner cocked one eyebrow. "Livvie?" He stopped loading his briefcase and studied Joe with his head tipped to one side and a sly grin curving his mouth. "Well now. Are you interested in the lady yourself, by chance? Or maybe you've already got something going with her and you don't want any competition? Is that what this is all about?"

"No. Of course not."

Reese's grin widened. "I think you do. Or at least you would like to."

Seeing a way to possibly get his friend to back off, Joe grabbed it. "I did meet her first, you know," he challenged, without really admitting anything. "That should count for something."

"Maybe. I'll tell you what I'll do. For the next couple of months or so I'm going to be out of town more than I'm here. You've got an open field for that long. But I'm giving you fair warning, if you two aren't an item by then, it's every man for himself."

"Dammit, Reese. This isn't a game."

"Sure it is. It's called the mating game. And either you play or you sit on the sidelines. In which case, you don't get to call the shots."

He picked up his briefcase and headed for the door. "You know, we haven't competed over the same girl since college. Cheer up, pal. This should be fun."

Seven

The workspace allotted to Olivia was next to Joe's office, and linked to it by a connecting door.

"This is very nice," she said as her gaze wandered over the walnut desk and comfortable chair. There was also a matching wooden filing cabinet and, not one, but two state-of-the-art drafting tables. Affixed to the slanted surface of one was the set of blueprints that Joe had promised.

"I'm glad you like it."

Olivia shot Joe a curious glance. He'd been unusually quiet ever since they'd parted company with his partner.

In the reception room he had paused long enough to formally introduce her to the two secretaries. Then he'd taken her on a tour of the building and introduced her to most of the staff. In a few of the offices the occupants had momentarily stepped out and they had missed them. One of those bore a nameplate that read Blair Desmond, General Assistant.

Olivia wondered if the employee could possibly be her old friend? Barely had the thought occurred to her than she dismissed it as absurd. Blair hold down a job? No matter how hard Olivia tried, she could not picture her childhood friend working, not even at her brother's company.

At the end of the tour Joe had escorted Olivia back to the third floor and shown her his own office, then led her into the connecting room and announced, "This is where you will work when you're in Savannah."

She caught Joe's eye and smiled. "I have to admit, I was expecting something more along the lines of a broom closet."

"You're an important member of our team. We want you to be comfortable."

"I see." She fiddled with the clasp on her purse, feeling oddly unsettled and not sure why.

The line of windows that graced both Joe's and Reese's offices also ran along the outside wall of this one. Growing uneasy with his long silences, Olivia wandered over to the windows and gazed out at River Street and the Savannah River. "I've always thought that one of the nicest things about a warehouse conversion is that it gives you a lot of light," she said to break the awkward silence.

Joe said nothing. She turned back and found that he was watching her, his expression thoughtful. Her nerves tightened another turn. "Frankly, I'm surprised that such prime office space was available."

"It isn't usually. This is my personal drafting room. Since we're going to be working so closely together on this project, I thought it would be more convenient to set you up in here. We moved the desk and filing cabinet in for your use, so feel free."

"I see. Are you sure I won't be in your way?"

He gave her a long, steady look. "Sweetheart, you've never been in my way in your life."

On the surface it was an innocuous statement, but

something in his tone and the look in his eyes made her chest tighten and sent her heart into overdrive.

"Very well then," she replied briskly. "I'll do my best not to be in the future, as well."

He continued to stare at her in that unnerving way, and she could see in his eyes that her response had disappointed him. Finally he nodded toward the door on the far wall.

"That door is a private entrance from the side hall. I often use it to come and go if there is someone in the reception room I want to dodge, so don't mind me if I dash through here once in a while. Also, from time to time I'll work in here at the other drafting table. Otherwise, you'll have this space to yourself."

"I'm sure that will work out fine." She took a seat behind the desk, laid her briefcase on the top and dropped her purse into the bottom drawer. Ignoring the uncomfortable tightness in her chest, she folded her hands together on top of the desk and sent him an expectant look. "Shall we get started?"

For the better part of the afternoon they went over the blueprints. Joe pulled his drafting stool up beside hers and explained each rendering, pointed out the changes he planned to make to the original structure and the ideas behind them, and explained any problems still to be solved.

She had worked with enough architects to know that he was very good. More than good; his ideas were innovative yet practical, even inspired, and at the same time stayed true to the period.

At first Olivia was nervous and extremely conscious of Joe's nearness, his scent, the feel of his shoulder rubbing against hers each time he turned a page. Soon, however, she became so engrossed in the project that she forgot everything else. It wasn't until Ms. Lumis tapped on the connecting door and stuck her head inside that they became aware of the time.

"Sorry to interrupt. I just wanted to know if you need me to do anything before I go?"

Joe flicked back his cuff and checked his watch. "Damn, I didn't realize it was so late. You should have taken off a half hour ago, Martha."

"I don't mind staying late."

"I know, but tonight it won't be necessary. Olivia and I are going to wrap up here and head for the island. I'll be there for the rest of the week, if you need me."

"Very well. Good night, sir. Miss," the woman said, nodding politely to Olivia as she closed the door behind her.

"Before we leave for the island, we'll have dinner." Joe rolled up the blueprints and slipped them into a cardboard cylinder. "That will give us a chance to talk some more about the changes to the employees' quarters."

Olivia would have preferred to confine the time she spent with Joe to office hours, but she'd been in business long enough to know that a great deal of work was handled over dinner or cocktails. "All right. Whatever you think best."

Joe looked around. "Where are your bags, by the way?"

"I left them downstairs with the receptionist."

"Good. Is the Cotton Exchange okay with you for dinner? It's on River Street and just a short walk."

"That's fine."

"Great. First I want to make a quick stop by my apartment. Then we'll be on our way."

Olivia shot him a startled look. "Your apartment?"

"Relax. I don't have seduction in mind."

"I never thought you did," she replied in a frosty tone. She glanced out the window. Already the setting sun had glazed the river's surface a fiery red and cast a rosy glow over the buildings on the opposite bank. "It'll be dark soon. I assumed you'd want to get going before it gets too late."

"If you're worried about taking the boat out at night, don't be. I can navigate in the dark. And I have the loft apartment on the top floor of this building. All I have to do is throw a few clothes together. It won't take long."

"Oh. I see."

Joe led her out the side door. At the end of the hall, he unlocked a folding iron grill, and they took the ancient freight elevator to the top floor. To her surprise, the elevator opened directly into his apartment.

"I'd give you a tour, but since we're in a hurry we'll save that for another time," Joe said, stepping inside the open loft.

Murmuring a noncommittal "Mmm," Olivia followed and glanced around, curious in spite of herself.

The loft was huge, almost cavernous. The ceiling soared to at least twenty feet overhead. A line of windows marched around the perimeter of the apartment on three sides, flooding the space with the rosy light of the setting sun and highlighting the dark patina of wide-planked wood floors and massive beams.

With no walls separating them, the main rooms all flowed together. Backed up against the elevator shaft's sidewall, the kitchen was set off by a long, half-hexagonal bar, and the living room and dining areas were defined by the placement of furniture, anchored on large Oriental rugs. The only interior wall was made of brick and at its center was one door, which Olivia assumed led to the bedroom area.

"Make yourself at home," Joe said with a wave of his hand, heading in that direction. "There's iced tea in the fridge. Or beer, if you want one. I won't be long."

Olivia remained beside the elevator, just inside the apartment, too uneasy to move, expecting Selina to appear at any second. She wasn't going to be pleased to find her husband's first wife in her living room. Olivia only hoped that Selina had outgrown her penchant for throwing tantrums.

As she looked around it occurred to her that this place was a far cry from the tiny garage apartment that she and Joe had rented when they were married. She had furnished the rental with castoffs and garage-sale and flea-market finds, but a little imagination, ingenuity, paint and elbow grease had turned the poky little apartment into an inviting home. At least, she'd thought so.

Gradually, it occurred to Olivia that the loft apartment, though spacious and tastefully furnished with expensive items, did not seem like a place where Selina would live. It wasn't formal enough or ostentatious enough to suit the spoiled girl she remembered. Although, maybe she was being unfair. Maybe Selina had grown up since she'd last seen her.

The more Olivia looked around the more she wondered if Joe's wife had ever so much as visited this apartment? As far as she could tell, there was no trace of Selina—or any woman—anywhere to be seen.

Perhaps it wasn't their primary residence. Maybe

Joe kept this place as a convenience for when he worked late.

Feeling a bit more at ease, Olivia left her purse, briefcase and coat beside the elevator and wandered into the living area, curious, in spite of herself, to see how Joe lived.

The windows had been left unadorned. The furniture was sturdy and overstuffed and definitely masculine. Throughout this part of the loft the colors were neutrals—various shades of brown and beige with touches of navy and copper.

There was no doubt in Olivia's mind that the place had been professionally decorated. Everything about it was immaculate and tasteful, perfect down to the last detail, but it did not look like Joe. At least, not the Joe she remembered, the young man who had liked warm colors and all the homey touches she had given their tiny garage apartment. The man who had kicked off his shoes and propped his socked feet on the coffee table. The man who had left newspapers scattered on the floor.

That man had valued tradition and had possessed a deeply ingrained love for the beauty and elegance of the past.

That Joe lived in this historic old building did not surprise her, but the loft's impersonal ambience did. Its design looked and felt as though it had been planned for a man on the go who was seldom there. This was a place in which to sleep and change clothes and maybe grab a bite to eat in between business trips. A place that required little maintenance or fuss beyond a weekly maid service. Even the houseplants were silk.

Poor Joe, Olivia thought. He led such a hectic existence that this apartment was apparently little more than a way station for him.

Catching herself, Olivia chuckled. Lord, how easy it was to fall back into old patterns. It was ridiculous of her to feel sad for Joe or concern herself with his happiness. She'd already wasted enough of her life doing that.

This place might be a bit sterile, but it fairly shouted money and success, Olivia thought, wandering over to the windows in time to see a freighter gliding by on the Savannah River. Plus, it had a magnificent view.

The activity on the river was mesmerizing, and as she watched, Olivia let her thoughts drift. Maybe Eleanore had been right all those years ago. Maybe she *had* been all wrong for Joe. This was where he belonged. In this world of money and power and decision-making, of gracious living and beautiful homes. Not working in a lumberyard for minimum wage and living in a cramped garage apartment, barely scraping by.

Would he have achieved all this if they'd stayed together? Perhaps. Like the old saying—the cream always rises to the top. Joe may have been born to money, but he was also smart and hardworking, a born achiever. However, had Eleanore stuck to her guns, his road to success would have been a lot tougher and longer had they remained married.

His mother's first reaction when Joe had told her that they were married had been full-blown hysteria. Olivia shook her head, remembering how Eleanore had shrieked and wailed and fluttered around the parlor like a Victorian-melodrama heroine with a case of the vapors.

* * *

Failing to elicit a sympathetic response from her son, Eleanore sank down on the sofa and wept into her hands, repeating over and over, "How could you do this to me? How could you?"

"I haven't done anything to you, Mother," Joe replied. "This isn't about you. This is between Livvie and me."

Eleanore jerked her head up and shot him an accusing look, her mouth quivering piteously and her blue eyes drenched with tears. "Not about me? Not about *me?* How can you say that? If my friends hear about this I won't be able to hold my head up in public ever again. Why...why, I'll probably be drummed out of the Married Ladies' Card Club. Imagine, a Connally, my very own son, married to the housekeeper's daughter," she whined, as though Livvie and her mother were not even in the room.

Joe reached for Livvie's hand and gave it a squeeze, but the gesture did little to help. She felt as though she'd been slapped.

Livvie glanced at her mother to gauge how much the remark had hurt her, but Flora merely stood in the doorway looking worried and a bit sick, silently wringing her hands.

"Well," Eleanore declared with a decisive huff. "There's only one thing to do now." She fluttered the laced-trimmed hankie she was clutching toward the door. "You're just going to have to fly right back to that awful place and have the marriage annulled. At once, before anyone finds out."

"No, Mother, we're not going to do that. I told you, Livvie is expecting my child."

"Well you didn't have to *marry* her. If you had

just come to me first, I would have given her money for an abortion.''

Livvie gasped and tried to take a step backward, but Joe slipped his arm around her waist and stopped her. ''I...I could never do that.''

''I see. Very well, then I'm willing to pay for your medical expenses, provided you agree to annul this marriage and give the child up for adoption.''

In an unconscious, protective gesture, Livvie splayed her hand over her flat belly. ''Give up my baby? I...I couldn't.''

Joe tugged her tighter against his side. ''Take it easy, sweetheart. You won't have to do that.''

Ignoring him, Eleanore tried to appeal to Livvie. ''Surely you can see that this marriage will never work?''

''I...I'm sorry, Mrs. Connally. I know you blame me for this, but—''

''No, that's not true. I blame myself. I have nothing against you personally, child. I hope you know that. Actually, I'm quite fond of you. But I see now that I should never have allowed a friendship to develop between you and my daughter. Associating with Blair, having the free run of this house all these years, has obviously given you ideas beyond your station. The truth is, you are simply not a suitable wife for my son.''

''Mother!''

''It's true. For heaven's sake, Joseph, you were raised at Winterhaven. You know how important bloodlines are.''

''Dammit, Mother. We're people, not horses.''

Eleanore lifted her chin. ''It makes no difference. Breeding is everything.''

Livvie flinched. The insult cut deep, but what hurt even more was, she knew that her own mother agreed.

Flora was a simple country woman who firmly believed that everyone should accept their lot in life. She felt that if you were born into a working-class family then that was where you belonged. To her way of thinking, ambition or any sort of desire to better yourself was an affront to the Almighty who had made you what you were and only led to discontent and disaster.

Livvie knew that her mother's attitude came, in part, from being married to Sean Jones. Her father had been Flora's exact opposite, an optimistic man who'd considered himself any man's equal and thought all things were possible. He had wanted more than the hardscrabble life of his parents and grandparents, and he'd believed with all his heart that if you wanted something enough, and worked hard enough, it would eventually be yours.

Olivia had vivid memories of her parents arguing about her father's unending efforts to get ahead. He had worked at the docks as a longshoreman and made a decent income, but he was always taking night classes at the community college, or learning various new skills, all with the hope of someday going into business for himself and making it big. Her mother had complained incessantly about the money spent on tuition and books, and had spent hours on her knees praying that her husband would be cured of his foolish ambitions.

When Sean Jones had dropped dead of a sudden heart attack at age forty-five, Flora had seen it as God's vengeance.

Knowing the root of her mother's attitude did not make her disapproval any easier to take, however.

"I'm sorry you feel the way you do, Mother," Joe replied, "but Livvie is my wife now, and that's not going to change."

Eleanore dropped her Southern belle persona like a lead cloak. Her face hardened and her eyes narrowed. "I'm warning you, young man. You will not live in this house with that girl."

"I hadn't planned to. I'm taking Livvie back to Princeton with me. We'll live in my apartment."

"I think not. You'd do well to remember that I control your trust fund until you are twenty-five. If you persist in this folly I will cut off your monthly stipend, and I will not pay next fall's tuition."

Livvie felt Joe stiffen. "You'd do that when you know how much store Dad put in an education? When I have only one year left to graduate?"

Eleanore shrugged. "If you want to get your degree, you know what you have to do."

"That's blackmail."

"Perhaps. But a mother has to use whatever weapons are at her disposal."

A muscle rippled in Joe's cheek as he engaged in a stare-down with his mother. They were two strong-willed people, neither willing to give an inch. His young face looked as though it were carved from stone. His mother, on the other hand, appeared supremely confident, like a woman who believed she held all the cards.

They were silent so long Olivia began to squirm. Guilt overwhelmed her. To satisfy his code of honor and protect her, Joe was about to throw away his education, his whole future. She couldn't let him do that.

She touched his arm, and discovered that his biceps were knotted and his fists clenched at his side. "Joe, maybe we should talk about this. I can't bear for you—"

"There's nothing to talk about. She's made her decision and we've made ours." He took Livvie's hand and tugged her toward the foyer. "C'mon, let's get out of here."

Almost trotting to keep up, Livvie glanced over her shoulder in time to see Eleanore's smug expression collapse.

"Joseph! Where do you think you're going? You come back here, young man!"

Joe kept walking, and his mother hurried after them.

"Don't be a fool. How are you going to get by? You don't have any money of your own yet. You won't gain control of your trust fund for another four years. You don't have a place to live or a job, and no one's going to give you one that will support a family. Not without a college degree. For heaven's sake, Joseph, if you stay with that girl you'll ruin your life!"

In answer, Joe ushered Livvie out the door and slammed it shut behind them.

It was snatched open again seconds later as Joe helped Livvie into his car. "You'll be back!" Eleanore shouted. "Just mark my words. When you discover what it's like to be poor, you'll leave that girl and come back here where you belong."

Those words had rung in her ears the night she and Joe had driven away from Winterhaven. Absently watching a pleasure boat speed past a freighter headed upriver, Olivia relived the panic she had felt all those years ago.

What would she do if Joe left her? Where would she go? she'd wondered. Neither her mother nor her sister could take her in, living on Eleanore's property, as they were. She would be on the street. Alone and penniless. And pregnant.

Her worry had proved unfounded, of course. Joe had not abandoned her nor given any sign that he regretted their marriage. The night they left Winter-haven he had gone directly to his aunt Tilly for assistance, and the dear old soul had welcomed them without hesitation. She had wanted to let them live in her garage apartment rent free, but Joe insisted on paying her the rent she usually got for the place.

The very next day he had begun searching for a job, but after applying to several companies owned by family friends and acquaintances it became apparent that Eleanore had put the word out that no one was to hire her son. In the end, the best job he had been able to find was at the lumberyard.

Olivia recalled how guilty she had felt, watching Joe come home to their tiny garage apartment each night, hot and dirty, covered with sweat and bone tired. She had fluttered around him, worried that he wouldn't like the economical meals she prepared, which was all their pitiful budget would allow, and trying her best to see that he was comfortable.

Strangely enough, Joe hadn't seemed to mind the work. He'd even claimed that he enjoyed the physical labor.

She hadn't believed him, of course. In the back of

her mind she kept hearing his mother's hysterical cry, "If you stay with that girl she will ruin your life!"

Olivia was still lost in thoughts of the past and absently watching the traffic on the river when the rumble of the freight elevator descending, then rising again, interrupted her reverie.

When the doors opened, she looked over her shoulder, and her heart began to pound as a tall, gorgeous woman stepped out of the cubicle into the apartment.

Eight

"Hey, Joe! It's me! I heard the elevator go up so I know you're he—" Spotting Olivia, she stopped short. "Oh! I'm so sorry. I didn't realize Joe had company."

Olivia turned slowly as the woman came toward her with a cordial smile, her hand outstretched.

She was wand-slim and stylishly dressed in a berry-colored suit that complemented her coloring and screamed money. Olivia recognized the pearls around her neck and adorning her earlobes as Connally family heirlooms. She wore her abundant dark hair pulled away from her face and secured in a chignon high on the back of her head. On most women the severe style would have been a disaster, but it merely emphasized her perfect features and gave her an elegant, patrician look.

"Hello. I'm Blair Desmond. Joe's sis…ter…"

Almost comically, a few feet from Olivia, the woman's smile collapsed and her words and steps faltered in unison until she stood stock-still, slack-jawed and wide-eyed.

"Li-Livvie?"

"Hello, Blair. It's been a long time."

"Omigod! It *is* you."

"Yes. I'm afraid so."

Blair's gaze darted around. "But...but...what are you doing here?"

"Waiting for Joe. We are on our way to Mallen Island, but he had to pick up some things first."

Olivia knew she was being deliberately obtuse, but she couldn't seem to help herself. That Blair was less than thrilled to see her was obvious, and that hurt more than she could have imagined. Surely she was entitled to pull her chain a bit.

This time Blair's gaze darted toward the door through which Joe had disappeared, then back to Olivia. "Joe is taking you to Mallenegua? I don't understand. Why? I mean...how did that happen? What are you doing back in Savannah? How did you two happen to run into each other?"

Olivia had to suppress a smile. In a small way, it helped to see her former friend so befuddled. "We didn't 'run into each other.' I was invited here. I've been awarded the design contract for the Mallenegua project."

"Wha-a-at? You...you're..." Blair closed her eyes and drew a deep breath. When she focused on Olivia again her smile was strained. "You're kidding, right?"

"No, not at all."

Speechless, Blair looked more horrified than ever. Abruptly, she spun away. "Excuse me. I have to speak to my brother."

"Have you completely lost your mind?"

Joe looked up as his sister barged into his bedroom and slammed the door behind her. He cocked one eyebrow. "Ever heard of knocking? Why are you still here, anyway? The office closed more than an hour ago.'' He tossed another pair of socks into the bag and headed for the bathroom.

''I was waiting for you,'' she replied, stomping after him. ''Mother is expecting you at Winterhaven for dinner. Remember? I thought we could ride out there together.''

''I can't make it tonight. I called Mother earlier and canceled. And why are you trying to bum a ride? Did your car break down again?''

Joe shook his head. When he'd given his sister a job at AdCo it was with the understanding that she had to live on her earnings. However, things like budgets and setting aside money for emergencies or unexpected expenses, such as car repairs, were foreign concepts to Blair. That her financial situation was such that she had been reduced to living at Winterhaven with their mother and driving a five-year-old car was sacrifice enough, to her way of thinking.

Blair no sooner reached the bathroom door than Joe reemerged and brushed past her with his shaving kit in hand.

''That's beside the point,'' she said to his back, dogging his heels. ''And don't try to sidetrack me. I want to know what's going on?''

''I'm packing for my trip to Mallenegua.''

''Very funny. You know perfectly well that's not what I meant.'' She gestured toward the living area. ''Livvie is out there. *Livvie,* for Pete's sake!''

''I'm aware of that.''

''She said she was given the design contract on the Mallenegua project. Is that true?''

''Of course it's true. When have you ever known Livvie to lie?''

Blair groaned. ''Why would you *do* that?''

Joe retrieved two clean shirts from the dresser and added them to the case, then cocked his head to one side and gave his sister a quizzical look. "You know, I find it curious. You two used to be inseparable. I thought you, of all people, would be happy to see her again. But you're not, are you?"

Blair looked away, her expression switching from anger to a mix of chagrin and guilt. Joe's eyes narrowed. "Why is that?"

She shrugged. "You're my brother. I can hardly be friends with your ex-wife."

"Why not? I can. This is Livvie we're talking about. She's been part of our lives since we were all kids. Blair, the divorce just happened. It wasn't her fault."

She looked at him then, her eyes flashing. "But the marriage was. She trapped you."

"How can you say that? You know as well as I do that Livvie doesn't have a devious or manipulative bone in her body. Getting married was my idea."

"She could have refused you. She *should* have."

"Why?"

Blair looked away again and shrugged. "Because."

"Not good enough. Because why?"

"Because she's not right for you," she snapped.

That startled a laugh from him. "Not *right* for me? What the devil does that mean?"

Looking uneasy again, Blair fiddled with a cuff link lying on his dresser and avoided his eyes. "You know..."

"No. I don't. Why don't you explain it to me?" Still holding a silk tie, Joe fixed her with a steady look.

"She's...she's from a different background."

"You mean, she has no money."

"Or family," Blair fired back, on the defensive now.

"Everyone has a family, Blair. And you couldn't find a more decent human being than Flora Jones. She's the salt of the earth."

"You know what I mean. For heaven's sake! Face it, Joe, Livvie is just not one of us."

Almost imperceptibly his eyes narrowed. He stared at his sister so long that she began to squirm. "Hell," he spat, tossing the tie into the case with the others. "You sound more like Mother all the time."

"That's a rotten thing to say!"

"Maybe. But it's true."

Her chin came up. "Mother can be difficult. No one knows that better than I. But did it ever occur to you that maybe sometimes she's right?"

"Not about this sort of thing." Joe shook his head. "For Pete's sake, Blair. You and Livvie were like sisters. You told each other everything, shared everything—from clothes to your most intimate secrets. How can you think for one minute that she's inferior to you?"

"I don't! It not like tha— Oh, forget it. You wouldn't understand." She looked away again, her expression turning mulish.

"What blows me away about all this is you were the one who talked me into taking Livvie out in the first place."

"Yes, on a *date*. I didn't expect you to marry her."

"Why did you even bother to set us up?"

She cut her eyes around and shot him a sullen look. "If you must know, I'd had a horrible fight with Mother, which I lost, and I wanted to get even. I knew she'd hate it if you went out with the housekeeper's daughter.''

The admission caught Joe like a fist to the gut, knocking the breath right out of him. The whole course of his life and Livvie's had been altered by something so trivial?

Why was he even surprised? he wondered. His sister had always been impulsive and self-centered, and she and their mother had been butting heads ever since Blair could crawl. Even more curious, why did hearing her reason for arranging his one and only date with Livvie make him feel so rotten?

"I see. So, out of spite you used me and your best friend to strike back at Mother, without giving a thought to possible repercussions.''

"Whoa. Wait just a minute. Surely you're not blaming me for what happened? How was I to know—''

Joe cut her off with a raised hand. "Let's just drop it, okay? I really don't want to get into all that.''

"Fine. So back to my question. Why in God's name did you invite Livvie to bid on Mallenegua?''

"She's a sought-after interior designer now. And she came highly recommended.''

"By whom?''

Joe zipped his suitcase shut and straightened. Experiencing the first flicker of amusement since his sister had barged into his bedroom, he looked her in the eye and grinned. "Mother.''

"*Wha-aat?* That's impossible. She would nev— omigod!'' Blair clamped her hand over her mouth, her eyes growing round as saucers over the top. "Livvie is *Olivia?*''

"Funny, that's exactly the reaction I had.''

"You mean you didn't know when you issued the invitation for her to work up a proposal?"

He shook his head. "No. I didn't make the connection. Even now I'm still having a hard time reconciling that sweet little Livvie and the stylish businesswoman out there in my living room are one and the same."

"Well, why didn't you say so in the first place, instead of putting me through that third degree?" Nibbling the tip of one berry-red acrylic fingernail, Blair began to pace. "Well...you're just going to have to tell her that you and Reese have changed your minds, that you've decided to go with one of the other designers."

"We can't do that."

"Why not?"

"For one thing, Livvie's design plan is the best one."

"So? You'll just have to settle for second best. I mean, you obviously can't give her the contract. Mother wouldn't stand for that."

"Last time I checked, Mother wasn't a partner in AdCo. She has no say in the matter, one way or the other."

Blair stopped pacing and looked at him as though he'd lost his mind. "Surely you're not saying you're going to go through with this? That you're actually going to *hire* Livvie?"

"It's done. We signed the contract an hour ago. And just so you know, I'd hire Lucifer himself if he had the right vision for the project. Reese and I have too much invested in Mallenegua to settle for less than the best."

"But, Joe—"

"Drop it, Blair. This is none of your business."
She opened her mouth to argue more but he stopped
her with a look.

"You do realize that Mother is going to pitch a
hissy fit when you tell her about this, don't you," she
said after a while.

"I know." He pointed his index finger at his sister.
"You're not to say a word to her about this, you hear?
I will tell her myself when I'm ready."

"But, Joe—"

"You heard me. You keep quiet or you can find
yourself another job."

She gasped. "You'd actually fire me? Your own
sister?"

"That's right. If I so much as suspect that you've
run to Mother about this or anything else concerning
my business or my personal life, you're out of here.
I didn't tolerate her interference when Livvie and I
were married and I won't tolerate it now."

"But, Joe—"

"I mean it, Blair."

She glared at him. He could see her temper rising
like mercury in a thermometer that had been plunged
into boiling water. "Fine," she spat finally. "Have it
your way."

She spun around and stomped out of the room. He
heard her mumble something to Olivia. A moment
later the ancient elevator clanked and rumbled downward.

Abandoning his suitcase, Joe went in search of
Olivia. She looked up when he entered the living area,
her expression revealing what he'd feared. "How
much of that did you overhear?"

"Enough to know that Blair doesn't want me

here.'' Joe winced, and she hurried on. ''I'm sorry. I wasn't trying to eavesdrop, but I couldn't help but hear when you raised your voices.''

''That's okay. I'm just sorry you had to hear that.''

''Joe, if this arrangement is going to cause you problems with your family, I'll bow out.''

''No. I don't want that.'' He rubbed the back of his neck with his hand, frowning in thought. ''Would you mind if we skipped dinner and put off going to the island until tomorrow? I think I should deal with this now.''

''Of course. If you feel that's best. I'll check into the Hyatt for the night and meet you in your office first thing in the morning.''

''Great. And thanks for understanding. C'mon, I'll walk you to the hotel,'' he said, reaching for her bags.

''You don't have to do that. It's just down the street.''

''Sweetheart, you may be an independent woman these days, but there is no way I'm going to let you walk alone down River Street in the dark carrying three suitcases. So there's no use arguing.''

''Evenin', all,'' Joe drawled, strolling into the living room of his family home at Winterhaven Farm an hour later.

''Joseph, dearest,'' Eleanore exclaimed. Rising, she went to him, her hands outstretched. ''What a lovely surprise. You changed your mind and decided to join us after all.'' She turned to her daughter with an aggrieved expression. ''Why didn't you tell me, Blair?''

''She didn't know. It was a spur-of-the-moment decision.''

Blair rolled her eyes and mouthed "thank you" to her brother, but wisely kept silent.

Another sign that his sister was growing up, Joe thought. A few years ago she would have flared back at Eleanore for the oblique accusation and within minutes the two would be embroiled in a heated argument about nothing.

After kissing his mother's proffered cheek, Joe went to the drinks tray and poured himself two fingers of bourbon. He had a feeling he was going to need it before this evening was over.

Turning, he met his brother's amused gaze and raised his glass. "Luke. Good to see you."

"You, too, bro." Luke sat sprawled in a fireside chair, long legs outstretched, his drink balanced on his flat belly, silently watching the interaction of his family in his usual detached way.

"Well, no matter," Eleanore went on with an airy wave of her hand. "I'm just delighted you're here. Blair, be a dear and go tell Mrs. Bonner that Joseph is joining us for dinner. And don't let her give you any sass, you hear."

"Yes, Mother," Blair replied in a long-suffering tone, executing another eyeroll.

"I do declare, that woman is impossible. She's not half the housekeeper or cook that Flora was, yet she talks back to me and complains constantly. Honestly, anyone would think that she was the mistress of this house. I wish you would talk to her while you're here this weekend, Joseph. I swear, I don't know why Flora had to go and leave me. I'll never find a replacement half as good."

"She didn't 'leave' you, Mother," Joe replied.

"She retired. Flora is getting up in years. She deserves to take it easy in her golden years."

"Fiddle-dee-dee. Flora is just a few years older than I am, and you don't see me slacking off."

Joe wanted to say there was a big difference between chairing a couple of charity fund-raisers and the Cotillion Ball and playing bridge once a month, and cooking and cleaning every day, but he didn't. One battle at a time, he reminded himself.

"Mrs. Bonner says dinner is ready," Blair announced from the doorway.

As Luke unfolded his lanky frame out of the chair, Joe drained the last of his drink, placed it on the cart and offered his mother his arm.

"Thank you, dearest," she murmured, flashing him her fragile-damsel smile, and they led the way at a decorous pace to the dining room on the opposite side of the wide central hallway.

Eleanore had always been a stickler for proprieties. At Winterhaven they dressed for dinner each night. For family dinners the men wore suits and ties, tuxedos if they had guests, and the women wore long dresses. At seven they met for cocktails in the living room, at eight they moved to the formal dining room for dinner.

His mother belonged to all the right clubs and charity organizations. She golfed at the country club twice a week and lunched with her friends afterward. She was one of the sixteen members of the exclusive Married Ladies' Card Club, which had been founded in 1893, and she was exceedingly proud that her late husband had belonged to the all-male, equally exclusive Madeira Club and the Oglethorpe Club.

Like everything about Eleanore, Brian Connally

had thought her insistence on "maintaining proper standards" was cute and endearing and he had humored her every whim.

If Joe and his siblings sometimes felt the rituals were pretentious, unnecessary and a general pain in the ass, they went along out of respect for their mother's wishes. *And* to avoid the wailing, walleyed case of the vapors that was sure to occur if they didn't.

After seating his mother at one end of the table, Joe sat down at the opposite end. In his absence, Luke occupied the chair, but Eleanore insisted that her eldest son take his place at the head of the table whenever he was home, even though Luke ran the farm now. He and his brother had long ago given up arguing with her about the matter.

"So, how is the Mallenegua project coming along?" Luke asked when Mrs. Bonner had finished serving and left the room.

"So far so good. The marina is almost finished, and by next week we should be going full bore on the house restoration."

"Does that mean you've chosen a designer?" Eleanore asked.

Blair choked on a spoonful of soup. She snatched up her napkin and covered her mouth while she coughed. Over the top of the cloth her eyes met Joe's.

"Yes. We have. Reese and I chose Olivia."

"I knew it, I knew it!" Eleanore clapped her hands daintily. "You see? Didn't I tell you her work was marvelous? Oh, I'm dying to meet her. So are all my friends. We all want to hire her. But I suppose that now she's working on your project it will be a while before she's available. Oh, I know. Why don't I throw a party in her honor?''

Blair choked again, and Eleanore shot her a disapproving glance. ''Really, Blair, must you? If you'd mind your manners and not eat your soup so fast you wouldn't embarrass yourself.''

Joe swallowed a spoonful of soup, patted his mouth with his napkin and leaned back in his chair. ''Actually, Mother, you already know Olivia.''

''Really?'' She thought for a moment, then shook her head. ''No, I don't think so. She had already finished Dorothea's home and returned to Atlanta when I visited last summer. I didn't get a chance to meet her.''

''Mother, Olivia is Livvie.''

''Livvie? Livvie wh—'' She sucked in a sharp breath and her soupspoon dropped from her fingers with a clatter. She put her hand over her heart as though she was about to faint. ''Are…are you saying that Olivia, the designer that everyone is raving about, is…is…''

''That's right. None other than our very own little Livvie Jones. My ex-wife.''

Luke threw his head back and let loose a string of delighted guffaws. ''Oh, man! This is rich.''

Blair buried her face in her hands and groaned.

''Oh, my Lord! I don't believe it. This is terrible. Just terrible. This can't be happening! It has to be a nightmare. Please tell me I'll wake up soon.''

''Nope. It's real, all right. Livvie started on the project today.''

Eleanore glared at her son down the length of the table. ''Why in God's name did you hire her? You must have discovered her identity before you actually awarded her the contract!''

''Yeah, I did. But her ideas were the best—hands down.''

''Oh, for heaven's sake! What does that matter? She's your *ex-wife!* You can't have your ex-wife working for you. Just think of the talk that will stir up. She has to go. That's all there is to it. You may have to buy out her contract, but it will be worth it to have her gone.''

''Livvie isn't going anywhere. Except back and forth between Savannah and Mallen Island.''

Eleanore looked as though she were about to have apoplexy. She was so angry she was quivering, and the tendons in her neck stood out like ropes. ''Joseph! You can't be serious.''

''I'm dead serious. Frankly, I don't know why you are so upset. First of all, Livvie is one of the nicest, sweetest people I've ever known. And second, who does or does not work for AdCo is not the business of anyone other than Reese and myself. I have no problem whatsoever working with Olivia. That's all that matters.''

''That most certainly is *not* all that matters. Think of the gossip. The speculation. The—''

''I don't give two hoots and a holler about those things. All I care about is having the best person for the job. And that person is Livvie.''

''But—''

''It's settled, Mother. I don't want to hear any more about it.''

Eleanore clenched her jaw. She glared at him, breathing so hard her chest heaved. Frustration radiated from her like a red aura. After a moment she tossed down her napkin and stood up. "In that case, I'll say good night. I've lost my appetite."

She walked out of the room with all the stately dignity of an offended duchess, her back ramrod straight, her chin in the air.

The three left at the table said nothing, giving her time to climb the grand staircase. When they heard the distant sound of her door closing Luke gave a low whistle.

"Damn, bro. *Livvie?* You couldn't find another designer whose work you liked just as well?"

"Possibly. But Livvie is the one I want. Do you have a problem with that? If so, let's hear it now."

Luke held up his hands, palms out. "Hey, not me. I was just making an observation." He grinned slowly. "I'll give you one thing, bro. You're usually a peaceable guy, but when you decide to stir up trouble, you don't mess around." He laughed again. "Livvie. Oh, man, it's going to be interesting around here for the next few months."

Nine

The oldest restaurant on River Street, the Cotton Exchange occupied a cotton warehouse that had been built in 1799. Olivia had been there only a few times for lunch with Blair, but it had been one of her favorite places. She was happy to see that it had changed very little over the years.

After canceling their plans the evening before, Joe insisted on taking her to dinner before they left for the island.

That he was a regular and favored customer became obvious when he exchanged greetings with several people on the staff. It was early yet for the dinner crowd, so only a scattering of tables were occupied. Even so, several of the other patrons waved and called to Joe as they followed the hostess to their table, all the while casting curious glances Olivia's way. She could tell by their puzzled expressions that they were trying to place her.

Savannah's elite tended to live in an insular little world of their own that consisted of "the right" people, descendants of the old Southern aristocracy, mostly—even those currently living in genteel poverty—with a few nouveau riche thrown in, so long as they fit into polite society and knew their place in the pecking order. "A little new blood now and then never hurts," Olivia recalled Madeline Owens, one of Eleanore's friends in the Married Ladies' Card Club, saying on more than one occasion.

They all knew one another and kept track of who was seeing whom. People like Joe, who were born into this privileged set, were expected to date and marry within their group or the equivalent from some other Southern town, though, of course, a Savannahian was preferable to an outsider, even another Georgia native.

Amused, Olivia had to fight back a smile. Speculation about Joe Connally's dinner companion would be a hot topic for a few days. It was inevitable that word would soon get around that his ex-wife was working for him. When it did, the gossip mill would go into overdrive, but she couldn't let that concern her.

After taking their order, the waiter returned within moments with the bottle of wine that Joe had ordered, ceremoniously filled their glasses and retreated.

"I'm very pleased to have you working on this project, Olivia. Welcome aboard." Joe lifted his glass. "Here's to a long and mutually gratifying association."

Olivia clinked her wineglass to his and took a sip. After returning the flute to the table, she toyed with the stem. "It's obvious that not everyone shares that sentiment. Blair, for one. And I'm sure your mother is no happier. How did she take the news when you told her?"

Joe snorted. "Not well. But there's nothing she can do about it. As for Blair, I'm truly sorry about the way she's behaving. Darned if I don't know what her problem is, but I hope you won't let her attitude bother you."

"Don't worry. Years ago, when Blair didn't answer any of my letters, I got the message that our friendship was over."

"You wrote to her? I didn't know that." Joe frowned. "I don't get it. Blair is spoiled and flighty at times, but she does have good manners. It's not like her to be rude. Or disloyal. I'll have a talk with her and get to the bottom of this."

"Oh, no, please don't." Without thinking, Olivia reached across the table and touched his arm, her eyes pleading. "I don't want to stir up trouble for anyone, Joe. It all happened a long time ago. It doesn't matter anymore. Truly."

His frown faded. Covering her hand with his free one, he smiled. "It matters to me. But don't worry. There won't be any trouble."

Becoming aware of the warmth of his touch, Olivia pulled her hand free and sat back in her chair. "Correct me if I'm wrong, but I got the impression that Blair works for you now. Is that right?" At his nod she chuckled and shook her head. "Well, well. Will wonders never cease? Blair Connally actually has a job. How did *that* happen?"

"It's Blair Desmond now. After graduating from college she finally gave in and married a man whom mother deemed 'suitable.'"

Leaning back, Olivia sipped her wine. "Meaning from the right sort of family. Preferably rich, of course, or at least he had prospects. Correct?"

"You got it. Mother never changes."

Olivia would have bet money on that. "I'm surprised at Blair, though," she said. "I didn't think she would ever give in to Eleanore's badgering. When we were kids she practically made a hobby out of defying your mother.''

"I know. But something happened to Blair after you left. All her old fire and spirit just sort of drained away. When she married Colin, things got worse. She seemed to have lost all sense of herself as an individual. She became subservient to him. And withdrawn and jittery.''

"Subservient? Blair? That doesn't sound like her at all,'' Olivia murmured. "Granted, we didn't talk long, but when I spoke to her the other night she seemed like the same old Blair.''

"She's perked up some recently. As it turned out, the marriage was a disaster,'' Joe went on. "Blair stuck it out for almost ten years, but about eight months ago she finally worked up the gumption to defy Colin, and mother, and file for divorce.

"Mother was outraged. Never mind that Colin is an alcoholic, arrogant snob with a mean streak a mile wide.''

"You mean he abused her?'' Olivia asked, angered on her old friend's behalf in spite of everything.

"I'm not sure, but I suspect as much. Whenever I ask, Blair clams up and says she doesn't want to talk about it.

"Anyway, even though she was obviously unhappy, mother tried in every way she could to get Blair to go back to her husband. When she wouldn't, typically, Mother cut her off without a cent. So far, though, for the first time in a long while, Blair is standing her ground.''

"Why should she be dependent on your mother for support? What about her trust fund?''

"Unfortunately for my sister, she didn't gain control of her trust at age twenty-five like Luke and I did. That won't happen until she is thirty-five."

"That hardly seems fair."

Joe held his hands up. "Hey. Don't blame me. I agree with you. But Dad worried that Blair wouldn't be mature enough by age twenty-five to handle that kind of responsibility. He was also concerned that she might fall for the first smooth-talking fortune hunter who came along."

"It still isn't fair. And I think your father grossly underestimated Blair."

"God knows, she couldn't have done much worse than Colin Desmond. Anyway, I told Blair that if she applied herself and did a good job, and lived on her own salary, she could work at AdCo. To manage, she lives at Winterhaven with Mother.

"It's an arrangement that neither of them likes, but Blair can't afford to live anywhere else, at least not in the style to which she's accustomed, and Mother can't refuse to allow her to live at home. I inherited the house, and Luke and I each own a third of the farm now. The other third is Blair's, but it's tied up as part of her trust, which Mother controls."

"I see."

Olivia fell silent and sipped her wine while she digested everything he had told her. It didn't seem possible that the lively girl she'd known would allow herself to be a doormat for anyone. When they'd been kids it had always been Blair who had taken the lead and instigated their childish shenanigans, then boldly faced her mother's disapproval.

Leaning back in his chair, Joe looked at Olivia and

smiled. "So, tell me. What have you been up to since you left Savannah?"

Olivia shrugged. "Nothing all that exciting. I went to college. When I graduated I got a job with a Dallas decorating firm. I stayed there for two years. Then I was lucky enough to land a job with a well-known Boston firm that specializes in traditional period decor. After working there for two years I decided it was time to go out on my own, so I moved to Atlanta and started my own decorating business."

Joe grinned. "I should have guessed that you'd go into decorating. You always had a real flair for it. I remember how attractive you made our apartment on a shoestring budget. I was really proud of you."

Olivia experienced a dart of surprise. She didn't think he'd noticed. Or cared. The most he'd ever done was murmur a tired "Hmm, that's nice" when he came home after work and found she had fixed up a new flea-market find or painted a room or made new curtains. It was a bit unsettling to find out all these years later that he had approved.

To change the subject, she asked, "And what about you? How did you end up in construction? All these years I've assumed that you were running Winterhaven Farm."

"Luke is better suited for that job. He loves it. I prefer building things. Your story and mine are similar. After we split I went back to Princeton and finished my last year of studies.

"Reese and I shared an apartment at college. We'd been roommates since our freshman year. Our mothers had met at college and have remained friends all these years, even though the Addisons live in Charleston. Reese's mother and mine had always planned for him and me to room together in college. Growing up, we'd met a few times, but we really didn't get to know each other until college. Luckily, the friendship took.

"Shortly after graduating, Reese's father passed away, and he inherited, among other things, a small construction firm. Like me, he was interested in historic preservation, and he decided to specialize in that type of construction. The idea sounded great to me, so when he asked me to join forces with him, I accepted. I've never regretted that decision. We've restored everything from old warehouses and factories to entire neighborhoods. It's very satisfying work. Not to mention profitable."

Olivia took another sip of wine and rolled it on her tongue while she pondered her next question.

"How did your family react to your decision to go out on your own?"

Joe grimaced. "As you can probably imagine, Mother wasn't happy about it. Luke, on the other hand, was delighted that I was leaving the running of the farm to him. Blair didn't care one way or the other, so long as we didn't sell her horse. Though why she'd think we would get rid of Prince Rupert, I have no idea. Dad gave her that horse when she was a kid."

"Yes. For her tenth birthday. Surely she can't still have him. He'd have to be…what…twenty-three by now?"

"Uh-huh. But we lost him three years ago. It was a blow to Blair. She loved that horse more than anything or anyone in the world."

"Yes, I know."

Olivia fiddled with her wineglass and fought a silent battle with herself. Finally, though, her curiosity won out. "How did Selina react to your career choice? And how is she, by the way?" she asked as casually as she could manage.

"Selina? You mean Selina St. Clair? I wouldn't know. I haven't seen her in years. The last I heard she was working on her fourth marriage. This one is to some Italian count or something. I think they live on the Riviera."

"Oh, I'm sorry. I had no idea that the two of you had divorced." Her mother hadn't said a word to her about the split.

Joe looked taken aback. "Selina and I were never married. What made you think we were?"

"But…I heard… That is, I assumed…I…" Feeling like a fool, Olivia closed her eyes for an instant, then marshaled her composure and waved aside the matter with a flutter of her hand. "Never mind. I must have misinterpreted something I was told years ago."

"Which was?"

Though softly spoken, Olivia knew the question was not one that she could dodge. Everything about Joe said he intended to have an answer.

"Just that your mother was planning your wedding."

"Is that all? Honey, my mother's been planning my wedding for the last fifteen years. And Luke's and Blair's, too, for that matter. She wants to see the next generation of Connallys before she takes her place beside Dad in Bonaventure Cemetery." Ever so slightly, his gaze softened, and his voice dropped to a velvety pitch. "You are the only wife I've ever had."

"You never remarried?" she asked, stunned right down to her toes.

"Nope. How about you?"

"No. I've been too busy. With my business and all." She stared at the surface of her wine, trying to adjust her thinking. She couldn't believe that all these years her mother had let her believe that Joe was married.

"Have you had any serious relationships?"

Olivia looked up and met Joe's gaze with a challenging stare. "Have you?"

He grimaced. "Right. None of my business. Sorry."

He gazed at her in silence for several moments. "There," he said finally. "That wasn't so bad, was it?"

"I beg your pardon?"

"We actually carried on a pleasant conversation for a full two minutes without you freezing me out once."

Olivia looked down at her fingers, turning her wineglass around and around by the stem. "I have no idea what you're talking about."

"C'mon, Olivia. You've been distant toward me ever since we met again. As though you're angry with me about something. What's wrong?"

"Nothing is wrong. You're imagining things."

"I don't think so." He took another sip of wine, watching her all the while, letting the silence stretch out again. "What happened to us, Livvie?" he asked after a time. "Where did we go wrong?"

The questions startled a mirthless laugh from Olivia. One thing about Joe, he didn't pussyfoot around. When he wanted to know something he got straight to the point.

"Us? Don't you understand? That was the problem. There never was an 'us.' Not really."

"How can you say that? We were married for almost five months."

"Yes, but not for the right reasons."

Joe frowned. "I wouldn't say that."

"Oh, please. Let's be honest, Joe. If I hadn't been pregnant with your child, you would never have married me."

He gazed at her thoughtfully across the table. "You know, that's something I've always wondered about. That night when we went out, why did you...?"

"Let you make love to me?" she finished for him. She felt her face heat, but she met his gaze squarely over the flickering candle in the middle of the table. She had hoped to avoid this discussion, but Joe obviously wasn't going to let it go until he had some answers.

And maybe he was right. During the brief marriage they'd both been too young and too unsure of each other to delve very deeply into such things as feelings. Maybe it was time to clear the air and put this behind them, once and for all.

"You were eighteen and hadn't been with anyone. That must have been a conscious choice. So...why me?"

Olivia sighed. This was so embarrassing. There was no easy way to explain except to come right out and say it. "The answer to that is so obvious I'm surprised you didn't guess. I was madly in love with you. I had been since I was nine years old."

Joe's first reaction was shock. Then his face lit up. "Really?"

The waiter arrived with their salads. As soon as he left Olivia picked up her fork and shot Joe an annoyed look. "Don't let it go to your head," she drawled, stabbing a bite. "And don't look at me like that. I got over it a long time ago."

"Shoot. Just my luck."

"That's not funny," she grumbled.

They ate in silence for several minutes. Then, out of the blue, Joe asked, "Do you ever wonder what would've happened if we'd stayed together?"

The question jolted Olivia, and her answer was a bit sharper than she'd intended. "No."

At least…she hadn't allowed herself those kinds of thoughts in years.

"I have," Joe said. "I've thought about it a lot. I guess it's always bothered me that we threw in the towel so early. I did care about you, Livvie."

She gave a little huff of disbelief. "Oh, right. Surely you're not going to try to tell me that you were in love with me."

"No. Well…maybe. Ah, hell. I don't know exactly what I felt back then. All I'm sure of is I was happy being married to you, and I wasn't ready to give up on us."

The statement stung. Olivia put down her fork and fixed him with a stare. "Oh, really? So, let me get this straight. You wanted me *and* Selina?"

"Selina? That's the second time you mentioned her. What's she got to do with us?"

"Oh, please, Joe. What do you take me for? An idiot? You were with Selina while I was in the hospital,'' she accused. ''That night, just hours after I'd lost our baby.''

''What! That's not tr—'' He stopped, wincing. ''Aw, hell. I remember now. Look, I did see Selina that night, but I wasn't 'with' her. Not the way you mean. I just drove her home after—''

An arrested look came over Joe's face. ''Wait a second. How did you know I'd seen Selina that night?''

''Your mother paid me a visit at the hospital that evening before you returned.''

''What! *My* mother?''

Olivia nodded. ''Along with your sister and my mom. Eleanore insisted that since I'd lost the baby, there was no longer a reason for us to be together, and that I should do the right thing and let you go.'' Her mouth twitched. ''She couldn't wait to tell me that you were with Selina.''

''Of all the conniving—'' Joe looked away, a string of low profanity spewing from between his clenched teeth. Olivia could see the muscles along his jaw knot and ripple.

When he'd regained control he turned back to her. ''I'm sorry she hurt you, Olivia. But why didn't you tell me? And why in God's name did you believe her? You knew what Mother was like.''

''Don't try to put all the blame on me. I don't recall you protesting or trying to talk me out of getting a divorce.''

''How could I? I'd gotten you pregnant, then forced you to marry me. When you said you wanted out I couldn't make you stay.''

''And I was young and insecure and afraid. I knew that the only reason you had married me was for the baby's sake. Trust me, I didn't want to believe Eleanore. But what was I supposed to think? You were hours late, and Eleanore swore that you and Selina were back together. Not only that, both my mother and Blair backed up her story.''

Joe looked as though he'd been slapped. ''They actually told you that I'd taken up with Selina again? While my wife lay in the hospital after losing our baby?'' At her nod he shook his head. ''Why would they *do* that? Blair, especially. She was your friend. And she was there at dinner that night. She knew that wasn't true.''

Olivia's gaze held disbelief, her expression softening not one iota.

Joe leaned in closer, and his voice dropped to an urgent pitch. ''Listen to me, Olivia. After I left the hospital that day I went home to the apartment and grabbed a few hours' sleep. Then Mother called and hinted that she wanted to mend fences. That's the only reason I accepted her invitation to dinner. But when I arrived at Winterhaven Selina was there.

''I knew that Mother was up to her old tricks, and I probably should have set them both straight right then, but I was so worried about you I couldn't think about anything else. The minute dinner was over I told them that I had to get back to the hospital and excused myself.

''Mother insisted that I drive Selina home. Since her place was on the way, I couldn't very well refuse. But I swear to you, all I did was drive her home. Nothing happened.''

''Do I really look that gullible to you, Joe? Your mother was at the hospital around eight-thirty. You didn't arrive until ten. And you had Selina's lipstick smeared all over your face and the collar of your shirt.''

"Ah, hell," Joe groaned, closing his eyes. "All right, I admit that as soon as we got into the car Selina made it clear that she wanted us to get back together. I told her I wasn't interested. When I stopped the car in front of her house, the next thing I knew she was all over me.

"Apparently, she thought if she seduced me I'd change my mind. But I wasn't going to let that happen, so she threw one of her tantrums. You know what Selina is like. It took me more than an hour to calm her down and get her out of the car."

Before Olivia could stop him, Joe reached across the table and took her hand, holding it between both of his. "Look at me, Olivia," he urged when she lowered her gaze to the half-eaten salad in front of her. "Look at me."

The deep timbre of his voice tugged at her, at something deep inside that she thought she'd conquered long ago. It seemed she was wrong. Reluctantly she did as he asked.

"I swear that's the whole truth. I lied to you that night about the car breaking down. I shouldn't have. If I had told you the whole truth then…who knows? We might still be together."

Olivia frowned and tried to pull her hand free. "Joe, don't…"

"But I promise you, Olivia. I will never lie to you again. You have my word on it."

The sincerity in his voice, in his eyes, was difficult to dismiss. Still…Olivia wasn't altogether convinced. She wasn't sure she wanted to be. She had been hurt badly, but she had accepted the past as she'd believed it to be and moved on with her life. The possibility, however unlikely, that she and Joe might have had a chance together was too painful to contemplate.

Yet, she could not deny that he had been right to force this discussion. Finally getting everything out in the open—well, almost everything—had alleviated the awful tension she experienced whenever she was around him.

Except when he touched her, as he was doing now.

To her relief, the waiter arrived with their entrées and Joe released her hand.

"There is one other thing you should know," Olivia said when they were alone again. "Your mother gave me a check for fifty thousand dollars to leave Savannah and never see you again."

Joe put down his knife and fork and stared at her. "She did *what?*"

"Just so you know, I didn't cash the check." She pulled her wallet out of her purse and took a folded square of paper from it and handed it to Joe. "Here it is. I've carried it with me all these years as a reminder of the most painful, humiliating experience of my life. I don't know if this makes sense to you, but whenever I get discouraged, or life deals me another slap, just looking at that check spurs me on."

"Just wait until I see my mother. She's got some explaining to do. And when I'm through with her, I'm going to have a long-overdue talk with my sister."

Olivia experienced a rush of panic. The last thing she wanted was to get Eleanore stirred up again. "Please, Joe, don't do that. Just let it go. It was a long time ago. None of it matters anymore."

"The hell it doesn't. Dammit, Livvie, Mother interfered in our lives. She didn't care how we felt or how much she was hurting either of us. All she cared about was getting her own way. She can't be allowed to run roughshod over people."

"Joe, please let it drop. For my sake. I don't want to anger Eleanore. Maybe you haven't thought of this, but my business depends on word of mouth, and your mother is in a position to hurt me in that regard. Let's face it, she's one of the mavens of Savannah society and has influential connections all over the South."

"Don't worry about that. I can control Mother. I'll make sure she never tries to harm you in any way ever again. I love my mother, but I'm fed up with her trying to control my life."

He looked away, his jaw tight, then his gaze snapped back to her. "It was because of my mother's lies that you called it quits that night, wasn't it?"

"Well…yes. But the irony is, she was right."

"What! How can you say that?"

"I'll admit, in the beginning I was heartbroken and miserable. But as the years passed and I matured, I realized that to succeed, a marriage had to be built on a lot more than just an adolescent crush. Face it, Joe. Sooner or later we would have ended up exactly as we are now. Divorced."

Ten

At first glance, Olivia thought that the movement along the top of the cliffs was fog rolling in.

The almost-full moon hung low over Mallen Island, ringed with a misty halo. Oblivious to the buck and bump of the boat over the water, Olivia gazed at the glowing orb and felt a chill ripple through her.

Old Minerva's warning whispered through her mind. "Beware de pale moon risin' over Mallen Island, chile," the old voodoo priestess had warned in her raspy Jamaican accent. "Dat's when de spirit fog shrouds de land with bad mojo and evil stalks de unwary."

Minerva, a skinny black woman of indeterminate age, had been married to one of the stable hands at Winterhaven Farm when Olivia had lived there. The self-proclaimed priestess had practiced the voodoo of her native land.

Though the woman had scared them both half out of their wits, and Eleanore had issued strict orders for Blair to stay away from her, her friend had often sneaked off to seek Minerva's advice on her love life, and Olivia had tagged along.

The scary woman always wore flowing caftans, colorful turbans and blue mirrored sunglasses. She concocted potions, made voodoo dolls, cast and removed spells, predicted futures, and generally scared the bejesus out of a lot of people. Even nonbelievers were wary of her "magic."

The boat edged up to the pier and bumped the piling, drawing Olivia from her reverie. Joe cut the engine and she glanced up at the cliffs again, in time to see the roiling white tendrils of mist take the shape of a man.

She caught her breath, and the suitcases she'd just hauled up from below deck dropped from her nerveless fingers. Rooted to the spot, she stared, open-mouthed.

Her heart began to pound. Unconsciously she groped for the boat's railing for support.

Walking along the edge of the cliffs was a ghostly figure in a frock coat and top hat, the same apparition that she had seen on her first visit to the island.

"Here we are."

Gasping, Olivia jumped and swung around to see Joe nimbly descending the steps from the bridge.

"Just let me see to the mooring lines and I'll carry those bags for—" He stopped when he got close enough to see her face, his dark eyebrows snapping together. "Are you all right? You look as though you're about to faint."

"N-no, I'm fine. I, uh... It's just that I thought I saw a man up on the cliffs."

"A man? I don't think so." Joe glanced upward. "There's no one on the island but the two of us and Mrs. Jaffee." He scanned the clifftop in both directions. "I don't see anyone."

"You're right. It was probably just the fog playing tricks on my eyes," Olivia agreed with a nervous smile. But she knew she wasn't seeing things. There had been the ghostly figure of a man standing on the cliff's edge, staring down at the boat.

Joe put his arm around her shoulder and gave her an affectionate squeeze, grinning. "Hey, don't let those old stories get to you, sweetheart. Mallen Island is just that—an island. And Mallenegua is just an old mansion. That's all."

"I know. You don't have to worry about me. I don't believe in ghosts."

"Good girl." After another squeeze, he picked up her cases and tossed them onto the pier. He then vaulted over the side, tied up the boat, fore and aft, and offered his hand to Olivia.

At the base of the cliff Joe flipped an electrical switch, and a line of lights curving up the cliff face flashed on, illuminating the stone steps all the way to the top. Side by side, they started the climb. Two-thirds of the way up Joe cautioned, "Careful. The rest of the way is going to be tricky." An instant later they were swallowed up in the fog, and the lights became no more than glowing dots in the swirling cloud.

If the eeriness of the scene in any way unnerved Joe, he didn't show it. As though he had built-in radar, he guided her up the worn stone steps and along the nearly obscured path to the front entrance.

Inside the mansion, they found Mike Garvey waiting for them, pacing the entrance hall like a caged beast.

"Thank God you're here," he said, hurrying forward.

"Mike. What're you doing still here?"

"Waiting for you. We've got trouble, boss."

"Did you happen to go outside while you were waiting?"

"Only every few minutes."

Joe turned to Olivia with a smile. "There, you see. It was most likely Mike you saw when we pulled up."

In a frock coat and top hat? She didn't think so. But she knew if she pushed the issue she'd just wind up looking like a fool. Instead she smiled and murmured, "I'm sure you're right."

Joe looked back at Mike. "So. What's up?"

"Like I said, we got trouble. The workers quit."

"What! All of them?"

"All but a handful. And the only reason those few didn't was because they were below deck when the ghost was spotted."

"Ah, hell. Not that again," Joe groaned.

"I'm afraid so. It was just after quitting time, right at twilight. The conditions were right. The moon was rising, all hazy and eerie-looking, and the fog was creeping in. The men were boarding the *Lady Bea* for the trip back to the mainland when somebody hollered, "Look! There's old Theobald!""

"Theobald? You mean…Theobald Mallen?" Olivia asked, feeling a little sick to her stomach.

"Yeah. It's the second time this has happened," Joe replied. "When I first brought a skeleton crew out here to start work on the new marina one of the guys claimed that he saw Theobald's ghost. His hysteria spread among the others like wildfire. They hightailed it back to the mainland like the demons from hell were after them."

"Yeah, well, I doubt that this bunch has any more backbone than the first," Mike grumbled. "We're probably gonna have to hire a whole new crew."

Joe cursed under his breath. "Damn those stupid stories. And I don't know what the hell that bunch of ninnies is so afraid of, anyway. This is Savannah, for Pete's sake. Or at least, the Savannah area. Half the homes around here are supposedly haunted, and the owners are proud of their ghosts."

"I think Theobald's reputation, along with the rumors about the things that were supposed to have happened on this island over the last hundred years, is what spooks them," Mike offered.

"Whatever." Joe raked his hand through his dark brown hair. "Well, there's no choice. You and I are going to have to go back to the mainland first thing in the morning and either talk some sense into the guys or hire others to replace them. We need to get cracking on this project."

He gave Olivia an apologetic look. "I'm sorry. I hate to leave you alone here again, but I have to see to this."

"Don't worry about it. I understand."

"I know we were going to put our heads together and start working out the changes, but that will have to wait until I get this problem under control. Do you think you could work on your design plans until I get back?"

"Actually, I thought I'd start taking inventory of the pieces you have, both in the rooms and in the attic. Then I'll know what I have to purchase to fill in."

"Good idea."

"I'm sure you two have a lot to talk about, so I'll leave you to it," she said, heading for the stairs.

"Oh, by the way, Olivia," Mike said. "Before you go, I should tell you Joe asked me to find someone to assist you with manual-labor jobs, so I hired a big, strapping young guy named L.J. Nye. He's a jack-of-all-trades type, so anything you want done, any heavy moving, draperies hung, that sort of thing, he'll provide the muscle. He should be here in the morning.''

"Thank you, Mike. You, too, Joe. He can move things around in the attic for me and help take inventory.''

"Great. And when you don't have work for him, he can fill in on one of the other crews.''

"That should work out fine. Now, if you'll excuse me, I'll say good night.''

"You don't have to rush off on our account. Stay and have a brandy with us.''

"Thanks, Joe, but it's been a long day. I think I'll turn in early. I assume I'll be in the same suite as before?''

"Yes. I told Mrs. Jaffee to prepare it for you.''

"Thank you. Good night.''

"Hold on a sec," Joe said, turning to Mike. "Why don't you wait for me in the front parlor. I won't be long. I'm just going to see Olivia to her room.''

She jumped at the announcement. All things considered, so far things had gone well. She and Joe had worked side by side and they had managed to rub along together amicably, but she didn't think it wise to get too chummy.

Joe was, after all, a handsome, intelligent and charming man, and she wouldn't lie to herself—though she didn't love him anymore, she still found him attractive. She was a mature woman now and capable of appreciating animal attraction for what it was—a purely physical thing—but she was also a sucker for courtly Southern charm, which Joe possessed in such abundance it practically oozed from his pores. The last thing she needed was for him to escort her down a dimly lit hallway to her room.

"No, please. That won't be necessary. Really. I can find my own way."

Before he could argue, she bid him and Mike good night again and hurried across the foyer.

From the corner of her eye she saw Joe watching her, and as she climbed the grand staircase, she felt his gaze boring into her back, but she kept her eyes focused straight ahead and kept climbing.

As Olivia started down the hall on the second floor it occurred to her that maybe she'd been a bit hasty in refusing Joe's offer.

There was something unnerving, even downright spooky, about the mansion at night. Olivia told herself she was being silly. There was nothing to be afraid of. It was just a big old house. That was all.

Wall sconces hung beside each door on either side of the wide hall, but only one in every three or four contained a bulb, and those barely provided enough dim puddles of light to allow her to negotiate the corridor. More of Miss Prudence's economy measures, Olivia assumed.

"Oof!"

The sound burst from her as she slammed into a solid object.

In the dim light she saw a four-foot-high pedestal with an ornate urn on top. Both teetered in front of her nose and threatened to topple at any second.

"Oh, for—" Grabbing the urn with one hand, she steadied the wobbling column of marble with the other. As soon as the stand and art object were restored to their normal place, she slapped her hand over her heart and exhaled a long sigh. When she'd regained her composure, she took a cautious sidestep and moved out into the center of the Oriental runner that ran the length of the hallway.

It was darker in the middle of the corridor, but safer. The pedestal was only one of many that stood outside the curtain-draped alcoves spaced at regular intervals along the length of the hall. She wasn't an expert on porcelain, nor had she examined the accessories closely yet, but she knew enough to be sure that the vases and other art objects were valuable. The last thing she needed was to break a priceless piece.

First thing, when he returned, she would have to have a talk with Joe about the lighting, she decided.

The farther she went the darker and eerier the hallway seemed to become. The prickly sensation crawling over her skin intensified.

A floorboard creaked behind Olivia, and the hair on her neck stood on end. She whirled around. "Who's there?"

Nothing.

"Mrs. Jaffee? Is that you?" Olivia's gaze searched the shadows, but still no one answered and nothing moved.

Cautiously, Olivia turned back and headed for her room at a faster pace, her heart thumping.

She had almost made it when, light as thistledown, something brushed across her hair. Olivia gave a strangled cry and flung her arms over her head.

"Stop it! Stop it right now!"

Sinister laughter, so soft it was barely audible, sent panic racing through her. She spun around again, but again, no one was there. "Who *are* you? *Where* are you? Why are you doing this?"

Silence.

Olivia stood absolutely still, one hand fisted over her thudding heart, the other splayed across her throat. Her wide-eyed gaze darted all around, searching the shadows. The only sounds she heard were the rasp of her own breathing and the thunder of her pulse pounding in her ears.

"Whoever you are, if this is your idea of a joke, it *isn't funny!*"

Again, there was only silence.

Olivia backed away slowly, her gaze making a constant sweep of the shadowy hall. Finally reaching her room, she snatched frantically at the doorknob, but she was shaking so hard it took three fumbling attempts before the door opened. With a cry of relief, she stumbled into the room, slammed the door shut again and locked it.

"Dear God," she gasped, and leaned her forehead against the heavy walnut panel. She stayed there for several seconds until she regained a modicum of control. Then, with a sudden renewed sense of alarm, she whirled around and pressed her back against the door and anxiously looked around the room.

Mrs. Jaffee had left lamps on beside the bed, on the desk, and on the end table beside the fainting couch, giving her enough illumination to see even into the corners of the room. No one was there, and as far as she could tell no one had been in her room. Still leery, she crept to the bathroom door, reached inside and flipped on the light switch. The room was empty.

Olivia released the breath she'd been holding. She recrossed the room, sat down on the Victorian fainting couch and slumped against the hard backrest. Had fright caused her imagination to run wild?

Old as it was, the house could creak and pop on its own, but could she have imagined that touch? That awful laugh? Maybe, she conceded. It had certainly seemed real, but she could have been jumping at shadows. It was possible that a draft had played with her hair, and God knew, old houses made all manner of weird sounds.

Shaking her head at her lapse of common sense, Olivia unzipped her boots and pulled them off. Standing, she stripped off her pantsuit and hung it in the closet, peeled off her panty hose and headed for the bathroom dressed only in bronze satin bikini panties and matching bra. She'd let the stories she'd heard as a child cloud her reason, Olivia decided. There were no ghosts. Here or anywhere else. And certainly no one was stalking her.

After showering and getting ready for bed, Olivia double-checked that the door and all the windows were locked before she crawled into the massive four-poster bed. She settled into a comfortable position and closed her eyes, determined to banish Joe from her mind and get a restful night's sleep.

It wasn't to be. She tossed and turned and punched her pillow frequently, but sleep eluded her for hours. Long after turning out the lights she heard Joe and Mike pass by her room, talking softly, then, far down the hall, a door closed, then another.

Sometime during the wee hours of the morning Olivia finally drifted off out of exhaustion, but almost immediately a disturbing dream began to torment her. In it, a man, wearing an 1890s frock coat, somehow slipped into her room and, bold as brass, walked over to her bed.

Try as she might, Olivia could not scream. It was as though her vocal cords, and every other part of her body, were paralyzed. She could only lie there, heart pounding, and watch him through slitted eyes, unable to move or make a sound as he came toward her.

For the longest time the man stood in the shadows beside her bed, watching her. Then, as silently as he had come, he turned and walked away, disappearing into the shadows.

Olivia awoke from the dream with a cry and jack-knifed into a sitting position in the middle of the enormous bed, clutching the covers to her breasts. Trembling and struggling for breath, her eyes wide with fright, she darted a look all around. There was only darkness and inky shadows and absolute stillness and silence.

With a long sigh, she flopped back against the pillows. It had been a dream. Just a dream. That's all. Turning onto her side, she pulled the covers up to her chin and tried to will her thundering heart to calm. Still…it had seemed so real, she thought, staring into the darkness.

She had not seen the man's face clearly, but his muscular build and dark coloring had been the same as Joe's.

"Are you satisfied with this lot?" Joe asked, looking over the two dozen or more men milling around the Savannah pier next to the *Lady Bea*. The group included seven men from the old crew whom Joe had shamed into coming back to work, but most were new hands. He suspected that many of them were nervous about working on Mallen Island, but the incentive bonus that he offered to every employee who stuck with the job for six months was too good to pass up.

"Yeah," Mike replied, nodding. "They've all got experience and references. I think they know what they're doing."

"That's all well and good, but do you think they'll turn tail and run at the least little thing?"

"I don't think so. But it's hard to tell. I explained to all of them about the sightings, and that we think it's just someone playing tricks on us. Every man laughed it off, but who knows how they'll react if they think they've seen a ghost?"

"I guess that'll have to do. Why don't you take them to the island and put them to work. We've wasted enough time on this nonsense."

"Sure thing, boss. What about you? You coming?"

"Not just yet. I've got a personal matter to see to. Tell Olivia that if I'm not back tonight I'll call in the morning."

Joe left Mike issuing orders to the new crew and walked down the river promenade to the AdCo office building.

"Oh there you are, Mr. Connally," his secretary exclaimed when he strode through the outer office. "I didn't know whether or not you'd be back today. You've had several calls—"

"I'll get to those later." He paused at the door to his office just long enough to add, "First I want you to buzz Blair and tell her I want to see her in my office. Now."

Martha Lumis's eyes widened. She'd worked for Joe long enough to recognize that tone. It spelled trouble for someone.

A few minutes later Blair breezed into Joe's office, looking chic in a powder-blue semifitted blazer and silky skirt that fluttered around her knees. "Martha said you wanted to see me. What's up?"

Sitting back in his chair, Joe looked at her through narrowed eyes for a full ten seconds before pointing to one of the chairs in front of his desk. "Sit."

"Uh-oh. This sounds serious." His sister flashed a cheeky grin. "Did I park in someone else's spot or something?"

"I want to know why you betrayed Livvie."

"What? Betrayed Livvie? Don't be absurd. I've only seen her once since she's been back. In your apartment, Monday evening, and that was for only a few seconds. How could I have betrayed her in that short time?"

"I'm talking about fourteen years ago. In her hospital room. The night after she lost the baby. Mother told Livvie that I was out with Selina, and you and Flora backed her up."

Blair's grin wavered and collapsed. "Oh, God," she groaned, slumping back in the chair. "She *told* you about that?"

"I pried it out of her, yes. Now answer my question. And don't give me any of that nonsense about you thinking she wasn't good enough for me. If I thought for an instant that you truly believed that, I'd boot you out on your spoiled little ass before you could blink. So spit it out. Why did you turn on your best friend?"

"Joe, please, do we have to—"

"Damned right, we have to. Start talking."

Blair grimaced. "All right, all right. It's true. I sold

Livvie out. But Mother left me no choice. She said if I didn't go along with her, she would have Prince Rupert put down. I couldn't let that happen.''

"So you chose your horse over your best friend?"

"Don't look at me like that," Blair cried. "Daddy gave me that horse. I loved him. I couldn't let Mother destroy him."

"Maybe not. But you could have come to Luke and me."

"What could you two have done? Mother had all the power."

"Only with regard to our trust funds. You forget, I was over twenty-one at the time. If reasoning with her failed, I could have filed charges on your behalf and stopped her. Everyone knew that horse was yours."

Blair's eyes widened almost comically. "Oh, Lord. I can just imagine the brouhaha that would have caused within the family."

"Since when has that ever stopped you? Anyway, with Mother there will always be some sort of drama going on. Hell, even Dad knew that. One of the last things he said to me was, 'Your mama is a handful, God bless her. I'm depending on you and your brother to protect her from herself when I'm gone.'"

Blair gave a little huff. "As though you could have. These days, yes. But we were all just kids back then."

"Trust me, Luke and I would've stopped her—although I doubt seriously that she would have carried out the threat. Mother may be willful and manipulative, but first and foremost she's a horsewoman. I doubt that she would put down a championship horse out of spite."

"Yes, well, I couldn't take that chance."

Joe simply looked at her without a word. He was silent so long that Blair squirmed in her chair. "You're more like Mother than you know," he said finally.

Blair bristled. "That's not tr—"

"Oh, it's true, all right. You want things your own way all the time and you never think before you act. Your selfishness not only betrayed and hurt Livvie, but you hurt me as well."

"*You!* I was doing you a favor. I was getting you out of an unfortunate marriage with a girl you didn't love."

"Is that what Mother told you?"

"Yes." A surprised look came over her face. "Are you telling me now that you *were* in love with Livvie?"

"Who knows? As you said, we were just kids back then. We may have gotten there eventually. But thanks to you, Mother and Flora, we'll never know."

Blair's lower jaw dropped. "I never dreamed…that is…oh, Joe, I'm so sorry, I—"

"Save it for Livvie. She's the one to whom you owe an apology."

"You want me to apologize to Livvie. I…I *can't!* Not after the terrible thing I did."

"That's the whole point, Blair. If you hadn't done something terrible you wouldn't need to apologize. Hell, I'd think you'd want to get this off your chest, if for no other reason than to possibly salvage your friendship. Wouldn't you like to have your friend back? Correct me if I'm wrong, but it seems to me that you could have used the support of someone like Livvie these past years."

"Of course I would love to have Livvie's friendship back, but that's not going to happen. Not after what I did."

"You don't know that. I'm not saying it'll be easy. It may take time for you to earn her trust again, but have you ever known Livvie to hold a grudge for long?"

Blair shook her head. "You don't know what you're asking, Joe. It's been too long. It…it would be too humiliating, and I feel so…so…"

"Guilty?" he supplied.

She shot him a sour look. "All right, yes. Guilty. I did a terrible thing and I'm sorry. I've regretted my part in the whole thing every day for the past fourteen years. But don't you understand? I just can't face Livvie."

Joe's stare pinned her to her chair. Then he shook his head. "I could drag you out to the island kicking and screaming, but I won't. However, if you have as much backbone and honor as I think you do, you'll do what you know is right." He rose, signaling the discussion was over. "When you work up the gumption, you know where to find Livvie."

Catching her lower lip between her teeth, Blair rose without a word and headed for the door, thoroughly chastened. Once there she paused and cast a sheepish look her brother's way, then scurried from the room.

"Excuse me, ma'am. I'm L.J. Nye. I was told to report for work here this mornin'. The lady who answered the door said to come see you."

"Yes, of course." Leaving the drafting table, Olivia came forward with her hand outstretched. "I'm Olivia, the designer on this project. It's nice to meet you, L.J. Mike said you'd be here this morning. I hope you're ready to dive right in.''

''Oh, yes, ma'am.'' He sent her a shy smile and shifted from one foot to the other, all the while turning his baseball cap around and around in his hands. ''Anything you want done, you just tell me. I'm not afraid of work and I've got a strong back.''

That she could believe. Mike had said the man he had hired was brawny, and he hadn't been kidding. L.J. looked like a bodybuilder. She guessed his age at somewhere around twenty-five or six. He stood a little under six feet and had dark hair and the tanned skin of one who spends a lot of time outdoors. He spoke with the soft drawl that identified him as a native Savannahian and appeared to be mannerly and extremely shy, blushing every time he met Olivia's eyes.

''Good, I'm glad to hear that,'' she replied. ''Because today I'd like to get started taking inventory of everything that's stored in the attic. I took a peek earlier, and you're going to have to move things around in order for me to examine the pieces and decide what to do with them. It will probably take several days just to work our way through the attic. When we're done there, we'll start on the rooms.''

''Yes, ma'am. Whatever you say. Just lead the way.''

Eleven

After only one day of working with L.J., Olivia was so pleased she wanted to find Mike and give him a kiss. The young man was a tireless worker and so amiable and mannerly he was a joy to have around. Though it was dank and chilly in the attic, and by the end of the day they were both covered with the accumulated dust and grime of more than a century, he didn't seem to mind. From his attitude, one would think she was doing him a favor by letting him work for her.

The second morning Olivia awoke early. She'd had a restless night, waking often to strange sounds she couldn't identify. Finally, unable to sleep, she dressed and went downstairs just as dawn was breaking. Mrs. Jaffee was putting on the coffee to brew when Olivia entered the kitchen and poured herself a glass of juice and filched a bagel.

"Here, now. What're you doing in my kitchen?" the housekeeper protested. "Breakfast will be ready in a half hour and not before."

"That's all right, Mrs. Jaffee. This is all I want. If you need to find me, L.J. and I will be in the main attic again, taking inventory."

"Humph. Young people. Don't have a lick of sense. Don't eat enough to keep a bird alive and expect to work all day. Don't blame me if you pass out from hunger,'' she grumbled as Olivia sailed out the door.

She was surprised to find L.J. waiting for her in the library. "How did you get here so early? Cappy usually doesn't arrive until somewhere between seven and eight."

"Oh, I have my own boat. It's just a little fishin' skiff." He shrugged self-consciously. "I don't like dependin' on others for transportation. Besides, I figure in the evenings, on the way home, I can stop and do a little fishin' if I feel like it." He paused and looked worried. "I hope it's all right if I don't ride the tug? I wouldn't want to break any rules."

"I don't see why it wouldn't be. I'm sure that as long as you get here on time Mr. Connally will be happy."

She finished her bagel and juice and picked up her clipboard. "Since you're here, we may as well get started."

They worked steadily for hours. L.J. moved various trunks, boxes and assorted junk out of the way so that Olivia could examine each furniture piece, put it on her list and tag it with a color-coded sticker. Red meant the item was to go to the refinisher, blue to the upholsterer, purple to both, green was usable as it was, orange would be sold and yellow was destined for the trash bin.

Mid-morning, Joe called to tell her that he was in Nashville, handling an emergency on another job. "Reese insisted that I fly up here, but it wasn't that serious. Our foreman could have handled it. I should be back tonight or, at the latest, in the morning."

"That was the big boss, huh?" L.J. asked when she said goodbye and turned off her cell phone.

"Yes. He'll be here tonight. Why? Are you nervous about meeting him?"

"Yes, ma'am. Important men make me jittery and clumsy, an' I don't want to do something stupid and lose this job. I like workin' for you," he added, blushing to the roots of his hair.

"Well, thank you, L.J. I like you, too. But technically, you don't work for me. You work for AdCo."

"Yes, ma'am." He ducked his head and went back to moving boxes.

Late that afternoon Olivia was looking over a half-tester bed when she heard heavy footsteps on the attic stairs.

Olivia glanced at L.J. "I wonder who that could be?"

"Probably that crabby housekeeper. She gives me the willies," he muttered.

As if on cue, Mrs. Jaffee appeared in the doorway. She collapsed against the jamb, panting and holding her hand to her heart.

"My goodness, are you all right?" Olivia asked, rushing to the old woman's side.

"I wi-will be, s-soon as I catch my br-breath. You c-couldn't work on the f-first floor? You had to make an old lady cl-climb all the way to the r-roof?"

"I don't know what you're doing up here, Mrs. Jaffee, but surely it could have waited until I came down for dinner."

"Do you think I woulda climbed all those stairs if it could have?" she snapped. "That Mr. Addison is here. He wants to see you in the library."

"Reese? Here?" She looked down at her grimy

clothes and made a face. "I'd better go wash up and change clothes."

"No, he said to come right down. It was important."

"Oh." Olivia dusted off her shirt and jeans as best she could, but there was nothing she could do about her grimy hands or the smudges on her face. Loping down the stairs, she pulled the bandanna off her hair and shook it out. What could be so important to bring Reese to the island? Joe had said he would be tied up with other matters for several more weeks.

Reese stood by the library's French doors with his back to the room, gazing out at the terrace garden.

"You wanted to see me?"

He turned, and she knew immediately that something was wrong. His expression held none of the flirtatious charm that he had lavished on her only a few days ago. His face looked as though it had been chiseled in stone, and his gray eyes were as cold as the Atlantic in winter.

"Yes. Won't you sit down, Olivia," he said, gesturing toward one of the chairs in front of the desk.

She did so reluctantly, and after he sat down at the desk, Reese folded his hands together on the top. "I'm not going to beat around the bush, Olivia. As of today, your contract is terminated."

"What?" Shock jolted through her. She had feared that he was about to tell her that something had happened to Joe. This was the last thing she expected. "You're…you're firing me? Why? You can't be unhappy with my work. I've barely started."

"I had a visit yesterday from Eleanore Connally."

Olivia closed her eyes. Her shoulders slumped and she expelled her breath in a fatalistic sigh. "I see."

"I had no idea you were Joe's ex-wife. Hell, I didn't even know that he'd been married. But if I had, I would not have agreed to hire you. Eleanore told me the whole story. How you set a trap for Joe and forced him to marry you."

"That's not true."

Reese held up his hands. "Please. I have no wish to get into the sordid details again. It comes down to your word against hers, and frankly, I've known Eleanore all my life."

"I see. Does Joe know you're doing this?"

"No, but I'm sure when he finds out he'll be relieved to have you out of his hair. He's told his mother how awkward it is for him having you here and how miserable it's making him."

"If that's true, why did he choose me as the designer?"

"Simple. Because I did. Joe is the fairest, most decent guy I know. We issued the invitation, and he was determined to honor it and not hold the past against you. But apparently being around you again is making him miserable."

"That's not the impression I get from him."

"But then, he wouldn't let you see that, would he? I understand from Eleanore that you've known Joe since you were children. In which case you must know that he is the consummate gentleman. When he gives his word, he honors it. And he'd sooner cut out his tongue than tell a woman that he can't tolerate being around her—even an ex-wife."

Olivia couldn't argue with that. Joe was chivalrous to all females, no matter who—or what—they were.

Olivia's hands were curled into fists so tight that her fingernails cut into her palms, but she didn't notice. What a fool you are, Olivia, she silently berated herself. What a naive, head-in-the-clouds fool. Did you really believe Eleanore would let you have this job? You should have known better.

"My boat, *Footloose,* is tied up at the pier. I'll be heading back to Savannah in a couple of hours after I talk to Mike and take a look at what's been done so far. Can you be ready to go by then?"

What choice did she have? "Yes. I'll go pack."

"That would be best. Oh, one more thing, Olivia. We will, of course, pay you for the time you've spent on this project, plus a breach-of-contract settlement."

"Oh, you bet you will," she stated emphatically, making his eyebrows shoot upward. "You'll be hearing from my attorney."

The sun sank below the horizon in the west, streaking the water with shades of orange, red and pink as Joe docked *Fleeting Dreams.* He quickly jumped onto the pier's new plank boards and tied up the boat. Noticing Reese's boat moored at one of the other new piers, his eyebrows shot up. What was *he* doing here? He was supposed to be in Alexandria today. Whatever the reason, it couldn't be too urgent or earth shattering, otherwise Reese would have called him on his cell phone.

Not unduly alarmed, Joe hurried up the cliff steps and around to the front door. No one was in the entry hall or the library, so he headed for the kitchen. "Do you know where Reese is?" he asked Mrs. Jaffee, sticking his head inside the kitchen.

The woman jumped and let out a squawk. "Goodness gracious me," she gasped with her hand over her heart. "Scare a body to death, why don't you? I didn't know you were back."

"I just got here. I'm looking for Reese." He knew Mrs. Jaffee would know his whereabouts. She kept an eagle eye on anyone who came into the house. He suspected that she eavesdropped, as well.

"He's up in the attic, looking at the new quarters you're building."

"I see. And Olivia? Is she with him?"

She slanted him a sly look out of the corner of her eye. "Don't think so. I believe she's in her room."

"Thanks."

Joe glanced at his wristwatch, heading for the stairs. It was a little shy of normal quitting time.

He took the stairs two at a time. On the second-floor landing, instead of continuing up to the attic level he turned toward Olivia's room. Not because he couldn't wait to see her again, he told himself. He was simply making sure she wasn't ill, that was all.

He knocked on her door and called, "Olivia. It's me. Joe."

In seconds she opened the door, but neither her face nor her eyes held one iota of welcome. "What are you doing here? I thought you wouldn't be back until late tonight or tomorrow."

"I got lucky and caught an earlier flight." He looked beyond her to the open suitcase on the luggage rack and raised one eyebrow. "Going somewhere?"

She turned away and went back to packing, adding another garment to the case from the stack of things on the bed. Joe sauntered into the room behind her, hands in his pockets, looking around with interest.

"Yes. I'm going home to Atlanta. Reese fired me."

Joe was taking in the feminine accoutrements on

the dressing table—perfume bottles and little pots and vials of mysterious female potions. Then his gaze fixed on the neat stack of silken lingerie on the bed. It took a moment for Olivia's statement to register on him. When it did, his attention snapped to her.

"What? What did you just say?"

"Reese fired me," she repeated in a lifeless tone. She didn't bother to look at him, merely folded another garment and added it to the case. "He's taking me back to Savannah as soon as I finish packing."

She might as well have tossed a lighted match into a keg of gunpowder. Joe exploded.

"The *hell* you say!"

He spun around and stomped toward the door like an enraged bull. He started to step into the hall, then stopped and jabbed his index finger toward her. "You stay right there. You hear? Don't go anywhere. And unpack that damned suitcase. I'll be right back."

"Joe, what are you going to do? Joe. Joe! Wait!"

She could have saved her breath. He barely heard her.

He took the stairs to the third floor, three at a time. At the base of the attic stairs he roared at the top of his voice, "Reese! Reese! Damn you, Reese, get down here! Now!"

He had started up the narrower flight of stairs when Reese stepped out on the landing above him. "You bellowed?"

"I want to talk to you," Joe snarled.

Mike Garvey stuck his head around the attic door, and behind him were three nervous-looking workmen. "Something wrong, boss?"

"Hell, yes, there's something wrong. But it's between Reese and me."

"Yes, sir. Me'n the guys, we'll, uh…we'll just get back to work," Mike stammered, retreating into the attic.

"Do you want to duke this out here on the stairs or go to the library?" Reese drawled, and his nonchalance inflamed Joe's temper even more.

"Neither." Despite the red haze of fury that engulfed him, he still retained enough sense to know not to air his grievance with his partner where others could hear. He looked around. "Come with me," he ordered, leading the way back to the third floor and entering the first room he came to.

The room was musty and filled with sheet-draped furniture. Cobwebs hung from the ceiling and the chandelier, and a thick layer of dust covered everything.

"Charming," Reese drawled. He fastidiously sidestepped several grimy objects and walked to the middle of the floor where there was no danger of touching anything. "So what's got your shorts in a twist?"

Leading with his chin, Joe walked right up to Reese until they were nose to nose. "I want to know why the hell you went behind my back and fired Olivia," he snarled.

"And I want to know why the hell you didn't tell me that the reason you'd dropped out of college that time was because you got married," Reese fired back, not giving an inch. "And why the hell you didn't tell me that Olivia was the one you'd married. If I'd known that we wouldn't be having this shouting match now, because I wouldn't have hired her in the first place."

"Well *I* would have!" Joe roared back, thumbing

his chest. "She was the hands-down best and you know it. Hiring her was the correct move."

"For the business, yes, but not if having her around is going to make you miserable. Right now you're having a knee-jerk chivalrous reaction, but your mother assured me that once Olivia is gone and out of your life again you'll feel different."

Joe's eyes narrowed. "My mother?"

"Yeah. We had lunch together yesterday, and she told me the whole story—how Olivia had tricked you into marriage, then lost the baby. How unhappy you are now, how you hate every minute you have to be around her, but that you're too much of a gentleman to fire her."

"And you believed her?"

"Of course. Why wouldn't I? That's typical Joe behavior. Added to that, you've been acting strange for a couple of months. Like you're preoccupied about something."

"Let's get this straight. Olivia did *not* trap me. *I'm* the one who insisted she marry me. She is the sweetest, most honest and guileless female on the face of the earth. Nothing about Olivia—*nothing*—makes me unhappy. To the contrary, I'm delighted that she's here. And she's staying. You got that?"

An arrested look came over Reese's face. "Well, I'll be damned. When Eleanore told me about Olivia I thought the reason you didn't want me making a play for her was you were worried she'd try to trap me into marriage, too. But that's not it, is it. You want her for yourself. You're in love with her."

Joe looked taken aback. "What?"

"You heard me. You're in love with your ex-wife."

At a loss, Joe stared at his partner. Finally he heaved a sigh and raked his hand through his hair. "Yeah, I am. And do you have any idea how it makes me feel to know that she was once mine, but I lacked the good sense and maturity to realize that she was the love of my life and I let her go without a fight?"

"Yeah, that's rough," Reese agreed, but his eyes twinkled. "I guess you'll just have to win her back and marry her all over again."

"Damned right," Joe growled. "And *you* are going to apologize to her."

"Right. No problem."

"And after you do, you stay away from her, you hear?" He spun around and stalked toward the door.

"Where are you going?" Reese called after him.

"To talk to Olivia."

Joe went down the stairs to the second floor a lot slower than he'd raced up them, his mind whirling. It wasn't going to be easy, winning Olivia back. He and his family had hurt her badly. It would take patience and subtle maneuvering to breach that protective wall she'd built around herself.

He was going to have to move slowly and carefully, but that prospect did not discourage him. On the contrary, when he thought back to the rushed marriage ceremony that had briefly bound them together fourteen years ago, and the reason for it, he wanted to cringe.

Olivia deserved better, he told himself angrily. She was a lovely, desirable woman who should be romanced and pursued and wedded for herself. This time around he was going to court her as he should have done all those years ago. No matter how long it took, he would not give up until she was his again.

She was pacing the room when he walked in through the open door. Spotting him, she rushed to his side, her expression anxious. "Joe! What happened? Did you and Reese have a fight? I could hear you yelling all the way down here."

His smile was rueful. "Let's call it a loud discussion. But everything is settled now. You're staying.

"Turns out that Mother put him up to this. She told him her version of what happened between us, which, of course, was a pack of lies. He had no reason not to believe her, but I set him straight, and he understands now that, contrary to what Mother claims, I'm very fond of you."

He could see that Olivia was not as convinced as he'd hoped she would be.

"Oh, Joe, are you sure you want me to stay? Eleanore isn't ever going to be okay with this arrangement."

"She going to have to be. It's what I want. I'm heading back to the mainland now to hash this out with her, once and for all."

She opened her mouth to argue, but he placed his forefinger over her lips, silencing her. "Don't argue, Livvie. It has to be done."

During the boat trip back to Savannah and the drive to Winterhaven Joe thought about all the meddling his mother had done, all the manipulating and mischief, and with each mile he grew more angry. When he strode into his family home he didn't mince words.

"Mother, I want to talk to you."

"Joseph, darling. What a lovely surprise." Eleanore smiled fondly and extended her cheek for a kiss. Joe pretended not to notice, and a wary look came over her face. She waved to the chair opposite hers. "Sit down, dearest. I was just about to have my tea. Just let me ring Mrs. Bonner for another cup."

"Don't bother. I won't be staying long."

"Oh, dear. You really shouldn't rush around so. It's not good for your health, you know."

"I didn't come here to talk about my health. I'm here to talk about the little stunt you tried to pull, going behind my back and talking Reese into dismissing Olivia. Did you really think you could get by with that? Did you think I wouldn't notice she was gone?"

"Really, darling, do you have to be so disagreeable?"

"Answer me, Mother. Why did you do it, after I specifically told you to leave Olivia alone and stay out of my business?"

"You're my son. Your happiness is important to me. I thought that once that girl was gone you'd see that it was for the best. That you'd actually be glad. I certainly didn't expect you to kick up such a fuss."

"Well you were wrong, weren't you? Just like you were wrong fourteen years ago."

"Wha-what do you mean?"

"I know what you did after Olivia lost our baby, Mother. You set me up and you lied to Olivia and coerced her mother and Blair to lie, too. It's because of you that Livvie and I divorced."

Like a tragic heroine, Eleanore splayed her hand at the base of her neck. "She…she told you about my visit? That wicked girl. She shouldn't have—"

"She didn't want to tell me," Joe interrupted. "I

pried it out of her, and I'm glad I did. You had no right to do that, Mother. No right at all.''

"It's a mother's right to help her children any way she can. That's all I was trying to do."

"Horsefeathers. You were trying to have your own way, as you always do."

"Before you say something you will regret, there is something you should know about your precious Livvie. Her price for letting you go was fifty thousand dollars. I wrote her a check that night, which she took gladly."

"Oh, really. Show me the canceled check."

"What? Well, I, uh…I can't put my hand on it right this minute—"

"Nonsense. All our financial records, including canceled checks, going back to day one are stored in filing cabinets in the basement. It won't take me but five minutes to find it." He pretended to head for the door. "Let's see, that was fourteen years ago, right?"

"Joe, wait," Eleanore called. "You won't find the check down there. I…I destroyed it years ago. I couldn't stand to be reminded of that girl and how she almost ruined your life."

Joe strolled back into the center of the room, jingling the change in his pockets, a sardonic look on his face. "Nice try, Mother, but it won't work. I know that Olivia never cashed the check, although I wouldn't blame her if she had. I saw it with my own eyes. She still has it."

"No! What you saw…it…it must have been a forgery."

"It's no use, Mother. You're caught."

Eleanore's mouth firmed into a thin line, and her eyes burned with resentment. "Oh, all right. So she didn't cash the check. What does it matter, she still *took* the money.''

''No more. Not another word.'' He bent over her, bringing his face down to within inches of hers. ''Listen to me, Mother, and listen good. If you ever—and I mean *ever*—try to harm Livvie again, or try to run her off, or ruin her business, or make life miserable for her, if you so much as make a negative remark about her, you can pack your bags and move into town, because you will no longer be mistress of Winterhaven.''

Eleanore sucked in her breath. ''You can't throw me out of this house. This is my home.''

''No, Mother. It's *my* home. Dad left it to me.''

''Y-you would actually put me out? Your own mother?''

''In a heartbeat if you try to harm Livvie again. And don't try to make it sound like you're a penniless waif being tossed out into the cold. You can afford a place of your own. You have more money than you could ever spend.''

''I can't believe this. You would side with that girl over your own mother?''

''You'd better believe it. I mean it, Mother. This is no idle threat. You try to harm Livvie in any way, or by any means, and you're out of here.''

Twelve

Unable to sleep, Olivia heard Joe return sometime around one in the morning. She lay in her bed, staring into the darkness, wondering what had transpired between him and his mother. One thing was certain, Eleanore would not have been happy.

After yet another night of strange noises and interrupted sleep, she awoke later than usual the next morning and arrived in the dining room to find that Joe had already eaten and gone.

"He's been down at the pier talking to Mike for nigh on to two hours already," the dour housekeeper informed her with a sniff. There was no mistaking the disapproval in her voice, or in the pointed look she cast at the mantel clock.

Olivia could have informed the woman that the hours she kept were none of her concern, but she held her tongue. Her own mother would never have presumed to admonish a guest in the Connally home, no matter how obliquely.

Ignoring the old woman, Olivia helped herself to the toast set out on the buffet and poured a cup of coffee.

"That all you gonna eat?" Mrs. Jaffee demanded as Olivia sat down at the long dining table.

"Yes. It is."

"Humph. Young girls these days," the housekeeper muttered, transferring serving dishes to a tray. "Always worrying about your figures and lookin' to catch a man."

Olivia almost chuckled at that. Catching a man was not high on her list. And it had been at least ten years or more since she'd been called a "girl."

"And don't think I haven't noticed how you're always glancing at Mr. Connally when you think he doesn't know," the woman continued when she failed to get a rise out of Olivia. "Well, let me tell you, missy, if you're hoping to snag that man, you're wasting your time."

Olivia choked on her coffee, but Mrs. Jaffee continued as though she hadn't noticed.

"According to the society section of the newspaper, better women than you have tried and failed over the years. High-society women with money and breeding on their side."

When Olivia stopped coughing she blotted her lips on the linen napkin and gave the woman a cool look. "Let me put your mind at ease, Mrs. Jaffee, once and for all. I am not now, nor will I ever be, interested in 'snagging' Mr. Connally, as you put it. Or any other man, for that matter. I have no wish to marry. Ever."

Mrs. Jaffee's eyebrows rose. Then her eyes narrowed. "So. You're one of those, are you? I never would have guessed it, you being so pretty and feminine and all." She picked up the loaded tray. "I always thought your kind were tough and mannish," she added in a disapproving tone, and disappeared into the butler's pantry.

"What? Oh, no. You misunderstood. I'm not—"

Flabbergasted, Olivia found herself staring, slack-jawed, at the swinging door.

She rose halfway out of her chair, intending to follow the woman and set her straight, then thought better of it and sat back down again. What did it matter? If the old crone wanted to jump to conclusions, that was her problem.

Mike had left a note on the desk in the library saying that he needed L.J. to assist the electrician that day, so after breakfast Olivia set to work on one of the specific design plans for the employee apartments. Now and then, through a window directly in front of the drafting table, she could see Joe down at the far end of one of the new piers. A couple of times he came into the library to use the fax machine or check on something in the files, but they were both busy and barely spoke.

At one point he took the time to look over her shoulder at her rendering of a room. He stood with one hand braced on the back of her chair and the other on the edge of the desk, bent so near his warm breath stirred her hair and caused her scalp to prickle.

"Nice," he murmured.

"Thank you. I'm glad you like it. I've designed four different floor plans. They will all be similar in style, but individual in terms of color and decor." She turned her head to look up at him and was shocked at how close he was.

Joe smiled. "That's good, but I was talking about your hair. I've always loved the way it smells. I've never forgotten that scent."

"It's…it's just shampoo."

"Maybe so, but on you it smells delicious." Deliberately, he nuzzled his nose in the hair over her left ear. "Hmm, heavenly."

"Joe—"

He straightened. "Gotta go. I'll catch you later."

He strode out the door, leaving Olivia befuddled and unsure of what had just happened.

She did not see Joe again until lunch, and he was so rushed he barely spoke. He hurried through his meal and excused himself immediately afterward.

"Sorry, I don't mean to be rude, but I have to run," he said, rising from the table. "I've got an appointment in Savannah in less than an hour and fifteen minutes. See you later."

Not until Monday morning, Olivia thought, watching him rush out the door. It was Friday, and she had no intention of spending the weekend alone on this island with Mrs. Jaffee.

She had thought about flying home to Atlanta, but she had checked in with her office that morning, and according to Mary Beth, Janie and Maggie, there was nothing urgent that needed her attention.

Olivia sighed. She had put off visiting her mother for as long as she could, but it looked as though the time had come. As Mary Beth had pointed out, she'd run out of excuses.

After lunch she walked down to the pier and told Cappy that she would be going back to the mainland with him and the crew that evening. On her return to the house she worked on her design plans for a few more hours then went up to her room, took her sea-sick medicine and started packing.

Half an hour later she was bent over, zipping up the weekend carryall when the tugboat's whistle blasted.

Olivia's head snapped up. "The boat! Oh, no!"

She ran to one of the windows, threw it open and leaned out as far as she could, waving her arms and yelling, "Hey, wait! Wait! Don't leave! Wait for me!"

Not only was she too far away for anyone to hear her, between the wind, the surf and the noise of the tug's engines, catching anyone's attention was hopeless.

Even from that distance, Cappy's white beard and massive build made him recognizable, but she couldn't see him anywhere, which meant he was probably already in the pilothouse. The *Lady Bea's* powerful engines were rumbling, the propellers churning up the water at the tug's stern.

All of the workmen appeared to be onboard. Several had disappeared below deck, and on the pier, two of Cappy's crewmen were casting off the mooring lines.

Making a distressed sound, Olivia ducked back inside, slammed the window shut, grabbed her coat, purse, briefcase and the tow handle on her suitcase and took off at a dead run.

She met Mrs. Jaffee coming up the main stairs carrying an armload of bed linens. Olivia flew past the astonished woman like a bat out of hell, her suitcase bouncing down each step behind her.

Olivia thought she heard the housekeeper mutter "Good riddance," but she was too frantic to care.

Stony-faced, the old woman stood on the stairs and watched Olivia race across the foyer and out the front door.

From the deck of *Fleeting Dreams,* Joe watched Olivia scramble down the cliff steps. Grinning, he crossed his arms over his chest and leaned back against the side of the cabin, chuckling at her head-long, single-minded dash.

By the time she reached the pier the *Lady Bea* was a hundred yards out into the cove. Olivia was so intent on the tugboat she seemed unaware of anything else.

Calling and waving her briefcase in the air and towing her bouncing suitcase behind her, she ran down the pier right past *Fleeting Dreams* without noticing the boat or him.

"No! Come back! You forgot me! Wait! Wait! Come back!"

The tugboat chugged on at the same plodding speed.

A short way down the pier, past Joe's cruiser, the hopelessness of the situation seemed to sink in, and Olivia's footsteps faltered and came to a halt, her shoulders slumping.

"Oh, damn! Damn, damn, damn, *damn!*"

"Why, Livvie Jones, your mama would wash your mouth out with soap."

She spun around, astonishment dropping her jaw.

Even with the wind tearing at her hair and clothing and looking frazzled and angry, she was lovely, Joe noted.

"Joe! What are you doing here?" she demanded in the most ungracious tone that he'd ever heard her use. Before he could answer, her temper surged again and she shook her briefcase in the general direction of the tugboat and snarled, "Look at that. That cantankerous old captain of yours left without me."

The display both surprised and intrigued Joe. The

Livvie he'd known had always been such a sweet, meek little thing. Never, not once during the five months of their marriage, or for that matter, in all the time he'd known her, had he ever seen her in a full-blown temper. Hell, he hadn't known she had one. But he'd be damned if she wasn't cute as hell when she let fly.

"Yes, I know." Stuffing his hands in his pockets, Joe left the boat and strolled down the pier. He stopped directly in front of her and smiled. "I told Cappy to go ahead, that I'd take you back to Savannah."

"You'd take me? But...but...why are you still here? I thought you went to Savannah."

"I did. Now I'm back. I came to get you."

"You came all the way back here for me? Oh, Joe, you shouldn't have done that. Ms. Keeton specifically told me that I was to take the *Lady Bea* back and forth to Savannah. I don't want any special treatment."

"Too bad," he drawled, his grin widening. "You are special to me, sweetheart. You always will be. Anyway, I thought you'd be more comfortable on my boat than on the tug. Plus *Fleeting Dreams* is a lot faster. We'll cut the commute time in half.

"Unless, of course, you'd rather spend the weekend here with Mrs. Jaffee," he added slyly, and almost laughed at the revulsion that flickered over her face.

"No! I mean...I can't do that. I'm going to visit my mother this weekend."

Disappointment flickered through him. He had hoped that by the time they reached the mainland he could have talked her into having dinner with him.

And if he was really lucky, over dinner he would finagle his way far enough into her good graces that she'd consent to spending at least part of the weekend with him.

"Well, then, we'd better get going." Hiding his letdown behind a smile, he hefted her suitcase and offered his other hand to help her up the short gangplank.

Her hand was warm and smooth as silk against his palm, the bones so fragile he dared not grip too tight. A hint of perfume wafted to his nose as she stepped past him onto the deck. He inhaled deeply and smiled, experiencing a wave of intense pleasure. Funny. He'd forgotten how delicately she was built, how utterly feminine she was. How good she always smelled.

"Wait here. I'll be right back," he told her. "Just let me stow your things below deck, then we'll go up on the bridge."

"Un, if you don't mind, I'd prefer to lie down for a while."

Joe shot her a sharp look. "Are you ill?"

"I have a headache." The tension in her shoulders and neck had been building ever since she'd made the decision to visit her mother, and now there was a persistent throbbing up the back of her head. "I took something for it, but between that and the seasick medication I took a half hour ago I'm getting terribly drowsy. I'm afraid I might fall overboard if I don't lie down somewhere."

Joe studied her, wondering if she really was woozy from medication or she was just using that as an excuse to avoid talking to him. Although, now that he thought about it, he did recall that as a child she had suffered from severe motion sickness.

"Sure," he said finally. "You can use the bunk in the cabin. Follow me."

Below deck he showed her the small galley and the head and pulled out a couple of extra blankets for the bunk. "There, that should do. If you need anything else or start feeling worse, just use the intercom. It'll connect you to the bridge."

"I will. Thanks."

"You rest, and I'll see you later."

So much for his brilliant strategy, Joe thought, going up on deck to cast off the mooring lines. He'd had it all worked out, or so he'd thought. He'd use the commute time back to Savannah to get her to talk about something other than business, get reacquainted, maybe knock a few holes in that protective wall she'd built around herself.

Ha! She'd foiled all his plans before they'd so much as pulled away from the pier. Had it been deliberate?

No matter. Before they reached Savannah he intended to come up with plan B.

The instant the cabin door clicked shut behind Joe, Olivia sat down on the edge of the bunk, propped her elbows on her knees and held her head in her hands. Her headache pounded in earnest now.

She roused herself enough to unzip her boots and pull them off. Moving slowly, she shook out the blankets, then crawled into the bunk and pulled the cover up to her chin, closing her eyes with a weary sigh.

They snapped open again almost at once when Joe's familiar scent invaded her nostrils. Oh, Lord, she was resting on his pillow.

The engine started and she felt the boat ease away from the pier and pick up speed.

Lying motionless, Olivia closed her eyes and listened to the drone of the engine and the slap of the waves against the hull. She told herself to turn the pillow over or toss it aside. Instead she burrowed her face deeper and drew in the evocative scent.

Joe's annoyance, along with any doubt he had about the veracity of Livvie's excuse, vanished a few minutes after he eased the boat into its slip on the Savannah River and went below deck.

Olivia lay curled on her right side, the blankets pulled up to her chin and her face burrowed into the pillow, sound asleep. Not even the change in speed when they had entered the harbor, or the cessation of motion and noise when he brought the boat alongside the dock and cut the engine, had roused her.

For a moment, Joe stood beside the bunk and studied her, experiencing tugs of nostalgia and tenderness. Livvie had always been a heavy sleeper. Awake, she was an active, energetic person, but once sleep claimed her she surrendered to the arms of Morpheus with the complete abandon of a small child. He grinned, remembering how some mornings he'd had to pull her out of bed by her ankles.

"Olivia. We're here."

Nothing.

Chuckling, Joe bent over to the bunk and gave her shoulder a shake. "Hey, wake up."

A sleepy smile curved Olivia's mouth. She gave a long "Mmm," and arched her entire body in a slow, sinuous stretch. When done, she sighed contentedly and snuggled her face back into the pillow again.

Desire slammed through Joe with the speed and force of a runaway train.

Whoa. Careful, Connally, he cautioned. Retreating to the foot of the bunk, he lifted the blankets to grab her ankles, but before he could something glittery caught his eye and his hand stilled.

She had removed her sexy high-heeled boots but had otherwise remained fully clothed, and her long, straight skirt had ridden up above her knees. A chain, so fine it was barely more than a golden thread, encircled her left ankle. Suspended from it, dangling provocatively over her anklebone, was a tiny golden heart about the size of a pea.

Joe stared, unable to tear his gaze away. It was ridiculous. The piece of jewelry was simple and understated, so delicate it was barely noticeable, yet it was the sexiest damned thing he had ever seen.

Heat surged through him in a powerful tide and settled, hot and heavy, in his groin. At that moment Joe wanted nothing so much as to crawl into that bunk with Livvie, strip her naked and make love to her until neither of them remembered their names.

He wanted to watch her while he moved inside her, the way he used to, to see her face flushed with innocent ardor, those green eyes darkened to emerald and slightly out of focus.

Dammit! He wanted to kiss and caress every inch of her, to slowly work his way down and take that sassy little heart into his mouth while his teeth nipped her slender ankle.

He shook his head to clear it. "Get a grip, will you?" he ordered. It was one thing to love her awake when they were married, but something told him if he tried that now, Livvie would brain him with the closest heavy object she could lay her hands on.

None too gently, he grabbed her ankle and shook it.

Other than a reflexive jerk of her foot, she didn't respond.

"Oh, great." Joe stepped back to the head of the bed and gave her shoulder a rough shake and barked in her ear, "Wake up!"

Olivia stirred, and her lashes fluttered. Beneath heavy lids her green eyes glowed, slumberous and inviting, and slowly the corners of her mouth tilted in a sleepy smile.

"Mmm. Mornin', Joe," she mumbled in a provocative bedroom voice, and reached up with one hand to stroke his cheek.

The gentle caress was nearly his undoing. Joe groaned and gritted his teeth. Ah, damn, Livvie. Honey, you're killing me, he thought a bit desperately, capturing her hand before it could curl around his neck.

He knew that she wasn't aware of what she was doing. On top of being groggy from seasick medication, Livvie always came awake in stages, going from comatose to semiconscious to full alert like someone fighting their way through a heavy fog. In that state she tended to be amorous and did and said things that, back when they were married, she'd been much to shy to do awake. He'd considered it one of her most endearing traits.

Her other hand lifted to slide around his neck, and Joe snared it, too. "Okay, now, enough of that," he managed to say in what he thought was an admirably pleasant tone, given that he spoke through clenched teeth. "Time to wake up."

He tried to fold her hands across her midriff, but all the while Olivia tried just as hard to slip them around his neck. "No. Now, stop that. Cut it out. C'mon, Livvie, behave yourself."

"But, Joe…"

Olivia froze. A second later she jackknifed into a sitting position, her eyes wide. "Joe!"

He fought not to laugh. "Yep, it's me, all right. How're you doing?"

"I…I'm okay." She became aware that his fingers were wrapped around her wrists like manacles. She snatched her hands free and scooted backward to put space between them. Avoiding his eyes, she raked one hand through her hair and pushed the tumbled mass back over her shoulder. "Sorry. I, uh…I must have fallen asleep."

"I'll say. You were out like a light. You always did sleep like the dead." And, more often than not, she woke up in an affectionate mood.

Many a morning, his efforts to rouse her had resulted in a round of hurried lovemaking before he'd left for his job at the lumberyard. All warm and rosy, rumpled from sleep and amorous, Livvie had been difficult to resist.

To his amusement, a blush rose from beneath the collar of her sweater, climbed up her neck and spread over her face all the way to her hairline. He knew that she was remembering, too.

Not quite meeting his eyes, she raked her hand through her hair again. "Was there something you wanted?" she asked, then frowned and looked up at the overhead. "Shouldn't you be upstairs driving the boat?"

Joe chuckled. "Honey, it's called above deck, not upstairs. And I came down to tell you that we've arrived."

"In Savannah? Already?" At his nod, she asked, "What time is it?"

"Almost six."

"Oh, dear." Olivia swung her legs over the side of the bunk and shot to her feet. She snatched up a boot and, hopping on one foot, stuffed her other foot into it, muttering under her breath as she struggled with the zipper.

"Hey, take it easy. What's your rush?"

"I don't have much time. I have to rent a car. Which means I have to get to the Hyatt before the concierge leaves for the day."

"Is that all? Don't bother. I'm going to Bella Vista. I'll give you a ride to Flora's." The decision was spur of the moment, but she didn't need to know that. Since she'd shot down his original plan he figured he might as well take care of other business.

Olivia stopped in the act of pulling on the second boot. "I couldn't ask you to do that. It's too much trouble."

"You didn't. I volunteered. And it's no trouble at all. I'll be going right by your mother's place. Within a couple of blocks, anyway."

"That's kind of you, Joe, but I'll still need a car."

"Why? You can walk anywhere you want to go in Bella Vista."

"Yes, but I have to get back early Monday morning to catch a ride back to the island with Cappy, and

I don't want to ask Mom to take me. Driving in Savannah makes her nervous.''

"Then we don't have a problem. I'll be spending the weekend at Winterhaven. I'll pick you up on my way into town and take you back with me.''

He picked up her coat and held it open for her. "Now, then, shall we go?''

Darkness had fallen by the time Olivia and Joe arrived in Bella Vista. He drove directly to Flora's home without asking for directions, which was fortunate, since Olivia had never been there before. Her mother had purchased the house at 204 Elizabeth Lowe Street two years ago when she had retired.

Of course, unless the town had changed dramatically, Olivia could have found her mother's new home with little effort. Bella Vista covered less than two square miles, and she knew every street, alley, riding trail, walking path and shortcut.

"Here we are." Joe stopped his car in front of the small frame house and turned off the engine.

The white picket fence that surrounded the yard glowed an eerie pale blue in the moonlight. Olivia could make out the outline of flower beds bordering the inner perimeter of the fence and lining the walkway and the foundation of the house. Most of the plants were still dormant, but the branches of the crepe myrtles and camellias were heavy with buds and a few early bulbs were sprouting here and there.

Olivia smiled. If her mother had to live in the middle of the Sahara Desert she would somehow manage to have a flower garden.

She glanced at Joe. "Thank you for the ride." Giving him a faint smile, she reached for the door handle.

Her plan was to hop out, grab her suitcase from the back seat and scoot. With any luck, he would drive away before her mother opened the door.

She should have known that Joe was too much of a gentleman for that. He climbed out of the car and sprinted around to her side, and before she could grasp the bag he reached around her and plucked it up. "Here, let me get that for you."

"That's not necessary. I can manage. Anyway, I'm sure you're anxious to get home to Winterhaven."

"Chicken," he teased, grinning. "C'mon. Time to face the music." He grasped her elbow and started up the walkway.

Olivia sighed and went along. She would have preferred to tell her mother about the Mallenegua job *before* she saw her with Joe, but obviously that wasn't going to happen.

"As for going home," Joe continued, "this is one of my obligatory visits to the farm. Although, after our donnybrook last night, Mother probably isn't speaking to me. Anyway, if I don't work a visit in now and then she becomes impossible. Luke is perfectly capable of running the place, but she still insists that I go over the books periodically and double-check everything he's done."

"I don't imagine your brother appreciates that very much."

"No, and I can't say that I blame him. Trust me, it's not one of my favorite ways to spend a weekend, either."

With each step Olivia's nerves tightened. Too late, she realized that she probably should have called to let her mother know that she was coming. Each day she had made excuses—she was too busy, she would get around to it later, her cell phone needed recharging—but in her heart she'd known that the real reason for her procrastination had been fear of hearing her mother tell her not to come.

The shock on Flora's face when she opened the door did nothing to alleviate that fear.

"Livvie! What are you doing here?"

"Hi, Mom. I was in the area on business, so I thought I'd stop by."

"You should have told me that this was a surprise visit," Joe said, stepping out of the porch shadows. "I would have waited by the car while you sprang it."

Flora gasped, and even in the weak light spilling through the open doorway, Olivia saw her mother's face pale.

"Joseph?" Her gaze darted back and forth between him and Olivia. Unconsciously, she splayed her hand over her bosom. "Oh, dear. Oh, my. Wh-what are you two—"

"Who is it, Mom?" Olivia's sister stepped into the tiny foyer and peered over Flora's shoulder. First her eyes widened, then narrowed. "Olivia."

Victoria spoke her name in a flat tone that was more accusation than greeting. "What are you— Oh. Hello, Joe. I didn't see you standing there." She sent Olivia a sharp look, but a shuttered expression came over her face as she turned back to Joe and inquired politely, "What brings you here?"

"Just giving Olivia a lift home."

"Livvie, you should have called. Vicky or I would have come and picked you up at the airport," Flora scolded. She turned to Joe with an apologetic expression. "I'm sorry she put you to so much trouble, Joseph."

"It was no trouble. I was coming to Winterhaven for the weekend, anyway."

"Oh. I see."

Her tone said she didn't "see" at all.

Flora shifted from one foot to the other. Having a Connally on her front porch, particularly Joe, made her nervous and uncomfortable. Olivia could see that her mother was at a loss as to what to do or say next. "Um, would you like to come inside?" she finally offered.

"He can't stay. His mother is expecting him," Olivia said, jumping in before Joe could speak.

One raised eyebrow and the droll look in his eyes told her that he knew he was getting the "bum's rush," but he went along.

"Yes, I'd better be on my way. But thanks." He looked at Olivia's sister. "It was nice seeing you again, Victoria. You, too, Flora. Take care now." He turned to Olivia and winked. "And you I'll see around six Monday morning. Be sure to set your alarm, sleepyhead, or I'll come inside and haul you out of bed myself. And you know what that leads to."

The teasing comment brought a gasp from Flora, and from the corner of her eye Olivia saw her mother and sister exchange shocked looks.

Damn you, Joe, that wasn't funny, she fumed in silence, watching him walk away down the sidewalk and climb into his car. Perversely, though she had wanted him to leave, the instant he drove away Olivia missed his support.

"What did he mean, he'd see you Monday morning? And that he'd pull you out of bed? What's going on between you two?''

Olivia cocked an eyebrow at her sister's tone. ''Do you mind if I come inside before we start the interrogation?''

''Gracious, what was I thinking? Come in, child, come in,'' Flora urged, holding the door open wide.

Once inside, Vicky barely gave her a chance to put down her briefcase and weekender bag.

''Well?''

''It's very simple. We both have to be back in Savannah early Monday morning, so Joe is giving me another lift. That's all.''

Flora's eyes brimmed with distress. ''Oh, Livvie. Child, what are you doing?''

''What do you mean?''

Vicky snorted. ''Yeah, right. Like you don't know. She means what are you doing back here? And with Joe, of all people?''

''As I told Mom, I'm here on business. I don't know if you've heard, but Joe and his partner bought Mallenegua and they are going to turn it into an exclusive spa.''

''We heard. One of those chi-chi places where jet-setters with more money than sense go,'' Vicky sneered.

''Everyone in town is talking about it.'' Flora shivered. ''For the life of me, I can't imagine why anyone in their right mind would go near that place. Everyone knows it's haunted.''

''Oh, Mom, surely you don't believe those old stories?'' Olivia chided.

''I most certainly do. I know people who have actually seen Theobald walking along the cliffs. Anyway, it's not just the ghosts. For more than a hundred and thirty years Mallen Island has been known to be an evil place. I've heard tales about what goes on out there, and believe you me, they could curl your hair. Torture and murder. Even cannibalism.'' Flora shivered again and rubbed the gooseflesh on her arms. ''You couldn't pay me to go anywhere near Mallen Island.''

''Strange as it sounds, it's exactly those kind of stories that will bring guests to the spa. The island's reputation will be the drawing card, the twist that none of the other exclusive spas have.''

''What does all this have to do with you hanging around Joe again?'' Vicky demanded.

Olivia ground her teeth. ''I am not *hanging around* Joe, as you so elegantly put it. I'm working for him. I've been hired as the interior designer for the project.''

Instead of alleviating her mother's concern, she seemed to have distressed Flora more than ever. ''Oh, Livvie. Child, you aren't seriously considering taking the job?''

''I already have. The contracts are signed. I just spent an entire week at Mallenegua.''

''Oh, my word.'' Flora put her hand over her heart and plopped down on the sofa as though her knees had buckled beneath her. ''You *went* there? You actually *slept* in that horrible place? Praise the Lord I didn't know about that. I'd've been a nervous wreck if I had.''

''It was an interesting experience. I slept in the master bedroom, in the very bed that Theobald Mallen used.''

''Oh, Livvie!''

Olivia chuckled. "Relax, Mom. It was perfectly safe. Nothing happened."

Well…not unless you counted a couple of ghost sightings, she amended silently. However, she had no intention of telling her mother about either of those incidents. The more she had thought about them, the more convinced she'd become that she had let her imagination run away with her. Relaying the stories would only upset her mother and lend credence to the silly ghost tales.

"You'll just have to quit," Vicky declared. "You should never have taken the job in the first place."

"Quit? Don't be ridiculous. I'm not going to pass up this opportunity. This is the dream of a lifetime for an interior designer."

"That may be, but your sister is right. You can't possibly work for Joe."

Olivia gritted her teeth. Despite everything, she loved her mother. She had hoped to talk to her calmly and avoid a head-on confrontation, but she'd had enough of other people interfering in her life.

"Why do you say that? Joe doesn't have a problem with it, nor do I."

"Right off the top of my head, I can think of several reasons," Vicky charged. "First and foremost, his mother will be furious."

"She is, but that's her problem, not mine."

"Oh, please. You know that she'll make it yours. And ours. My husband still works at Winterhaven, remember? She could fire Travis and cut off Mama's pension."

"That won't happen. Joe and Luke are in charge of the farm now. They wouldn't let her get away with that."

"Even so, Mama and I have to live in this town. If you continue with this, all the nasty talk will start again. People will whisper and laugh at us behind our backs. Do you have any idea how embarrassing it was for Mama and me the last time you got involved with Joe Connally? Do you know what people here call you? That low-class gold digger, that's what. They all say you lured Joe into your bed and got pregnant on purpose so that he would have to marry you. That you just wanted to get your hands on all that lovely Connally money."

"That's not true. I would have married Joe if he hadn't had a dime, which he didn't when his mother cut him off. I loved him."

"Love!" Flora made a disparaging sound. "What fairy-tale nonsense. You always were a romantic dreamer, just like your papa. And that's what worries me. I'm afraid if you're around Joe too much you'll fall in love with him all over again.

"Child, when are you ever going to get it through your head? The Joe Connallys of the world are not for the likes of simple people like us. Especially not in Savannah or Bella Vista. Here old money marries old money. Trust me on this, baby. I'm your mama and I know what's best for you. I'm just trying to keep you from getting hurt again, is all."

"I promise you, that's not going to happen. I got over Joe years ago. I'm sorry, Mama, but I'm not going to give up this opportunity. I have my business to think of."

"Ah, here it comes. I knew that sooner or later we'd get around to your precious 'business.'"

"What does that mean?"

"Now, Victoria, there's no need to get nasty."

Their mother nervously looked from one daughter to the other.

Vicky ignored her. "You just love to throw it in our faces, don't you? 'Look at me,' she mimicked in a mincing falsetto. "'*I* went to college. *I* have my own business. And a pricey car. And a fancy-schmancy town house. I make oodles and oodles of money and associate with society types.'" She shot Olivia a searing look. "You think you're better than us. You always have."

"That's not true," Olivia protested, but she could have saved her breath. On a roll, her sister barreled on.

"Oh, yes it is. Even as a child you were never satisfied. You were just like Papa, always dreaming about a better life, always wanting more than what you were born to."

"If by that you mean I wanted to do something with my life, to get an education and accomplish something on my own, then you're right. But I never claimed to be better than you. I just wanted something different."

"Huh. Everyone knows what you wanted. You wouldn't have dreamed of marrying a horse trainer like my Travis, or any other poor working stiff. Oh, no. That wasn't good enough for Papa's little princess. Why don't you admit it? From the day we moved to Winterhaven Farm you set your sights on the big house and someday becoming its mistress."

"That simply isn't true."

Vicky gave a derisive snort. "Yeah, right."

Olivia felt as though she'd been cut to the bone. All of her life, Vicky's attitude toward her had vac-illated between affection and resentment, but until now she hadn't understood just how deep her sister's envy and rancor ran.

Olivia lifted her chin. "I didn't realize that you disliked me so much. Or disapproved of my ambition quite so strenuously. If I had I wouldn't have come here tonight."

She sat down in her mother's easy chair and reached for the telephone on the side table. "Does Truman Perkins still operate that taxi service back and forth between Bella Vista and Savannah?"

"Yes. Why?"

"Given the hatred you feel toward me, I think it would be best if I left. I'll get a hotel room in Savannah."

"Oh, child, don't leave. Please," Flora pleaded, wringing her hands. "Your sister doesn't hate you. Tell her, Victoria."

For a moment Vicky's expression remained sullen, but finally she sighed and relented. "Oh, of course I don't hate you."

With reluctant affection, she bent over and gave Olivia a hug. "Don't be silly. You're my baby sister. I love you. Stay, stay. You and Mama can have a nice visit over the weekend. And I'll drop by again after church on Sunday with your niece and nephew. You won't believe how they've grown." She checked her watch. "But right now I have to run or I'll be late picking the kids up from the movie."

She gave Olivia another hug, pecked Flora's cheek and sailed out the front door. Seconds later came the rumble of a diesel engine as the pickup truck reversed out of the driveway. Then the sound faded into the distance.

With forced cheerfulness, Flora slapped her palms

against the tops of her thighs. "There now, you see? Everything's going to be just fine."

"How'd it go?" Joe asked when Olivia climbed into his car on Monday morning.

Groaning, she leaned her head back against the neck rest and closed her eyes.

"Tough weekend?"

She opened one eye and shot him a pithy look.

"That bad, huh? I take it your mother didn't approve of our arrangement any more than mine did?"

"You could say that. She and Vicky are afraid I'll make a fool of myself over you all over again and embarrass them."

"Honey, you've never made a fool of yourself in your life. You have far too much dignity and class for that."

"Try telling that to my family. I explained that there was zero chance of anything of a romantic nature happening between us, that I wasn't in love with you anymore, but they didn't believe me."

"Ouch. Zero? Damn, sweetheart, you really know how to cut a guy off at the knees. I was kinda hoping my chances were better than that."

She opened both eyes this time and skewered him with a baleful stare. "Not funny, Connally."

He smiled, but his dark eyes glittered with a determination she remembered from long ago. "It wasn't meant to be. It wasn't a joke."

"What's that supposed to mean?"

"It means that I'm attracted to you. Very attracted. More than I've ever been to any woman." Over the weekend he'd decided to ditch the subtle approach. It wasn't his style and didn't seem to be working for him anyway.

She laughed and rolled her eyes.

"You can't be serious."

"Oh, I'm very serious."

"Oh, please. If you're attracted to me—which I don't believe for a minute—it's nothing more than propinquity."

"Propinquity?"

"It means I'm handy. You know, like the old song says, 'When I'm not near the girl I love, I love the girl I'm near.'"

"I *know* what *propinquity* means. I just can't believe you'd think that."

"Face it. You're working almost twenty-four/seven on an island where I'm one of two women, and the other one is a crone. And you're a normal male with a healthy sex drive. Ergo…"

Joe threw his head back and let loose a booming laugh. "Oh, baby, you're priceless," he sputtered. "I gotta admit, though, you would know."

Olivia's cheeks burned, and he chuckled again. "But you couldn't be more wrong. Trust me, if all I wanted was a woman—*any* woman—all I would have to do is take a quick boat ride to Savannah." He gave her a look that made her toes curl. "I want you," he stated in a deep, sexy rumble. "And for more than just sex."

Her jaw dropped, and for several seconds all she could do was stare at him with her mouth open.

Outside the windows the dewy Georgia countryside flew by and the rising sun tinted every tiny droplet with gold, but she didn't notice. "That's…that's insane."

"Why?"

"Because…"

"Because why?"

"Because…we have a history. Not a pleasant one at that. We're divorced, for heaven's sake. You surely don't believe that you and I can ever have any sort of romantic relationship."

"Why not? I'm single. You're single. And we're different people now. We're no longer a couple of green kids. We're mature adults who know what we want." He grinned and winked. "At least I do. An attraction this strong doesn't come along all that often. We'd be fools not to see where it leads us.

"Furthermore, I don't think the attraction is all one-sided. The physical side of our marriage was spectacular, and that electricity is still there. I can feel it crackling between us whenever we're in the same room, and I think you can, too."

"Joe—"

"C'mon, sugar, I'm not blind. Don't even try to deny it."

Flouncing back in her seat, Olivia folded her arms over her midriff and stared straight ahead. "I never said I didn't find you attractive," she said with as much hauteur as she could muster. "Just that I no longer loved you." Her heart pounded against her rib cage as though she had just run a marathon, and she felt flustered and confused, but she couldn't let him see that.

"Well, then, I guess I'll just have to see if I can change that."

"Trust me, you'd be setting yourself up for failure. Once you've gotten over those kinds of feelings, there is no going back."

"Hmm. Maybe. But then, I'm a determined kind of guy." He angled a smoldering look her way. "You don't mind if I give it a try, do you?"

Olivia turned her head and met his gaze. "And what if I said I did mind?"

"Then I'd have to ask why. If you're so sure that your feelings for me are dead, what are you afraid of?"

Olivia narrowed her eyes. Oh, he was clever. Very clever. "I'm not afraid of anything. Certainly not you."

"Good. Then go out with me next weekend."

"Next weekend I'm going to look for an apartment."

"Great. I'll help you. Then afterward we'll take in a movie."

"A movie?"

"Okay, if you don't want to see a movie, we could go dancing. Or I know this little place where we could just sit and listen to the piano player."

"Joe, I don't think that's a good idea. To allow any sort of romantic relationship to develop between us would be entering dangerous territory. Even a casual fling would be foolish."

"A fling, huh? Now, there's a thought. I think we should have a courtship first, though, don't you? But let's get back to next weekend. If you don't want to go to a movie or dancing or pub crawling, we could go roller blading."

Olivia blinked at him. *"Roller blading?"*

"Sure. Why not? I've never tried it, but it looks like fun. And they say you haven't lived until you've skated around the squares on Bull Street at midnight. How about it? You game?"

Olivia lips twitched. She couldn't help it. She tried not to laugh, but she had a mental picture of the courtly, well-mannered Joseph Connally whizzing around Montgomery Square, and the elegant homes that surrounded it, on roller blades in the dead of night. Finally, giving up, she laughed out loud.

"A movie sounds more my speed, but—"

"Great. A movie it is."

Thirteen

The following week Olivia had little time to worry about Joe or his intentions. On the drive into Savannah she had tried to discourage him and get out of the date he had tricked her into, but he managed to cleverly override all her arguments. Finally she'd closed her eyes and pretended to ignore him, and once on *Fleeting Dreams* she'd again claimed drowsiness from her seasick medication and retired below deck.

Once they reached Mallenegua they found the island a beehive of activity. Except for a few last-minute touches on the bait house and marina shop, work on the new piers was finished. Now the crews had turned their attention to the house.

A landscaping firm was cleaning out the debris in the gardens and pruning and tagging shrubs and plants that were to be either removed or transplanted.

Inside the house a demolition crew had already started knocking out walls and reinforcing floors in the attic servants' quarters.

For the next three days Olivia and L.J. continued to take inventory of the items stored in the attic. It was dirty work and Olivia dressed accordingly in jeans, a sweatshirt and tennis shoes, her hair pulled back in a ponytail with a bandanna covering it. One afternoon she was perched on a stepladder, inspecting the carving on a tall armoire, when a deep masculine voice drawled, "Now, that's the Livvie I remember."

Olivia twisted around and saw Joe standing a few feet away, his arms crossed over his chest, grinning up at her.

"Joe. What are you doing here?"

"I came to see what you were up to. And to tell you it's lunchtime."

"Oh, dear. I lost all track of time." Olivia started to climb down the ladder, but Joe clamped his hands around her waist and lifted her down as though she weighed no more than a feather. He placed her on her feet before him but kept his hands clasped around her waist.

"Be still," he commanded, pulling a white handkerchief from his pocket. "You've got a smudge on your nose. While I think you look cute as a speckled pup, Mrs. Jaffee might object." He wiped the tip of her nose with the handkerchief, then leaned back to inspect his handiwork. "There. You look fine." He dropped a quick kiss on her lips and deftly turned her toward the door, slipping his arm around her waist. "Shall we go?"

"I…I guess so. Oh, wait."

She stopped and looked at L.J., and found that his sullen gaze was fixed on Joe. If looks could kill, Joe would have been felled on the spot. When L.J. noticed that she was watching him, he quickly turned away and pretended to be busy.

"It's time to break for lunch, L.J. I'm going down to the dining room. I'll see you back here in about an hour. Okay?"

"Okay. Sure," he mumbled, not looking at her.

"Hmm. Looks like I have competition," Joe murmured as he and Olivia started down the stairs.

"Don't be silly. L.J. is just shy, is all."

At least she hoped that was all it was. The last thing she needed was to have a lovesick assistant following her around.

Midweek, just after breakfast, while Joe went upstairs to consult with Mike, Olivia remained in the library and made several telephone calls to suppliers and antique dealers. She had just hung up the receiver when someone tapped on the frame of the open door.

"May I come in?"

"Blair. How did you get here?"

"I rode out with Cappy."

Cappy and the crewmen had arrived on the island nearly three hours ago. Where, Olivia wondered, had Blair been all that time?

"I see." To hide her discomfort, Olivia picked up a stack of papers and tapped the edges against the desk to straighten them. "You'll find Joe upstairs in the attic of the southwest wing."

"Actually...I didn't come to see Joe. I came to see you."

"Me? I don't believe we have anything to talk about, Blair. You made your feelings about me being here fairly clear last week at Joe's apartment. If you came here to try to talk me into quitting, don't bother. I won't do that."

"That's not why I came."

"It's not?"

"No, but good for you. I hope you do stay."

Olivia didn't try to hide her skepticism. "Then why are you here, Blair?"

''To tell you that I'm sorry. For what I did fourteen years ago. For not answering your letters. For how I've behaved since you've been back.''

She paused and looked expectantly at Olivia, but she merely gazed back, her expression unchanged. Blair grimaced and fiddled with the strap on her shoulder bag. ''Would it be all right if I came in?''

Olivia wanted to say no, that she didn't want to dig up the past or remember the hurt the betrayal had dealt her, but her former friend looked so miserable she didn't have the heart. She nodded. ''Sure. Come in.''

Blair sat down on one of the twin settees in front of the fireplace, placing her bag and a folder on the cushion beside her. Olivia moved to the opposite settee. Looking down at the settee's silk damask upholstery, Blair traced the tone-on-tone pattern with her crimson fingernail.

''What I did was terrible,'' she said softly, not meeting Olivia's eyes. ''We were best friends. I should have defied Mother and told you the truth.''

''So why didn't you?''

Blair gave a little huff of mirthless laughter. ''Believe it or not I had a reason, although now it seems kind of lame. Mother threatened to destroy Prince Rupert if I didn't back up her story.''

''I see. I knew you loved that horse but, silly me, I would have assumed that I counted for more—that our friendship counted for more.''

''You did! It did! I panicked, is all. And...''

''Yes?''

''And at the time I was angry with you for not confiding in me about what had happened between you and Joe. And for running off and getting married without a word to me. We were best friends, and up until that point, we'd shared all our secrets." She shrugged one shoulder. "I know now it was silly of me to expect you to confide something so private, but I was hurt."

"So you struck back."

. "I guess Mother's threat gave me the excuse I needed."

Her honesty took Olivia by surprise. After all this time the fact that the girl she'd known was finally examining her motivations and delving into her psyche to discover the truth about herself was remarkable. Still, Olivia kept her guard up.

"I regretted what I'd done the minute the words were out of my mouth," Blair continued. "That's why I didn't answer your letters. I felt too guilty. That's also why I was upset when I saw you again. I couldn't bear to face you."

"So what has changed? That was only last week. Why the sudden confession and apology? What do you hope to gain by all this?"

A half smile of chagrin twisted Blair's mouth. "You know me so well, don't you. You're right. There is something I'm hoping to get out of this. I want us to be friends again."

"Oh, Blair, I don't think—"

"Wait. Hear me out before you say no. Please."

Olivia hesitated, but she couldn't withstand Blair's pleading gaze. "Oh, all right. Go ahead."

Blair shifted on the settee and plucked at a loose thread in the piping. "Well, you see…last week Joe called me into his office and reamed me out good for what I did to you."

"What! I asked him not to do that. I'm sorry, Blair. He shouldn't have."

"Oh, no. I'm glad he did. He said something that made me realize that I had to face you and ask your forgiveness."

"Oh? What was that?"

"He reminded me that I could have used a friend like you these past ten years."

"You mean during your marriage?"

"Yes. I know that it's all my own fault. I'm the one who ruined our friendship. But if I'd had you to talk to, your shoulder to cry on, I probably wouldn't have wasted ten years with a man who used me as a punching bag. Heck, I wouldn't have married him in the first place."

"Oh, Blair. I am sorry. No one should have to go through that. But why didn't you tell Joe and Luke? They would have gotten you out of there and given him a taste of his own medicine while they were at it."

Blair spread her hands in a helpless gesture. "It's a long story. Suffice to say that abusers have ways of making their spouses feel powerless and alone. And terrified. Besides, I was afraid that if I went to my brothers they would end up in jail for assault."

Leaning forward on the settee, she gazed at Olivia, everything about her—her expression, her eyes, her body language—a silent plea. "I know what I did was awful. I shattered the special bond we had, and that was unforgivable. But you've always been a forgiving person, Livvie. That's why I'm hoping that you'll find it in your heart to at least let me try to make up for what I did."

"I don't know, Blair. It's impossible to go back

and undo past events. What's done is done. To be brutally honest, I don't see how I could ever trust you again.''

''I understand. And I don't blame you. You have every right to feel that way. But I swear to you on my daddy's grave I will never let you down again. No matter what. Please, Livvie. Won't you give me another chance? I want my friend back.''

Torn, Olivia turned her head and looked out the French doors at the terrace garden. Two workmen were busy pruning trees and bushes and carrying away litter. Blair seemed genuinely sorry, but Olivia didn't trust her. She felt bad for the uncharitable thought, yet she could not help but wonder if this attempt to get back in her good graces was a ruse so that she could carry out some scheme of Eleanore's.

Part of Olivia wanted to tell her former friend that she wasn't interested in being pulled back into the past and old relationships. She had put all that behind her years ago and had moved on. But she had to admit, there was another tiny part of her that yearned for the special bond that she and Blair had shared as girls.

In the end, she couldn't bring herself to look at Blair's beseeching face and say no.

''All right. I'm willing to give it a try. Just don't expect too much too soon. Okay?''

''I won't, I swear. Oh, this is wonderful!'' Blair bounced up off the settee and hurried to Olivia's side and flung her arms around her. ''Thank you, Livvie. Thank you so much. You won't regret this. I promise.''

I hope not, Olivia thought, tentatively returning the impulsive hug.

"Hey, what's going on in here? I didn't expect to find you two together."

At the sound of Joe's voice, Olivia disentangled herself from Blair's embrace and his sister bounced up again and hurried to meet him as he strode into the room. "Oh, Joe, I have the most wonderful news. Livvie and I talked, and she's accepted my apology. She's going to give me another chance." She hugged her brother and looked at Olivia with a fond smile. "You were right. Livvie is a sweetheart."

"Great. I'm glad you two have patched things up. Your friendship was too special to lose."

He aimed a piercing look at his sister. "Now, then. Why don't you tell me what you're doing here during the middle of the day. Shouldn't you be at work?"

Blair looked at Olivia and rolled her eyes. "We're working for a slave driver. It so happens, I *am* working. Caroline sent me out here to get your signature on these contracts." She retrieved the folder from the settee and gave it to him.

"Uh-huh. After you talked her into it so you'd have an excuse to come out here."

"Now, I ask you, would I do that?" Blair asked with extreme innocence, fluttering her eyelashes.

He gave her an under-the-brow stare, but it was obvious he was pleased that she had made the effort to see Olivia.

Blair stayed for lunch, during which she wheedled her brother into giving her a tour of the mansion. Throughout the meal, though Olivia remained cautiously quiet, she could not help but smile at Joe's vivacious sister.

As always, Blair dominated the conversation. She was the Scarlett O'Hara of her day—brunette, beautiful, coquettish and brimming with sass and daring and feminine wiles. She may have gone through some rough times in her marriage, but basically she was the same old Blair.

After lunch, Olivia excused herself and went to her room to refresh her lipstick and call her office on her cell phone. She was halfway across the bedroom when the envelope propped against one of the pillows on the bed caught her eye. Curious, she went to investigate.

Affixed to the outside of the plain white envelope were letters that looked as though they'd been individually cut from magazines, spelling out OLIVIA.

Feeling more uneasy by the second, she opened the flap and pulled out a sheet of folded paper. The message it contained had been constructed in the same fashion. Simple and to the point, it read YOU ARE NOT WANTED HERE. GET OUT. NOW.

Olivia stared at the note, her heart pounding. Who could have done this? It didn't take long for an answer to come to her. The only one who wanted her gone was Eleanore. And possibly Blair. And Blair had been on the island for several hours before she had stopped by the library.

She started to toss the note in the trash can, but something told her to hold on to it, and she slipped it into a bureau drawer instead. So much for reconciliation.

Olivia made herself scarce the rest of the day until she was certain that Blair had left the island. Briefly, she considered showing Joe the note, but something held her back. He'd said he was attracted to her, however, that, too, may have been a ruse to put her off guard. But it didn't make sense that Joe was in any way involved with the note; why hire her if he didn't want her around? And if he'd changed his mind, he could have done nothing when Reese fired her.

Her thoughts went around in circles until Olivia grew annoyed with herself. In the end she decided that the best way to handle the situation was to ignore it—and to keep her guard up around Blair.

That evening during dinner Joe discovered that Olivia played chess. Afterward he coaxed her into a match. He was an excellent player, which was no more than she expected, but the level of her expertise seemed to come as a surprise to him. The first game he beat her, but just barely. "Where did you learn to play so well?" he asked halfway through the second game.

"One of my professors in college taught me. He was a former national champion and mad for the game."

"Oh? It's a little unusual for a professor to take that kind of interest in a student, isn't it? How old a guy was he?" he asked a shade too casually.

Olivia looked up. "I worked as his assistant. And he was a silver-haired old gentleman in his sixties who walked with a cane. He'd also been married to the love of his life for forty years." She moved her bishop. "Checkmate."

Joe looked over the board, frowning. "Damn. You're good."

"Thank you. Now, if you'll excuse me, I think I'll turn in."

"So early? You can't quit now when we're even. How about a tie-breaker?"

"Some other time. I have a headache. I'd better

take something and have an early night before it gets out of hand.'' It wasn't a fib. The tension of the day was catching up with her, and the muscles in the back of her neck and shoulders were wound as tight as a fiddle string. A dull throbbing had already started at the base of her skull.

Joe jumped up. ''You should have said something earlier. C'mon, I'll walk you to your room.''

''Joe, that's not necess—''

''Shh. Don't argue.'' He put his arm around her shoulders, pulled her close against his side and led her from the room.

His broad shoulder was right there, so inviting and strong, and when he reached around and tenderly cupped her head with his other hand and guided it down to rest against him, she didn't resist. She felt lousy and drained, and it had been so long since she had had a shoulder to lean on—not since before her father passed away—so for those few moments she let herself enjoy the novel sensation of being protected.

At her door he turned her to face him, holding her shoulders in a firm grip. ''Are you going to be okay?''

''Yes. It's just a tension headache. I get them now and then. My doctor gave me a prescription for them. I'll be fine by morning.''

''Good. You'll call me if you need anything, won't you? I'm in the last room at the end of the hall on the same side.''

''Joe, I'll be fine.''

He scowled, and she blew out her breath in an exasperated huff. ''Oh, all right. I'll come bang on your door if I need anything. I promise. Happy now?''

His scowl changed to a wicked grin. ''Not yet, but

I'll get there,'' he murmured, and lowered his head. His lips settled on hers, hot and soft and oh so seductive. Releasing her shoulders, he wrapped his arms around her and pulled her close—so close their bodies seemed to fuse together from shoulder to knee.

At first Olivia went utterly still, too surprised to react. Then, as his lips rocked over hers with barely restrained hunger, she shivered from head to toe.

The tiny reaction seemed to inflame Joe. A low growl rumbled from his throat, and he widened his stance. Sliding one hand down to her lower spine, he brought her hips tighter against the hard evidence of his desire.

A tiny, helpless whimper escaped Olivia. Seemingly of their own volition, her arms looped around his neck, and she sagged against him, giving herself up to the voluptuous kiss. It was hot and carnal, and tugged at a need in her so long denied.

Somewhere in the recesses of her mind the logical, sensible part of her nagged to be heard—this was insane, reckless, self-destructive—but common sense and caution had no chance against the intense pleasure. It had been so long since she'd been held like this, kissed like this, desired like this. It had been so long since she'd felt Joe's arms around her, his body pressed to hers.

With a suddenness that was shocking, Joe broke off the kiss and set her away from him. Vaguely, Olivia was grateful for the support of the door at her back. Every cell in her body was vibrating and her legs had the rigidity of cooked noodles.

Joe's chest heaved. Even in the dim light she could see the desire burning in his eyes and in the dark flush of his skin.

"I'm sorry, sweetheart," he gasped out between raspy breaths. "But if I don't stop now, while I still can, in about thirty seconds you and I are going to be naked in that big bed in there. Mind you, there's nothing I want more, but I would be less than a gentleman if I made love to you when you're not feeling well."

He bent and gave her another quick peck on the lips. "Good night, sugar." Before Olivia could gather her wits or utter a word, he turned her around, opened the door and gave her a little shove. "Take your medicine and go to bed. And if that headache isn't gone soon, come get me."

The next thing she knew she was inside her room leaning back against the door. Dazed, she blinked several times. Headache? She'd forgotten all about her headache. Tentatively, she touched the nape of her neck, but the sickening throbbing had slackened to barely a tap.

Closing her eyes, Olivia leaned her head back against the door. Sweet Mother Mary and Joseph. At twenty-one Joe had been a wonderful lover, but at thirty-five the man was positively lethal.

At first Olivia thought she had imagined the sound, or had dreamed it, but there it was again—the stealthy tread of footsteps crossing the floor. She lay on her right side, facing away from whoever was sneaking across the room.

A board creaked, and the footsteps stopped. The hair on the back of Olivia's neck prickled. She lay still, pretending to sleep, not daring to move. After what seemed an eternity the footsteps sounded again, this time much slower. She realized the intruder was moving away from the bed.

Deliberately, she made a sleepy sound and turned over, and the steps halted again. Snuggling her face deeper into the pillow, she pretended to sleep until finally the footsteps started up again. Olivia barely opened her eyes, but could see nothing but shadowy blackness. Through the veil of her lashes, she looked at the luminous green dial on her travel clock sitting on the bedside table. It was three forty-eight in the morning.

For an indeterminable time the only sound she heard was her own breathing and the drum of her heartbeat reverberating in her ears. Was he walking on the rugs? Or had he slipped out without her hearing?

She waited, checking the clock every few seconds. When twenty minutes had passed with no more sounds, she screwed up her courage, threw back the covers, swung her legs over the side of the bed and sat up. She waited to the count of ten, her heart booming like a kettledrum. Then she reached out and turned on the bedside lamp.

There was no one there.

The next morning Joe received an urgent call from Reese and had to fly to Alexandria. He apologized profusely for not being able to keep their date that weekend.

"I really am sorry, Olivia. I'll make up for it next weekend. I promise."

"Don't worry about it. As it turns out, I need to go home this weekend. One of my best clients wants to consult with me about redoing her guest house. She won't deal with anyone else." Actually the client wasn't in any hurry, but the project gave her an excuse to go home.

"That sounds like a big job. You're not taking on too much, are you?"

"Not at all. I'll meet with the client, work up a design plan, and if she approves it, Mary Beth can handle the execution."

"Okay, fine." Joe checked his watch. "Damn." He cupped his hands around Olivia's shoulders and looked at her with unabashed hunger. "I'd much rather stay here and go to the movies with you, but I can't. I don't know when I'll be back, but be sure to keep next weekend open, okay?"

Before she could reply he bent and kissed her full on the lips, a long, possessive kiss that fired her blood and made her toes curl inside her Italian pumps. "See you in a few days." For good measure he gave her another quick kiss, then he strode out the door, leaving Olivia staring after him, breathless and dazed.

The next day Olivia flew home to Atlanta for the weekend. She needed to get away from Mallenegua, and from Joe, and touch base with her real world and the safe, familiar life she'd built for herself. She met with her client on Friday evening, and by the end of the weekend she had a rough presentation worked up for the guest-house renovation.

On Saturday night she went to dinner with friends and spent the rest of the weekend working and returning telephone calls from clients.

As a respite, however, the weekend was a failure. At night her dreams were dominated by a shadowy figure that hovered over her bed, and during the day, no matter what she did, thoughts of Joe kept creeping in.

On Monday she returned to Mallen Island and learned from Mike that Joe was still in Alexandria and didn't know when he'd be back.

Since he had scheduled the renovations to start at the top of the mansion and work down, while he was gone, Olivia, with L.J.'s help, spent the time in one of the attic's west wings, measuring and sketching the existing staff quarters and working in the library at the drafting table.

She studied the blueprints in detail. In the staff attic space Joe's plans called for knocking out walls to double the size of each room, and adding a few more bathrooms at intervals along the hallway. The spec detail indicated that insulation and central heat and air-conditioning were to be added as well.

The improvements were sorely needed, but to Olivia's way of thinking the plan stopped short of what should be done.

Wasting little time worrying about how he would react to her suggestions, she set to work on plans of her own for the space. Joe, after all, had said that he wanted her input. Well he was going to get it.

She spent three days working from dawn until dark, coming up with ways to expand and reconfigure the staff quarters into small but comfortable apartments and to add the expected modern amenities, plus an employees' lounge and recreation room.

The fourth morning, Olivia entered the dining room and had just taken her seat when Mrs. Jaffee marched in from the butler's pantry carrying a serving tray.

"I know you usually eat like a bird, but you're having eggs and sausage this morning, like 'em or not," she said ungraciously, plunking a plate piled high with food down in front of Olivia. "Cappy's bringing more supplies today and I had to cook these up."

"Eggs and sausage will be fine, thank you."

"Good. You ask me, you could use some meat on those bones of yours."

"Mmm," Olivia replied, taking a sip of coffee.

Meals at Mallenegua were not something that she enjoyed. Not that the food was inferior, far from it. Mrs. Jaffee was an excellent cook. However, since Olivia's first morning on the island the housekeeper had insisted that she was a guest and must be treated as such, which meant she must eat in one of the mansion's formal dining rooms. Olivia had chosen this one, which was quaintly called the family dining room, only because the twenty-by-thirty-foot room was the smallest of the lot.

The idea of eating alone at the long table for twelve was so unappealing that, in desperation, Olivia had made the mistake the first morning of asking Mrs. Jaffee to join her. The suggestion so scandalized the housekeeper that anyone would have thought Olivia had committed heresy. Nor would she allow Olivia to eat in the kitchen with her.

During each meal Olivia sat in isolated splendor at the long table feeling foolish, which, she suspected, was exactly what Mrs. Jaffee wanted.

Olivia ate all she could of the hearty breakfast and was taking her last sip of coffee when the housekeeper returned to collect the dishes.

"You've hardly stepped outside all week," the old woman grumbled. "You've let three days of great weather slip by without taking advantage of it. Now the winds have kicked up and there're dark clouds on the horizon. You oughta take a break and get some fresh air while you can, before things turn nasty again.''

Olivia suspected that Mrs. Jaffee was merely trying to get rid of her, but the idea did have appeal. She had finished a rough draft of her plans for the attic space and could use a break. The ocean breeze would help clear her head before she went back to work.

If nothing else, it would be a relief to be by herself for a while, to not feel Mrs. Jaffee's disapproving stare boring into her back or see the flutter of a black skirt disappearing around the corner at every turn.

Olivia went in search of L.J. to tell him she was going for a walk before she started the day's work. She found him in the staff's quarters, already working, taking up where they had left off the day before.

''Good idea,'' he told her. ''You need to get out of this house for a while. And don't worry about me. I can measure these rooms on my own.''

''Thanks, L.J. I won't be gone long. Just an hour or so.''

The instant Olivia stepped outside, the wind whipped her coat around her, plastering it to her body, and sent her hair flying every which way. She looked up, squinting her eyes against the glare. Mrs. Jaffee had been right; the sky threatened rain and the wind off the Atlantic carried a nip. All the same, it did feel invigorating to be outside after being cooped up for days.

She bundled her coat closer around her body, wrapped a long, green wool scarf around her head and neck and set off.

For a while she wandered through the courtyard and gardens. Then, on impulse, she decided to venture out a bit and do a little exploring.

She set off through the meadow behind the house, heading toward the line of trees on the opposite side that marked the beginning of the pine forest. From that point the forest floor began a gentle five-mile slope downward, all the way to the opposite end of the island. There a horseshoe-shaped, white sand beach wrapped around both sides of the southern point until it reached the cliffs, which rose, stark and threatening, from the churning sea.

Hoping she might find a trail through the woods that would lead her to the opposite end of the island and the beach, Olivia explored along the perimeter of the forest. By the time she reached the top of the cliffs on the windward side, it became obvious that either the trails had grown over, or there had never been any in the first place.

Cautiously, Olivia inched closer to the cliff edge and peeked over. One look and she jumped back, her heart pounding. Already she was beginning to regret the impulse that had brought her here.

Tucking a strand of whipping hair back under her scarf, she looked around at the desolate scene. There was something sinister and forbidding about this part of the island, she realized. An aura of violence and waiting danger that was almost palpable.

Maybe it was the constant roar and crash of the surf, or the howl of wind, or the damp cold that created the malevolent atmosphere. Or maybe it was simply the unyielding harshness of the terrain. Whatever, there was something about the cliffs that made Olivia's skin crawl.

An icy blast of wind lifted her hair off her neck. She turned up her coat collar, and with her arms hugged tight against her body, she crept to the edge again and peered over.

Olivia shivered. Far below, ocean waves crashed over jagged boulders with an unending, vicious fury, then churned and swirled around the rocks before being sucked out to sea again.

This must be where Theobald Mallen fell to his death more than ninety years ago, she thought. She shivered again.

The wind was out of the northwest, biting and damp, blowing across the island in powerful gusts. Hunching her shoulders, Olivia hugged her arms tighter and took a step back from the edge.

The next instant a powerful gust slapped her back like a hand, and sent her stumbling forward with a terrified cry.

Pebbles clattered over the precipice and dropped as though in slow motion into the churning waters far below. Teetering on the edge, Olivia made desperate little sounds and windmilled her arms, her horrified gaze fixed on the razor-sharp rocks at the base of the cliff.

They seemed to call to her mockingly, exerting some sort of magnetic pull. The wind caught one end of her scarf and unfurled it like a banner. A low, keening wail of purest terror tore from Olivia as she flailed her arms and fought as hard as she could against the twin forces of gravity and momentum dragging her, inexorably, over the edge.

She was toppling over the edge when her flailing right hand came in contact with something. Her fingers closed around the object, latching on like grim death. An instant later, her heart in her throat, Olivia realized that she had managed to snag a low-hanging branch of a pine sapling.

The young tree's trunk was not much bigger than a fishing pole and bent almost double under Olivia's weight. She hung by one hand, feet braced against the side of the cliff, as though trying to rappel down the face, her body angled out over the deadly two-hundred-foot drop.

Olivia knew the sapling would not hold her for long, but every attempt she made to pull herself up against the punishing wind failed. Worse, she had grabbed hold of a clump of slick pine needles at the end of a branch, and slowly but surely she was losing her grip.

Fourteen

Where could she be?

With growing concern, Joe asked himself that question while striding along the edge of the woods, peering into the tangled undergrowth, looking for any sign that she had entered. He didn't think Olivia would be foolish enough to try to reach the beach by cutting through the forest, not in the shape it was in, but where else could she be? Mrs. Jaffee had said that she'd gone for a walk, and he'd checked everywhere else.

He cupped his hands over his mouth. "Olivia! Olivia, where are you?" He waited a couple of seconds but heard nothing. Which didn't surprise him. The wind snatched his words away the instant they left his lips. "Dammit, Livvie! Where *are* you?" he bellowed, cresting the slight rise just before the cliff's edge. "Answer me!"

Something caught his eye. It looked like a green banner flapping and popping in the wind from just beneath the cliff's edge. It looked like a woman's scarf. "Holy—"

Joe's heart stopped, then kicked into overdrive with a tremendous thump. He raced toward the cliff edge. When he got within ten feet he spotted her.

Holding on for dear life to a spindly sapling, Olivia

hung over the side of the cliff, feet braced against the side, her body ramrod straight, as though she were attempting to walk along the perpendicular wall of stone. Her fiery hair and long green scarf waved in the wind.

He was still a short distance away when, without warning, Olivia's precarious lifeline dropped her another six inches. Her scream raised the hairs on the back of Joe's neck. Assessing the situation as he sprinted the remaining few feet, he realized that the sapling's immature taproot was pulling out of the ground.

In one continuous motion, he jerked to a halt at the cliff's edge, grabbed the sapling trunk with one hand and clamped his other around Olivia's wrist.

Olivia's scream cut off. Her eyes widened. Shock, disbelief, then hope raced across her face as she looked up into his face. "J-Joe? Oh, Joe—" she sobbed.

"I've got you. I've got you. Just keep your feet braced. That's it. Okay. Don't let go of the branch. That's it. Good girl," he praised as he did the same and grasped her arm with both hands. Leaning back with his feet braced wide, he never took his gaze from hers.

"Now, on the count of three I'm going to pull you up and over. When I say 'three' put all your weight on your left foot and step forward with your right. Got it?"

Olivia swallowed hard and nodded.

"Okay. Here we go. One. Two. Three!"

His biceps bunched, and with one mighty jerk she came flying up over the edge and against Joe's chest. His arms closed around her as momentum sent them stumbling backward a few steps. When they regained their balance, Joe pulled her still farther from the edge, but his protective embrace never slackened.

"Oh, Joe. Joe. Thank God." Sobbing, Olivia clung to him, her hands clutching his shirtfront, then slipping around him to dig into his broad back muscles. She burrowed against his chest as though she could not get close enough, as though his arms offered the only safe harbor in the world.

Holding her close, Joe hunched over her. "You're okay now. You're okay. I've got you, sweetheart." He slid one hand up over her back and neck, threaded his spread fingers through her hair and cupped the back of her head, holding her cradled against him. "That's all right, baby. You go ahead and cry. I've got you. You're safe now." Tenderly, he rubbed his cheek against the top of her head and murmured soft words of comfort. The silky strands of her hair caught in his beard stubble and slid back and forth with each caressing movement.

He could feel her heart pounding like a wild thing against his chest, his own beating a thunderous counterpoint.

They stood that way for what could have been minutes or hours, clinging together for mutual comfort and strength. Joe couldn't remember ever being so terrified as when he'd spotted her dangling over the side of the cliff, or so weak in the knees, once he had her safe in his arms.

After a while Olivia's sobs began to taper off into hitching breaths, and finally, watery sniffles. Then she began to tremble. She shook from head to toe, like someone in the grips of a hard chill.

Delayed shock, he thought. He knew he needed to

get her back to the house and take steps to combat the reaction, though he hated to let her go.

Reluctantly, he relaxed his embrace and grasped her shoulders. "C'mon. I'm taking you back to the house and putting you to bed. You need to get warm and drink some sweet coffee. As for me, I could use a good stiff drink."

Joe bent to scoop her up in his arms, but Olivia stopped him. "Oh, no, please. You don't have to carry me. I'm a little shaky, but I can walk."

"You sure?"

"Yes. With your help, I'm sure I can make it."

Joe wrapped his arm around her shoulders and pulled her close against his side, and Olivia looped her arm around his back. She leaned heavily against him, letting him bear much of her weight. Her wobbly legs barely kept her upright as they set off slowly across the meadow.

Around them the undulating waves of grass emulated the restless breakers rolling in from the ocean. Joe knew that Olivia had noticed the similarity as well, when she burrowed her face in the curve of his shoulder and shivered harder.

"Joe?" Olivia asked meekly against his jacket as they tromped through the grass.

"Hmm?"

"How…how did you happen to be there?"

"At the cliffs?"

She nodded.

"Pure luck. When I arrived Mrs. Jaffee told me you'd gone for a walk, so I decided to go look for you. I came up over the rise and saw your scarf blowing in the wind."

"Was there…that is…did you happen to see anyone else nearby?"

"No. Why?"

"I, uh…never mind. No reason, really."

Except she could have sworn that someone had
pushed her.

Half an hour later Olivia still couldn't stop thinking
about what had happened on the cliffs.

After hanging her slacks in the closet and putting
her folded sweater away in a drawer, she made her
way cautiously across the room on wobbly legs. She
slipped out of the lace-and-satin negligee that
matched her nightgown, tossed it across the footboard
and climbed into bed, as per Joe's instructions.

On their arrival back at the house he had hustled
her into the kitchen past an astonished Mrs. Jaffee and
seen to it that she downed a cup of hot, vilely sweet
coffee. Then, before she'd realized his intent, he'd
swooped her up in his arms and carried her upstairs
to her room. He would have undressed her himself if
she hadn't protested.

"Honey, I've seen you naked before," he argued.

"Not in a long time."

"So? From what I can tell, nothing has changed."

"What's changed is we're not married now. Joe,
stop that," she snapped, batting his hands away when
he tried to unbutton her shirt. "Just get out of here.
I am perfectly capable of undressing myself."

"Dammit, Livvie, just let me—"

Olivia pointed toward the door. "Out. Now."

Joe went, but he was not at all happy at being
shooed from her room and issued strict instructions
for her to get into bed and stay there for the remainder

of the day. He left her saying that he would send Mrs. Jaffee up in a few minutes with some brandy.

Olivia would have argued that he was making too big a fuss, that she was fine now and perfectly capable of working, but the truth was, she wasn't fine. Not only did she feel shaky and weak, she was racked with doubts and questions.

Piling several pillows against the massive headboard, Olivia leaned back against them and pulled the covers up, smoothing them over her hips. Her fingers plucked restlessly at the top sheet as she waited for the housekeeper's knock.

She supposed it was possible that a powerful gust of wind had sent her stumbling over the edge of the cliff. The winds had been strong, and she had been daydreaming.

Still…that shove against her back had felt more like the flat of a hand than a blast of wind. Trouble was, she could not swear to either, thanks to her thick coat and the chunky sweater she'd had on underneath.

If her worst suspicion was true and someone *had* pushed her, and she and Joe had been the only ones by the cliffs…

No. No, that didn't make any sense. Why would he try to kill her? She wouldn't put it past his mother, but not Joe. Such a vicious act was completely out of character for him. Besides, if he didn't want her around he'd had plenty of opportunities to be rid of her. And if he *had* pushed her, why had he then turned around and saved her?

No. No, if she had been pushed, someone else had to have done it. But who? And why? And where had they disappeared to?

A light tap at the door broke into her thoughts and Olivia called out, "Come in, Mrs. Jaffee."

"I'm not Mrs. Jaffee, but I'll take that as an invitation," Joe said, shouldering open the door.

Olivia's first impulse was to snatch the bedcovers up to her chin. Don't be a ninny, she silently scolded, watching him stroll toward the bed carrying a tray holding two snifters of brandy. You're decently covered, she told herself, but she glanced down at the dark blue satin-and-lace bodice of her nightgown just to be sure.

Her shoulders were bare except for two spaghetti straps, but that could hardly be considered indecent exposure. Some formal attire showed more skin than her nightgown revealed. You're a mature woman, not a jittery teenage virgin, Olivia reminded herself. For Pete's sake, act like one.

"Mrs. Jaffee was busy cooking so I brought your brandy up."

"You didn't have to do that. I don't really need—"

"Yes, you do. And it wasn't any trouble, so don't fuss."

Joe put the tray on the bedside table, handed one snifter to Olivia and picked up the other. "And since it would be rude to let you drink alone, I brought one for myself as well. To tell you the truth, my nerves could stand a bit of soothing, too."

Casual as can be, he hitched up one knee and sat down on the side of the bed, facing her. "I've never been so scared in my life as when I saw you hanging from that spindly sapling. Sweet Jesus, Livvie, you nearly gave me a heart attack."

His nearness made Olivia so nervous she barely heard him. Remotely it registered that he had called her Livvie again and that she should object, but with the top of his thigh rubbing against her hip she couldn't seem to gather her thoughts. All along her left side she could feel the heat from his body.

She could also feel heat rising over her chest and shoulders and climbing up her neck. Quickly, she took a sip of brandy, hoping he would blame the drink for her flush.

In her haste she swallowed too fast, and the fiery liquid went down the wrong way.

"Whoa, there. Take it easy," Joe said as she coughed and sputtered. He took the snifter from her and put it and his own on the bedside table. Grasping her upper arms, he pulled her toward him until her head rested on his shoulder, and proceeded to pound her soundly on the back.

When her coughing fit eased he rubbed his hand in circles over her back. "Didn't anyone ever tell you you're supposed to sip brandy?" he teased, and she could hear the amusement in his voice.

She was more concerned, however, with other sensations. Like the moist warmth of his breath seeping through her hair, just above her left ear, prickling her scalp and making her shiver, the clean, masculine scent of him invading her nose with every breath she took, the toned strength of his body.

Olivia was also acutely aware of Joe's palm against her bare back. His touch seemed to sear her flesh like a branding iron. She forgot all about the burning in her lungs and windpipe.

Marshaling her wits, she stiffened and pulled back, and resorted to annoyance to cover her embarrassment. "Believe it or not, I *do* know how to drink brandy. I simply swallowed the wrong way, is all," she said, making a production of fluffing the pillows before settling back against them.

Joe handed her the snifter again, smiling at her prickliness, which made Olivia suspect that he knew just how nervous he was making her.

Leaning forward, he grasped a stray tendril of her hair and tucked it behind her ear, letting his fingertips graze the side of her neck and shoulder. Her skin prickled in the wake of his touch, sending another shiver rippling through her.

Damn you, Joe, she thought, though she managed to keep her expression unruffled. What do you think you're doing?

"Why did you go to the cliffs, anyway, sweetheart?" he asked softly. "It's dangerous there. One of the first things Reese and I intend to do is install a four-foot iron railing all along that section. And believe me, after today, I'm putting a crew on that job tomorrow."

Olivia looked down at her hands, which were needlessly smoothing the covers. "I didn't set out to go to the cliffs at all. I was walking along the edge of the forest looking for a trail to the beach when, suddenly, there I was."

"What happened? Did you get too close and the edge crumbled under your feet?"

Biting her lower lip, Olivia looked up at him. The words "Someone pushed me from behind" hovered on the tip of her tongue, but she wasn't ready to confide in Joe. Even if she felt comfortable doing so, she wasn't sure he would believe her. Instead she shrugged and murmured, "The wind knocked me forward. I guess I wasn't paying attention."

"Do me a favor, will you? Stay away from there.

At least until we can get a safety railing installed. Okay?''

"Don't worry. I'm not going anywhere near those cliffs ever again.''

"Good.'' He drained his snifter and put it on the tray. "Finished?'' he asked, and at her nod he took hers and placed it on the tray as well.

"It's time for you to get some rest.'' His gaze wandered over her face, feature by feature, then dropped down to her bare shoulders and the lush ivory swells of her breasts visible over the top of the nightgown. "You look pale,'' he murmured. "Beautiful. And sexy as hell, but pale.''

The look in his eyes and his tone made her heart skip a beat. "Joe, are you flirting with me?''

"Oh, yeah.''

"Well, stop it. You're making me nervous.''

"Good. That's progress at least.''

"Joe—''

Laughing, he stood and lifted the covers partway. "C'mon, scoot down in the bed and I'll tuck you in.''

"For heaven's sake. I'm not a child.''

He stilled. His dark eyes smoldered and grew heavy-lidded. "Sweetheart, no one knows that better than me. And trust me, now is not the time to remind me of that fact.''

The comment, uttered in that deep, raspy voice, rendered her speechless. Too stunned to reply, Olivia scooted down in the bed, her wide-eyed gaze fixed on Joe's face as he tucked the covers around her shoulders.

When done, he remained bent over her, his hands braced on either side of her pillow. For a time his gaze held hers, and Olivia was powerless to look away. "Sweet dreams, sweetheart," he murmured, and then he leaned down and placed a lingering kiss on her mouth.

It was the softest of caresses, a slow rub of lips, an exchange of warm breaths, the merest stroke of the tip of a tongue, but the kiss packed a wallop that Olivia felt all the way to her toes.

Joe raised his head and smiled. "Now, go to sleep. I'll see you later."

"Oh, Joe, I almost forgot. I left L.J. working up in the staff's quarters. He's probably finished by now. Would you send someone up to tell him that I won't be needing him anymore today, so he can report to Mike?"

"I'll take care of it. Now, stop worrying and go to sleep."

He dropped another quick kiss on the tip of her nose, then straightened and headed for the door.

Olivia watched him go, befuddled and bewildered. When the door clicked shut behind him, she touched her fingertips to her tingling lips and closed her eyes. "Sweet Mother Mary and Joseph," she whispered.

After that mind-blowing kiss, Olivia did not think she could possibly relax. She turned onto her side and snuggled into a comfortable position beneath the covers. If Joe truly was attracted to her as he claimed, how ironic and sad that would be, she thought drowsily.

His kiss may have curled her toes and set her hormones to percolating, but that was only natural. A woman would have to be dead not to respond to a man like Joe, she thought, burrowing deeper into the pillow. But the girlish love she had felt for him for so long was no more.

* * *

A little after five o'clock that evening, Olivia awoke from a deep and dreamless sleep, feeling herself again. She splashed her face with cold water, refreshed her makeup, dressed in a pair of camel slacks and a black turtleneck sweater and left her room. She was halfway down the stairs when Joe came striding in through the front door with Cappy Baines on his heels, yammering away.

"I'm telling you, you're makin' a huge mistake."

"I don't agree," Joe replied absently over his shoulder.

Not wanting to interrupt, Olivia stopped, assuming the men would continue on into the library or some other part of the house.

"You're just askin' for trouble," Cappy insisted. "This here's an evil place. Pure evil."

Joe stopped by the hall table beside the stairs and tossed down a stack of mail, which she assumed Cappy had brought from the mainland, before turning to face the old man. "And on what do you base that opinion? A few hysterical sightings of a so-called ghost? C'mon, Cappy. We both know there's no such thing. It had to be wisps of fog. There's no other explanation."

"I wouldn't be so quick to dismiss something you don't understand if I were you. People been seein' old Theobald on them cliffs for nigh onto ninety years now."

"Correction. People have been seeing what they wanted to *believe* was Theobald. It makes for good storytelling and adds to the mystique of the area."

Cappy shook his head and gave Joe a pitying look. "I'm telling you, if you're smart you won't put another dime into this place. Forget this highfalutin idea of yours and get outta here, before something really bad happens. You said yourself that pretty little designer gal was nearly killed today. Ain't that enough to convince you?''

''I told you, Olivia slipped. It was an accident.''

''Accident, my arse. That was old Theobald what pushed her. Don't you see? He's trying to send you a message, an' that's to get off his island.''

''Look, Cappy, I'm going to say this one more time,'' Joe warned, pronouncing each word with strained patience. ''I don't believe in ghosts. Or voodoo. Or bad mojo. Whatever you want to call it. I bought this property with the intention of restoring the mansion and grounds and turning the island into a first-class getaway. And that's exactly what I'm going to do. If you don't like it, or you're afraid to come here, then I'll find myself another tugboat and captain. Just say the word.''

Cappy's mouth compressed into a thin line. ''Don't you worry none about me. I'll do my job. I was just trying to save you a lot of headache and trouble.''

From where she stood Olivia could see Joe softening. He grinned and cuffed the older man's shoulder. ''I know, Cappy. I know. And I appreciate it. But everything is going to be fine. Trust me.''

''Humph! Just don't say I didn't warn you,'' Cappy declared, and stomped back across the foyer and out the door.

Chuckling, Joe turned toward the library, but he spotted Olivia and stopped. ''Hey. You're up. How do you feel?''

''Good as new,'' she said, starting down the steps again.

He braced one hand against the fancy carved pine-apple pediment that adorned the top of the newel post and watched her, his eyes simultaneously assessing her condition and glinting with male appreciation. "Good. I'm glad to hear it. I've got to admit, you do have roses back in your cheeks."

"What was Cappy upset about?" Olivia asked, stopping on the second step from the bottom, on eye level with Joe.

"Oh, don't pay any attention to him. He's all caught up in the ghost stories and rumors about this place. He's convinced that we're all heading for doom and damnation if we continue with this project."

Before she could comment he changed the subject. "While you were sleeping I glanced at your proposal for the staff's quarters. Do you feel like going over them with me? We have a couple of hours before dinner."

"Certainly."

"Good. I have a number of questions." He stepped aside and motioned for her to accompany him.

Olivia hadn't known what to expect. At first she had been concerned that Joe's recent kisses, particularly the one he'd given her earlier, had changed something between them, but apparently she had nothing to worry about. From the moment they settled in the library and began going over her drawings and notes, Joe was all business. In no time at all she relaxed. She chalked up today's kiss as nothing more than his panicked reaction to the scare she'd given him.

For the next two hours they went over her design plan in detail. Joe, as she'd expected, was dubious about the apartment aspect.

"If you want to keep a quality staff, particularly on an isolated island, you must provide them with more than a single room," Olivia insisted. "These quarters will be their homes for extended periods of time. They should at least be equivalent to a city apartment. I would even suggest that you make a few of them larger, perhaps two or three bedrooms, for married couples and their families. Maybe even provide a day-care facility for their children. The Mallens' children's nursery would be perfect for that use."

"Good grief, Olivia. This is supposed to be a luxury retreat for the guests, not the staff."

She stiffened, and Joe raised his hands.

"Now, before you get all huffy and defensive let me say that, in principle, I agree with you. But there's not enough space in the staff's quarters for the number of apartments that would be needed."

"In the existing staff's quarters, no. But there's plenty of attic space over other wings that is currently not being used. Convert that."

"Do you have any idea how much that would cost?"

"As a matter of fact, I do," Olivia said, pulling a sheet of paper from her briefcase. "I worked up a cost estimate."

Taking the paper from her, Joe shot her a wry look. "Why am I not surprised?"

Throughout dinner, and for a couple of hours afterward, they continued to discuss her plan, debating her reasoning, the cost effectiveness and feasibility. At times they even resorted to shouting, each arguing their point of view with no holds barred.

There had been a time when Olivia would not have

dreamed of challenging Joe or expressing her opinion so forcefully. Now, however, she found the exchange exciting and exhilarating.

In the end she won some major concessions, they compromised on others, and a few frills she wisely let go. By the time they said good-night and parted company, she was feeling well pleased with herself.

Fifteen

The next day Olivia saw little of Joe. The renovation was in full swing, and the house was a beehive of activity. The sounds of power saws and hammers reverberated throughout the mansion. From outside came the rumble of heavy equipment as a crane moved construction materials from the dock and deposited them on the top of the leeward cliffs, while a bulldozer leveled off part of the meadow behind the house for a golf course.

Inside, men tore down walls and put up others. Plumbers, electricians, carpenters, plasterers, stonemasons and wood craftsmen and their various helpers swarmed through the halls carrying pipes and wires, wood, rolls of insulation, buckets of mortar and sundry tools.

Trying to stay out of the way, Olivia worked either in the storage section of the attic with L.J. or in the library, refining her design plans and making a list of pieces to look for on her next buying trip. Every now and then she'd catch a glimpse of Joe striding through the vast entrance hall carrying a rolled-up blueprint under his arm, gesturing and giving instructions to various crew bosses or to Mike. He was so busy they spent little time together except during meals, and not always then.

One Friday, she had almost finished lunch when he came striding into the dining room and, much to Mrs. Jaffee's disapproval, made himself a sandwich out of a roll and the glazed ham she'd baked for lunch.

"Sorry. I don't have time to sit down to a meal," he said in response to her sputtering protests.

"According to the weather service, a storm is going to blow in this afternoon," he went on, turning to Olivia. "I'm letting the crew go early. L.J.'s working with you today, right?"

"Yes. We're still taking inventory."

"If you would, tell him he'd better take off soon, since he's in that small skiff."

"I will, just as soon as I finish lunch."

"We want to get to shore before it hits, too, so be prepared to leave by three-thirty. Okay?"

"All right. I'll be ready."

"How about you, Mrs. Jaffee? Do you want to spend the weekend in Savannah or stay here?"

"Humph. What would I do in Savannah? Many's the storm I've ridden out in this old house. I reckon I can ride out this little ole puny one, too. The weatherman on the radio said they're not expecting it to amount to much. Not even hurricane strength."

"Suit yourself. Mike and a couple of his top men will be staying over the weekend, so you won't be alone."

Joe had finished eating his sandwich while she talked. He quickly made himself another one and headed out the door. "Remember," he called to Olivia over his shoulder. "Be ready to go by three-thirty. And take your seasick pills. It's going to be a rough ride."

Olivia found L.J. waiting for her in the library. When she relayed Joe's message, he frowned.

"I don't like the idea of leaving you here with a storm coming."

"Don't worry about me. Joe is taking me to Savannah before the storm hits."

"Oh. I see," the young man said, staring at his work boots. "I guess you'll be going out with the big boss tonight then, huh?"

"Not with a storm coming. I plan to get a room at the Hyatt. I'll probably spend the weekend working. Or if the weather clears, looking for an apartment."

"Oh. Okay, well in that case, I guess I'll head for home before the waters get too rough. You sure you're going to be okay?"

"I'm sure. Now go."

"Yes, ma'am," he said, flashing her a shy smile.

At three, Olivia went upstairs to her room to pack for the weekend. The instant she opened the door she spotted another note propped against her pillow. On the outside it appeared identical to the first one.

Experiencing a mixture of dread and anger, she tore open the envelope and pulled out the single sheet of paper. This one read, GET OUT NOW, WHILE YOU STILL CAN. IF YOU DO NOT HEED THIS WARNING YOU WILL PAY THE PRICE.

With trembling fingers, Olivia stuffed the sheet of paper back into the envelope. Who was doing this? Blair had not been on the island that day. At least, she didn't think she had. She hadn't seen her, at any rate. Still…she supposed Joe's mother could have hired someone else to deliver the warnings for her.

Annoyed, Olivia stuffed the note into the drawer with the other one and started snatching clothes out of the closet. If Eleanore and Blair thought their scare tactics were going to drive her away, they could think again.

Joe was right. As Olivia hurried down the cliff steps it began to sprinkle, huge droplets that splatted against the recently finished piers, dotting them with water spots the size of golf balls. By the time *Fleeting Dreams* pulled away from the new marina, slanted sheets of blowing rain pockmarked the surface of the water in the harbor cove and obscured the mouth of the inlet.

Down in the cabin, Olivia looked out a porthole and shuddered. She hoped that Joe's instruments worked well and that he knew how to use them. Visibility was almost zero.

The minute she'd stepped aboard the boat he'd scowled at her wan appearance. "What's the matter? Are you ill?"

"No, I just had a bad night. I couldn't sleep." Which was the truth, as far as it went. She hadn't slept a wink after hearing footsteps in her room again, and the paleness of her skin and dark circles under her eyes showed it.

"Go below and get some sleep on the trip," Joe yelled over the increasing patter of rain.

Olivia stripped off her boots and snuggled under the blankets in the bunk, but the rough sea made sound sleep impossible. Every time she dozed off, the boat would pitch and roll, nearly dumping her onto the deck.

About halfway to shore they outran the storm, but when they docked in Savannah the wind had begun to gust and you could smell the advancing rain in the air.

"We'd better hurry. The storm will be here soon," Joe said, hustling her down River Street toward the elevator at the back of the Hyatt.

Minutes later they stepped off the elevator into an unusually crowded lobby. "What the heck is going on?" Joe wondered out loud, guiding her through the crowd to the registration counter. "We'd like a single room for the lady, please," he said to the clerk on duty.

"I'm sorry, sir, but we're full up."

"Oh, dear," Olivia murmured. "I guess I should have called ahead and booked a room. Could you please call around and see if you could locate a room for me in another hotel?"

"I'd love to, ma'am, but I've already done that for another customer. I'm afraid there's not a room to be had in town. There are three large conferences booked this weekend."

"Oh, dear." She cast Joe a worried look and they walked away from the desk. "What am I going to do? We can't go back to the island in a storm."

"That's easy. You stay with me at my place."

"I can't do that!"

"Sure you can. I've got a guest room. Actually, I have a couple."

"Joe, for heaven's sake. If it got out that I was staying with you, people will assume that we're..."

"Having an affair?"

"Yes."

"Sugar, I hate to tell you, but that rumor has already made the rounds. As soon as word got out that you were working for me, the assumption was we were hitting the sheets.''

''Wha-at?''

''Why are you surprised? This is Savannah, remember.''

''Well there is no reason to add fuel to the fire.'' She thought for a moment, then said, ''I guess I could stay on your boat. That is, if you don't mind.''

''Honey, even tied up to the pier, that boat will be rocking so hard you'll be tossing your cookies within an hour.'' He gave her a wicked, ''step-into-my-parlor'' grin. ''Looks like you're stuck with me.''

Grasping Olivia's arm, Joe hustled her into the hotel's River Street elevator. By the time she could gather her wits they were outside, heading toward the AdCo building.

''Joe, wait,'' she protested, trying to hang back. ''I can't stay with you.''

''Sure you can. I've got plenty of room.''

''That's not what I meant, and you know it.''

She dug in her heels and he stopped and turned to face her. The winds had kicked up, and people were scurrying for shelter, flowing around them like water seeking its course. ''Look, sweetheart. You don't have a choice. Unless you'd rather I drove you to your mother's, that is.''

Olivia almost winced at that. She didn't think she could tolerate another weekend of tension and disapproval from her mother and Vicky. Debating, she caught her bottom lip between her teeth and at the same time struggled to keep her gored skirt from blowing up. A raindrop splatting on her cheek seemed to settle the matter. ''I guess you're right.''

''Good. Let's go before we get soaked.'' He

grabbed her hand and hauled her along at a pace so fast Olivia had to trot to keep up.

They almost made it. They were about half a block from the building when the rain hit, blowing and whipping in wavy sheets and striking the pavement and brick courtyards in thousands of tiny geysers.

Olivia let out a squeal and Joe sprinted for the building at full tilt, towing her along with him. They reached the back entrance, he got the door unlocked and they stumbled inside, laughing and gasping. Both were soaked to the skin.

"C'mon, let's get upstairs and out of these wet clothes," Joe urged when they'd caught their breath.

In his living room he helped her out of her soggy jacket and steadied her while she pulled off her wet boots. Water ran in rivulets down her body and dripped from her hair and clothes. Her hair hung in wet strings around her face and she was painfully aware that her silk blouse and flared skirt were plastered to her body, outlining every dip and curve.

Joe led her through the door to the bedroom area. Though the loft apartment was spacious and the hallway unusually wide, suddenly the atmosphere seemed too close. Too intimate.

"Here we go. This is the best guest bedroom. It's right across the hall from mine, if you should need me for anything. You'll find plenty of towels in the adjoining bathroom."

"Thank you," Olivia said, and took her bag from him and slipped into the bedroom.

Like the rest of the apartment, the room was tastefully decorated, this one in three shades of sea-foam green, accented with touches of terra-cotta, but it appeared soulless.

Heading for the bathroom, Olivia had to smile when her gaze encountered the bed. Like all big men, Joe obviously considered a king-size minimum standard.

After a hot shower she discovered that the rain had seeped into her weekender bag and a few of her clothes had damp spots. She hung them on hangers in the bathroom to dry and donned the smaller of the two terry-cloth robes that hung on the back of the bathroom door.

The garment was miles too big for her. It puddled on the floor around her feet and she had to overlap the front edges by a foot and cinch the belt tight to preserve her modesty. As she was rolling up the sleeves she wondered how many other women had worn the robe.

"Never mind, Olivia," she scolded her reflection in the bathroom mirror when she realized the direction her thoughts had taken. "Joe's love life is his business. If he wants, he can have a harem for all you should care," she told herself, marching barefoot out of the room.

The only trouble was, the thought had left her with a sick little knot in the pit of her stomach.

Olivia had barely stepped into the hall when she detected a delicious aroma. Following her nose, she found Joe in his open kitchen, grilling steaks. She noticed that he had mopped up the trail of rainwater they had dripped onto the floor.

"Mmm, something smells heavenly," she said, hitching herself up on a bar stool on the opposite side of the granite counter from him. He wore faded jeans and an old sweatshirt and, like her, he was barefoot. Still damp from the shower, his hair was slightly disheveled. He smelled of soap and shampoo and maleness.

"My housekeeper left us steaks and salads, but I'm afraid I'm going to have to microwave the potatoes. I'm too hungry to bake them the old-fashioned way."

"That's fine. But tell me, how did she know to leave enough for two?"

Unabashed, Joe grinned. "I called her earlier, just in case I could persuade you to stay here with me."

Olivia narrowed her eyes at him. "Did you plan this whole thing?" she demanded, sweeping her arm toward the wall of windows, where the rain was striking the panes in a frenzied assault. At that moment, lightning lit up the sky in jagged forks. A few seconds later a boom of thunder vibrated the glass.

"Yes, and no. I'm mighty glad you think I'm powerful, but sugar, no one can control the weather. I'll admit that when I found out the storm was coming I called my housekeeper and asked her to pick up a couple of steaks and potatoes and salad fixings."

"Did you also bribe that desk clerk to say there were no rooms available?"

"No. I did call ahead to book you a room and learned the hotel was full, but I knew you wouldn't take my word for it so I let you find out for yourself. That's absolutely all I'm guilty of."

She kept her eyes narrowed. She wanted to be angry, but she couldn't. "It had better be," she replied, trying to sound annoyed.

"I can't recall how you like your steaks."

"That's because I'd never had one when I was around you. We couldn't afford steaks back when we were married. But I like them medium rare."

"Ah, great. Same way I like mine. Which means we can eat our salads while these cook."

Joe had already set out the salads and lit the candles on a small table by the windows. It wasn't until they were seated that Olivia realized that at some point he had turned off all the lights except for the one above the sizzling steaks.

Rain pattered against the panes. Through the downpour she could see the fuzzy lights of a cargo ship silently gliding by, heading upriver. Soft, mellow jazz poured from hidden speakers around the room, and the candles cast a small circle of flickering light around them, as though they were the only two people in the world.

Joe filled their wineglasses and offered a toast. "Here's to happiness."

Olivia clinked her glass to his and took a sip. When she looked at Joe again he was grinning. "What's so funny."

"That robe seems a bit large for you."

"Yes. Apparently all your lady friends are taller than I am."

"I keep those robes for guests. Actually only two women have worn that one, and both are very dear to me."

"Oh. I see." If suspecting that he had a whole string of girlfriends had caused her discomfort, hearing that two held a special place in his heart made her chest tighten painfully, though why she couldn't imagine. Shame on you, Olivia, she silently scolded. You're acting like a dog in a manger; you don't love him or want him, but you don't want anyone else to have him, either.

Some of her feelings must have shown in her face.

Chuckling, Joe reached across the table and squeezed her hand. "Don't look so glum, sweetheart. The only women who have worn that robe are Blair and you."

"Oh. Well, if you bought it to fit Blair no wonder it's so long on me."

"Yeah, every now and then she or Luke spend the night here if they're in town late. The other robe is for him."

"How is Luke?"

"The same. Quiet, laid-back, still a bit of a rebel. And still a horse man through and through.

"When he heard you were back and a designer now he was happy for you. He said he'd like to come out to the island and see you when he got a chance. To tell you the truth, I think Luke always was sweet on you when we were kids."

"Luke? Don't be ridiculous. He tormented me every chance he got."

"Sugar, that's what little boys do when they like a girl. Didn't your mama ever teach you that?"

Immediately it occurred to her that Joe had never teased her when they were youngsters, although he seemed to be making up for that now.

Not in her wildest dreams could Olivia imagine cocky, wildly popular Luke Connally nursing a secret crush on her. However, if Joe was right about his brother, how ironic it would be that all the years she had been mooning over Joe, Luke had been doing the same over her and she'd never even noticed.

"Don't worry about it. He got past that stage long ago." Chuckling at her chagrined expression, Joe scooped up the empty salad plates and took them to the kitchen. He returned moments later with their steaks and baked potatoes and a four-compartment condiment dish.

"So, tell me about your life," Joe said, cutting into his steak.

"What do you want to know?"

"For starters, where do you live? In a house or an apartment?"

"I own a small town house. Being that I'm out of town a lot, it seemed more practical. But I do own a post-Civil War Victorian cottage that I use to house my offices and workshop."

She told how she'd rescued the derelict cottage when the area was still run-down. She explained about all the red tape she'd had to plow through to get grants from state and federal historical societies, and how she'd practically had to get down on her knees and beg bankers to loan her enough money to finish the project.

"It took a year and a lot of hard work to do the restoration right, but it was worth it. It turned out beautiful. It stands out like a jewel, surrounded by a bunch of soulless steel-and-glass boxes. I've been offered a small fortune for the property. If I sold out, I'd never have to work again."

"But you won't do that, right?"

She shook her head. "No. I can't stand the thought of the house being demolished. Or even moved to another location. It just wouldn't be the same. Besides, I love my work. It's always a challenge. Every house, every room, every client is different. I wouldn't know what to do with myself if I didn't have my career. Besides, there are several other people who depend on me to provide them with jobs."

"Yeah, I know that feeling," Joe commented.

Throughout dinner and the cleanup afterward the conversation flowed. When the dishes were done Joe topped off their wineglasses and they moved to the sofa. He told her in detail about some of the projects that he and Reese had done—old warehouse conversions, factory revampings, entire slum neighborhoods they'd restored. He did not say so but, from his tone, Olivia could tell that he enjoyed the residential projects the most.

They talked nonstop, about anything and everything, until almost one in the morning. Olivia was surprised at how easy it was, how effortless, how enjoyable. It was too bad that they hadn't had the maturity or courage to talk to each other like this years ago when they were married, Olivia thought, listening to Joe describe the first job that he and Reese had taken on.

"I guess all of this just proves that our divorce was a good thing," Olivia said after a while. "You wouldn't have accomplished what you have if we had stayed together. And I certainly would not have."

"Oh, I don't know about that," Joe countered. "It may have taken longer, but eventually I would have gained control of my trust fund and finished school. And I like to think that I would have supported you in whatever you wanted to do."

"Mmm," she replied sleepily, and took another sip of wine. "Maybe so. But, I don't know, it just seems more of an accomplishment that…well…"

"That you did it all on your own," Joe finished for her, smiling with understanding.

"Yes. It makes everything I have, everything I've done all the more precious to me. If that makes me prideful, so be it."

"Not at all. You have every right to be proud of all you've accomplished. I'm proud for you. You set your sights high and went for your dream. And you made it. With no help from anyone. And I say, good for you."

Olivia experienced a warm rush of emotion as she looked at him over the top of her glass. He understood. He truly understood. He didn't fault her for her ambition or daring to dream. He applauded her for it. And he acknowledged the struggle it had taken. He had no idea how much it meant to her to have his support and understanding.

"Thank you," she murmured. "That means a lot, especially coming from you."

"Sugar, I've always been proud of you. Even as a little girl there was something special about you. You were smart as a whip and cute as a button and talented. I remember when you were about twelve years old you did a pencil drawing of me on my horse, Thunder. It was really good. I still have that drawing."

"Really? I'd forgotten all about that."

"It's hanging in my bedroom. Wanna see?" he asked with a wicked grin.

Olivia laughed. "I think I'll pass, thanks," she said, trying to stifle another yawn.

"Okay, we'll save it for another time. Now, though, I think it's time we both turned in. You're fading fast."

"Mmm, sounds like a great idea." After hours of stimulating conversation and three glasses of wine, she could barely hold her eyes open.

At her door, Joe cupped her face between his palms and smiled. "Good night, sweetheart," he whispered, and placed a soft, lingering kiss on her parted lips. By the time the kiss ended they were both trembling. He pressed his forehead to hers and closed his eyes. "God, how I want you."

"Joe—"

"I know, I know. You don't think it would be a good idea. But if you change your mind, you know where to find me." After another quick peck on the cheek he disappeared inside his room, leaving Olivia weak in the knees and filled with yearnings.

The next morning the rain still fell in torrents and showed no sign of letting up. Olivia prepared a breakfast of pancakes and sausage, and after they ate and cleaned the kitchen she and Joe lounged around the living room, still in their robes, and read the morning paper and drank coffee.

Almost like an old married couple, Olivia thought. Except that when they *had* been married they hadn't come close to achieving this level of ease with each other.

When she finished reading the paper Olivia went through the Apartments for Rent section of the classifieds, even though Joe had already convinced her that today wasn't the day to start a search for a place. When the deluge ended, though, she wanted to be ready.

She made an irritated sound when a perfect-sounding place turned out to be in the wrong part of town.

Joe lowered his newspaper partway and looked at her over the top. "How's it going?"

"It's slim pickin's. It's impractical to bring my car here or to rent one, so I'm going to be on foot. That means whatever I rent must be in this area, close to the office and the river. All I need is an efficiency or a really small place, preferably not too pricey, since I won't be there but now and then.''

"Why bother renting a place at all? Stay here.''

"Now, Joe. Be serious. I can't live here with you when I'm working in town.''

"Why not? We live in the same house on the island. Our rooms are just a few doors apart. Anyway, it's the perfect solution. This place is convenient to the office. All you have to do is ride the elevator down a floor. And the river is right outside. When you need to go to the island you just walk to the dock and board a boat. The apartment is roomy. It's comfortable. And it's free. What else could you want?''

"Your mother, and mine, would have a stroke. And can you imagine how people would talk?''

"Do we care? And anyway, that ship has already sailed. Like it or not, we're the hot topic among Savannah society. Look, we get along great, so it won't be a hardship. You're comfortable here, aren't you?''

"Yes, of course.''

"And last night wasn't so bad, was it?''

"Well…no, but that was a special circumstance.''

"To tell you the truth, I kinda rattle around in this place by myself. We can keep each other company. Anyway, once the project gets under way I'll be traveling some, too. We probably won't be here at the same time very often. Why rent another place when this one is just sitting here unused for the most part?''

She had to admit, she was tempted. His apartment was a lovely place. It was roomy and comfortable, and it was certainly convenient. Maybe too convenient.

Deep down, she knew it probably wasn't wise to spend so much time with Joe, especially in such an intimate situation. He had made it clear that he desired her.

Not that she was worried that he would take advantage or force himself on her. He was too much of a gentleman for that. But the plain truth was, though she no longer loved him, she did find him attractive. And she was human, after all.

"I don't know. Let me think about it."

"Sure. Take all the time you want." He went back to reading his paper with a satisfied smile on his lips, thoroughly pleased with himself.

As it turned out, apartment hunting was not in the cards that weekend. Rain lashed the Georgia coast for three straight days. Olivia and Joe stayed in the apartment. They talked endlessly, played numerous games of chess and watched the college basketball playoffs on television.

Surfing through the channels, Olivia discovered that one station was having a "chick flick" marathon. After much moaning and groaning from Joe, he agreed to watch one romantic movie with her for every western or action movie she watched with him.

They teased each other unmercifully over their taste in films and poked fun at the stories, the acting and the impossible stunts, but in truth, they both enjoyed the movies, and each other, tremendously.

By the time they said good-night and parted company at Olivia's door after another long, sizzling kiss, she felt wonderfully content. She could not remember ever experiencing such an enjoyable and relaxing weekend. Oddly, the weekend with Joe had done much more to relieve her tension than being at home had. And that bothered her.

On Monday morning, after spending an hour in the AdCo office so that Joe could confer with key people on his staff, he and Olivia boarded *Fleeting Dreams* in a gray drizzle. The leaden skies stayed with them all the way to the island.

There they found that outside jobs had been temporarily shut down due to the weather, but work on the inside of the mansion continued at full speed.

After carrying her bag upstairs, Joe set off in search of Mike. Olivia pulled the suitcase into her room, intending to unpack and change clothes. The first thing she saw was the white envelope propped against her pillows.

She stopped and stood stock-still, staring at the envelope as though it were a poisonous snake. Oh, Lord. Not another one.

Without enthusiasm she crossed the room and picked up the note, slitting the envelope open with her thumbnail as she sank down on the edge of the bed. With unsteady hands, she unfolded the single sheet of paper. Short and ominous, it read, YOU'VE BEEN WARNED.

She put the note in the drawer with the other two and debated whether or not to tell Joe about them. She no longer had the least suspicion that he had anything to do with this effort to drive her out, but she couldn't say the same for Blair and Eleanore. If this proved to be their doing he was sure to be upset. Maybe the best course was to just ignore them. Despite the tone of the notes, she didn't believe Eleanore would actually cause her physical harm.

Work progressed at a rapid pace the following

week. Being built of stone, the mansion was basically sound, so with the exception of rewiring and installing new plumbing, moving a few walls and adding new staff quarters, most of the work was cosmetic.

Except at mealtime, Olivia saw little of Joe. He was so busy he seemed to be going in ten directions at once, overseeing all the varied jobs that were under way, dealing with suppliers, inspectors, shipping companies, workmen and temperamental craftsmen brought in to do specialized work. He also had to respond to calls and faxes on other ongoing AdCo jobs.

During that week two more notes were left in her room, each more threatening than the last.

At night she often awoke to the sounds of footsteps, or creaking doors, or even more frightening, heavy breathing close by her bed and low, chilling laughter. Items had also begun to disappear from her room—a ring she had taken off and left on the dressing table, a candy bar, a roll of breath mints, a nail file. Other things seemed to have been moved around, with no attempt made to hide the mischief, as though someone—or something—was taunting her.

Olivia grew more edgy and tense by the day. Merely entering her room made her uneasy, and sleep was almost impossible. She dozed fitfully through the night, waking with a start at the tiniest sound.

Coffee kept her going, but she had dark circles under her eyes, she was cranky and she had roughly the energy level of a sloth and had to drag herself through each day. By Thursday she was looking forward to the weekend with an intensity she hadn't experienced since her high school days. She had half a mind to check into the Hyatt and hang out the Do Not Disturb sign until Monday morning.

Joe, of course, noticed her pallor and commented on it. So did Mike and L.J., and even Mrs. Jaffee, all with varying degrees of concern, but Olivia brushed aside their comments and assured them that she was fine.

Some of the new workmen had reported seeing a ghostly figure in eighteenth-century dress in the tower room on several evenings as the *Lady Bea* had chugged out of the harbor. Invariably, Joe reacted to the reports with annoyance and disbelief, making Olivia more hesitant than ever to mention the notes and the mysterious things that had occurred in her room at night. She didn't want to add to his burdens, nor did she want him to think of her as a hysterical woman.

Joe was so snowed under with work he didn't seem to realize the weekend was upon them until Thursday night at dinner when she mentioned that she would be gone until the following Wednesday.

His fork stopped halfway to his mouth and he shot her a startled look. "Gone? Where are you going?"

"For starters, I'm going home to Atlanta for the weekend. Then I'm going to spend Monday and Tuesday going to a couple of estate sales. I'm hoping to pick up some prime pieces to replace some of those that Miss Prudence sold."

And, once again, she needed some down time, away from this place. She desperately needed to return to her real life, where there were no ghosts or crotchety old housekeepers or spooky mansions. Where there was no Joe stirring up memories and feelings best forgotten.

"Couldn't you put that off?" Joe asked. "I was hoping we could spend the weekend together and unwind."

"I'm sorry, but I can't. Estate sales won't wait, and I do need to check on my own business from time to time, you know."

"Hurry back, will you? I'm going to miss you."

Feeling a tad uneasy and not sure why, Olivia laughed. "Oh, right. You've been so busy this past week you've hardly known I was here."

Joe put down his fork and took her hand. His dark eyes caressed her, and his voice dropped to a deep rumble. "Don't you believe it, honey. Wherever you are in this house, I'm aware of your presence. Just knowing that you're nearby makes me happy."

Those words played in Olivia's head like a stuck audiotape the whole time she was gone. She had no idea what she was going to do about Joe. His unexpected, impossible attraction to her seemed to be growing stronger.

She was flattered, of course. Merely knowing that he found her attractive made her entire system hum with excitement. She had to admit, seeing that predatory gleam in his eyes and knowing that she had put it there was a balm for her ego and wounded spirit. She was only human, after all. And yes, he did make her go weak in the knees when he touched her, but she didn't love him.

She wouldn't love him. Not again.

Sixteen

Olivia picked up some gorgeous pieces at the estate sales—at one a cherry-wood bedroom set in the Eastlake style, a couple of twelve-foot pier mirrors with marble bases and ornately carved walnut frames, at the other a magnificent Oriental rug and a fainting couch.

The weekend at home was less successful.

She couldn't seem to relax, no matter what she did. The more she thought about those threatening notes, the more she wondered if someone *had* pushed her that afternoon at the cliffs.

Her strategy of ignoring the perpetrator was not working. Olivia had hoped he or she would get tired of the game and go away, but apparently that was not going to happen. Soon she would be left with no choice; she would have to tell Joe about the notes and her suspicions about his mother and sister. She was not looking forward to the brouhaha that was going to create.

Late Wednesday evening, following the buying trip, Olivia emerged from the jetway in the Savannah Airport, took three steps and stopped short. A few feet away, leaning with one shoulder propped against a post, arms crossed over his chest, stood Joe.

"Joe. What are you doing here?"

He pushed away from the post and sauntered toward her. Before she realized his intent he pulled her into his arms and kissed her—a long, searing, curl-your-toes kind of kiss that could not possibly be mistaken for anything but what it was—a man declaring to the world that "this is my woman." The kiss was hot and devouring, and it stunned Olivia so completely she was helpless to resist.

"Joe, have you lost your mind?" she gasped when he at last raised his head. She cast a worried look around and stepped back out of his arms. At least, she tried. "You can't kiss me like that in public."

"So it's okay in private, huh?"

"No! Oh, you know what I mean." She glanced around again. "The gossips will have a heyday."

"Let 'em." He took her garment bag, hung it over his shoulder hooked by one finger, looped his other arm around her waist, pulled her against his side and headed for the parking area. "I'm glad to see you, and I don't care who knows it."

"Well I care. What if the talk gets back to your mother? I don't want to get her all riled up. Especially over nothing."

He laughed and gave her a squeeze. "Don't worry, sugar, it won't be over nothing."

"Joe, will you be serious?"

"I would, sweetheart, but I don't think you're ready for that yet. Now then, let's go home. We'll stay at the apartment tonight and go to Mallenegua in the morning."

"I was going to check into the Hyatt."

He chuckled at her frosty tone. "Now you don't have to. See, aren't you glad I picked you up?"

* * *

Over the next week, Olivia learned just what Joe had meant when he'd said he was a determined kind of guy. He was relentless. He teased and joked, disarming her with heart-stopping smiles and mischievous winks and comments. He touched her whenever possible—a pat on her arm, a caress as he brushed a strand of hair off her cheek, an arm draped casually over her shoulder at opportune times—nothing too intimate or aggressive, but enough contact to keep her off balance and her nervous system humming.

She wanted to be angry and, at times, tried to work up a good head of steam, but the truth was, Joe was so charming that she could not. To have a man as handsome and dynamic as Joe look at you as though you were the most beautiful, desirable creature on the planet was enough to turn any woman's head.

Olivia wouldn't lie to herself; she wanted him, too. She may not be in love anymore, but she would always care deeply for Joe. She could remember exactly what it was like to make love with him, and her body clamored for that exquisite pleasure.

In her weaker moments she even thought that maybe she should quit fighting the attraction. She was thirty-two years old and, except for that one slip fourteen years ago, had always lived a sensible, circumspect life. Maybe it was time she went a little crazy and indulged in a mad, passionate affair. If so, who better to do it with than her ex-husband, the only man she had ever loved?

Olivia half expected to find another note waiting for her when she returned from the buying trip, but to her vast relief, there was none. When almost a week passed with no more threatening messages, she began to relax. It looked as if whoever was responsible was giving up after all.

She began to sleep better and felt more at ease during the day. Despite a rash of accidents and vandalism and unforeseen delays, construction on the project was forging ahead.

Olivia planned another extensive buying trip to New York and the New England area, and she had a consultation scheduled the following month with a designer at a California wallpaper company that could replicate historic patterns for the mansion. L.J. was busy crating all the items that were to be shipped to various restorers. All things considered, especially from her end, things were moving along quite nicely.

So well that she was surprised in early April when, for the first time in weeks, she was startled out of a sound sleep around midnight.

She lay still and let her eyes adjust to the darkness, her heart palpitating. The room was quiet and still. After a moment she thought it must have been another dream that had woken her. Then she saw something move.

At first it was just a slight fluctuation of the darkness, like the ripple of a curtain in the wind. Olivia squinted her eyes and stared. Gradually the object took shape—the shadowy figure of a man, creeping across her room.

So she hadn't imagined those footsteps before. Nor had it been bad dreams that had disturbed her sleep. And tonight there was only one man in the house.

Anger exploded inside her, overriding any fear she might have felt. She did not stop to think. All at once, she had simply had enough.

She sat up. "Joe, what are you doing in here? If this is your idea of a joke, it's *not* funny!"

Abandoning stealth, the figure took off. He snatched open the door and, for a split second, Olivia saw him from behind, silhouetted by the weak light in the hall. All she caught was a glimpse, but it was enough to tell that the person wasn't Joe.

"Stop! Come back here, you!" she yelled, but he pounded down the hall. Olivia tossed back the covers and tore after him. By the time she reached the hall there was no one in sight, but she was almost certain he had run toward Joe's room so she took off in that direction. She'd gone only a short way when the few hall lights left burning went off.

Olivia screamed and came to a halt. An icy sensation trickled down her spine. She shivered, and the fine hair on her arms stood on end. The recklessness of her actions occurred to her then, but it was too late.

"Who are you? What do you want?" she cried, straining to see in the stygian darkness.

A low, sinister laugh came from somewhere behind her and to her right.

"Livvie! Livvie!" Joe shouted from far away, and footsteps came pounding up the main stairs. "Livvie, are you all right?"

"Joe! Joe, help me!" she screamed. "Help m—aaah!"

Just as she took a step to the left, groping for the wall, something hard struck her and pain exploded across the top of her right shoulder. The impact sent Olivia staggering forward and she went down, sprawling on all fours. She cried out again when she took too much weight on her right arm and collapsed onto her other side. Sobbing, she clutched her shoulder and curled into a ball, expecting to be struck again at any second.

Instead she heard the muffled thumps of someone running away down the carpet runner that covered the middle of the floor, followed by a door clicking shut.

"Livvie? Livvie, where are you?" Joe called from near the top of the stairs. His voice held a frantic note. "Liv— What the hell happened to the lights? Livvie!"

"He-here. I'm here," she managed to gasp.

"Where? I can't see you. Hold on a sec. There's a light switch around here somewhere."

After a short delay, the lights came back on. Olivia lay in the semidarkness between two dim pools of light.

"I still don't see—"

She groaned and he took off toward the sound. "Holy—" Joe skidded to a stop and knelt down beside her. "Aw, Livvie. What happened, sweetheart?"

"I...I woke up and...and saw a man in my room."

"A man. Honey, that's impossible. I'm the only man on the island right now, and I was downstairs working in the library."

"I...I know. But at first I thought it...was you. That's why I confronted him. He ran out of my...my room and I ran a-after him. Then the lights...went off and I heard him laugh, just...a few seconds before he struck me with s-something heavy."

"Struck you? Sugar, are you sure? Could you have woken from a dream and thought it was real? And when you ran into the hall you bumped into something?"

"You don't believe me," Olivia said in a stricken voice.

"No, no, it's not that I don't believe you, exactly."

"Then what, exactly?"

"It's just that you, Mrs. Jaffee and I are the only ones on the island. I can't see her dressing up as a man and creeping around your room in the middle of the night."

Anger and hurt combined to partially block out the throbbing pain in Olivia's shoulder. "I'm telling you, there was a man in my room."

"Okay, sugar. We'll figure it all out later. Right now let's get you in some light and take a look at the damage. Tell me where you're hurt."

"My right shoulder," she replied in an offended tone.

Joe started to scoop her up from her left side, but even that much jostling made her cry out, and he stopped. "Sorry. Did I hurt you?"

"I'm all right. If you'll just help me up I'm sure I can walk. It's just my shoulder that's injured."

Joe did as she asked. His bedroom was closest, so he led her there. Olivia did not object. She felt exposed and vulnerable in the hallway and the quicker she could get behind a locked door, the better.

The instant they were inside the room Olivia clutched Joe's arm and begged, "Please, lock the door."

"Honey, there's no need. No one is going to hurt you."

"Please, Joe."

"Okay, okay. Don't get upset. I'll turn on the chandelier, too, so I can see how badly you're hurt."

As she did each night in every occupied room, Mrs. Jaffee had turned down the bed and left the bedside lamp on. While Joe went back to secure the door and turn on more lights, Olivia made her way to the bed and sat down on the edge.

"Okay, the door is locked. Now, let's have a look." Joe came to the bed, intending to sit beside her, but at the first glimpse of her shoulder he stopped short. "Holy— What the hell! Someone *did* strike you. With something heavy, by the look of it. You don't get an injury like that from a fall."

An ugly red mark about three inches wide covered the top of her shoulder. It was angry-looking and beginning to swell, and already a livid bruise was forming around the wound.

"I told you someone hit me. It was just pure luck that I stepped to the left just as he swung, or he would have hit my head, which I assume was what he was aiming for. That would have done a lot more serious damage."

"It would probably have killed you," Joe snarled through clenched teeth. "The dirty son of a—when I find out who did this I'm going to tear him apart." He eased down on the bed next to her, examining the wound closer. "Is anything broken?"

"I don't think so. I think it's just badly bruised."

"Can you move your arm?"

"I think so." Olivia caught her lower lip between her teeth. Tentatively, she rotated her shoulder, then raised her arm until it was at a right angle to her body.

"How does that feel?"

"It hurts like the devil, but it doesn't feel as though anything is broken or out of place."

"I'm going to probe around a little. It's going to hurt, so brace yourself." Gingerly, he pressed on the angry area with the tips of his fingers.

His touch was exquisitely gentle, nevertheless

Olivia could not suppress a groan when he applied light pressure to the injured flesh.

"Sorry." Joe's teeth were clenched so tight the muscles in his jaw rippled. A tic twitched just under his left eye, and Olivia knew that the temper that Blair had told her about was simmering just beneath the surface, barely held in check.

"I think you're right. It's badly bruised but not broken. I'll run down to the kitchen and get an ice pack for you." He started to rise, but Olivia grabbed his arm.

"No! Don't leave me here alone."

"Sweetheart, calm down. You need ice on that shoulder, and I want to check the marina to see if there are any strange boats docked."

"Then I'm going with you."

"No. Absolutely not. You've just been attacked. You're injured and probably in shock. Look, I want you to lock the door after I go. If it'll make you feel better you can brace that chair under the doorknob, as well. Then get into bed and stay there until I knock. And don't open it for anyone but me. Okay?"

"O-okay," she replied in a trembling voice. She didn't want to be left alone, but she knew that Joe was right. Already she was beginning to shake.

"Good." He rummaged around in a bureau drawer and pulled out a pair of binoculars and a long, heavy flashlight that looked like a club.

Olivia followed him to the door, hugging her arms close to her body and biting the inside of her cheeks to stop herself from begging him to stay.

"I'll be back as quickly as I can. Lock this door behind me." Joe gave her a quick kiss and slipped out into the hall.

He may have been kidding about the chair, but Olivia didn't care. She pulled the Gothic wooden chair from in front of the secretary desk and wedged it under the doorknob, then crawled into the bed. Too frightened and nervous to lie down, she snatched the afghan from the foot of the bed and wrapped it around her shoulders and pulled the covers up to her waist.

She sat huddled in the middle of Joe's bed, shivering, her teeth chattering, for what seemed like an eternity, her gaze glued to the door. She jumped at every creak and pop the old house made. Once, when a tree branch screeched against a windowpane, she cried out and ducked under the covers.

She was beginning to think that something had happened to Joe when he tapped on the door and said, "Livvie, it's me. Open up."

She scrambled out of bed and flew across the room. After removing the chair, just to be sure, she pressed her ear against the door and said, "Joe?"

"Yeah, it's me."

He stepped inside the room carrying the flashlight in one hand and a plastic zipper bag full of ice in the other. His hair was windblown and standing up in spikes. Olivia threw herself at him and wrapped her arms around his lean middle. There was something hard and lumpy under his shirt, but she didn't care. At that moment he represented safety and strength, and she needed both.

"Oh, Joe, you're back. Thank God."

"Take it easy, sweetheart. I was only gone ten minutes." He settled her back in the bed and handed her the ice pack. "Keep that on your shoulder." After unlooping the binoculars from around his neck, he placed them and the flashlight on the bedside table and sat down on the side of the bed facing her. "How do you feel?"

"Better, now that you're here."

He smiled tenderly and cupped his hand to the side of her face. "It's nice to be needed, but I was talking about your shoulder."

"It's okay. The pain is easing."

"Good. That ice should help." Unbuttoning the top two buttons on his shirt, he pulled out a heavy jade statue about twelve inches high. "I found this on the floor in the hall. I'd say it's what he used to hit you," he said, his voice tight with controlled rage.

Olivia shivered and rubbed her upper arms.

"I went out to the landing and checked the marina, but there aren't any strange boats tied up. Then I went up to the tower room and scanned the ocean with the binoculars for boat running lights heading back to the mainland, but the only thing I saw was a freighter. That means whoever this guy is, he's still in the house.

"Easy. It's okay, it's locked," he assured her when she shot a panicked look toward the door.

Joe's expression turned uneasy. "The guy in your room, did he try...that is...did he touch you?"

"No. No, he didn't try to molest me. He was just creeping across the room. I think he was trying to scare me."

"Scare you? What for?"

"To make me leave this project."

"Why would anyone—" The look on Olivia's face gave him his answer. "Aw, hell. You think Mother is behind this."

"I can't rule her out. Or Blair, either. Can you?"

"You suspect Blair, too? Why? She apologized, and I think she was sincere."

"Joe, the first note appeared in my room the very day that Blair came out here to apologize."

"Note? What note?"

Olivia caught her lower lip between her teeth and looked at him with apprehension. She hadn't meant to blurt out the information about the notes that way. To minimize Joe's anger toward his mother and the backlash that, in turn, Eleanore was sure to direct her way, Olivia's intention had been to broach the subject to him matter-of-factly. She had intended to downplay her own reaction, as though she viewed the matter as more of an irritating prank than a threat, but she was so shaken by the attack that the words had come tumbling out before she thought.

"Well?" he demanded.

Olivia grimaced. "Notes telling me to leave, or else, that I'm not wanted here, that I'll be sorry if I don't do as they say. That sort of thing."

"*What!* Why the devil didn't you tell me about this?"

"I'm sorry. I was going to tell you at breakfast in the morning. Honestly. I didn't at first because you had so much on your plate already, and because I thought if it was your mother she would eventually give up and try something else when she realized the tactic wasn't working. I was certain she was merely trying to frighten me away."

"Good Lord, Livvie! Someone threatens your life and you don't say a word about it to me!"

Her chin quivered and fresh tears filled her eyes, banking against her lower lids. "Don't yell at me. I said I'm sorry."

"Ah, hell. I didn't mean to upset you more. Come here, sugar." He cautiously put his arm around her and drew her close. Olivia nuzzled her face against his chest, feeling safe for the first time since she'd awoken.

"Joe."

"Mmm."

"There's something else you should know." She felt him tense.

"What's that?"

"That day on the cliffs. I don't think it was the wind that caused me to fall. It felt like someone pushed me from behind."

"What?" Putting a finger beneath her chin, he tipped her face up until she had to look at him. His eyes were ablaze with horror and exasperation. "Why didn't you...?" He closed his eyes and shook his head. "Never mind."

"I couldn't be sure. I still can't. There was no one there when you found me. But that's what it felt like," Olivia rushed to tell him, then added meekly, "I just thought you should know."

"Thanks," he said, his voice reeking with sarcasm. "Anything else?"

She shook her head like a chastised child, and with a long-suffering sigh he pressed her face back against his chest.

"I'm probably wrong," she mumbled against his chest. "There wasn't anyone around when you found me hanging over the side of the cliff."

"He probably ducked into the woods after he shoved you," Joe theorized, rubbing his cheek against the top of her head. "He may have been watching the whole time I was pulling you up."

Olivia shivered. "Oh, don't say that."

"Take it easy." He rubbed her arm and back, being careful to avoid her injured shoulder.

"You know," he mused after a few minutes of silence, "this whole thing with you could also be just part of an attempt to stop this project. Like the so-called ghost sightings, and the mishaps and accidents that have been plaguing this job."

Olivia's chest squeezed with sympathy. Desperate to believe that his mother had had nothing to do with the notes or the attack, he was searching for any alternative motive. She couldn't blame him for that.

"It's possible," Olivia agreed, though privately she had her doubts. "There are plenty of people who oppose this project. Mrs. Jaffee, for one. And Cappy."

"Yeah, and there are plenty of people in Savannah who objected when we announced our plans. The consensus is, we're messing with things that are best left alone. At the time I dismissed the complaints as silly superstitious nonsense, but when people get stirred up, there's no telling to what lengths they will go."

"So how are we going to find out who is behind all this? Without proof, it's all just speculation."

"Do you still have those notes?"

"Yes. They're in my room." She clutched his shirt with both hands. "You're not going to leave me again to go get them, are you?"

"No. We can get them in the morning."

"I don't think they'll be much help. They're constructed from words cut out of magazines, pasted on paper."

"I want to take a look at them, anyway." He fell silent again, but after a while he asked, "How often did you get these notes? Did they come at regular intervals?"

"Not really. At first they were frequent. Then they seemed to taper off. I had begun to think whoever was responsible was about to give up."

"Obviously he hasn't."

They fell silent again, but after a while Joe muttered a soft "Damn" and raked his hand through his hair. "It's true that Mother wants to get rid of you, and I guess it's possible that Blair is involved, but I can't believe that either of them would do you any physical harm."

Olivia felt so sorry for Joe. She could see him wrestling with the possibility that his mother or sister might be behind the notes and the attack. He didn't want to believe it, but he was far too honest and straightforward to allow family loyalty and love to blind him.

"Maybe Eleanore didn't intend for this to happen tonight," she suggested. "Maybe things just got out of hand."

"That's possible, I suppose. Did you get a look at the guy by any chance? Or have any idea who he is?"

"Not really. I just saw him from behind."

Joe fixed her with a hard look. "Just so we're clear on the matter, until we catch this guy, you're sleeping in here with me. I'm not leaving you alone."

Joe looked like a man braced for a fight, his expression daring her to argue, but Olivia had no intention of balking. She would swim back to Savannah before she'd stay in that bedroom alone again. "Okay." She looked around. "I can sleep on the fainting couch."

"No, I'll sleep there. You'll take the bed."

"Joe—"

"Don't argue with me, Livvie. I'm this close to losing it, just thinking about what could have happened to you," he warned, holding up his thumb and forefinger just a hair's width apart. "Let's just go to bed and get some sleep."

"Are you sure the door is locked?"

"Yes. I can wedge the chair under the knob, too, if you'd like."

"Yes, please. Mrs. Jaffee has keys to all the rooms."

While Joe secured the door Olivia used the bathroom, then climbed into the bed. Joe pulled a pair of pajama bottoms from the bureau drawer and disappeared into the bathroom.

Olivia heard the shower running. She pretended to be asleep when he came out a few minutes later dressed only in silk pajama bottoms. As she peeked at him over the top of the covers, Olivia's mouth went dry.

Joe's physique had matured from that of a youth into that of a well-developed man in his prime. His torso was muscled and bronzed, with bulging biceps, broad shoulders and a wide chest that tapered down to a washboard-flat abdomen and narrow waist. The mat of dark hair on his chest formed an inverted triangle that narrowed to a thin line that whorled around his navel, then continued downward and disappeared beneath the low-slung pj's.

Through the veil of her lashes, Olivia watched him get a blanket from the top shelf in the closet and the other pillow from the bed. He turned out the chandelier, then the bedside lamp, and after a bit of rustling and creaking of the fainting couch, the only sounds were the wind around the eaves, and the soft sibilance of their breathing.

The silence did not last long. Within moments she heard Joe shift on the couch, then shift again. He rose up and punched his pillow and plopped back down. A second later he rolled over onto his back.

In the faint crack of moonlight spilling in through a gap in the velvet drapes, Olivia could see that his feet and ankles hung over the end of the fainting couch.

Making a restless sound, Joe flopped over onto his stomach.

Olivia could not stand to listen to his fidgeting another second.

She sat up. "Joe, for heaven's sake, that couch is too small for you to sleep comfortably. If you won't let me sleep there, then come get in the bed. It's a king-size. There's plenty of room on it for us both to sleep."

In the shadows she saw him sit up, and felt his gaze pinning her through the darkness. "Baby, if I join you in that bed, we'll be doing more than just sleeping. And even if you were willing, with your sore shoulder I don't think that's advisable."

The low, sexy texture of his voice slid over Olivia's skin like warm velvet. Gooseflesh popped out all over her body, and she shivered from head to toe. Debating for only a moment, she tossed back the corner of the covers closest to him. "Then you'll just have to be gentle, won't you."

Seventeen

Joe sat perfectly still, and Olivia heard his breathing grow heavier. "Are you sure?"

"I'm sure. I need you, Joe," she said just above a whisper.

It was all the invitation he needed. In one graceful movement he stood up, skimmed off the pajama bottoms and kicked them aside. He went to the nearest window and shoved the heavy drapes wide, letting moonlight pour into the room. "I've been going crazy, waiting for this. I want to see you."

He moved to the bed, and Olivia felt the mattress dip as he slid in beside her. Then she was in his arms and he was kissing her as though he would devour her.

Olivia wrapped her arms around him and gave herself up to the rapacious kiss, much as she'd done the first time he'd held her like this. What she was doing was reckless and irrational, and there was a good chance she would live to regret this decision, but at that moment she didn't care. She had almost been killed tonight, and she needed to be close to someone, to feel a tender human touch, to feel wanted, to feel alive.

And if on some level she was indulging her pride, then so be it. After years of idolizing Joe from afar, then the insecurity of knowing that he'd married her out of a sense of duty and honor, it was heady stuff, indeed, to find herself the object of his desire.

She reveled in the freedom to touch him, running her hands over his naked flesh. She tested the broad muscles that banded his back. She explored the trench that marked his spine, pausing along the way to let her fingers dance over each bony knob, working slowly downward until she encountered the enticing clef at the base. She explored his waist, the slight indentations just beneath on either side of his backbone. Then she grasped his tight buttocks with both hands.

Joe groaned. He pressed his hips hard against her, letting her feel how much he wanted her.

He broke off the kiss and propped up on one forearm. Breathing hard, he looked her over and a slight smile curved his mouth. "By the way," he murmured, tracing the curving neckline of her satin gown with his forefinger. "I neglected to tell you before, but I like your nightgown. Now take it off."

Olivia twined her fingers through his chest hair. "Why don't you do it for me," she whispered. "I'm not sure I can pull it off over my head without hurting my shoulder."

Joe pushed one spaghetti strap and then the other off her shoulders, slipped them down past her elbows and carefully eased her arms free. He worked the bodice down to her hips, pausing long enough to lavish attention on her breasts, circling each rosy nipple with his tongue, then suckling the turgid buttons until Olivia cried out and arched her back, clutching fistfuls of his hair.

In a sudden move, Joe threw back the covers and

moved to the foot of the bed, grasping the hem of the gown.

"Lift up your hips," he ordered in a raspy voice. Olivia obeyed, and the satin garment slithered down her body. Joe stopped and stared.

Olivia lay still, letting him look his fill, delighted beyond measure that she had put that ravenous look on his face. She could see his chest heaving, the hungry glitter in his eyes. Without taking his gaze from her, he tossed the nightgown over his shoulder. It landed on the rug with a whisper soft swish, and settled into a shiny puddle of emerald in the moonlight.

A glint of gold caught his attention, and he sat back on his haunches and lifted her left leg. He kissed her instep, her toes, the top of her foot, working his way up to the tiny heart hanging from the gossamer chain that encircled her slender ankle. Joe mouthed the chain and batted the heart with his tongue. Then he nipped her anklebone, and Olivia made a restless move and groaned.

Releasing her ankle, Joe kissed his way up her legs, pausing to nuzzle the triangle of silky auburn hair at the apex of her thighs, to trail a thin wet line with the tip of his tongue on the tender skin where her legs and body met, to explore her belly button, the soft undersides of her breasts, the aroused nubs at the center of each areola. By the time he reached her collarbone, then the side of her neck, Olivia was almost delirious.

Turning her head from side to side on the pillow, she clutched handfuls of his hair. "Please. Oh, please." She trembled all over, need pounding through her.

Lying cradled between her thighs, Joe braced up

on his forearms. "Look at me, Livvie," he ordered in a gravelly voice. "Look at me. I want to see your eyes when I make love to you again."

Her eyelids lifted slowly, as though they were weighted with lead. The tone of his voice, the heat and intensity in his eyes, made Olivia feel as though she were melting inside.

She framed his face with both hands. "Oh, Joe," she whispered.

Never taking his gaze from hers, he tilted his hips and she felt his sex nudging her. Then he pushed forward, and in a single, silken stroke, he slid into her.

Joe stilled and closed his eyes, his jaw clenched tight, his heart thundering against Olivia's breasts. "At last," he murmured with heartfelt relief.

Opening his eyes, he smiled and lowered his head. He kissed her lovingly, with so much tenderness and feeling that emotion flooded Olivia's chest until it felt near to bursting, until the sweetness of it was so great it was almost pain.

Then the movement began, the rhythm as old as time, the feelings as new as the moment. He loved her tenderly, almost reverently, savoring each slow stroke, each small sound of pleasure, the overwhelming feeling of rightness, of homecoming, of souls entwined.

Making love with Joe had always been wonderful, but for Olivia, this time—this time it was almost spiritual. The need was all-consuming, the sense of fulfillment, of completion, soul deep, the joy endless. This felt preordained. This felt heaven sent.

Before long, as surely as the sun rises each morning, the pleasure built, and with it the urgency. A slow savoring was no longer possible. Hearts beat faster, breathing became labored, desire became desperation, and the slow, sweet rhythm became driving demand. Low moans turned to gasps, hands that had stroked and caressed now clutched and clung.

Together, Olivia and Joe climbed higher and higher, and when the journey became too exquisite to bear, as one they went over the precipice, calling out in delicious agony.

A while later, when thundering hearts had slowed and breathing became normal, they floated back to earth, boneless and replete.

Bracing up on his forearms, Joe smiled down at Olivia ruefully. "I swear, making love with you short-circuits my brain. I get so worked up I forget all about everything else. Only twice in my life have I ever been with a woman without using protection, and both times I was with you."

His expression changed from rueful to caressing. "The first time resulted in a baby. How would you feel if history repeated itself?" he asked, watching her closely.

His words brought a burst of joy to Olivia's heart. For fourteen years she had grieved for the child she had lost, and she longed for another chance at motherhood. To have a second chance at bringing a child of Joe's into the world would be a blessing and a miracle.

This time, however, there would be no need for him to marry her. This time she was not without options or resources. Emotionally and financially she was capable of raising a child on her own.

For a few seconds she allowed herself to imagine the deliciousness of that possibility, but after a quick calculation reality took over and she realized that it wasn't to be.

"I don't think we have anything to worry about on that score," she assured him, fighting down her disappointment. "It's the wrong time of the month for me to conceive."

"Oh," Joe replied, and Olivia could almost swear that she'd heard disappointment in his voice.

The first thing Olivia saw the next morning when she awoke fully was Joe's face, just inches from her own. They lay on their sides, facing each other, and the instant her eyelids fluttered open she found herself looking into his dark eyes.

"Morning," he murmured.

"Mmm. Morning," she whispered back. "How long have you been watching me sleep?"

Smiling, Joe traced the curving line of her cheek with his forefinger, his touch as light as thistledown. "Not too long. Enough to know that you're the most gorgeous woman I've ever seen."

"Joe, please. I'm not wearing a speck of makeup, my hair has to be a mess, and I probably have sleep marks on my face."

"So? You look beautiful to me," he insisted, and to prove it he gave her a lingering kiss.

When the kiss ended he pulled back, and this time he looked at her with concern. "Any regrets?"

"No. None at all." She breathed deeply and stretched, arching her back like a contented cat. Waking up next to Joe again was novel and enthralling, yet it felt so...so normal. She felt enveloped by his warmth, by the clean male scent of him, by the wonderful feeling of security she used to experience whenever she was around him.

Noticing the bright sunlight flooding in through the curtains he'd opened the night before, she asked, "What time is it?"

Joe skimmed his forefinger down the side of Olivia's neck and along her collarbone. "A little before nine," he answered absently, his exploration now centered on the enticing slope of her breasts.

"Mmm" came her lazy reply, followed instantly by a stunned "*What?* Oh, my word! I missed breakfast. Mrs. Jaffee will be madder than an old wet hen."

After the events of the previous night Olivia had not expected to sleep a wink. Which, she supposed, proved just how potent Joe's lovemaking could be.

She sat up, intending to scramble out of bed and make a dash for her room, but Joe hooked an arm around her waist and hauled her back down beside him.

"Whoa. Where do you think you're going?"

"Joe, let me go. It's late. L.J. is probably in the library already, waiting for my instructions. And Mrs. Jaffee will be up here any minute to make up the beds and clean the rooms."

"So? L.J. can wait. And if Mrs. Jaffee comes to this door I'll tell her that you and I are sleeping in this morning and she can come back later."

"Joe! You wouldn't dare."

"Wanna bet? Honey, Mrs. Jaffee doesn't run things around here. I do. If I want to cuddle with my lady until noon, I will, and if she doesn't like it, too bad."

Olivia stared at him. Then she began to giggle.

"What's so funny?"

"Mrs. Jaffee is going to be so shocked when she

finds out about this,'' Olivia sputtered between giggles, gesturing back and forth between herself and Joe. ''She thinks I'm a lesbian.''

''What? You? Where did she get a crazy idea like that?''

''Once, when she accused me of trying to catch you, I told her I wasn't interested in getting married, ever, and from that she assumed…''

''I see. And you didn't bother to correct her.''

''Why should I? If she wants to jump to conclusions, that's her problem.''

''Uh-huh. And you figured if she thought you were gay she'd give you a wide berth. Nice try, honey.''

Olivia laughed. ''It worked for a while.''

They lay without speaking for a few moments longer, gazing into each other's eyes, enjoying the closeness. Finally, Joe trailed his fingertips down Olivia's arm and said casually, ''So. Never?''

''Pardon?''

''You never want to get married again?''

Olivia felt a twinge of uneasiness. ''Not really. I've built a good life for myself. I'm content as I am.''

''But what about a husband and kids? And don't try to tell me that you don't want a family, because I know better. There's no woman more maternal than you.''

''I'm thirty-two years old. That's a little late to be planning a family.''

''But not too late. Lots of women—''

''Joe, could we drop this, please? I really don't want to discuss it.''

He hesitated, and she could see in his eyes that he did not want to let the matter go, but after a few seconds he shrugged and said, "Sure. Whatever you want.

"There is something else I want to talk to you about," he added. "Before you woke up this morning I did some thinking about what happened last night, and I think I've got an idea how we can catch whoever has been leaving those notes."

"Really? How?"

"I'm going to get the guy who heads up security for AdCo out here and have him install a hidden camera in your room. No one outside of the three of us will know anything about it, not even Mike. Provided we didn't scare that guy off last night, the next time he delivers one of those threatening messages we'll nail him."

"That's a great idea, except that after last night I doubt that he'll try that same tactic again."

"Maybe not. But you're still going to be staying in here with me until we have this guy under lock and key."

He threw out the last statement almost as a challenge. Olivia could tell that he expected her to argue, but the truth was, she was relieved.

Now that she knew for certain that she hadn't imagined or dreamed those sounds at night, that there actually *had* been someone sneaking around in her room, she didn't think she could bear to sleep alone in there. Not to mention the idea of spending her nights in Joe's arms was extremely enticing. Still, she felt obligated to point out a few things he may not have considered.

"Joe, are you sure you want to do that? A single night is one thing, but if I spend every night with you, word is bound to get around. Not just here on the island, either. Soon everyone in your circle will know. You know how juicy talk spreads among Savannah society.''

"Sweetheart, if people want to talk, let them. I don't give a rat's behind. I want you with me. Besides that, I'm sure as hell *not* leaving you alone with this nutcase running around loose. I've also decided that I'm going to hire a security guard to stay with you during the workday.''

Olivia chuckled and stroked his cheek. "I appreciate the thought, Joe, but that won't be necessary. I won't be alone. L.J. is going to be working with me for the next few weeks, getting items ready to ship to the restorers."

"I'm not crazy about that idea, either. You ask me, that young pup is sweet on you. He looks at you like a lovesick teenager."

"You're being ridiculous. For heaven's sake, L.J. is just twenty-six."

"So? What's your point?"

"My point is, he wouldn't be interested in a woman so much older than he is."

"You can't be serious. Good grief, Livvie. You are one helluva talented decorator and an excellent businesswoman, but when it comes to men you're still as naive as ever. I hate to burst your bubble, sweetheart, but when a woman is as gorgeous and sexy as you, age doesn't enter the picture."

"Well, I think you're wrong. L.J. is a sweet, shy young man who is simply eager to please. He also happens to be built like a professional wrestler. No one would dare harm me with him around. So you can quit worrying."

* * *

Joe wasted no time setting his plan into action. Using the pretext of needing to discuss a break-in at another AdCo construction site, Joe contacted the head of the company's security, Arthur Westcott, who arrived midmorning by boat. By noon the camera was installed, cleverly hidden in what appeared to be a jewelry box atop the dresser in Olivia's bedroom.

Arthur joined Olivia and Joe for lunch. During the meal he explained that the video camera was the latest in top-quality security equipment.

"It's motion activated and will tape only when someone goes near the bed," he explained. "I suggest that you check the camera several times a day. If any tape has been used, play the video immediately."

Joe insisted that Olivia tell the security man every unusual or suspicious thing that had happened to her since she first arrived on the island. Reluctantly, Olivia did as he instructed. When she related the first time she saw the ghost, Joe looked thunderstruck.

"What's this?" he demanded, interrupting her. "This is news to me. You didn't say the person looked like a ghost. Why the devil didn't you tell me before now?"

Arthur's gaze switched back and forth between Olivia and Joe, his interest caught by both her story and the undercurrent of emotion Olivia knew he sensed between her and his boss.

"Because I knew you wouldn't believe me," she replied. "I saw how you reacted when the workmen reported seeing a ghost."

"Your workers have seen ghosts, too?" Arthur asked Joe.

"So they claim."

"There, you see? That's what I'm talking about. You don't believe them. Why would I think you'd believe me?" Olivia challenged.

"Because I trust you, and I know you're not prone to hysterics. Now, is there anything else I should know that you've neglected to mention?"

"Actually…" She went on to tell Arthur about the night she and Joe had arrived on the island and she saw what appeared to be Theobald Mallen walking along the top of the harbor cliffs, and of the unnerving incident that happened that same night in the hall outside her bedroom.

The more she talked, the more frustrated and upset Joe became. She knew he was restraining himself only because Arthur was present.

"Do you still have the notes that were left in your room?" Arthur asked her.

"Here they are." Joe pulled a small stack of white envelopes from the inside pocket of his suede jacket. "I picked them up from Olivia's room this morning and went through them."

The security man scanned through the notes, frowning. "Do you mind if I hold on to these? I doubt we'll find any fingerprints, but I'd like to go over them for other clues. Also, we'll need them for evidence."

"Sure."

"You know, Mr. Connally, I don't believe in ghosts or the supernatural. I've always thought the tales about Theobald Mallen were a bunch of hooey, but if several of your employees have spotted him, maybe all those people who reported sightings over the years did see something."

"C'mon, Arthur. Not you, too. There's no such thing as ghosts."

"Right. But there are holograms. I'd like your permission to search this place for hologram projectors."

Joe groaned. "A hologram. Of course. It makes perfect sense. Sure, you can search the place. But be discreet. I don't want to tip off our man that we're on to him."

"The job is going to take several days, even with a team working. How about I go back to Savannah and bring back a couple of my men who are good at searching. We'll tell everyone that we're going over the place so we can custom-design a security system."

"Sounds good. Get right on it, will you?"

"You bet." Arthur downed the last of his after-lunch coffee and blotted his mouth with his napkin. "Before I leave, though, I think we should check the video."

After what had happened the previous night, Olivia doubted that the man would return to her room again. She fully expected they would find that the camera hadn't recorded a thing. Joe, however, was so focused on catching the man that she didn't want to be negative, so she accompanied the men upstairs and let them into her bedroom.

The first thing Olivia spotted when they walked into the room was the white envelope on the bed, propped against the pillow. She stopped in her tracks in the middle of the room, her gaze glued to the small white square.

"Dammit," Joe snarled, and stomped over to the bed and snatched up the note. He ripped it open and scanned the paper, his jaw clenched tight.

"What does it say?" Olivia asked in a wavering but determined voice.

Joe shook his head. "Same old stuff."

"Joe, tell me."

His mouth folded into a grim line, but he sighed and read, "'YOU'VE IGNORED ALL MY WARNINGS. NOW YOU WILL PAY WITH YOUR LIFE.'"

Olivia had told herself that no matter what the message, she would not let it bother her, but she could not control the gasp that escaped her.

Cursing, Joe thrust the note into Arthur's hand and snatched her into his embrace. "Easy, sweetheart. Don't let this guy scare you. I won't let him hurt you."

"This note was delivered within the last hour. That means we should have our man on tape," Arthur said, tucking the envelope into the inside pocket of his suit coat, along with the others. He ejected the tape from the machine hidden in the false bottom of the jewelry box and a look of hard satisfaction came over his face. "Just as I thought. We got him."

"Great. Let's have a look," Joe said.

They went into the sitting room and Arthur slipped the cassette into the VCR, and after a few seconds of "snow" and static, a picture appeared on the television screen. The three of them watched, mesmerized, as one of the construction workmen came into view.

"Why, that's Clyde Shoemaker," Joe said. "He's one of our carpenters."

The man's body language gave him away. He crept into camera range like a burglar, stopping every few steps to listen and look over his shoulder. He reached the bed and looked around again. When he was sure it was safe, he pulled a white envelope from inside his sawdust-covered jean jacket and propped it against Olivia's pillow.

"Gotcha, you bastard," Joe growled.

"I don't understand. How did he get a key to my room?"

"Oh, that wouldn't be difficult. These old locks are easy to pick and it would be almost as simple to find a skeleton key that worked in most of them," Arthur explained.

"Okay, that settles it. You're sleeping in my room with me for the duration of this project," Joe informed Olivia.

"Joe! For heaven's sake," she gasped, turning the color of a beet.

Arthur cleared his throat. Pretending a sudden interest in a fringed lampshade, he turned away to examine it more closely.

"I don't give a rat's behind if Arthur or anyone else knows about us. Soon everyone in town is going to know, anyway. Hell, I'd like to shout it from the rooftops myself. The important thing right now is to keep you safe. Now that we know who the culprit is, I think my foreman ought to be let in on what's been going on. I'll meet you two in the library as soon as I round up Mike and Shoemaker."

Olivia and Arthur did not have long to wait. Within ten minutes Joe and Mike returned with a nervous-looking Clyde Shoemaker in tow.

Joe's jaw was clenched. He was so enraged he didn't trust himself to speak, and Olivia could see that he was itching to take a swing at the man.

"Uh, is something wrong, boss?" Clyde murmured in an aside to Mike. "What am I doin' here in the big boss's office?"

Hearing him, Joe barked, "Just shut up and watch this. Then you'll know." He stuck the tape in the

VCR, folded his arms over his chest and fixed Clyde Shoemaker with a laser-beam stare.

The instant the tape started playing the man turned pale.

"Look, boss, I can explain—"

"Go ahead," Joe snarled. "Explain to me how you broke into Olivia's room and left threatening notes. How, at night while she slept, you crept around in her room with the express purpose of frightening her. What did you do, sneak away from the others at quitting time and hide out in one of the empty rooms until you were sure Olivia was asleep? It would be easy enough to do. With that many men on board, who would notice someone was missing? If they did you could always say you'd caught a ride home with L.J."

"No, sir! I ain't never—"

"Last night when she chased you out into the hall you tried to kill her by hitting her with a jade statue," Joe barreled on, ignoring Clyde's protest. "And you were the one who pushed her over the cliff."

"What! No, sir! Not me!" Clyde denied vehemently. "I never did none of that stuff. I swear to God I didn't. All I did was deliver a few notes for a friend. I didn't even know what was inside those envelopes."

"You expect me to believe that?"

"It's the honest-to-God truth. I'll swear to it on my mama's grave."

"What's this so-called friend's name?" Arthur Westcott interjected in his calm interrogator's voice.

"Travis. Travis Dawson. Actually, I did it as a favor for his wife, Vicky."

"Vicky," Olivia gasped. The statement hit her like

a slap in the face. "Oh, my Lord! *Vicky* sent those notes?"

"I take it you know a Vicky Dawson?" Arthur said.

"I…I…" Olivia sank down on the nearest settee and buried her face in her hands, too upset to speak.

Hunkering down beside her, Joe put a comforting hand on her back and shot Arthur a grim look. "Vicky is her sister."

"Yeah, that's what Travis's wife said. And that she just wanted to pull a joke on her sister. I didn't know she was sending her threatening notes. I swear. Heck, I never woulda done it in the first place, except I owed Travis a favor."

"What about the rest?" Joe demanded. "The creeping around in her room at night, the attempts to murder her? Did Vicky ask you to do that, too?"

"No, sir. An' I didn't do none of that stuff. I just delivered the notes like Travis's wife asked me to, and that's all. I wouldn't hurt nobody. Especially no woman. I swear."

"How did you gain entry into Olivia's room?" Arthur asked.

"Vicky, she gave me a bunch of those big old-fashioned keys. She said there was probably one in the bunch that would open the door and, sure enough, she was right. But shoot, even if there hadn't been, those old locks are a joke. A kid could pick one with a paper clip."

"You stay right where you are. Don't move," Joe ordered, and signaled for Arthur and Mike to come with him to the other side of the library. "I want this guy thrown in jail," he told the other two men as soon as they were out of earshot.

"I understand how you feel," Arthur replied cautiously. "The problem is, you don't have much of a case. He was working on the island as one of your employees, and Olivia's own sister gave him some notes to deliver. I'm telling you, even if the sheriff's office will let you file charges, the case will never go to court."

"I think Mr. Westcott's right," Mike said. "Looks like your only option is to fire his ass."

"That's it? He can conspire against Olivia and scare her half to death, and nearly kill her, and all I can do about it is fire him?"

"You can prove only that he left the notes," Arthur pointed out reasonably. "You have no evidence that he committed the other offenses. Just your suspicions. I'm afraid that's not enough for a court of law."

"Damn," Joe spat. He fumed for a moment, then signaled to Arthur and Mike and stomped back to where Clyde stood, turning his cap around and around in his big workman's hands.

"You're getting off easy, Shoemaker," Joe informed the nervous man. "If I could I'd have you thrown in jail, but I've been advised that I can't do that. So pack your tools and get off my island. You're fired. Mr. Westcott was about to leave. He'll take you back to Savannah in his boat."

Eighteen

"I still don't think this is a good idea. I shouldn't be here."

Joe brought his car to a stop in the circular drive in front of the Connally mansion and switched off the engine. He turned to Olivia with a determined look that told her she hadn't a chance of dissuading him.

"This is exactly where you belong. Where I go, you go."

He reached for the door handle. "This won't take long. I'm going to be blunt and to the point. Before we go head-to-head with Vicky and Flora, I need to find out if my mother put them up to their tricks.

"But I understand that you don't want to subject yourself to Mother's sharp tongue. You can either wait here or take a walk down to the stables. I'll find you when I'm finished." He leaned across the center console and kissed her. "Don't worry. Everything is going to be all right."

For a few minutes after Joe disappeared through the front door, Olivia sat staring at the Colonial-style mansion. For nine years she'd had the run of the place. She knew every room, every nook and cranny. Now she felt like an intruder merely being in the driveway.

The elegant old house looked exactly as it had the

last time she'd been here, which didn't surprise her. Places steeped in tradition like Winterhaven Farm never changed. The brick siding and pillars were still painted a crisp white, the shutters, window trim and doors dark emerald. The ornate ironwork furniture on the veranda was green as well, with white-and-green cushions in a leafy pattern, and a pot of red roses and baby's breath sat on the glass-top table.

The lawn formed a smooth green carpet around the house and low, precisely trimmed hedges marked its boundaries, thanks to Moses Odem, the gardener at Winterhaven for the last thirty years or more.

As they had for more than a hundred and fifty years, the azalea and camellia beds provided a vivid display of color—from the darkest reds to pink and salmon to lavender and white—around the base of the house and veranda. Forsythia and althea bushes at each corner added splashes of gold and purple.

Olivia looked away from the house. Being there made her nervous, but she knew the worst was yet to come. When they left the farm they were going to pay her mother and sister a visit.

After Mr. Westcott had left Mallen Island with Clyde Shoemaker, Olivia saw firsthand just how right Blair had been about Joe's temper. She had never seen anyone display such quiet, lethal fury.

Considering the black rage he'd been in she knew she could count herself lucky that she'd managed to persuade him to put off the showdown with her sister for a few days.

At first he wouldn't hear of waiting.

"To hell with that," he'd said in a frighteningly soft voice. "Now that we know who is responsible, why wait?"

''So that you can cool down and handle the situation rationally and calmly. You're so angry right not there's no telling what you'll say or do. I want us to be in complete control when we face Vicky.''

Joe had argued some more, but Olivia eventually wore him down, especially after pointing out that if they waited until Sunday afternoon to deal with her sister they could have a pleasant, leisurely three-day weekend together before things got ugly.

It had taken a lot of pleading and shameless feminine wheedling on her part, but in the end he'd given in.

They had spent three glorious days at Joe's apartment, making love, watching movies and going for long walks around the squares, which were at the peak of their spring beauty.

They'd had countless chess matches and slow-danced barefoot in his living room to old Sinatra records. On Saturday night they went to a club and listened for hours to a piano player who had a seemingly endless repertoire. Around one in the morning they'd walked home, Joe with his arm around her shoulders, she with hers around his waist, and, once there, they'd made love again.

Olivia glanced back at the house and the long windows that opened onto the veranda. If Eleanore and Joe were in the front parlor they had a clear view of the car and of her. Growing uneasy, she got out of the car and headed for the stables.

Memories flooded back as she walked down the drive and looked out over the miles of intersecting white-board fencing and green pastures dotted with moss-draped oaks and sleek Thoroughbreds. In the pasture next to the drive, under the watchful eyes of their mothers, impudent spring foals ran on spindly legs and kicked up their heels for the sheer joy of being alive, drawing a smile from Olivia. Spring on the farm had always been her favorite time of year.

There appeared to be no one around when she reached the stables. She strolled along beside the row of white-washed stalls. Several magnificent horses poked their heads out over the half doors, hoping for a treat or a bit of petting. One beautiful mare the color of dark mahogany captured Olivia's attention. She stopped and scratched between the mare's eyes.

"Well, now, aren't you a beauty. Yes you are," she cooed, and the animal whickered softly and nuzzled Olivia's arm.

"I'm sorry, girl. I don't have any treats to give you."

Looking around, she spotted a pail of oats sitting beside the next stall door and scooped up a handful. Dainty as a Savannah debutante, the mare plucked the offering from Olivia's palm with velvety lips.

"Oh, what a mannerly girl you are," she praised. The animal bobbed her head as though agreeing, and Olivia laughed. Leaning her forehead against the mare's, she patted her neck. If only humans could be as uncomplicated as horses, she thought.

"I been waitin' for you," a raspy voice grated in her ear.

Olivia started and spun around, her heart in her throat, and saw herself reflected in a pair of blue mirrored sunglasses. Topping the grizzled head and wrinkled face was a scarlet and gold turban.

"Miss Minerva!" Olivia put her hand over her booming heart and closed her eyes. "My goodness, you scared me half to death."

"I come to warn you, chile. You listen to ole Minerva, an' listen good. The danger, she ain't passed."

"Wh-what? What do you mean?"

"The pretender, he don't want you there. None of you. You is interferin' with his evil b'ness. And he be running out of time. He'll strike at Mr. Joe through you agin. And soon," she warned in her lilting Jamaican accent.

"Through me? I—I don't understand."

"Here, you take dis talisman." The old woman handed Olivia a small jagged rock that looked like a flintstone. "It has powerful good mojo, an' I done sanctified it during the dark of the moon, just for you. It will protect you. But you must keep it with you always, you hear?"

"Minerva, I'm not sure about this."

"You don't got to be sure. Minerva be sure. You just mind what I say."

Olivia turned the shard over in her hand and gave the old voodoo priestess a wan smile. "Well, I don't suppose it could hurt."

"De pale moon be risin' soon. You best beware, chile. Just you beware. And remember, keep dat talisman with you."

As suddenly as she had appeared, Minerva turned and walked away, her colorful caftan flapping around her skinny legs.

"Miss Minerva, wait!"

The old woman kept going and merely raised her hand and called, "Beware the pretender, chile."

Olivia stared after the scary woman, barely able to breathe. Minerva disappeared around the corner of the row of stalls, and Olivia shuddered.

* * *

Joe found his mother and brother in the office at the back of the house. He could hear them arguing before he reached the door of the paneled room.

"I disagree," Eleanore said in her most imperious tone.

"Disagree all you want. I'm still buying the horse. I'm telling you, he's a good investment."

"How can you say that? He has yet to win a race."

"But the potential is there. All he needs is training."

"Is this a private argument, or can anyone join in?" Joe asked, striding into the room.

"Joseph."

"Hey, bro. What brings you here on Sunday afternoon?"

"You'll be staying for dinner, I hope," Eleanore said.

"No. I just stopped by to ask you something."

"Me? Of course, dearest. What do you want to know?"

"Did you enlist or coerce or pay or in any way talk someone into sending Livvie threatening notes? And before you answer, I should tell you that I can find out the truth from someone else."

"Uh-oh," Luke murmured. "This doesn't sound good."

"Certainly not. And I resent the question."

"How about hiring someone to eliminate her?"

"Eliminate?"

"Like push her off a cliff, or hit her over the head with a blunt instrument."

Eleanore's eyes widened. "Are you asking me if I hired someone to *kill* Livvie? Certainly not. How dare you even think such a thing about your own mother.

You should know that I would never harm Livvie. I
told you, I don't hate her, or even dislike her. I love
that girl like one of my own. I simply don't think
she's right for my son.''

"I have to side with her on this one, bro," Luke
drawled. "That's going a bit too far. Ma will do a lot
of things to get her way, but never murder."

"Thank you, darling. It's nice to know that I have
at least one son who loves me. And please, how many
times must I tell you, do not call me Ma."

Unmoved, Joe asked, "Will you put your hand on
a Bible and swear to me that you had nothing to do
with the notes or the attacks on Livvie?''

"Yes," she replied without hesitation. "If that's
what it takes."

"Whoa. Wait a sec, bro. Are you saying that those
things actually happened? Someone sent Livvie
threats and tried to kill her?''

"Yes."

"Why in God's name would anyone want to harm
Livvie?''

"I don't know, but I intend to find out."

Joe turned on his heel and headed for the door, but
his mother stopped him.

"Joseph."

He turned and cocked one eyebrow. "Yes?''

"I hope you realize that this means I'm not the
only one who wants Livvie gone from here."

Wordlessly, Joe stalked out.

"Hey, wait up, bro, and I'll walk with you," Luke
called, unfolding his long, lanky frame from his
slouched position in the chair.

"So what's going on?'' he asked, falling into step
beside Joe in the hall.

"I told you, I don't know. And I don't have time to talk about it now. Livvie and I have another stop to make."

"Livvie's here? Hell, man, why didn't you say so? Where is she?"

Olivia stood with her arms resting on the top board of the paddock fence, absently watching a black stallion prance up and down the far fence line, bobbing his head and whinnying. Her mind, however, still wrestled with old Minerva's strange warning.

It didn't make any sense. Who was the pretender? What evil business was he supposedly conducting? There was nothing clandestine or illegal going on at Mallen Island, just crews of workmen restoring an old house.

"Well, as I live and breathe. If it isn't little Livvie Jones."

Recognizing the voice from the past, she turned around and saw Luke and Joe strolling toward her.

Like his brother, Luke had matured into manhood during her fourteen-year absence. At thirty-three he was long and lean and whipcord tough. He resembled Joe more than she remembered. He had the same dark hair, the same eyes and nose, but his face was a little thinner than Joe's, the features sharper and craggier, his skin more weathered beneath his broad-brimmed hat.

Luke had the pared-down look of a horseman whose everyday work kept him in shape, whereas Joe looked exactly like what he was: a successful, always-on-the-go businessman who kept fit through jogging and regular trips to the gym.

Olivia waited as Luke approached, expecting a

handshake, or at most a quick hug. She wasn't prepared when he let out a whoop, picked her up and swung her around in circles, then planted an exuberant kiss on her mouth.

She was still recovering when he set her on her feet, grabbed her hands and held them wide, looking her over from head to toe.

"Damn, Livvie. If I'd known you were going to turn out this good I would've married you myself."

"The hell you would've," Joe growled, stepping between Olivia and his brother. "As for that kiss, I'll let it pass this once, but if I ever catch you kissing her again, you'll be eating teeth."

Luke grinned at Olivia. "He always was a selfish bastard."

"Yeah, well, I'm sorry to cut this reunion short, but Olivia and I have to be going."

"C'mon, we can talk on the way to the car," Luke said congenially. Looping his arm around Olivia's shoulders, he shot Joe a taunting look over the top of her head.

All the way back to the house Luke peppered her with questions about her life; where she'd gone after she'd left Savannah; where she'd attended college; where she lived in Atlanta; was she seeing anyone? He slipped the last one in as they reached the car, and before Olivia could say a word Joe answered for her.

"Yes, she is. Me. So whatever is going on in that head of yours, little brother, forget it."

Luke laughed and opened the passenger door for Olivia. "Hey, you can't blame a guy for trying."

Vicky's pickup truck was in the driveway, just as Olivia had expected. Ever since their marriage, Vicky and Travis, and later their kids, had eaten Sunday dinner at Flora's. Afterward, while mother and daughter visited and the kids played in the backyard, Travis spent the afternoon watching sports on TV.

Joe wasted no time. He banged on the front door with the side of his fist.

"Livvie. Joseph. What a surprise," her mother said, hastily drying her hands on her apron.

"We're here to see Vicky," Joe informed her.

"Yes, of course." Flora stepped back. "Come in."

In the living room to the left of the tiny entrance hall, Vicky's husband, Travis Dawson, sat watching television. He glanced over his shoulder to see who had dropped by, then did a double take and jumped to his feet.

"Mr. Connally. What are you...that is...I didn't expect to see you here. Is something wrong with one of the horses?"

"No. I'm here to see your wife."

"Vicky? About what?"

"I don't intend to go over this but once. If you want to know, I suggest you go get your wife."

"Yes, sir. Right away."

Travis returned in less than a minute with Vicky in tow. Her face was pale and her eyes had the wild look of a trapped animal. Olivia knew that her sister had guessed why she and Joe were there.

"Travis said you wanted to talk to me. I can't imagine what about."

"Knock it off, Victoria. I'm sure by now you've heard from Clyde Shoemaker. He told us all about how you had him put those threatening notes in Olivia's room. What I want to know is why?"

"Oh, dear," Flora murmured, wringing her hands. "I told you not to send those notes. I *told* you."

"You were in on this, too, Mama?" Olivia's gaze went back and forth between her mother and sister, her eyes brimming with infinite sadness. "How could you do that to me? Either of you?"

"Oh, no, child, no. This was all your sister's doing," Flora vowed. "I swear. I had nothing to do with any of it."

"But you knew what she was planning yet you didn't say a word to me. You could have warned me."

"Well...I...I..."

"Wait a minute," Travis broke in. "Vicky, you had Clyde deliver threatening notes to Livvie? That's not what you told me was in those envelopes. You said the whole thing was just a joke."

Vicky set her jaw and looked away, refusing to look at her husband or Olivia.

Olivia watched her sister. All her life, whenever Vicky had been caught doing something she shouldn't, she reacted defensively with belligerence and aggression, and this time was no different.

She saw her sister's face harden and her chin jut out. "Well, *somebody* had to wake her up," she snapped at Joe. "I was merely trying to keep her from making a fool of herself over you all over again."

Vicky shot Olivia a searing look before refocusing on Joe. "She obviously didn't learn a thing from that fiasco fourteen years ago. From what I've heard, this time around she crawled right back into your bed the first chance she got."

"Hardly. But that's really none of your business, is it?" Joe said with chilling calm. "But back to my question. You're saying you threatened your sister's life for her own good? And of course your actions were in no way intended to benefit you, right?''

Vicky's expression turned even more sullen. ''I was also hoping to save Mama and me more embarrassment. So what? Livvie isn't the one who has to live here and put up with all the tittle-tattle and snickers and snide comments about how the housekeeper's daughter was warming the young master's bed, and how she snared him with the old baby-in-the-oven trap.

''Livvie always did have high-flown notions. She won't accept that we're working class and that you and your family are upper crust, and that the two just don't mix. Especially not in Bella Vista or Savannah.''

Joe drilled Vicky with a hard stare. ''I can almost understand how Flora could feel that way. Almost. She's from another generation that had different ideas. But not you. I think you're just plain jealous of Olivia and always have been. She's prettier and smarter and she was your father's favorite. Never mind that you were Flora's pet, you were jealous of their relationship. She had the gumption and get-up-and-go to make something of herself, and you couldn't stand that, could you. So now you're lashing out, trying to wreck her life any way you can.''

''That's not true,'' Vicky denied. ''I love my sister.''

''Yet, by your own admission, you were willing to have her killed in order to save yourself a little embarrassment.''

''Killed! What are you talking about? I never wanted Livvie killed.''

"Uh-huh. Then you didn't tell Shoemaker to get rid of her?"

"I don't remember, exactly. But if I did I only meant that I wanted her to quit the Mallenegua project and go back to Atlanta. I wouldn't tell him to harm her. She's my sister, for God's sake."

"Yes, I know. That's the only reason I haven't already turned this over to the sheriff."

"The sheriff! Oh, Lordy," Flora gasped. "Now you've gone and done it," she scolded her eldest daughter.

Flora burst into tears and Vicky and Travis began to talk at once.

"Quiet!" Joe roared, and the babble shut off as though someone had turned a spigot. "Now, listen to me, all of you. I'm giving you all fair warning. If any harm comes to Olivia during the duration of the Mallenegua job, if she receives any more threats or gets so much as a paper cut, I'm going to hold you and your mother responsible," he said to Vicky. "And believe me, the next time I won't hesitate to call in the authorities. Is that clear?"

Vicky and Flora nodded and mumbled yes.

Joe's eyes narrowed and his frighteningly soft voice grew softer still. "And once and for all, I want to get something straight. I don't give a tinker's damn what Savannah's blue bloods think, or about any of their arbitrary rules. Nor do I want to hear any more of your antiquated ideas about class, or Olivia 'trapping' me, or being a gold digger, or having ambitions above her station. Is that clear?"

Chastened, the two women nodded again.

"Good. Because Olivia is the classiest woman I've ever known. She's bright and talented and beautiful, and sweet through and through. Instead of doing everything you can to tear her down and sabotage her happiness, you should both be busting with pride over all she is and all she's accomplished.

"And as long as I'm setting the record straight, you might as well know that I happen to be very much in love with her. If she'll have me, I plan to marry her again just as soon as possible."

"Joe!" Olivia cried. "What are you saying?"

At the same time Vicky and Flora gasped in unison, "*Marry* her!"

"That's right. And this time if anyone dares to try to come between us, God help them."

"But you *can't* marry Livvie," her sister protested. "It…it isn't right. Can't you see that? And…and Mrs. Connally will be furious."

"She'll accept it eventually. She'll have to. She won't have a choice if she wants to see her son and if we're lucky, her grandchildren."

Olivia winced.

"Merciful heavens," Flora whispered, sinking down onto the sofa as though her legs would no longer support her.

"Joe. Joe, we have to talk," Olivia insisted, urgently tugging at his shirtsleeve.

"I know, sugar, I know, but not now." He gave her a rueful smile and patted her hand. "We'll talk at home. I promise."

Looking back to the others, his expression turned menacing again. "All of you remember, I meant what I said. Every word."

"Olivia, honey, I know you're upset with me, and I understand, but don't you want to talk about it?"

Joe asked, following her into his apartment. "You haven't said a word since we left your mother's house."

"Maybe that's because you left me speechless," she said wearily. She walked to the windows and stared out at the river traffic, feeling sick inside. She'd known in her heart that it was a mistake to get involved with Joe again. How could she have been so stupid?

"I swear, I didn't mean to blurt out everything like that," Joe said in a contrite tone. "My intention was to court you for six months or so, the way I should have the first time around. Then I was going to take you to Paris or Rome or some other romantic spot and propose. I'd planned to get down on one knee and do it right this time.

"But today I was just so furious with your sister and mother, and so fed up with their ridiculous ideas about class and who should and should not marry whom, that I lost it. That's all."

Standing with her arms crossed over her midriff, Olivia massaged her elbows with her fingertips. She shook her head slowly. "I wish you hadn't," she murmured. Oh, Lord, how she wished he hadn't.

"I understand. But, honey, just because it was the wrong time and the wrong place to make that declaration doesn't make it any less genuine. I do love you, Livvie," he murmured from somewhere close behind her. "With all my heart. And you would make me the happiest man alive if you agreed to marry me."

His hands closed around the curves of her shoulders and slid gently down to her elbows, then up again. She felt his warm, moist breath feather over her right ear. "Will you marry me, Livvie?" he asked in a husky whisper.

"Oh, Joe, if only you had kept quiet," she groaned.

"What?"

"My answer is no. I can't marry you."

"What are you saying?" He turned her around to face him. Stunned, he stared down at her. "Why can't you marry me?"

"I just can't."

"That's not good enough. If you're going to turn me down, I at least deserve to know why."

"Joe, please, can't you just take no for an answer and be done with it?"

"No, I can't. Give me a reason. Is it because we were married before? If so, so what? That was a long time ago and we're both different people now. Back then we were a couple of green kids. We're adults now. We know what we want out of life."

"That's partly it, but it's not the main reason."

"Then what is?"

Olivia lowered her gaze and concentrated on the third button on his shirt. "I'm not in love with you, Joe."

She felt him stiffen, and for the space of five agonizing seconds he did not speak. She could feel his dark gaze boring into the top of her head.

"I don't believe you," he said finally. "I've felt the way you respond to me when we make love. I've felt the love in your touch. I've seen it in your eyes."

"I never said I wasn't fond of you, Joe. I am. I will always have a deep affection for you. I'm just not in love with you anymore. I told you that at the beginning, when I first took this job."

"Our relationship has changed since then. We've

grown closer.'' Frustrated, Joe turned and walked away a few steps and raked his fingers through his hair. ''If you didn't love me, then why did you make love with me? Where did you think this thing between us was heading?''

''I didn't think about that. I...I just thought we were having an affair.''

''An affair. For how long? A month? Six months? The duration of the project? What?''

''I don't know,'' she cried. ''I guess I assumed we'd take it as it came.''

''I see. Okay, let's say we were still involved when the project was completed. What did you think would happen then? We'd say, So long? It was fun while it lasted? Then go our separate ways?''

''I didn't think that far ahead. I suppose I assumed that you'd visit me in Atlanta now and then.''

''A long-distance affair, huh? When both our schedules allowed I'd drop by and we'd have a nice roll in the hay, then we'd go back to our separate lives until the next time we had time for each other. Is that it?''

''Something like that.''

''Liar.''

''What?''

''I know you, Livvie. You're an old-fashioned girl at heart. You wouldn't be satisfied with an arrangement like that. Not for a minute. You want marriage and commitment. You want babies with a life partner who will love you forever. And I think you want those things with me. You love me, Livvie. I know you do.''

''No, you're wrong. I don't.''

''Then why can't you look at me?'' he demanded

taking hold of her arms again. "I won't believe you until you can look me straight in the eyes and tell me that you don't love me. I don't think you can do that."

Olivia looked up then. "Oh, Joe, don't make me do this. I don't want to hurt you."

"Say it, Livvie. If you can."

She caught her lower lip between her teeth. Finally, drawing a deep breath, she met his gaze squarely. "I don't love you, Joe."

She watched the determined glint fade from his eyes. For an instant she saw raw pain, then, like an invisible iron curtain, a protective shield came down. Releasing her, his arms fell to his sides and he seemed to put distance between them, even though he did not move.

"I see," he said. "Well...I guess there's nothing left to say."

Nineteen

Olivia and Joe left for Mallen Island aboard the *Fleeting Dreams* early the next morning. After lying awake all night, alone in the guest bedroom's huge bed, she felt exhausted. During the trip from the mainland she tried to nap in the cruiser's bunk, but she was too sick at heart to sleep.

Earlier that morning she had emerged from the guest room filled with trepidation about facing Joe again, but she needn't have worried. He was pleasant and friendly, the soul of politeness, and he treated her as though she was a welcome guest.

Yet for all his exquisite good manners, there was a distance and formality about his demeanor that made her so sad she wanted to cry.

Over breakfast she tried to talk to him about what had happened, but he cut her off.

"I'd rather not discuss it, Olivia," he said in a pleasant but adamant tone. "We said all there was to say last night. There's no point in rehashing it all again. Let's just forget that these past few days happened. Okay?"

He checked his watch. "Can you be ready to leave for the island in twenty minutes? I talked to Mike a little while ago and there are several things that need my attention."

And that had been that.

Other than an occasional "yes" or "no" or "excuse me" they hadn't spoken since.

Ever the gentleman, Joe offered his hand to assist Olivia off the boat and carried her bag up to the mansion and all the way to her bedroom door. On the way they had to pick their way around crews of workmen who were making repairs and stripping the banisters on the grand stairway and the woodwork along the second-floor hall.

"It just occurred to me that perhaps you feel uneasy about staying in this room," Joe said when they stopped outside her door. "In case you're wondering, the video camera has been removed. With Clyde Shoemaker gone you'll be safe, but if you'd like, I can have Mrs. Jaffee move you to a different room."

"Thank you, but that won't be necessary."

"In that case, I'd better go find Mike. I'll see you at lunch."

"Joe, wait. I've been thinking. In light of what's happened between us—"

"Olivia, I said I don't—"

"No, wait. Please, hear me out. I was just going to say that I think it would be best if I moved up my buying trip. I'll be gone for three or four weeks. Some time apart might make things easier for both of us."

"I see. When do you want to leave?"

"Today, if I can get a flight out. And if I can get a ride back to Savannah."

"All right. I'll tell Cappy to take you in my boat." Joe looked at her in silence, and in those brief moments she saw the raw pain in his eyes. Then, like a steel curtain, his protective shield came down, and all she saw was a polite mask. "Today is shaping up to be busy. If I don't see you again before you leave, have a nice trip.''

''Thank you.''

Watching him stride away down the hall, Olivia felt as though she had an anvil sitting on her chest, crushing her heart.

She knew the pain of unrequited love. She would give anything to spare Joe that heartache, but she had to protect herself. It would be so easy to fall in love with him again, but she didn't dare let that happen. It had taken her years to get over him the first time. She wasn't sure she would survive if she had to go through that again.

With a dispirited sigh she opened the door and pulled her weekender bag into the room.

While unpacking the small bag and sorting through the clothes she would take with her, she came across the talisman that Minerva had given her. Turning the sharp piece of flint over in her hand, Olivia shivered. Minerva claimed to practice only good magic, but the old woman still gave her the willies.

She had forgotten all about the strange encounter with the voodoo priestess. The showdown with her family, followed by the breakup with Joe, had pushed everything else out of her mind.

Olivia started to toss the stone into the trash can beneath the desk, but at the last instant she hesitated. She stared at the talisman. It was just a stupid piece of rock. It had no magic powers. Nevertheless, though feeling like a fool, she wrapped the shard in a tissue and slipped it into the pocket of her slacks.

An hour later Olivia had booked a flight to Boston, made hotel reservations, checked in with her office and was in the middle of packing when someone knocked on her door. Before she could move, the door opened and Blair stepped inside the room. Olivia's spirits sank even lower. The last thing she needed at this particular time was to be around another Connally.

"Blair, what are you doing here? If you brought more documents for Joe, I think he's with Mike."

"I've already seen Joe. I just spent the last hour wheedling out of him the reason why he's acting like a grizzly bear with an impacted tooth. He told me that you two broke up. Since I didn't know that you were back together, that was a bit of a surprise, but not nearly as much as the reason for the split."

"Blair, what happened is between Joe and me. This doesn't concern you."

"The heck it doesn't. My brother is in hell and my friend has obviously lost her mind. That makes it my concern."

"I assure you, I'm perfectly sane."

"Oh, yeah? Then would you please explain to me exactly what your problem is? For years you adored my brother as though he were some sort of god. Now, when he loves you back, you refuse his proposal. Honey, in my book, that's nuts."

"For heaven's sake, Blair, that was a childish crush and it was years ago. We all have them and we all get over them. That's part of growing up. I'm a woman now." Olivia turned back to her suitcase and added another silk blouse to the contents. "I know the difference between infatuation and love, and I don't love Joe."

"I don't believe you. A crush doesn't last ten or twelve years."

Olivia rolled her eyes. "You Connallys are so stubborn. What's it going to take to…'' She turned back to face Blair just as the door to the huge dressing room opened and a man stepped into the room.

"L.J.! What were you doing in my dressing room?" Olivia demanded in a startled voice. "For that matter, how did you get in there? I've been going in and out of that room for the last hour and you weren't there then."

The young man shook his head and smiled amiably. "Looks like you caught me," he drawled. Still smiling, he reached inside his workman's coveralls and pulled out a gun. "I'm sorry about this, ladies, but under the circumstances, I don't have a choice."

Blair let out a shriek of alarm, and L.J. swung the muzzle of the gun toward her, his demeanor going instantly from genial to vicious. "Shut up. You make another sound like that and I'll kill you where you stand."

Olivia edged closer to Blair and touched her hand. "Shh. Stay calm," she advised, never taking her gaze from L.J. Blair latched onto Olivia with both hands and clung like a limpet. Olivia could feel her shaking.

"I don't understand," she said. "Why are you doing this, L.J.? What could you possibly have to gain?"

"You'll find out soon enough. Right now I need to get you two out of here." He took a roll of duct tape from the pouch on his tool belt and tossed it to Blair. "You. Miss High and Mighty Connally. Take that tape and bind Olivia's wrists behind her back. And do a good job, because I'm going to check it when you're finished."

Olivia turned her back to her old friend. With her

left side to L.J., she surreptitiously slipped her right hand into her trouser pocket and closed her fingers around the talisman that Minerva had given her. With both hands balled into fists, she crossed her wrists behind her back.

Whimpering with every breath, Blair went to work. "Oh, God, oh, God, oh, God. He's going to kill us. I know he is," she blubbered. She managed to clumsily wrap the duct tape around Olivia's wrist three times and tear off the roll.

"All right, let's have a look." L.J. motioned with the gun for Blair to move aside, and he stepped behind Olivia and examined the tape.

Olivia held her breath and silently prayed that he would think her hands were clenched in fear.

"That'll do. All right, bitch, your turn," he said to Blair. "And knock off that sniveling. I hate weepy women."

Valiantly trying to hold back her tears, Blair followed his command and turned and put her hands behind her back. When he finished binding her, he herded the two women into the dressing room.

Theobald's dressing room was the size of most modern master bedrooms. The entire back wall held floor-to-ceiling shelving that had been divided into cubbyholes for such things as shoes, shirts and hats. To Olivia's amazement, L.J. ran his hand along the inside of a cubby and the entire middle section of shelving swung open.

He turned to the women and waved his gun. "After you, ladies."

Blair choked back a whimper, barely able to contain her terror as first she, then Olivia were prodded into what appeared to be a black hole.

Following close behind, L.J. closed the door behind

them, and Blair gave a strangled cry when they were enclosed in total darkness.

"I told you to shut up, bitch," L.J. barked, switching on the flashlight he carried on his tool belt. "I'm not going to tell you again. Now move."

Standing behind Olivia and Blair, he shone the flashlight over their shoulders, illuminating steep wooden stairs that led downward. They walked down single file. Whenever Blair moved too slowly, Olivia received a prod in the back with the gun barrel and L.J. growled, "Move it, bitch, or your friend gets a bullet right now."

The perpendicular shaft through which the stairs descended could not have been more than eight or ten feet in diameter. Every seven steps they reached a landing and the stairs turned back upon themselves. They went down so far that Olivia knew they had to be nearing basement level.

Finally they reached the bottom of the stairs, and she realized that they were in a long, sloping, cavelike tunnel carved out of the granite cliffs. To the left, in the dim peripheral light of the flashlight beam, she spotted what appeared to be a door. If Olivia's mental calculations were right the door likely led into the basement furnace room.

"This way," L.J. ordered, motioning to the right with the flashlight, where, ahead of the feeble beam of light, only blackness awaited them.

Having their hands bound behind them made walking over the uneven tunnel floor difficult, and several times both Olivia and Blair stumbled and fell, only to be dragged to their feet again by a cursing L.J.

After walking for about twenty minutes, the passageway ended at a door that looked like something out of a medieval castle. The door was made of thick planks of wood with heavy metal strapping.

The ancient brass lock was temperamental. L.J. cursed and jiggled the key until finally the tumblers clicked and he pulled the door open. He shoved Blair and Olivia through the opening and into a large cavern, lit by only one dim kerosene lantern.

"End of the line, ladies," L.J. said with a laugh. Olivia shivered, knowing he was referring to more than the end of the tunnel.

Instead of struggling with the recalcitrant lock again, he barred the door behind them with a thick plank, which he hefted into the iron brackets bolted to the inside.

While L.J. dealt with the door Olivia examined their surroundings as quickly as possible. Unlike the tunnel they had just traversed, which had obviously been man-made, the cavern room appeared to be the work of Mother Nature, carved out by the relentless surging of ocean waves over the millennia.

The cavern was a spacious oval cavity at the end of a finger of the ocean that had cut perhaps a hundred and fifty feet into the cliffs. At its widest point the cave appeared to be somewhere around sixty feet, and overhead a domed ceiling soared at least that high. Olivia shivered. It was as though a malevolent giant hand had reached in and scooped out a fistful of granite to create the space.

Like all caverns, the air was cool and humid. And noisy, she realized. Concentrating harder, she identified the constant background noise as water lapping against stone, accompanied by the more distant roar of waves pounding the cliffs.

Looking around, she noted that the stone floor of

the cavern extended only a little over halfway across the space. There it met a restless pool of water. Squinting her eyes in the semidarkness, Olivia realized that ocean water still surged into the cavern. The outside passageway that nature had gouged into the cliff side was much larger than the one they had taken from the house. From the entrance at the other end of the tunnel-like opening faint daylight seeped into the cavern room.

The tunnel must open to the sea on the east side of the island, Olivia calculated.

Could she and Blair escape by swimming out? she wondered, but she quickly dismissed that idea. Not only was she not a strong swimmer, at that point the sea was treacherous, and for a mile or so in each direction the shoreline was sheer rock cliffs. There were no beaches or even any boulders onto which they could climb, assuming they didn't get pounded to death on them first.

The only way into and out of the cave from the sea was by boat, and it would have to be small enough to negotiate the tunnel—a boat like L.J.'s sleek powerboat, which was bobbing in the pool of water just a few feet away, moored to one of the iron rings set in the rock floor.

Most likely even small craft could enter the cave only at precisely timed intervals around high tides.

Olivia thought back to the time when L.J. had told her that he liked to get in a little fishing on the trips to and from work, which was why he preferred to commute in his own boat rather than on the tug. He probably never left the island at all, she thought, but at the end of each work day merely circled around the south tip of the island to the east side, out of sight of the house, and entered the cave.

"You two sit down on that cot and don't move until I tell you," L.J. barked.

"Oh, God, we're going to die, Livvie. We're going to die," Blair whimpered when they obeyed.

"And no talking!"

L.J. began to move around the cavern, lighting more kerosene lamps, and Olivia took advantage of his inattention to take stock. The cavern contained a small wooden table, one chair, the cot on which she and Blair sat, a couple of coolers, several large cans of kerosene, six lanterns, a battered trunk and hundreds, maybe thousands, of plastic-wrapped, brick-size bundles, stacked all around the curving back wall of the room.

Olivia's gaze fixed on the latter, and her stomach sank. Was L.J. dealing drugs?

"I see you've noticed my merchandise," he said with a chuckle. "You're looking at millions of dollars in pure-grade heroin. I've been smuggling cocaine and heroin into the country through this island since I was sixteen. Just like my daddy and granddaddy before me." He laughed again. "I guess you could say it's a family tradition, handed down by none other than Great-Great-Grandpa Theobald himself. Only instead of rum and pirated goods, my family used Mallen Island as a distribution point for drugs."

"I thought Miss Prudence was the only living member of the Mallen family left," Olivia said.

"Well, I suppose if you want to get technical about it, my family's not blood kin to the Mallens. My great-grandmother married Theobald's son, Randolph, Miss Prudence's father, when her son—my grandpa—was a kid. Which I guess makes me Theobald's step-great-great-grandson, but I'm the closest thing to family that Miss Prudence has."

"*You're* Lennard, the one Miss Prudence let stay here in exchange for handyman work."

"Right. I've been waiting for ten years for that stupid old woman to die. Since I'm almost family I figured she'd leave the place to me someday, but instead she up and sold it out from under me.

"With two nosy old women around, I've had to keep my operation small, but after Miss Prudence fell I figured the old bat couldn't last much longer. I mean, she's in her late eighties, for God's sake. So I recently made a deal with a South American supplier. No sooner had we made the deal than Miss Prudence announced that she'd sold the place, lock, stock and barrel. The stupid old woman," L.J. raged. "The amount she received from the sale was paltry compared to the fortune I'll be making soon."

"Is Mrs. Jaffee in on all this with you?"

"That old scarecrow? Hell no."

"Then why didn't she tell us who you really were? She had to have recognized you."

L.J. shrugged. "I asked her not to. She never did like me much, but she liked you guys and what you're doing even less."

"Listen, L.J. or Lennard or whatever your name is," Blair interrupted. "If you'll contact either of my brothers, or my mother, they'll pay you quite a large sum for our safe return."

"Forget it. Kidnap for ransom is stupid. Those guys always get caught. Besides, whatever your family would pay would be chump change compared to the operation I'm soon going to be running outta here."

"You're the one who pushed me off the cliff that day, and the one who tried just last week to bash my head in, aren't you?"

"What?" Blair gasped, her eyes huge.

"Yeah," L.J. admitted. "But both times it was spur-of-the-moment. I didn't exactly plan to kill you. I'd been trying to stop the project by playing head games with you and the crew, and embellishing the ghost stories about the place."

He gave another cold laugh. "In their day, my grandpa and my old man used to dress up like old Theobald and walk along the cliff at night to scare away anyone who got too close. I've been doing the same thing for years by using hologram projectors. What people thought was Theobald's ghost in the tower room and walking along the cliffs was really a hologram of me." He laughed harder. "The trick scared the bejesus out of the workers, too, for a while, but in the end all it did was slow down the renovation work.

"Then that day I saw you by the cliffs, it occurred to me that if the big boss's ladylove died tragically on Mallen Island he'd probably shut the project down. I knew that he was walking along the forest edge looking for you and would be there any minute, and I thought, if I was really lucky, Connally would be accused of pushing you, you being his ex-wife and all."

"How did you know that?"

"I was listening outside the door when you came to the island the first time. That night last week when you chased me into the hall, the jade statue was handy and so were you, so I took a crack at bashing in your head.''

"Oh, my God," Blair whimpered.

"I see." Miraculously, Olivia's voice sounded a lot calmer than she felt. "Silly me. I thought you liked me."

"I do," he said, smiling evilly. He stepped close to Olivia and trailed his fingertips over her cheek and neck and down into the vee opening of her silk blouse. Olivia stared back at him, striving to remain stoic, but she couldn't suppress the shiver of revulsion that rippled through her.

L.J. laughed. "If things had been different, you and I could've had a good time together.

"But, in a way, I'm glad that I wasn't successful in shutting down the restoration. I've come up with a new plan that's going to work out even better. I've made a deal with my supplier. He's going to purchase Mallenegua through a third party and use the resort operation to launder drug money. I'll pretend to be the resort manager and handle the distribution end. Since I'm going to be living here, it'll be kind of nice to have the place fixed up.

"Of course, Mallenegua will actually be managed by a professional hotelier whose official position will be that of my assistant. Negotiations are already under way between my supplier's front man and AdCo."

Her mind racing, Olivia strove for a logical argument that would cast doubt on his plan, and perhaps change his mind about killing her and Blair.

"Your plan is flawed, L.J.," she warned. "Don't you see? As soon as the deal goes through, your supplier could eliminate you and put one of his own men in charge of Mallenegua."

He frowned. "That's not going to happen. I've got everything under control." He thumbed his chest. "I'm the one with the local contacts. Carlos needs me."

"L.J., listen to me," she pleaded. "You can't get away with holding us like this. Blair and I will be missed soon and Joe will have the whole crew out looking for us."

He merely laughed again. "They'll never find the secret door. My grandfather looked for it for years while he was growing up here. In the end, before he tossed Theobald off the cliff, he had to beat the old coot nearly to death before he got the location out of him."

The casual way he revealed the murder and the vicious nature of his family made Olivia's blood run cold. However, she clenched her jaw to keep from shivering, refusing to let him see how frightened she was. She raised her chin, her eyes snapping with defiance. "You're wrong. Joe will find the passageway if he has to tear Mallenegua down, stone by stone," she declared with a confidence she was far from feeling.

"Yeah, well by then it'll be too late. At high tide I'm going to take you and your friend out to sea and dump you overboard. When your bodies wash up on shore the authorities will think you fell from the cliffs and drowned. Just like old Theobald."

Blair hung her head, her shoulders shaking as she began to weep quietly.

Olivia knew he was probably right. Terror clawed at her throat, making further speech impossible, but somehow she managed to stare back at him all the same.

* * *

"We've found two of them so far," Arthur West-cott explained to Joe, who was examining the holographic projector hidden in the wall of the tower room. "This one and another in a second-floor hallway niche. There are probably more."

Joe turned to Mike. "Could Clyde Shoemaker have set up something like this?"

"I don't think so, boss. Clyde is an unskilled framing carpenter and, if you ask me, not too bright. Whoever set up this equipment did a meticulous job. He had to have a superior knowledge of electronics and expert masonry skills to hide it so well. We darn near missed it."

"I traced the serial numbers on the projectors, Mr. Connally," Arthur said. "They were purchased by a Lennard J. Ainsworth."

Joe's head snapped around toward the security man. "Ainsworth? That's the step-great-nephew who was handyman for Miss Prudence. Hmm, Lennard J.," he mused out loud. "L.J. I wonder…"

Joe had a bad feeling. Clyde Shoemaker had sworn vehemently that all he'd done was deliver notes for Vicky, that he had not knocked Olivia down or been responsible for any of the other mysterious things that had happened. Joe hadn't believed him. He'd been certain when he'd fired Shoemaker and kicked him off the island the mischief would stop, but apparently there was more than one troublemaker on his crew.

"Excuse me for interrupting, Mr. Connally," Cappy said from the door of the tower room. "But if Olivia ain't ready to leave soon I won't be able to get back here in time to ferry the men back to Savannah.

Frowning, Joe checked his watch. "She hasn't left yet?"

"I ain't seen hide nor hair of her. I even knocked on her door, but nobody answered."

"What about my sister? She went down to Olivia's room to talk to her more than an hour ago."

"Ain't seen her, neither."

The hair on the back of Joe's neck prickled. "I don't like the sound of this." His gaze swept over the other men. "Come with me."

On the second floor Joe banged on Olivia's door with the side of his fist. "Olivia. Are you in there? Open up."

Nothing.

Joe tried the doorknob and the door swung open. Her suitcase lay open and half packed on the luggage rack. On the bed were neat stacks of clothing and other items to be added to the case.

"Olivia? Blair? Are you in here?" Joe called, but no one answered. The men spread out, checking the dressing room, the bathroom and the adjoining sitting room, but the suite was eerily empty.

Arthur zeroed in on a notepad on the desk. "According to this, she booked connecting flights to Boston. The first leg is scheduled to leave Savannah in a little over an hour. She'll never make it now."

Joe strode out into the hall. "Have any of you men seen Olivia or my sister?"

The men working on the woodwork stopped what they were doing. "Miss Olivia went into her room right after you left her this morning," one of the men spoke up. "She hasn't come out since."

"Yeah, and Miss Blair, she went in there an hour

or so ago, and she hasn't come out, either," another man added. The others all nodded in agreement.

Joe's gut knotted. "Then there has to be another way in and out of that room, because they aren't in there."

A hidden door, he thought. One that someone had been using all along. Which would explain a lot.

"Mike, you and Cappy and the rest of your men start searching the house from the basement to the attics, just in case they happened to leave without anyone seeing them. Arthur, come with me. We're going to find that door if I have to tear that damned room apart with my bare hands."

"What do we do if they're not in the house, boss?"

Joe thought about the cliffs, and his mouth flattened into a grim line. "Then we fan out and search every inch of this island. Now go."

Joe and Arthur methodically worked their way around the bedroom, tapping on walls and checking the floor for a trap door. Having no luck, Arthur concentrated on the sitting room, while Joe turned his attention to the dressing room. Becoming more frantic with each passing second, he furiously tapped his way around the room. Out of necessity he had to duck under Olivia's clothes hanging on the rods to examine the walls, and the scent of her and her perfume haunted his senses.

By the time Joe reached the back wall he was so frantic he was ready to take an ax to the place, when suddenly his tapping produced a hollow sound.

"Arthur! Arthur, get in here. I've got something."

In seconds the security man skidded through the door.

"This wall is hollow," Joe told him, demonstratin

at the same time. "I'll get a power saw and we'll cut through it."

"Hold on. There has to be a latch hidden somewhere in here," Arthur said, running his hand over the surface of each cubby.

Impatient, Joe shifted from one foot to the other. "To hell with this. Let's tear the thing down."

"Wait, here it is." The middle section of the wall of shelves swung open. Joe darted past Arthur and through the opening before the other man could move.

"Damn, it's dark as a grave in here," the security man mumbled, and immediately regretted his choice of words when he turned on the penlight on his key chain and saw Joe's expression.

"There are some stairs," Joe said, and headed for them with Arthur on his heels. "No, wait. Give me that light and I'll see where these stairs lead. You go back and call the mainland for help—the sheriff, the FBI, the Coast Guard, whoever has jurisdiction. Then get some men and whatever weapons they can round up and follow me."

"Mr. Connally, I think you should wait for backup. You don't know what or who you'll find down there. It's too dangerous to go alone."

"Dammit, man, my sister and the woman I love more than life itself are down there. I'm going after them. Now go."

Without waiting for an answer, Joe tore down the narrow stairs, his heart beating double time.

Twenty

Time was running out. The tide was coming in. The roar of the surf was getting louder and the water in the pool had begun to churn, keeping the small boat bobbing at the end of its mooring line.

Olivia kept a wary eye on L.J. while she worked furiously to cut through the duct tape with the shard of flint stone. He was aboard his boat, filling the outboard motor with gas and checking the oil, getting everything ready to leave.

Olivia was so terrified she wanted to scream, but she kept sawing away at the tape and wouldn't let herself give in to the fear. Blair was already falling apart, so one of them had to keep her wits about her.

"We're going to die. We're going to drown in the ocean or be eaten by sharks," Blair babbled beside her. "Oh, God, how did I ever get into this fix?"

"Be quiet, Blair," Olivia whispered. "You don't want to anger him."

"What difference does it make if he kills us now or later? Either way, we're dead."

"We're not going to die if I can help it."

Blair looked at her with the first glimmer of hope in her tear-drenched eyes. "Do you have a plan?"

"Yes. But please be quiet. Don't attract his attention."

L.J. put the gas cap back on the outboard motor and headed for the front of the boat. "All set. You ladies ready for your last ride?"

Olivia sawed harder, and as he hopped onto the stone bank the tape gave way.

"Whatever you're going to do, you better hurry," Blair urged, the panic in her voice rising. "Here he comes. Oh, God."

"It's going to be all right," Olivia whispered, keeping her gaze fixed on L.J. "Do what he says, but be ready to run when I tell you. When we stand up, you go first and pretend you need help climbing into the boat. I'll take care of the rest."

"Okay. Okay," her friend panted, grasping desperately at any shred of hope.

"On your feet, ladies. Chop, chop."

Following Olivia's instructions, Blair went first. Olivia kept her hands behind her back as though they were still bound, praying that L.J. wouldn't notice the frayed tape.

"Oh, oh! Help me," Blair cried.

"Dammit, bitch, get in the boat."

"I can't. I can't keep my balance with my hands behind my back."

"Dammit." L.J. stomped forward. When he reached the water's edge Olivia made her move.

She wrenched her wrists apart, ripping off most of the tape, and charged L.J. Catching him off guard, she rammed into him, the flat of her palms striking him just beneath his shoulder blades.

L.J. gave a yelp and toppled, hitting the churning water in a breath-stealing belly flop.

"Run, Blair! Run!" Olivia yelled, grabbing her friend's arm and pulling her along.

"Cut my hands loose. I can't run like this."

"You'll have to. There's no time for that. Now run!"

Gripping Blair's arm, Olivia hustled her toward the door. Halfway there, Blair looked back over her shoulder and cried, "He's swimming to the bank! We'll never make it!"

"Shut up and run."

They reached the door and Olivia ordered, "Here, help me with this. Put your shoulder under it."

She lifted one end of the plank that secured the door and Blair put her shoulder under the other end. When the plank fell free and the door swung open, Olivia struggled to drag the heavy piece of wood out into the passageway.

"Oh, Lord, he's climbing out," Blair cried.

Olivia darted back into the cavern, grabbed the nearest lantern and darted back out again. "Help me shut this door. Hurry!"

Both women put their shoulders to the heavy door, and when it clicked shut Olivia wedged the plank against it at a forty-five-degree angle, bringing all her weight down on the top of the board to dig it securely into place.

"Let's go! Run!"

She grabbed the lantern with one hand and Blair's arm with the other and plunged headlong into the blackness ahead. They had barely run ten feet when L.J. thudded into the door.

Blair screamed, and the sound bounced off the stone walls of the tunnel in an eerie echo.

"Hurry. Faster, faster," Olivia urged, pulling the bound woman along with her. Behind them the thud struck the door over and over. Olivia knew it was jus a matter of time until he dislodged the plank. Then he would come after them. He had to. His entire operation depended on keeping the cavern and tunnels a secret.

They ran headlong for what seemed like forever, stumbling every few feet, constantly looking over their shoulders for any sign of a flashlight beam.

"C'mon, Blair, hurry. We have to go faster. We h-have to get to the door b-before he catches us."

"I c-can't run any f-faster," Blair gasped. "I'll f-fall. A-and I have…a st-stitch in my side." She stumbled to a halt and leaned against the wall, panting. "G-go ahead without me, Livvie. I can't…I can't run anymore."

"Now, you listen to m-me, Blair Connally. I'm not l-leaving without you. So just suck it up and g-get your butt in g-gear and run. I don't care how m-much your side hurts."

"Shh. Listen."

Olivia tensed and cocked one ear. From behind them came the distinct sound of pounding footsteps.

"He's coming," Blair cried. "We don't have a chance of getting away."

"Maybe not," Olivia conceded. "But we're not going to make it easy for him. C'mon. Move it."

They took off again, running flat out with little regard for Blair's balance. Behind them they could hear L.J.'s footsteps getting closer.

The tunnel curved to the left. They barely made it around the bend when the kerosene lamp flickered and went out. This time both Blair and Olivia screamed.

The two women clung to each other, shaking and fighting back hysteria.

"Livvie! Blair!" Their names echoed down the pitch-black passageway from the direction in which they were headed. "Is that you? Answer me!"

"It's Joe!" Olivia cried.

"Oh, thank God."

"We're here, Joe! Hurry! He's right behind us!"

"I'm coming."

A tiny beam of light appeared about fifty feet ahead of them. To the rear the pounding footsteps grew closer.

Olivia squeezed Blair's arm. "C'mon. We have to get to Joe."

They ran toward the pinprick of light with no thought for the uneven ground or whatever obstacles might be in their way. They reached Joe and fell into his arms, crying and chattering all at once.

"Oh, Joe. Thank God you found us," Olivia sobbed against his chest. "Thank God. It was L.J. all along."

"He was going to kill us," his sister wailed through her tears. "He was going to take us far out to sea and dump us overboard. It was horrible. If it hadn't been for Livvie we would have died."

"Are you two all right? Did he hurt either of you?"

"I'm bruised and my knees and palms are scraped from falling, but—"

"For heaven's sake! We don't have time for this now," Olivia cried. "He'll be here any second."

As if on cue, the flashlight beam came bobbing around the bend, heading straight for them.

Joe instinctively pushed the women behind him. "Take off, you two. And here, take the penlight."

"What're you going to do?" Olivia demanded. "You can't stay here. He's got a gun."

"Just go, will you? The men are on their way. You'll probably run into them before you reach the stairs. I can hold L.J. off until they get here. Go! Go! Now!''

Olivia and Blair did as they were told and took off. A hundred yards or so down the passageway they heard the footsteps of a gang of people coming toward them.

"Here come the men," Olivia said, coming to a halt. "You stay right here, Blair, and wait for them. They'll free your hands and take care of you. I'm going back to help Joe."

"What? Wait! Don't leave me here alone all trussed up like a Christmas turkey," Blair squawked. "Are you crazy? That creep has a gun. He's dangerous."

Olivia barely heard her as she raced back toward Joe. Before she saw the faint glow of artificial light she heard their voices. Dousing the penlight, she crept closer to Joe's back, staying to one side, close to the wall of the tunnel.

"Well, well, if it isn't the big man himself. Looks like there'll be three bodies instead of two washing up on the shore in a few days."

"Put down your weapon, L.J.," Joe ordered. "It's over."

"To hell with that. You can't stop me, Connally. After I shoot you I'll catch up with those women long before they get to the stairs. I know this tunnel like the back of my hand. I could run it flat out in the dark if I had to."

"You're too late already, L.J. My men are right behind me, and the authorities are on their way."

"Nice try, big shot, but I'm not falling for it." L.J.

raised his gun and sighted down the barrel. "Sorry I can't stay and chat, but I've wasted enough time. So long, Connally."

"No-o-o!" Olivia cried, and made a diving leap, throwing herself in front of Joe at the same instant the gun's report reverberated through the tunnel.

The bullet struck her chest like a fist while she was in midair and slammed her back against Joe.

"Livvie!" he yelled, sinking to the stone floor with her in his arms. "Oh, God, Livvie. Say something. C'mon, honey. Speak to me. Livvie."

He was only vaguely aware of L.J. standing a few feet away, repeatedly pulling the trigger on his jammed gun and getting only a "click, click, click."

Holding Olivia in his arms, Joe rocked her back and forth and pressed his folded handkerchief to her wound. Despite his effort to stanch the flow, an ever-widening circle of blood blossomed on her ivory silk blouse.

Behind him he heard footsteps pounding his way, and he yelled, "Help! Help me! Livvie's been shot!"

Mike and Arthur came pounding up behind Joe, guns drawn, followed by Cappy and about twenty men, each one holding a weapon of some sort.

Using a two-handed grip, Arthur aimed his gun at L.J. "Drop it. Now."

Mike knelt beside Joe and Olivia. "How is she?"

"I don't know. She's bleeding badly." He looked at the other man with pure, unadulterated hell in his eyes. "If we don't get her to a doctor soon she won't make it."

For three days Olivia floated on a sea of alternating pain and tranquillity. She clung to the fuzzy feeling that surrounded her, unwilling, on a subconscious level, to face what awaited her when she woke up.

Gradually, though, the doctor reduced the amount of painkiller injected into her IV and the fuzzy cloud began to disappear.

The first face she saw when she opened her eyes was Mary Beth's.

Her friend leaned over the hospital-bed railing and took her hand. "Hi. It's about time you woke up, Sleeping Beauty."

"M-Mary Beth. What...what happened? And what're you doing here? Who is...looking after business?"

Mary Beth rolled her eyes. "I might've known that would be your first concern. Don't worry, Janie and Maggie can hold down the fort for a few days. And where else would I be, I'd like to know? I swear, I send you down here to redecorate a house and what do you do? You go and get yourself shot. What am I going to do with you?"

"Shot?" Olivia croaked. "How did I get sh—"

Her eyes widened as her memory flooded back. She clutched Mary Beth's hand. "Joe? How is Joe?"

"He's just fine. Why don't you see for yourself," he said, nodding toward the opposite side of the bed.

Olivia turned her head slowly and found herself looking up into Joe's haggard face. Dark circles lay beneath his eyes, and the lines running from each corner of his mouth to his nose appeared to be etched deeper than before. The lower half of his face bore at least a three-day growth of beard and his hair was disheveled, as though he'd been constantly raking his hand through it.

"Joe. You're all right?" she said in her cracked voice.

"Yeah. Thanks to you. You saved my life," he said tenderly, holding a straw to her lips so that she could sip water. "And if you ever do anything that stupid again I swear I'll paddle your behind."

"H-how is Blair?"

"Hale and hearty and singing your praises. I wish I could say the same for you. You gave us quite a scare."

"Sorry." She took another sip of water from the straw Joe held to her lips then settled back, frowning. "I don't remember much after L.J. took aim at you. What happened to him? He didn't escape, did he?"

"Nope. The cavalry arrived seconds after he shot you and took him into custody. He's being held without bond and charged with a whole laundry list of crimes, starting with attempted murder and drug trafficking. My hunch is L.J. is going to be looking at the world through bars for a very long time."

"That's a relief." She glanced around at the monitors and tubes surrounding the head of the bed. "How long have I been in the hospital?"

"Three days."

"Mmm. When can I get out?"

"In another week or so. But even then you're going to need to convalesce for several months. So I thought the best thing for us to do is get married quietly and rent a villa in Italy or Spain for the summer."

"Married. Joe, we've been through this. I'm not going to marry you."

"Oh, yes you are. And don't you dare say you don't love me. No one takes a bullet for someone she doesn't love. Besides, you've been calling my name for the past three days.''

''Shall I leave?'' Mary Beth asked, grinning.

''No, stay. I want a witness when she finally admits that she loves me.''

''Joe—''

''You're never going to convince me that you don't so you might as well give up.''

Olivia caught her lower lip between her teeth and gazed up at him, her heart contracting as she relived the stark terror she had experienced when L.J. had taken aim at Joe. She had known in that instant that she loved him. Deeply. Irrevocably.

It wasn't fair, she thought with silent despair. She had put him out of her heart and mind years ago, and when they'd met again she hadn't loved him. She had liked and admired him and felt a nostalgic sort of affection for him, but she hadn't been in love.

In hindsight she realized how foolish—even arrogant—it had been of her to think for a moment that she could work around Joe without falling under his spell again. Over the last few months those very same qualities and virtues that had so beguiled her as a girl all those years ago had made her fall in love all over again.

Only this time she loved him with the deep, abiding love of a mature woman. This time she wasn't blinded by starry-eyed adolescent idealism and impossible dreams. This time she loved him not as some mythical Prince Charming, but as a mortal man—human, fallible and flawed, but whose decency and goodness far outweighed any shortcomings.

And sadly, this time she had no illusions that she and Joe could ever have a future together.

"Oh, all right," she replied in a defeated tone. "I'm in love with you. But that doesn't mean I'm going to marry you."

"Why not?"

"Why not? Because I don't want to ruin your life. My mother's ideas about class distinctions are outdated and just plain wrong, but the inescapable truth is, this is Savannah. And like it or not, here the old notions still apply. Things like family background count more than accomplishments.

"And the cold hard truth is, you and I come from different worlds. You were raised in a mansion, and I grew up in a tiny two-bedroom cottage. You and Blair and Luke went to Savannah Country Day School. I went to public school. You earned your degree from Princeton. I barely scraped together enough money to go to a state college."

"So?"

"Don't you see. Though those sorts of things mean nothing to me, I don't have the kind of pedigree that would make me acceptable to your circle of friends. If you married me you'd be ostracized. You'd never be invited to join the Madeira Club, or the Oglethorp Club, like your father was. And never in a million years would I be asked to join the Married Ladies Card Club. Socially, I'd be a liability."

Joe burst out laughing. He laughed so long and so hard he had to bend over and hold his side. "Oh, sugar, you're priceless," he sputtered when he finally regained control. "Do I strike you as the kind who gives a damn about those things? Hell, I couldn't care less."

Though a bit surprised that her argument did not make a dent in his determination, she was not rea to give in. "All right, even disregarding the social aspect, there's still your mother. She would be livid if we remarried. I love you, Joe, but I don't think I could put up with her constant disapproval for the rest of my life."

His slow smile was positively gleeful. "If that's the best you can do, sugar, we might as well make it official," he said, pulling a ring box from his pocket.

Olivia gaped at him, so taken aback by his insouciance she did not have the presence of mind to resist when he slipped a large diamond solitaire onto her left hand. His reaction was not at all what she had expected. After all, Eleanore's disapproval was something he could not change, ignore or deny.

Bending over, he gave her a lingering kiss, further short-circuiting her thought processes. When he raised his head he looked deep into her eyes, and Olivia's heart gave a thump at the emotion she saw reflected in his. "I love you, Livvie, and I always will."

"Oh, Joe, I love you, too." She raised one hand and stroked his jaw. "But if there's one thing I've learned, it's that ignoring a problem won't make it go away. And your mother will never accept me as a daughter-in-law."

"Wrong. Sugar, you saved not one, but two of her children. For the past three days she's been running all over town telling everyone what a heroine you are, how you took a bullet meant for me, and how you risked your life to get Blair out of a madman's clutches."

"You're kidding me. Eleanore?"

"Swear to God," he said, putting his right hand over his heart.

"Well. That's nice, of course, but that doesn't mean she wants me for a daughter-in-law."

"Honey, she's busy planning our wedding at this very moment."

Olivia blinked at him. "Are you serious?"

"Yep. I hope you like garden weddings."

"I...I don't know what to say."

"Say yes, for heaven's sake," Mary Beth advised. "While we were waiting for you to wake up, Joe and I got acquainted, and I like him. The man hasn't left your bedside since they brought you to the hospital. You can't let a great guy like this get away. Again."

Joy began to effervesce inside Olivia like champagne bubbles, but she remained cautious. "But my business is in Atlanta and yours is here in Savannah."

"No problem. Reese and I will open an AdCo office in Atlanta. Or, if you'd prefer, you can move your business here."

"You'd do that for me?"

Joe leaned over the bed rail and gave her another lingering kiss. When it ended, he smiled tenderly. "Honey, there isn't anything I wouldn't do for you."

Olivia gazed at Joe with stars in her eyes, her heart so full it felt as though it might burst. She cupped his whisker-stubbled cheek with her hand and smiled back. "I've always liked April weddings."

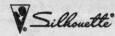

Carnival Elation
7-Day Exotic Western Caribbean Itinerary

DAY	PORT	ARRIVE	DEPART
Sun	Galveston		4:00 P.M.
Mon	"Fun Day" at Sea		
Tue	Progreso/Mérida	8:00 A.M.	4:00 P.M.
Wed	Cozumel	9:00 A.M.	5:00 P.M.
Thu	Belize	8:00 A.M.	6:00 P.M.
Fri	"Fun Day" at Sea		
Sat	"Fun Day" at Sea		
Sun	Galveston	8:00 A.M.	

TERMS AND CONDITIONS

PAYMENT SCHEDULE:
50% due upon booking. Full and final payment due by July 26, 2004.
Acceptable forms of payment are Visa, MasterCard, American Express, Discover and che
The cardholder must be one of the passengers traveling. A fee of $25 will apply for all retur
checks. Check payments must be made payable to **Advantage International, LLC and sen**
Advantage International, LLC, 195 North Harbor Drive, Suite 4206, Chicago, IL 60601.

CHANGE/CANCELLATION:
Notice of change/cancellation must be made in writing to Advantage International, LLC.

Change:
Changes in cabin category may be requested and can result in increased rate and penalti
name change is permitted 60 days or more prior to departure and will incur a penalty of
per name change. Deviation from the group schedule and package is a cancellation.

Cancellation:

181 days or more prior to departure	$250 per person
121—180 days or more prior to departure	50% of the package price
120—61 days prior to departure	75% of the package price
60 days or less prior to departure	100% of the package price (nonrefundabl

U.S. and Canadian citizens are required to present a valid passport or the original birt
tificate and state issued photo ID (driver's license). All other nationalities must co
the consulate of the various ports that are visited for verification of documentation.

<u>We **strongly** recommend trip **cancellation** insurance!</u>
For further details call 1-877-ADV-NTGE or visit www.GetCaughtReadingatSea.co

For booking form and complete information
go to <u>www.getcaughtreadingatsea.com</u>
or call 1-877-ADV-NTGE

Complete coupon and booking form and mail both to:
Advantage International, LLC
195 North Harbor Drive, Suite 4206, Chicago, IL 60

Harlequin Enterprises Ltd. is a paid participant in this promotion.

Visit us at www.eHarlequin.com

If you enjoyed what you just read,
then we've got an offer you can't resist!

Take 2
bestselling novels FREE!
Plus get a FREE surprise gift!

Clip this page and mail it to The Best of the Best™

IN U.S.A.
3010 Walden Ave.
P.O. Box 1867
Buffalo, N.Y. 14240-1867

IN CANADA
P.O. Box 609
Fort Erie, Ontario
L2A 5X3

YES! Please send me 2 free Best of the Best™ novels and my free surprise gift. After receiving them, if I don't wish to receive anymore, I can return the shipping statement marked cancel. If I don't cancel, I will receive 4 brand-new novels every month, before they're available in stores! In the U.S.A., bill me a the bargain price of $4.74 plus 25¢ shipping and handling per book and applicable sales tax, if any*. In Canada, bill me at the bargain price of $5.24 plu 25¢ shipping and handling per book and applicable taxes**. That's the complete price and a savings of over 20% off the cover prices—what a great deal! understand that accepting the 2 free books and gift places me under n obligation ever to buy any books. I can always return a shipment and cancel a any time. Even if I never buy another The Best of the Best™ book, the 2 fre books and gift are mine to keep forever.

185 MDN DN*
385 MDN DN*

Name	(PLEASE PRINT)	
Address	Apt.#	
City	State/Prov.	Zip/Postal Code

* Terms and prices subject to change without notice. Sales tax applicable in N.Y.
** Canadian residents will be charged applicable provincial taxes and GST.
All orders subject to approval. Offer limited to one per household and not valid to current The Best of the Best™ subscribers.
® are registered trademarks of Harlequin Enterprises Limited.

BOB02-R   ©1998 Harlequin Enterprises Limited